Praise for
You May Kiss the Bride
Book One of
The Penhallow Dynasty series

A *Publishers Weekly* Top Pick
A *Booklist* Top 10 Debut
A Barnes & Noble Top Pick
A *Washington Post* Romance Novel of the Month
A Sarah MacLean Recommended Romance
A *Kirkus* Best Read of the Year, Romance
An *RT* Reviewers' Choice Award Nominee

"A masterful Regency debut . . . A sheer delight."
—*Kirkus* (★**Starred Review**★)

"Berne's consistent, engaging writing and solid knowledge of the period make for a wonderful evening's reading."
—*Publishers Weekly* (★**Starred Review**★)

"Exceptional . . . Will dazzle readers with its irresistible mix of graceful writing tempered with just the right dash of crisp wit, splendidly captured Regency setting and atmosphere, and beautifully nuanced characters."
—*Booklist* (★**Starred Review**★)

"Delicious . . . Berne's debut is a lingering homage to the heyday of the Regency historical romance—a lovingly crafted story of opposites forced together by society's censure, quirky side-characters, and stolen kisses."
—Sarah MacLean, *Washington Post*

"Really fun! Very smart and engaging."
—Megan Frampton, author of *Why Do Dukes Fall in Love?*

"UNPUTDOWNABLE! This book consumed me. Truly one of the absolute best romances I've ever read!"
—*New York Times* Bestselling Author Sophie Jordan

"Prepare to be swept away! Lisa Berne's sensuous, richly imaginative debut will delight and satisfy you. I savored every page!"
—Lenora Bell, *USA Today* Bestselling Author

"Definitely recommended to Regency lovers."
—Historical Novel Society

By Lisa Berne

The Penhallow Dynasty

LISA BERNE

THE BRIDE TAKES A GROOM

THE PENHALLOW DYNASTY

AVONBOOKS

An Imprint of HarperCollinsPublishers

Untitled excerpt copyright © 2019 by Lisa Berne.

THE BRIDE TAKES A GROOM. Copyright © 2018 by Lisa Berne. All rights reserved. Printed in the United States of America. No part of this book may be used or reproduced in any manner whatsoever without written permission except in the case of brief quotations embodied in critical articles and reviews. For information, address HarperCollins Publishers, 195 Broadway, New York, NY 10007.

First Avon Books mass market printing: May 2018

Print Edition ISBN: 978-0-06-245182-8
Digital Edition ISBN: 978-0-06-245184-2

Cover design by Amy Halperin
Cover illustration by Anna Kmet
Cover photographs: ©Michael Frost Photography (main image);
© Dmitry Bruskov/Shutterstock (sky); ©PLRANG ART/Shutterstock
(background)

Avon, Avon & logo, and Avon Books & logo are registered trademarks of HarperCollins Publishers in the United States of America and other countries.
HarperCollins is a registered trademark of HarperCollins Publishers in the United States of America and other countries.

FIRST EDITION

18 19 20 21 22   QGM   10 9 8 7 6 5 4 3 2 1

For Cheryl Pientka, again

Acknowledgments

With warmest thanks to Lucia Macro, Katelyn Detweiler, and Sophie Jordan. And to Eloisa James, too, who kindly pointed me to the perfect phrase from Shakespeare, which appears on page 219.

A summer evening.

Overhead, a full, golden moon.

A soft masculine voice murmuring in her ear, *"Ma chérie, je veux te toucher."*

A hand, drawn across her bosom.

Pleasure. Refuge. Connection.

She pressed herself closer, and as she did so, to her drifted the faintest scent of lavender, carried gently on the breeze that rustled leaves, caressed flowers, stirred the light muslin hem of her gown.

Lavender, and . . . witch hazel?

A sudden, urgent warning sounded deep in Katherine Brooke's brain, but it was too late.

"Miss *Brooke!* Monsieur de la Motte! *What* is the meaning of this?" came the outraged voice of Miss Wolfe, headmistress of the very exclusive and even more expensive boarding school at which Katherine had been immured for two long, miserable years.

Germaine—Monsieur de la Motte—gave an audible gasp of horror, and before Katherine's equally horrified gaze the dashing music instructor who had been so bold, so eloquent, seemed abruptly to become a rather large pile of blancmange. He released her and pulled away as if he had just been holding in his arms a repulsive, bad-smelling troll he'd found lurking under a bridge somewhere, and gibbered:

"Oh, Mademoiselle Wolfe, forgive me—it was nothing—without significance—a brotherly embrace to comfort only—the poor *demoiselle* so lonely and far from home—and but this one time, I do assure you—it was that I felt so very sorry for her—"

"You lie, you—you *weasel*," interrupted Katherine hotly. If she'd had her wits about her, she might have gone along with his inane little story and maybe, just maybe, mitigated this rapidly unfolding disaster, but there was something about the way he was babbling on, as if *she* was nothing, as if *she* was without significance, that made a crimson mist of rage rise up in front of her eyes like a vengeful wraith. What had happened to all those bewitchingly romantic words of passion?

She wrenched herself around to face Miss Wolfe. "It's not the first time, we've been meeting in the garden for *ages,* and he's been *kissing* me!"

Germaine de la Motte, no doubt aware that his days at the Basingstoke Academy for Young Ladies had drawn to an immediate close, and that within mere minutes he would be booted out onto the street with nothing but his hastily packed valise in hand, gave Katherine a look of undisguised malice. "But recall, *mademoiselle,* how ardently you sought me out."

Oh, splendid, now the cat was well and truly let out of the bag, thus making things instantly go from bad to worse. Katherine could feel her fury dissolving with almost ludicrous speed and giving way to soul-shattering embarrassment and shame. "I—I thought you liked me," she faltered.

He smiled thinly and lifted his shoulders in a Gallic gesture of dismissal. *"Ma pauvre chérie."*

His words came at her like a slap in the face, cruel, patronizing, stinging. It had all been a lie. A malign and hard-hearted deception. So much for those embraces, the kisses, the furtive touches here and there, the exciting feel of a man's body against her own. How wrong and awful she'd been, how stupid, how *bad*—

And here, to emphasize just how bad, was Miss Wolfe again, very nearly sputtering in her fury:

"I can hardly believe my ears! That a pupil of mine would stoop so low! To *solicit* such a thing! To sneak about, like a sordid criminal! And you but fifteen, Miss Brooke! Be sure that I shall inform your parents by express first thing tomorrow."

Katherine hung her head. She *was* a low, sneaking, sordid, criminal sort of girl. Hadn't she known, underneath it all, that she was behaving dreadfully? "Yes, Miss Wolfe," she muttered, aware, to her further horror, that tears were gathering in her eyes, had begun to roll in heavy, wet, revealing drops down her cheeks. More ashamed of herself than ever, with a kind of desperation she scrubbed at the tears with her bare hands. Oh, she *hated* this place. If she was lucky, her parents would have her removed at once.

But as it turned out, she would stay on for four more long, miserable years at the Basingstoke Academy, Mother and Father agreeing with Miss Wolfe's expert (and, ultimately, costly) assessment that Katherine—so gauche, so inattentive—would need them in order to acquire even the most fundamental degree of polish, that essential and elusive *je ne sais quoi,* which would enable her to someday, one hoped, comport herself without committing further, dreadful gaffes.

Six years after the hushed-up incident at
* the Basingstoke Select Academy for Young Ladies . . .*
Somewhere near the Canadian border
April 1811

It had been a perfectly good day, tramping along the St. Lawrence River and leading his men in a jolly little reconnaissance through the woods, until all at once there was a *crack* and a slight whistling noise.

Then there was a sharp pain six inches down and to the right of his heart.

"Damn it to hell," said Hugo Penhallow, whipping around and in a single rapid motion bringing up his own musket, sighting the French sharpshooter two hundred paces away, and targeting him rather more effectively. He watched with grim satisfaction as the other man crumpled like a puppet released from its string, then sat himself down hard on the ground. His hand, pressed against the front of his red jacket, came away red also, but unfortunately with his own blood.

If he was lucky, the bullet that was now resident inside him hadn't struck anything of particular importance. It occurred to him now that he was very fond of his internal organs, as they'd functioned beautifully all his life, and he'd love for them to keep on doing exactly that.

Carefully, Hugo allowed himself to slide down into a prone position. Everything was getting all hazy and woolly, and just before he closed his eyes he saw the concerned faces of his men hovering over him. A nice bunch of chaps. He was fortunate to have a group like this under his command. Too bad for them they'd have to convey him all the way back to camp, but that, after all, was one of the hazards of military life, and he was sure they'd do a decent job of it.

The pain, he noticed, was getting worse. Well, this certainly was an annoyance. How he loathed those pesky

Frenchmen, and wished they'd stay in their own country where they belonged, kowtowing to that blasted little egomaniac Bonaparte and also making brandy which was, admittedly, of excellent quality. In fact, he wouldn't object to a long swallow of that right now. But, he suspected, he was soon to be losing consciousness, so all things considered, the brandy might well have been a waste.

His last sentient thought was gratitude for the fact that the reconnaissance had been a useful one. His men would be able to confirm that yes, of a surety, there were active enemies in the area, and here was their bloodied and insensate captain to prove it.

Chapter 1

*Six months after the eventful reconnaissance mission
   along the Canadian border . . .*
*Brooke House, five miles inland from Whitehaven, England
October 1811*

Many people would have considered Katherine Brooke
to be an exceedingly fortunate young lady.

She was rich—very rich indeed. Her jewels were of
a quality *and* a quantity that even a queen would envy.
Her gowns were made from the costliest fabrics. Her hats,
gloves, shoes, stockings, shawls, pelisses, reticules, and
parasols were delivered by the dozens. And her immense
bedchamber had been modeled, without thought as to expense, after the neoclassical style made fashionable by no
less a personage than the Prince Regent himself. It was a
marvel of a room, with a high domed ceiling, large gilded
mirrors, fireplaces artfully crafted so as to resemble the
fronts of ancient Roman temples, half a dozen busts of
eyeless long-dead emperors rendered in the purest of
white marble, and walls painted Pompeiian red.

It was here that Katherine stood with her back against the closed door, looking at her maid Céleste. "Do you have it?"

"*Oui, mademoiselle.*"

"Give it to me, please."

"*Je suis désolée, mademoiselle,* but it cost more than expected." Céleste's narrow face was impassive, her tone respectful, but her attitude was nonetheless imbued with every bit of her usual sly, self-satisfied insolence.

Here we go again, Katherine thought. "How much more?"

"It came all the way from London, *mademoiselle,* and as you know, secrecy is difficult to maintain across so many miles."

"I know it all too well. How much more?"

"*Le coût total* is one pound, eighteen shillings."

"That's absurd."

"*Mademoiselle* is concerned about *le coût?*" Céleste shrugged, glancing around the luxurious room as if she didn't, in fact, know just how much pin-money Katherine received. "*Quel dommage.* Rest assured, I can dispose of it elsewhere."

"I'm sure you can." Katherine reached into the satin reticule hanging from her wrist, her fingers slipping past the downy, fragile marabou feathers with which it was ornamented, and extracted two golden guineas which she held out to Céleste. "Here."

Céleste didn't move. "Would *mademoiselle* like back *les cinq shillings?*"

"Keep them." With effort, Katherine kept her face bland. Oh, tedious, tedious, this final extraction of money on top of what was doubtless an inflated fee, but one had to tread carefully with Céleste in these matters. She added, insincerely: "By way of a thank-you."

"*Mademoiselle* is too kind." Without hurry, Céleste took the guineas, then slid her hand into the pocket-slit at her waist and produced from within it a small rectangular bundle wrapped in cheap, plain paper.

Katherine snatched it from her, and Céleste smiled.

"It is always a pleasure doing business with *mademoiselle*."

"You may leave."

"But you are expected downstairs, prior to the dinner hour, and your hair is *ébouriffé*."

"Come back in twenty minutes, and fix it then."

"I shall come back in five."

"Ten." Her hands, Katherine noticed, were shaking a little with anticipation. But then, they always did at a moment like this.

"Five minutes, *mademoiselle*. Or *votre chère maman* will notice your absence, and she may well chide me for your lateness. I do not wish to be chided."

"Nor do I." A scanty patch of common ground between herself and Céleste. She said, "Have you ever wondered what would happen if Mother found out about our—ah—transactions?"

"I would doubtless be let go at once, and *sans références*," replied Céleste coolly. "One can only speculate as to your punishment, *mademoiselle*. Too, you would lose my services as an *intermédiaire,* which would be a punishment in itself, would you not agree? It is not so easy to find someone as resourceful, and as discreet, as I."

This complacent assertion Katherine could not dispute. It had been six years since that humiliating debacle at the Basingstoke Select Academy and the maid Céleste had been forced upon her; they had lived alongside each other locked into a vile dynamic in which their antipathy was mutual, yet each had benefited from their clandestine dealings. Céleste had been magnificently feathering her nest with all the money Katherine paid her, and as for herself—she almost brought the little package to her nose, to breathe in its heady fragrance, but instead said:

"Which reminds me. Where are the books I asked for?"

"The volume of Shakespeare's plays is *en route,* I am informed, *mademoiselle,* but the other—the Italian book—"

"La Divina Commedia."

"Oui. It is proving more difficult to locate in the original language. Rest assured, I have not forgotten." Céleste smiled, with a knowing sort of glimmer that made Katherine feel like her skin was prickling with shamed embarrassment. "Shall I leave you now, so that you might enjoy *votre petite gâterie?"*

"Yes. Do." Katherine stepped aside, and Céleste sauntered out of the room with what had to be deliberate insolence; the moment the door was shut Katherine leaned against it again and carefully unfolded the paper in her hands.

There. There they were. Saliva pooled in her mouth as she stared at the two dozen *diablotins,* the dark thin disks of chocolate covered with nonpareils, tiny, tasty white balls of sugar. For years Mother had forbidden her candy, insisting it made her spotty, but still Katherine had found a way.

Diablotin.

It meant *imp* or *gremlin* in French.

A defiant little smile curved her lips and she popped one of the disks into her mouth.

Oh, delicious. Delicious—exquisite—beguiling—magical—except that words couldn't even come close to describing it. She closed her eyes, savoring. The taste was both bitter and sweet, the chocolate smooth and rich on her tongue; the little nonpareils crunched between her teeth, yielding up a tantalizing contrast of textures.

But one wasn't enough. And time was short. Katherine opened her eyes and rapidly consumed three, four, five *diablotins,* waiting for the rush of pleasure that always came with eating chocolate. No wonder the ancient Aztecs believed that cacao seeds, from which chocolate was made, were a gift from the gods, or that they valued the seeds so greatly they used them as currency. She'd read that in one of her history books, at present hidden away in a locked box under her bed.

And speaking of books . . .

What excellent news that her contraband volume of Shakespeare's plays was on the way. At school they could only read the Bowdlers' version, *The Family Shakespeare*, edited—*eviscerated* was more like it—in a way that supposedly protected a maiden's fragile sensibilities. All the really good parts had been removed, the bits having to do with bad people using bad words, no doubt, and doing bad deeds. Katherine could barely wait to read them all.

She smiled, really smiled. She was feeling it now. For a few precious moments she would feel happy. Good. *Alive.*

Until Céleste came back, did whatever she was going to do with her hair, and she'd have to go downstairs. Ugh. Another excruciating evening spent with her parents and their—what was a good way to describe them?

"Guests" didn't quite do them justice. Katherine preferred "leeches in human form." Hovering a few rungs below Society's topmost echelon, they doubtless had received no better invitations elsewhere, and so here they flocked, the best her parents could do. They ate, they drank, they borrowed money, they expected the Brooke servants to wait on them hand and foot, and for all she knew they were smuggling the silver into their trunks.

This was bad enough, but it had also struck her that none of them appeared to have ever read a book from start to finish. And their conversation—if one could call it that— reflected this sad fact. Mealtimes were interminable.

But at least she would know, all throughout the next several hours, that concealed in her armoire, at the far end of a drawer beneath a pile of silk stockings, were eighteen more *diablotins,* waiting for her to come back.

At around the same time . . .
On the road to Whitehaven

Many people would have considered Captain Hugo Penhallow to be a man in trouble.

He had almost no money, and no income to anticipate; an old house was his only property. In addition, he had a large family to support: a widowed mother, a younger sister, and three younger brothers. His profession for the past eight years, in the Army, was no longer a viable one, for he had recently sold out. As the son of a gentleman, naturally he had no training for any other occupation. And, finally, several months ago he had badly broken his left leg and so now, when he was fatigued, he walked with an unmistakable limp.

Yet here was Hugo, riding north along the Longtown Road on this cool, cloudy afternoon, sitting his horse with casual grace and whistling cheerfully, giving all the appearance of a person without a care in the world.

This was, in fact, largely how he was feeling.

For one thing, he was on his way home, and he'd soon be with his dear and delightful family, whom he hadn't seen once during those eight years, as he had been sent to the annoyingly obstreperous territory along the Canadian border. Letters had helped bridge the distance between himself and home, although he was fairly certain that not all of them were delivered or received, it being not uncommon to have placed in his hands a missive that looked as if it had been in a battle itself, so bent and begrimed was it.

As for the financial difficulties, Hugo wasn't ignoring just how dire they were, but he *was* taking action: he had decided to capitalize on his two chief assets, both intangible but clearly of significant value in certain circles.

One—he was a Penhallow. It was an old and illustrious name that loomed large, extremely large, among the *haut ton*. The first Penhallow, it was said, had long ago come to England with the great Conqueror himself, and the Conqueror had humbly deferred to *him*. Although he himself was but a straitened member of the cadet branch of the Penhallow family, Hugo was fully aware of the effect his hoary surname exerted upon even the loftiest dukes and earls, permitting oneself to walk about trailing, as it were, clouds of glory. All rather comical, in his opinion, but there it was.

Two—the female sex evidently found him attractive, which would make his task easier. For years he had heard himself compared left and right to a Greek god which, as a modest fellow, he found extremely silly. He was one of those tall, fit sort of men, an attribute for which of course he was appreciative, but still, one couldn't help being born the way one was, and it was decidedly uncomfortable to be stared at as if one were an exotic beast on display.

Yet if his appearance assisted him in his quest, so much the better. And that quest was to marry into money. He had evaluated his limited options carefully, and all in all this seemed to be the best and the most expeditious way to solve the problem.

He *could* have continued to accept assistance from his older cousin, Gabriel Penhallow, who several years ago had not only generously purchased his commission but had also provided him income in the form of an allowance (which he'd had diverted to his stalwart mother, holding the fort back in Whitehaven). No, that sort of thing—charity—was all well and good for a single-minded, Army-mad youth, but he was done with that now. That bullet in his midsection back in April had resulted in a serious, lingering infection which had his kindly commander forcibly putting him onto a ship bound for home, and there was nothing like a long sea voyage when one was weak as a damned cat to inspire an extended period of introspection.

While Gabriel's assistance—which also included sending additional cheques to Mama—was gratefully received by both himself and the mater, the plain truth was that it wasn't sufficient to see the children adequately established in life. With Gwendolyn now fourteen, the twins Percy and Francis thirteen, and Bertram twelve, the issue had become rather more urgent. But he had no intention of asking Gabriel for anything more. Never in a million years could he imagine himself saying, *Thanks for all that you've done, Coz, and now could you give me many times that sum over again.*

It was, Hugo had concluded, a perfect time in which to take destiny by the shoulders and give it a good hard rattle.

And as luck would have it, a tremendous storm had blown up as the ship neared the western coast, forcing them to divert from Liverpool to Bude, where, his wound having reopened in spectacular style, he'd decided to hotfoot it to Gabriel's estate in Somerset, it being much closer than Whitehaven and the last thing he'd wanted to do was horrify his family by staggering home as a moribund invalid.

Once he got to Surmont Hall he had—in an embarrassingly dramatic fashion—toppled off his horse like a sack of turnips and nearly bled to death on Gabriel's enormous graveled carriage-sweep.

Some might have thought this a bad thing, but really, when you looked at it another way, it had all worked out beautifully. He'd been able to recuperate at his leisure, attended by a very capable doctor as well as by servants offering a tempting array of food and drink multiple times a day. Too, it gave him the opportunity to thank Gabriel in person for his generosity and insist that he both accept repayment for the commission and terminate the allowance; to write home alerting them to his arrival upon *terra firma;* and to receive in return a buoyant letter from his mother which contained along with her usual fond, rambling report of his siblings' health and activities a tidbit of neighborhood news that had caught his eye.

According to Cook, who had it from the butcher's wife who somehow seems to know everything that happens within a twenty-mile radius of White-haven, Brooke House is packed to capacity with guests along with, of course, Mr. and Mrs. Brooke as well as Katherine—your former playmate, such a sweet, lively little girl she was!—who had her first Season and received many offers (highly understandable given the extent of her fortune) but came home without, evidently, any of them being accepted. Cook also says that the butcher's wife told her that one of the custom officer's children very nearly drowned yesterday. Bertram says he knows the boy and that he'd been told many times to stay away when the waves are rough. How very frightening for his people. Also Cook mentioned—

Now here, to be sure, was another great piece of luck. An unwed heiress practically on his doorstep! And it was someone he knew, even better, and had, once upon a time, liked.

To own the truth, he hadn't thought of Katherine in years. It was well over a decade since he'd last seen her. He had been thirteen at the time, and had come home from Eton for Father's funeral. The Brookes, then, had lived next door, and more than once had little Kate—five years younger than himself, yet even so they'd been good friends—slipped between the line of bay trees separating their houses and come to console him.

He'd been grateful for her visits, for a hard time it was, very hard indeed: first the shock of Father's sudden death, and then its painful aftermath, with his three siblings so little, still in leading strings, and Mama pregnant with Bertram.

Their man of business, Mr. Storridge, had laid it out plain: the late Anthony Penhallow, always more interested in science than in money, had left behind very little for his family aside from the modest sum of eight thousand pounds invested in the five percents and their big old house overlooking the wide sandy shore that gave way to the blue-green depths of the ocean.

If the remaining Penhallows practiced the strictest economy, Mr. Storridge had said in his dry, precise voice, they would manage to get by. Hugo had immediately declared his intention to withdraw from Eton and spare Mama the expense of his keeping there, but this she had, in her gentle way, forbidden.

"Oh, my dear Hugo," she had said, smiling through the tears which seemed to flow continually during those dark days, "it was your papa's dearest wish that you receive the same education he did. He was so very proud of you! And wasn't it clever of him to pay your fees in advance? Almost—" And here she had paused to hold back a pitiful sob. "—almost as if he knew something would happen to him."

"Yes, Mama," he'd replied, "school's not a bad thing, but what about Gwennie, and the twins, and the baby? I'll make the headmaster give you back the money. And I'll find a job. I could become a sailor."

"And a marvelous one you'd be, too, darling Hugo. I can just picture you climbing a rigging like a monkey! But do, please, go back to school, and don't worry about the children. Everything will be fine."

Somehow he had managed to swallow a great lump in his throat, and say, "How will it, Mama?"

"It simply will," she had answered, confidently. "And look, I've just today received a letter from dear Anthony's cousin Henrietta Penhallow, with an invitation to spend

the summer holiday with her and her grandson Gabriel in
Bath. You and Gabriel will travel from school together.
Isn't that kind?"

He would infinitely rather have come home, but had
only said, "If it will save money, Mama, I'll do it."

"That's my brave boy," she'd said, and at that moment
he had felt that any sacrifice, large or small, was worth it,
if it could but lighten her load. It was a feeling that had
never left him, and now Hugo smiled a little, noticing with
pleasure the familiar tang of salt air, and the faintest hint
of the ocean's restless breeze.

Not much further now.

With luck, he'd be home by dinnertime.

Whistling again, gently he pressed his heels into his
horse's side, urging it to go just a little faster, and obligingly it picked up its pace.

Actually, by the time Katherine reluctantly made her
way downstairs, there were only fifteen *diablotins* hidden
in her armoire, as she had managed to eat three more
before Céleste had returned.

A light rain had begun to fall, and dusk was settling its
mellow hand upon the streets, buildings, and gardens of
Whitehaven, lingering softly upon the broad expanse of
sand and sea, as Hugo came to the old stable that stood
upon a corner of their property furthest from the beach.
He dismounted and thrust the horse's reins into the hand
of the aged groom who had cautiously emerged from the
stable and was now staring in evident amazement at the
master upon whom he'd not set eyes in quite some time.

"Hullo, Hoyt!" said Hugo amiably, "you're looking
exactly the same, I'm happy to see. Trust all is well?"

At the other's dumbstruck nod, Hugo went on, "Splendid! Do take care of this nag, will you? She's held up wonderfully well all the way here, bless her, and I'm no featherweight, am I? Well, I'm off to the house—hope I'm not too late for dinner. Good night, then."

He had already unstrapped from the saddle his neat leather rucksack, and so, after a friendly nod to the still-speechless Hoyt, walked with eager steps toward the large, rambling old house which looked, even to his own affectionate eyes, considerably more dilapidated than he remembered. The reddish clay bricks with which it was constructed were crumbling in places, the sloping slate roof looked extremely weather-beaten, and several windows on the uppermost story had been clumsily boarded up.

He took this in, and went lightly up the front steps onto the wide, welcoming portico.

He was home at last.

From inside he could hear dogs barking—they'd doubtless heard him come onto the portico—along with some odd screeching noises. Not bothering to bang the old iron knocker, Hugo opened the door and let himself in, into a large, high-ceilinged entry hall, shabby and familiar, and quite possibly the nicest place on earth. As he dropped his rucksack onto a bench, a pack of mongrels, all unknown to him and barking fiercely, surged down one of the halls, even as a maidservant scuttled in from the kitchen passageway, looking alarmed and gasping out:

"Oh! Sir! Was you expected? I'll just get the mistress, if you'll wait here, please—"

"Not to worry, I'll go to her," answered Hugo over the tumult of barks, yips, nails madly clicking on wood flooring, and loud hostile panting. "Are they all at dinner?"

"Yes, sir, but—"

"What's your name, then?"

"It's Eliza, sir, but—"

"Quiet!" said Hugo to the dogs who, recognizing the genial tone of authority, instantly subsided and sat on their haunches, wagging their tails and casting up at him looks of servile adoration. He counted them. There were only five, after all, although from their collective volume one would have thought there were at least a dozen, and altogether a motley lot—one was missing an ear, another seemed to have the head of a poodle set upon the body of a dachshund, and still another had eyes of a milky opacity which suggested severe vision problems if not actual blindness.

Hugo patted the biggest of them, an enormous white and brown Great Dane whose front legs were crooked, and said to Eliza:

"Tell Robinson to set another place for me, would you? I'll go in directly."

"Oh, sir, but Mr. Robinson's not here."

"Egad, not dead, is he?" Hugo hoped not, as he had been very fond of their old butler; he'd loyally stayed on after Father had died, despite having his wages drastically reduced.

"Oh no, sir, he's alive, but his palsy got so bad that the mistress pensioned him off, you see, and he's living with his daughter Nancy and her family, up on Roper Street. Very happy he is, sir. Takes a pint every day at the pub, and sings in the choir on Sundays."

Hugo was pulling off his greatcoat and hanging it on a peg. "Well, that's excellent news. I'll go see him later this week. See here, Eliza, I'm hungry as a bear. Can *you* set a place for me?"

"To be sure I can, sir! But—but—if you'll forgive me asking—who *are* you, sir?"

"Good God, didn't my mother tell any of you I was coming? No wonder poor old Hoyt looked as if he'd seen a ghost." He laughed. "Never mind. I'm the prodigal son, Eliza! The eldest, you know—Hugo."

Eliza looked astonished. "Oh! Sir! *You're* Mr. Hugo? We was all afeared *you* was dead!"

"Dead! Why?"

"Because the mistress said you'd been shot by a Frenchy, Mr. Hugo, and that you was laid up in your cousin's house—and then there wasn't any more letters from you! Cook says them French bullets have a special poison in them, sir, that drains the life right out of a person!"

Blast it all, he'd deliberately trivialized the nature of his illness when writing home, not wishing to worry them—and why hadn't Mama gotten the letter he'd written from Gabriel's house a fortnight ago, informing her that he was fine, and would soon be on his way? Well, he could allay their anxieties right now.

"I *was* shot," he said to Eliza, "but it would take more than some beastly Frenchman to kill me, that's for certain! Go on, now, and bring me some supper, that's a good girl."

She bobbed a curtsy and Hugo, favoring his left leg ever so slightly, went down the long, familiar hallway, the dogs trotting behind with the same pliant obedience the children of Hamelin might well have displayed while following the Pied Piper. He came to a pair of oak-framed double doors, brought them open, and strolled into the dining-parlor. "I say, I'm home."

Five golden-blond heads swiveled in his direction, five pairs of wide blue eyes displayed shocked surprise, and then pandemonium erupted.

Chapter 2

"**H**ugo!" cried Mama, "dearest Hugo!" Swiftly she rose to her feet, as did the others, and they all hurried toward him, their progress impeded by what seemed like a single swirling mass of dogs who gaily circled round their feet, loudly barking, which seemed to trigger that odd, raucous screeching intermixed with somebody begging, "Kiss me, you saucy wench!"

Hugo was enfolded in rapturous hugs which, laughing, he returned, interrupting the excited barrage of exclamations and questions to tell the dogs to behave (which they did) and to ask of no one in particular: "Who the devil wants to be kissed?"

"Oh, Hugo, it's my parrot!" said his sister Gwendolyn, flitting off to a primitively constructed wood perch set near the fireplace on which sat the ugliest bird Hugo had ever seen, a pitiful creature almost denuded of feathers and also sporting a large curved beak which looked fully capable of shredding to bloody bits the fragile-looking hand Gwendolyn held out to it. But it only stepped onto her finger and cackled. "Isn't he *beautiful,* Hugo?" she said lovingly, coming near so that Hugo might admire him better at close range. "I've named him Señor Rodrigo, el Duque de Almodóvar del Valle de Oro. Isn't that perfect? The sailor who gave him to me said he was called 'Stubby,' but I like this so much better! We call him 'Rodrigo' for short, and he doesn't seem to mind it. *Do* you, Rodrigo darling?"

The bird cackled again and Gwendolyn smiled approvingly. "Did you notice Rodrigo's perch, Hugo? Francis made the stand, and Percy nailed it all together. Isn't it splendid?"

"That it is," said Hugo, "and I can't think of a better name than Señor Rodrigo! Egad, Mama, why are you crying?"

"Oh, Hugo, my dear boy," his mother replied, dabbing at her cheeks with an absurd wisp of a handkerchief extracted from her reticule, "I'm not crying exactly—I'm weeping, you know, with joy! I'm so glad you're home! We were all so dreadfully anxious about you!"

Which reminded him. "I sent you a letter two weeks ago. Can't imagine why you didn't get it."

"Oh, I have it," said the youngest one, Bertram, pulling from his breeches pocket a wadded-up piece of paper, its wafer crumpled, and holding it out to Hugo. "Mr. Hodgson gave it to me and I forgot all about it."

"Bertram, how *could* you?" said Gwendolyn reproachfully.

He shrugged. "I meant to give it to Mama straightaway, but I was on my way to Grandpapa's—we had a lesson in metallurgy and then we did the most ripping experiment with charcoal. We nearly coughed to death, and Aunt Verena was very unhappy about what happened to the curtains. But we didn't care about that, of course. Or at least *I* didn't. Hugo, did you know that puddling was invented by Henry Cort in 1783, and lets you make bar iron from pig iron without any charcoal at all?"

"Now I do," answered Hugo. "Give the letter to Mama, will you? I say, Bertie, what happened to your hand?"

"Well, I was studying all about saltpeter last year,"

Bertram explained, "and so there was a jolly good explosion in one of the attics."

Hugo nodded, just as casually, as if this single sentence was entirely comprehensible. "Yes, Mama wrote me about the explosion, but she didn't mention that you'd lost parts of your fingers."

"Oh, that happened afterwards. It took a while to see what was going to happen. It was exceedingly interesting, Hugo, I do wish you could have seen it."

"Wish I'd been here, too. I'm sorry, Bertie."

"Sorry? Why should you be? I didn't have *all* my fingers amputated. And it was only the upper bits—see?" Bertram held up the afflicted limb and viewed it with clinical interest.

"Dr. Wilson said he's never seen someone so brave as Bertram," put in Mama proudly. "He didn't cry at all."

"What's to cry about?" Bertram's tone was scornful. "Besides, it was only the fourth and fifth fingers of the hand I don't use for writing and so on."

"And also, Hugo, when Bertram is all grown up, he'll be a perfectly tragic figure," said Gwendolyn with a satisfied air. "All the young ladies will recognize his noble sacrifice for the advancement of science, and fall in love with him."

"Oh, don't talk rubbish, Gwennie! Love!" Scowling, Bertram made a loud and extremely graphic gagging sound, as if the very word left a bad taste in his mouth.

"Hugo, how did you get here? Did you walk?" said one of the twins, and the other one interpolated:

"Walk? All the way from Somerset in those boots? He rode—didn't you, Hugo?"

Hugo smiled down at the twins. As alike as two peas in a pod they were, at thirteen both bidding fair to become as tall as himself someday, but at present still more wiry than muscular. "Percy's right," he said. "I rode. Old Hoyt's looking after my horse."

Gwendolyn gave a little bounce of delight. "Oh, Hugo, you knew right away which one was Percy and which one was Francis! *We* all know, naturally, but no one outside the family can *ever* tell them apart!"

"How did you, Hugo?" inquired Bertram.

"Never mind that," Percy said impatiently, "I want to hear about the horse! How many hands is he, Hugo? Is he a good jumper? You'll let me ride him, won't you? Can I do it tomorrow?"

"She's a nice, sturdy old roan I picked up in Bude," said Hugo. "Of course you can ride her—you all can—but not tomorrow. She needs a rest. Took me twelve days to get here. And no, she's not a jumper."

"Damn," said Percy.

"Percy, darling," Mama said.

"I'm sorry, Mama. But I *did* want to try jumping. It's just rotten luck."

"Having a horse is better than not having one at all," Francis pointed out philosophically.

Percy brightened. "That's true."

"Ah, Mr. Hugo, here you are!" said a gravelly voice, in whose resonant wake came its owner, an immense woman of indeterminate age in a neat gray gown and white ruffled cap, bearing in her meaty hands a tray on which reposed a large bowl of soup, a plate heaped high with bread, a pot of butter, and a tankard filled to the brim with ale.

"Cook!" said Hugo, "how do you do? You're looking very well."

"As to that," mournfully responded Cook, moving at a magisterial pace toward the table, "it's merciful of you to say, Mr. Hugo, but I doubt I'll last the winter."

"Oh, Cook, you say that every autumn," said Mama, who had had Cook with her for nearly three decades, and whose personality was in every way contrary to her own; yet they had for all these years lived under the same roof in perfect, inexplicable tolerance and harmony.

"That may be so, madam, but one of these autumns I'll be right."

"Pooh!" Mama retorted. "You'll outlast us all, I daresay. Let's sit down, and finish our supper."

Everyone went again to their places; Hugo took his at the head of the table. "I say, Cook, it's awfully kind of you to bring the tray yourself."

"Well, Mr. Hugo, that Eliza was so done in by your arrival, all sudden-like as it was, I'd wager a guinea she'd a' dropped your supper on the way here." Cook had finished setting out Hugo's meal, and now she lifted the tray and stood narrowly surveying her handiwork.

Hugo picked up his spoon, then paused. "What's in the soup?"

"Tripe, Mr. Hugo."

"That's what I was afraid of."

"It's what we can afford, Mr. Hugo." Cook heaved a deep, gloomy sigh, very much in the manner of Shakespeare's Prince Fortinbras arriving at Castle Elsinore only to find the corpses of Hamlet, Hamlet's mother, Hamlet's uncle, and so on, together representing the total collapse of the Danish monarchy. Heavily she left the dining-parlor, as one who simply couldn't bear it a moment longer.

"It's not so bad, Hugo," said Gwendolyn helpfully. "I pretend I'm eating *le jambon à la broche, avec la sauce au Madère.*"

"Tripe," Bertram said, "is made from only the first three chambers of a cow's stomach, Hugo, did you know that? They use the rumen, the omasum, and the reticulum."

"Thank you, Bertie," answered Hugo politely, putting down his spoon and reaching for a thick slice of wheaten bread which he proceeded to lavishly butter.

"Walk the plank, you lily-livered dog," said Señor Rodrigo, el Duque de Almodóvar del Valle de Oro, in a conversational tone from his comfortable roost atop Gwendolyn's slender, muslin-clad shoulder.

"Gwennie darling, put Rodrigo back on his perch, please," Mama said.

"Oh, but Mama, you often let Rodrigo join us for dinner, and it's *such* a treat for him." Gwendolyn turned huge, melting blue eyes on her mother. "Only *see* how happy he looks."

"Dead men tell no tales," remarked Rodrigo, and, bobbing up and down on his skinny little legs, giggled in a sinister way.

"Yes, but I always regret it afterward," Mama replied to Gwendolyn. "Rodrigo inevitably goes onto the table, where he wants to fight with the candle-flames, and then he expects me to share my supper with him."

"That's because he adores you, Mama. Isn't he the most delightful creature in the whole entire world?"

"Yes, of course, darling, but—"

"Oh, please, Mama, do let him stay. I promise I won't let him attack any candles."

"Well, I'd really rather you didn't, darling."

"But Mama—"

"Gwennie," Hugo said, "Mama asked you to do something."

Those big blue eyes were now fixed pleadingly on his face. "Oh, but Hugo—"

"Gwennie." Hugo's voice had lost none of its affable kindness, but there was a certain, subtle timbre in it that made Gwendolyn stare, then a little sulkily stand up and return Rodrigo to his perch near the fire.

"I say, Hugo," said Percy admiringly, "is that how you ordered your men around? It's *capital*."

Before Hugo could reply there came to their ears the distant sound of the front door's knocker being banged, and at once the dogs proceeded *en masse* to rush off, barking at the top of their lungs.

"I wonder who that could be," said Mama, but with such obvious nervousness that Hugo looked at her curiously.

"Odd time for a caller," he said, and Bertram commented dispassionately through a mouthful of very chewy tripe:

"It's probably that awful Mr. Bambers."

"Who's—" Hugo began, but was interrupted by Eliza poking her head into the dining-parlor to say anxiously, "Oh, madam, it's that Mr. Bambers for you again. Will you see him? He says he won't go away till you do, and he's dripping all over the entry."

Mama rose to her feet. "Everyone stay and finish their dinner," she said, draping her thin wool shawl more securely about her shoulders, "I'll be back in a moment." Swiftly she went away, followed by Eliza, and Hugo stood up. He had taken only a few steps when Francis stopped him with a hand on his arm.

"Hugo," he said eagerly, "did you bring some books with you? I've read all of ours, and most of Grandpapa's, too."

"Have you, Frank? That's splendid," returned Hugo. "I didn't bring any, but we'll see about getting you some more. Excuse me," and he patted Francis on the shoulder and went with a brisk, slightly limping step out of the dining-parlor, along the lengthy corridor, and into the entryway where he found his mother in discussion with a tall, cadaverous man in an ill-fitting black coat who was tilting toward her in a way Hugo didn't care for; nor did Mama, apparently, for on her pretty face was a look of outright distress. The dogs, Hugo noticed, though antagonistic were keeping their distance, leading him to think that the fellow was one of those nasty sorts who kicked dogs, or brutally wielded the huge umbrella he carried and which was, in fact, dripping all over the floor.

"Your account, ma'am, is overdue. Considerable overdue. I've been plenty lenient, ma'am, for months now, but it's getting to be a problem, d'you see?" He tilted a little closer. "A problem that needs to be fixed, if you know what I mean."

"Oh, yes, Mr. Bambers, you've been so kind," said Mama falteringly, "and we do so appreciate it. It's just that—"

"What's going on here?" Hugo said, and the children, who had slipped up behind him, looked at each other with suppressed excitement. It was the same tone he'd used on Gwendolyn. Hugo *sounded* perfectly easygoing, but there was, unmistakably, steel in that deep, calm voice.

"Oh, Hugo darling," Mama said, turning to him a white and worried face, "this is Mr. Bambers. He's the coalman. I'm afraid we owe him quite a bit of money, and even though it's raining dreadfully, he's stopped by to remind me."

Mr. Bambers straightened. "That's it," he said, adding with unpleasant emphasis, "Twenty-eight pounds, thirteen shillings, and four pence, *plus* interest accrued, that comes to twenty-nine pounds, seven shillings, and six pence."

"You'll have it soon enough," answered Hugo, "and in the meantime, don't come bothering my family again."

"Bothering?" For a moment Mr. Bambers was inclined to take offense, and then he seemed to look more closely at Hugo's height, and muscular breadth, and his overall air of unobtrusive self-assurance, after which he swallowed visibly, bowed, and said, "So sorry to have troubled you, sir. Thank you, sir. I'll wish you all a good night."

It was Eliza who sprang into action then, holding wide the front door and saying cheerfully, "Miserable evening to be abroad, ain't it, Mr. Bambers? Raining by the buckets out there! Hope you don't catch cold or nothing, sir."

Mr. Bambers glared at her and fled into the rain, Eliza shut the door behind him, and the children gathered happily around Hugo.

"Routed him, by Jove!" exclaimed Percy. "Usually he hangs about till Mama starts crying, and I wish I had a sword so I could run it right through him."

"Oh, Hugo, did you come home rich?" Gwendolyn said hopefully. "Did you win a lot of prize-money?"

"That's for sailors, not soldiers," Percy told her pity-ingly, then glanced up at Hugo. "But did you? It'd be aw-fully nice."

"I'd love a new gown," said Gwendolyn, eyeing her old muslin with distaste, and Francis breathed, "Books."

"A horse of my own," said Percy.

"A microscope," said Bertram, dreamily.

"Off you all go," Hugo said. "I want to talk to Mama. Is there a fire lit in any of the other rooms?"

"Yes, in the library," said Gwendolyn, "that's where we all go in the evening, but Hugo, can't we come with you? We had very nearly finished our supper when you arrived. And we'll be as quiet as mice, I promise you."

"No," he said, pleasantly.

"But—"

"Oh, Gwennie, give it up," said Percy. "Let's go wait in the dining-parlor," he told the others. Francis followed him down the hallway, and so did Gwendolyn, but drag-ging her feet; Bertram paused to knowledgeably inform Hugo, "Speaking of mice, we have them," then trotted after his siblings, the dogs frisking behind him.

Hugo and Mama made their way into the library, which was just as he remembered it, filled with books and paint-ings and comfortable old sofas and chairs, a big faded rug underfoot, and heavy drapes drawn tight against the chill of the evening. He sat on one of the sofas, and stretched out his long booted legs on an ottoman; Mama perched on the edge of a chair, sitting very straight.

"Oh, Hugo darling," she said at once, "I'm so sorry you had to see that."

"Nonsense. *I'm* sorry you've had to deal with that fellow. Mama, have you other debts?"

"Yes, and I'm afraid—well, I'm afraid there are quite a lot of them. There's the grocer, and the chandler, and dear Dr. Wilson, who's been absolutely *gracious* about it, I assure you! The influenza was horrid last year, and not only did Francis and Gwendolyn contract it, so did Eliza and poor old Hoyt. And your Aunt Claudia also! We quite feared for her life the entire month of November. Which reminds me—we needed a great many bones for broth, and pork for jelly, and so unfortunately we *do* owe the butcher a substantial amount."

She fidgeted with the ends of her shawl, then, clearly determined to give a full accounting, added, "There's the linen-drapers as well, for the children do grow so, and the expense of the animals—somehow they seem to find us, the poor darlings, and I simply *couldn't* turn them away. And I know some people might think it's ridiculously extravagant, given our circumstances, to pension off a servant, but dear Robinson shakes so dreadfully, and he's been so good to us all these years! How could I not? And last month I had to take Bertram to Hensingham, to get a tooth pulled—he still has it in a jar on his windowsill, and I'm sure he'll want to show it to you. Oh, Hugo, Bertram didn't even flinch! It was *he* who gave me my smelling-salts afterwards, as cool as you please!"

Hugo nodded. "Pluck to the backbone, isn't he? You all are. Mama," he went on, gently, "I didn't think you were flush, precisely, all these years, but what with your income from the Funds, and what I've been sending, and Gabriel, too—I hadn't any idea things were so difficult for you."

Mama's enormous blue eyes were shimmering with tears, which valiantly she tried to blink away. "Oh, my darling Hugo, how could I bother you with these trivialities? There you were, so far away, desperately fighting for your life in that horrible wilderness!" She drew a deep breath. "I've made a ghastly mess of things, haven't I? I haven't even mentioned the Sunday collection-plate, and the subscription to the indigents' charity! You have every right to scold me."

Hugo raised his eyebrows. "Scold you, Mama? Don't be silly. You've done magnificently."

She was dabbing at her cheeks again, with that same ineffectual bit of a handkerchief. Then she looked at him and smiled a little. "Have I, dearest? Have I really?"

Hugo crossed one ankle over the other, and repressed a wince; his leg was really hurting now. It had been a long day. If, he reflected, he were the type of person to indulge in pointless guilt, he'd be obliged to feel bad for having loved being a soldier and enjoying it vastly, when all the while he'd been ignorant of their severe money problems. But—luckily—he wasn't that type. Both he and the mater, in their separate spheres, had done their best, and wasn't it humorous that they'd concealed from each other some of the less pleasant aspects of their existence? His wounds, her debts. So he said, with sincerity, "Yes, Mama, you've been a brick."

"I'm so glad you think so! Oh, Hugo, now that you're home, safe and well, everything is going to be fine." Her smile was confident now.

"To be sure it is," he said easily. "By the bye, is there any news from Brooke House since last you wrote me?"

"From Brooke House? Why, no, darling, not that I've heard of."

"Ah." Hugo yawned hugely, and turned his gaze to the cozily flickering fire, listening with contentment as a gust of wind sent rain spattering against the windows. How splendid to be inside and warm and dry. Of course, other people might be worrying right now about how many leaks there were in the roof, but *he* wasn't, as he had no intention of tramping upstairs tonight to find out. Nor was he brooding, possibly with a certain sense of pressure, about the fact that their situation was quite a bit worse than he'd thought.

There was nothing he could do about it right now.

And tomorrow was a new day, filled with possibility.

Hugo yawned again and got up, saying, "Well, Mama, I'm to bed." Half an hour later, having said good night to everyone including Señor Rodrigo, who (according to Gwendolyn) gave every sign of wanting to kiss him also (he civilly declined the honor), Hugo was in his bed, utterly relaxed, and deeply, peacefully asleep.

"**W**ake up, *mademoiselle*."

Katherine didn't open her eyes, but only groaned, twisted onto her side, and tugged the soft, rich bedcovers up around her chin. "Don't want to," she muttered to Céleste.

"The morning is well advanced, *mademoiselle,* and breakfast will soon commence."

Katherine groaned again. "I'm tired."

"When you stay up very late, it is to be expected."

Céleste's tone was unsympathetic, which was hardly surprising given that she slept on a truckle bed right next to Katherine's own vast luxurious one, and so had endured—as she often did—the full blaze of a candelabra set on a side table while Katherine, propped up on pillows, read until her eyes grew too weary to continue. And not just reading; also ignoring Céleste's grumblings and rustlings. Countless times had she suggested that Céleste move the truckle bed to a nice shadowy corner of the gargantuan bedchamber. But Céleste always refused, saying, with the unnecessarily dramatic air of a martyred saint about to be lashed to the pyre, *I know my duty, mademoiselle.*

So if Céleste didn't feel sympathetic toward *her,* she didn't feel sympathetic toward Céleste, either.

Last night she had read nearly into the morning hours, which of course was why she was so tired: she'd been devouring Mrs. Radcliffe's *The Italian, or the Confessional of the Black Penitents.* A preposterous novel, filled with lurid and improbable plot twists, but nonetheless wonderfully entertaining. In the end, the beautiful heroine Ellena di Rosalba was released from the convent where she'd been held against her will, and also she learned that not only was she *not* of humble birth, as she'd believed all her life, she actually had royal blood running through her veins, thereby making her completely eligible to marry her noble and heroic love, the dashing Vincentio di Vivaldi, who more than once almost died for her sake. Plus, all the nasty villains were exterminated, in horrible and very satisfying ways.

Speaking of devouring, while she was reading she'd also eaten all the remaining fifteen *diablotins*. Really, now that she thought of it, *The Italian* was a kind of *bonbon* in itself—a delicious confection for the brain. And now she was hungry for more. Unfortunately, having finished *The Italian*, she'd have to reopen negotiations with Céleste for a fresh supply of chocolate *and* forbidden novels. Bother. Katherine frowned and twisted onto her back, wincing. Blearily she opened her eyes.

"What's the weather today? Is it still raining?" she asked Céleste.

"Oui, mademoiselle."

Katherine's frown deepened. It was pleasant last night listening to the rain pattering against her windows while she was tucked up snugly in bed, but rain this morning meant that Father and the other men wouldn't go out hunting and shooting; instead they would crowd into the drawing-room after breakfast, where they'd hang about complaining, drinking, making an elaborate pretense of reading the newspapers, and sleeping, thereby taking up a great deal of space on the best sofas as well as rendering Katherine's enforced interval among Mother and the other women doubly tedious.

The day stretched before her, predictably and endlessly. Katherine pulled the covers up over her head. Maybe, if she was lucky, she would suffocate here in bed, die a peaceful death, and ascend to heaven, in her mind a lovely, quiet place where no one nagged at you, kept you from doing the things you liked, made people you despised sleep in the same room as you, or woke you up before you wanted. In fact, maybe heaven was a place where you could be absolutely alone. Wouldn't that be a treat?

"Get up, *mademoiselle, s'il vous plaît, le friseur* will soon be here."

"What? Why?"

"*Votre maman* mentioned to me, earlier, that your *coiffure* requires immediate amendment."

"But she had it done over last week. And now I have a fringe and look just like a Shetland pony. Isn't that enough for her?"

"Apparently, *mademoiselle,* your appearance is not yet satisfactory."

Even though Céleste's voice was muffled due to the bedcovers over Katherine's ears, she could still hear within it a distinct note of malicious satisfaction. She said, more to herself than to Céleste:

"It never will be."

She was able to state this with some certainty. It seemed that for all her life from Mother, from Father, had issued an endless stream of remarks suggestive of some fundamental lack. Her hair, for example, or her posture. Her complexion, her attitude. And so on. And so forth.

It had been drearily familiar at school, too. *Pay attention, Miss Brooke. Head up, eyes forward. Do stop gnawing at your fingernails; it's most unseemly. What are you scribbling there? No, you may not have more ink. You would be infinitely better off, Miss Brooke, if you could only conform; that is, after all, why your parents have sent you here, so that you might model yourself after the other young ladies. If you behave as though your background is without stain, you may, at least, foster that illusion when among those of impeccable breeding. Will you kindly turn your attention, Miss Brooke, to the front of the classroom. This constant daydreaming really must stop. More candles? What for? The reading interval is over; put down that book at once, it's a scientific fact that excessive reading damages the delicate tissues of the female brain. So troublesome—again—really, Miss Brooke, it's most trying.*

The memories had come crowding in, and rage ran through her now, ran through her body like a storm—a savage, merciless storm that could turn the sky black, uproot trees, sweep away houses. At the same time, she was rapidly emending her idea of heaven.

It was a place where nobody wanted to change you.

Katherine waited for the rage to subside, bit by bit, and in the slow wake of its receding devastation came deep sorrow, loneliness, and another thought: there was a strong likelihood she'd never gain admittance to heaven, for really, she wasn't at all sure that she was a good person. For one thing, she was quite unfilial. She couldn't remember the last time she'd summoned a scrap of affection for either of her parents. For another thing, she furtively spent most of her pin-money on illicit goods. Also, quite frequently she made a pretense of listening to people when really she wasn't, occupying herself instead by thinking her own thoughts. No, it was the other place where she would probably end up, being prodded with a pitchfork by a devil who would look exactly like Céleste.

"Get up, *mademoiselle,* or else—"

"I *know!*" Katherine threw back the bedcovers. "Or else *ma chère maman* will chide us." She sat up, and her back began to hurt her even more. "Damn," she said, but very, very quietly, lest *chère* Céleste report to Mother that Katherine had been heard to utter a dreadful, low, vulgar word—*just* like the grandchild of a miner, which, undeniably, she was, a troublesome fact that Mrs. Brooke had for many years labored to conceal.

Having enjoyed breakfast with his usual hearty appe-
tite, and then unearthing a pair of his old brogues entirely
suited for a good tramp through the countryside, Hugo had
set off for Brooke House, cheerfully disregarding both the
light rain overhead and the mud underfoot. He was home,
he'd slept well, there was no tripe put in front of him this
morning, and here he was, quite literally moving forward
with his plan to fix things.

As he walked along the sodden lane, Hugo tried to
summon to his mind an image of Katherine Brooke. She
had dark hair, he remembered that, and *perhaps* her eyes
were dark also, but he could recall nothing else about her
appearance. In her letter, Mama had said that Katherine
was sweet and lively; this did align with Hugo's memory
of her. She seemed always to be chattering on about
books, dolls, kittens, flowers, and fairies, in such a droll,
engaging way that one couldn't help but be entertained
(despite generally preferring to discuss horses, fishing,
Army maneuvers, a seal carcass which had washed up on
the beach, that sort of thing).

He remembered, now, Mama once saying, *Poor little
girl, she's here so often it almost seems as if she wants
to live here. But of course I haven't the heart to turn her
away.*

There was more to be known about the Brookes, had
Hugo wished to consult his mother, or Cook, or Whitehaven's most fruitful source of information, the wonderfully knowledgeable butcher's wife.

At the time of which Hugo was thinking, the Brookes
had lived next door in a large, handsome brick house very
much like that of the Penhallows; it belonged to Katherine's grandfather, old Joseph Bugle, who had begun his
working life as a child joining his father in the coal mines,
and eventually—through relentless effort and ruthless
ambition—amassing ownership of a dozen mines and an

incredible fortune to boot. Having married the equally
humble daughter of a collier's agent, he'd shrewdly
snapped up the brick house on the beach when its unlucky
owner had fallen on hard times, and there established his
bride.

They were blessed in due course with one child only,
a daughter, Hester, who had inherited her father's soar-
ing ambition, except that hers was focused on the social
sphere rather than on the financial; at twenty she'd managed to leap up the ladder by eloping with Rowland
Brooke, the son of an impoverished Yorkshire baronet—
who had promptly disowned him for sinking so low as to
marry the offspring of a low-bred laborer. But Rowland
hardly noticed; he'd made his choice, had staked everything on his chances with the Bugles.

Never one to willingly part with his hard-earned
money, old Joseph had insisted that for the sake of economy Hester and her new husband live under his roof, and
for several years explosive acrimony had reigned within.

Joseph loathed his son-in-law Rowland, whom he cas-
tigated as a pretentious, dandified ne'er-do-well. Hester
resented this as an aspersion on her own cleverness,
and told her father so, deliberately throwing in French
phrases which he didn't understand and which rendered
him nearly apoplectic with rage. Rowland, for his part,
tolerated his father-in-law as one would a large primate
with whom one was trapped in a cage—a primate with a
finite life-span that happened to be sitting on a bulging
chest of gold coins.

Within weeks of their wedding Rowland and Hester
discovered that aside from a mutual interest in social
advancement they had nothing in common, and it
wasn't long before they were fighting about everything,
including whether the sky was really blue and if pigs
could fly, albeit in low tones so infused with vitriol that
in a way their arguments were worse than if they were
shouting.

Old Joseph's wife, wilting in this turgid atmosphere, quietly and gratefully passed away when Katherine was nine, and the next year Joseph was dead too, having tumbled into one of his own pits, an accident felt by many in the community to be cosmic justice.

The lawyers had barely finished articulating the terms of Joseph Bugle's will before Rowland, with Hester's eager assent, had sold the mines *and* the old brick house, and bought a large piece of land five miles past town, on which they proceeded to have built what they called "Brooke House" and quite a few of the Whitehaven wags termed "Broke House" due to its staggering expense.

Had such calumny come to their ears, Rowland and Hester would have ignored it, secure not only in the 300,000 pounds' worth of profit from the mines but also in the additional monies that were coming in from Rowland's new investments. Not all of them were successful, of course, but that was how business went, anyone with half a brain knew that. Why, only last week Rowland had suffered an aggravating loss in the wool market, but yesterday he had received a very satisfying cheque from the proprietors of the Swansea and Mumbles Railway, in whose daring venture he'd had the impressive foresight to invest.

Of this, naturally, Hugo was not aware, but all that really mattered to him was that the Brookes had a daughter, who was yet unmarried, with whom he had, in childhood, shared an affectionate friendship.

He smiled at the memory. Maybe, just maybe, there was still a reservoir of that attachment between himself and Katherine. Perhaps they could find real happiness together.

He walked on.

Absently Katherine eyed Sir John Bronrigg, who was seated in the chair next to hers and had been talking volubly, and at great length, about sealing wax, but as she had been pretending to be deaf, she now had no idea as to his current topic. Cabbages, perhaps, or the King's latest maniacal outburst. It occurred to her now, all at once, that Sir John reminded her of Monsieur de la Motte, late of the Basingstoke Academy; he was romantically slim, dark-haired, dark-eyed, plus he had a habit of quoting (inaccurately) from Robert Southey's epic poem *The Curse of Kehama* with a throwaway air that everyone said was positively mesmerizing.

Katherine waited uneasily for that deadly flicker of response, but there was nothing. No giddy flutter, no longing. No desire to bring him any closer than he already was.

Excellent.

She was completely in control. As cold as a block of ice, and as safe as any locked box.

Into her mind flickered a memory of herself at fifteen, rendered helpless with desire for Germaine de la Motte, and its ugly aftermath when they'd been discovered. What a silly little fool she had been.

But never again.

Katherine kept her gaze fixed on Sir John, idly wondering if, three or four years into the future, her parents would consider him an acceptable matrimonial candidate. Earlier this year, during her Season as unquestionably the richest young lady on the Marriage Mart, she'd received quite a few offers, but Father and Mother refused them all, as they'd been holding out for a duke, or a marquis at the very least.

None had been forthcoming. Naturally it didn't help that they hadn't received vouchers for Almack's, or invitations to the *ton*'s most select gatherings. Discreet *douceurs* (as Mother called them; bribes were what they were) to certain financially challenged hostesses had gotten them admitted to some of the better parties, but— alas, no duke or marquis had fallen on his knees before Katherine and offered her his hand and heart.

For Katherine's next Season, her parents had indicated, they would settle for an earl or a viscount.

Failing that, Katherine supposed, the year after *that* a baron such as Sir John would have to suffice or even, if all hope by then was lost, a hereditary knight.

And what came below that? She knitted her brows, thinking hard. There was a regular sort of knight, which, progressing from dukes downward, pretty much covered the nobility and the gentry, unless you factored in aristocrats from Ireland, Scotland, and so forth. What about the well-born from further afield? There was the rest of Europe, and Asia, and America (North and South, along with that interesting bit in the middle), and—

Katherine was mentally circumnavigating the globe and so missed the stately entrance of their butler Turpin, who announced in solemn tones, "Captain Hugo Penhallow," and also she failed to notice the awed ripple that swept throughout the room as well as the rather piquant sight of her parents surging forward to meet their unexpected guest, hailing him as a former neighbor and therefore a cherished member of their acquaintance, and jockeying for the privilege of being the very first to greet him.

It was only Sir John saying "Miss *Brooke*" in a loud voice that brought Katherine out of her reverie. He went on, more quietly but with a distinct note of awe:

"You *know* him?"

"Who?"

"Him," said Sir John, and she followed his gaze, to see an enormously tall, broad-shouldered man walking toward her, with thick golden hair cropped short and eyes the vivid blue color of sapphires. Goodness, she thought, surprised, how had a Greek god descended from Olympus and arrived in their hideously overdecorated drawing-room?

Even as that fanciful thought ricocheted through her mind, even as she stared at him—registering, in a second wave of heightened awareness, the stunning handsomeness of his face, the muscular strength of him and the easy grace with which he moved—an unwelcome, galvanic energy snaked its way through her body, supple and sinuous and merciless. Oh God, no, she'd *done* with this, she'd quashed this dangerous and humiliating tendency. Her feeling of safety evaporated, and a hot red flush rose up from her throat to her face, rendering her, she thought with awful self-consciousness, the exact shade of a ripe cherry. And why on earth was he *smiling* at her?

"Hullo, Kate."

Katherine blinked. The man had stopped before her, flanked by Mother and Father who had suddenly the aspect of guards keeping a prisoner in check. Although *he* was clearly so powerful he could—like mighty Zeus, say, or Apollo—flick them away like flies. It made for such an appealing image that she didn't respond, only gazed up at him as if entranced.

"Hullo," he repeated in a deep, pleasant voice, and then it came to her in a flash.

It was *Hugo.*

Hugo from her childhood.

Hugo Penhallow, whose memory, curiously enough, had surfaced in her mind once or twice during the Season, thanks to that dreadful old relative of his, and then sunk away into oblivion.

Still she said nothing as he bowed and added, "That is to say—Miss Brooke. How do you do?"

Reflexively, through long habit, suspicion rose within her, and Katherine steeled herself to resist that smile of his. That friendly charm, that impossibly glorious—horribly perilous—masculinity. What platitudes could she force herself to utter? Oh yes, the old fallback: "How do you do."

"I'm very well, thanks."

Think, think, you fool. Regurgitate another platitude. "You're in Whitehaven visiting your family?"

"Not a visit, no. I was in the Army for several years, but I've sold out and come home."

"Oh." Katherine wished he would go away, wished her fiery blushes would subside, wished she were safely tucked back in bed with a book—

Not with a book, but with him, came the wicked thought, *with Hugo,* and she scowled in an attempt to disguise her deepening fear as she reeled out of control.

"Katherine, do smile," said Mother. "Isn't it *merveilleux* that Captain Penhallow has come to call on us?"

Her lips were curved upward, noticed Katherine, in a simulacrum of a smile, but in her eyes was the icy alertness of a raptor. Mother was on the hunt again. Without waiting for Katherine to respond she went on with arch animation:

"We recently had the pleasure of meeting your esteemed relation in London. I refer, *bien sûr,* to Mrs. Henrietta Penhallow. Such graciousness, such *cordialité!* London was positively *abuzz* with rumors about her reasons for participating in the Season after such a long absence. So very titillating, don't you think so, Captain?"

Hugo Penhallow looked at her rather blankly. "I beg your pardon, ma'am?"

Mother's artificial smile widened. "Why, her search for a suitable bride for her grandson Gabriel. So *many* young ladies entertaining hopes! But one hears that a rather unexpected *jeune fille* somehow managed to dominate the field."

"As to that, ma'am, I can't say. I *can* tell you that my cousin's engaged to a fine young lady, Miss Livia Stuart."

"Yes, but who *is* she? No one's ever heard of her," said Mother, plainly hoping for confidential information (which could provide her with some status-elevating gossip), and Father put in, "You're the heir, though, aren't you, Captain? If Gabriel Penhallow doesn't have a son? Or happens to die soon?"

By now Katherine was plunged so deep in embarrassment that willingly could she have murdered both her parents. In front of all the gaping guests. With, say, the exquisite and expensive fan she held, on which the rosy figures of winged cherubs cavorted like idiots. If you used enough force, even delicate horn sticks would work, wouldn't they? *"Father,"* she muttered.

He glanced down at her. "What? Happens all the time, doesn't it? Life's like that. Unpredictable."

Brushing aside what she no doubt considered a pointless divagation, Mother jumped in again. "And what about yourself, Captain? Have you selected a fortunate *demoiselle* to call your own?"

Repressing a groan, Katherine slid down three or four inches in her seat. If she pretended she was boneless, maybe she could ooze off the chair, congeal in a puddle of shame, and be absorbed by the soft fibers of the luxurious Oriental carpet on which her kid slippers rested, thereby disappearing forever. Still, she couldn't keep from looking up at Hugo Penhallow, on whose handsome face was still that expression of courteous blankness.

"Ah—no, ma'am, I haven't," he said to Mother.

"What a loss to womanhood," she replied, brightening, "I do hope you'll remedy that *très bientôt*," and then she swung around to Sir John Bronrigg. "Oh, Sir John, I'm sure you won't mind giving way to *le cher* Captain Penhallow, will you? He and Katherine have so much to catch up on. Do get up, *s'il vous plaît*."

"What?—oh!—of course—" Sir John shambled to his feet and was instantly borne away by Father, while Mother stood at a remove of some five or six feet, her vigilant posture making it very clear to anyone of even the dimmest intelligence that her daughter and her distinguished guest were to enjoy an uninterrupted *tête-à-tête de la plus délicieuse*. Anyone might look, of course, but they had better not approach.

Or they might be very, very sorry.

Chapter 3

Hugo sat down.

For a moment he wondered which was worse: being stared at, or tripe.

It was an unanswerable question, and instead he looked over at Kate—at Katherine Brooke—hoping he'd done reasonably well at masking his surprise at her appearance.

Of course he hadn't come here expecting to find a little girl, he knew she'd be all grown up, but it was rather difficult to simply *see* her as she was now. One's attention was inexorably drawn to the large glinting jeweled ear-bobs, and to her dark hair, pulled up into a sort of high bundle around which strings of pearls and diamonds had been wrapped, leaving a thick straight fringe arrayed across her forehead with a stiff, crisp appearance. Also, Hugo was no judge of women's fashion, nor was he a critical sort of man, but it did seem that Katherine's gown had quite a lot of ruffles on it—running from her waist down to the hem, which had its own perpendicular set of them, along with multiple bands looping round the shoulders and at the wrists as well, giving Katherine overall a rather puffy look and also a sparkly one due to the diamonds in her hair and the three or four strands of them hung round her neck and which lay across her bosom in a glittering display.

Another thing he hadn't expected was her reaction to him.

She hadn't smiled, she hadn't seemed at all glad to see him, and altogether she gave the impression of being sorry that French sharpshooter hadn't done a better job of trying to annihilate him.

As he looked at her, she slid a little lower in her seat, her face flushed a bright red and on it an expression of sullen hostility. Puzzled, and conscious that her mother was well within earshot, Hugo said politely to Katherine:

"It's nice to see you again."

"Thank you," she muttered.

"Been a while, hasn't it?"

"Yes."

"Thirteen years, by my calculation."

"I suppose so."

"At my father's funeral."

"Yes."

"You were still living next door to us."

"Yes."

"Miss the ocean, and the beach?"

"I don't know. I never think about it."

"Enjoy living in the country, then?"

She shrugged.

"Did you like London?" he asked.

She shrugged again, and silence hung between them, almost like a physical thing. Hugo now wondered which was worse: being stared at, tripe, or sitting next to someone who disliked you.

He tried again. "So you met my Aunt Henrietta in London?"

"Not really."

"But . . ."

Here Mrs. Brooke darted forward. "The *charmante*

Mrs. Penhallow! *Quite* the first lady of London! I simply *dote* on her! Katherine, *ma douce,* I'm sure that Captain Penhallow would *absolument* adore seeing our new ruins. Why don't you take him for a little tour?"

Katherine glared up at her mother. "It's raining."

Mrs. Brooke gave a little tinkling laugh. "Oh, hardly at all! A bit of rain won't *melt* you, *après tout.*"

"Are we to go without a chaperone, Mother?" Katherine's tone was sardonic.

"Oh, you and the captain are old friends, *n'est-ce pas?* Most unobjectionable! Do go, *ma chère petite fille.*" And she gave Katherine a look which made it clear she wasn't asking, she was commanding.

"Fine," Katherine said dourly, then glanced at him. "If *you* want to."

It was less a question of wanting to view new ruins— and wasn't that an oxymoron, incidentally?—than being given an excuse to leave this stuffy crowded drawing-room. Hugo rose to his feet with alacrity. "I'd love to."

For a moment he would have sworn that Katherine was afraid of something—him? How could that possibly be?— and then she gave a deep, annoyed-sounding, entirely audible sigh and got up also, grimacing as if something hurt her. Quickly Hugo offered her his arm. "Miss Brooke?"

She actually leaned away from him, as if he were some kind of repulsive, bad-smelling troll she'd found lurking under a bridge somewhere, and dropped her unfurled fan onto her chair. "Let's go."

As they walked away, Hugo heard from behind him Mr. Brooke saying to someone in a loud whisper, "The Whitehaven branch of the Penhallows, you know, poor as church-mice, but still, a Penhallow's better than a duke any day," Mrs. Brooke saying, "Such a *handsome* couple, *ne sont-ils pas,*" as well as, inevitably, somebody else commenting, "Captain Penhallow looks just like a Greek god, doesn't he?"

Hugo resisted the impulse to growl at this last and all too familiar remark, and ignored the others. He and Katherine then passed an awkward mute interval in the cathedral-like Great Hall while they waited for a maid to bring her a pelisse and a hat, with the butler and his several satellites standing about. (They, at least, had the courtesy not to stare.) In the meantime, Hugo gazed up at the ceiling, which displayed an astonishing quantity of arched panels and gold leaf. This, he thought, wasn't so much a home as a sort of bizarre museum. A damned uncomfortable place to live, if you asked him.

In due course the maid arrived and assisted her mistress into a high-necked, crimson pelisse heavily trimmed with ermine and then placed over the high knob of Katherine's hair a red velvet hat festooned with lace and several large artificial flowers. She had brought with her soft kid gloves as well as a pair of half-boots embroidered with so much silver thread it was difficult to see the leather underneath. "If *mademoiselle* would step into the *salon* just over there," the maid said, "I shall help you with the boots."

Katherine seemed about to comply, but then she glanced up at him; an arrested look came onto her face and for several moments she simply stood there, stock-still, as if consumed by her own thoughts.

"Your boots, *mademoiselle*. If you would be so good as to come with me—"

"I don't want them."

"But *mademoiselle,* your slippers will be ruined."

"Very likely."

"Votre maman—" whispered the maid.

Katherine only shrugged. "Let's go," she said again to Hugo.

"Mademoiselle, your gloves."

"No. Turpin, the door, please."

"At once, Miss Katherine," and the butler signaled to a subordinate, who hastened to comply.

A cool, playful breeze from outside whirled to meet them, causing the white lace on Katherine's hat to flop wildly about, and together they crossed the threshold into a damp pungent world of scudding gray clouds high above, everywhere the rich smell of wet earth, and fallen leaves scattered at their feet in a wanton riot of red, orange, green, gold. They made their way along a wide, winding path toward a thickly clustered grove; once they had reached it, and followed along three or four of its long gentle curves, Brooke House disappeared from their view as if it had never existed.

Hugo looked over at Katherine. She was frowning a little, with her gaze fixed on the muddy ground in front of her, giving the appearance of one who was mentally a thousand miles away.

"Kate," he said, "do you really want to be out here? With me?"

Again he would have sworn he saw a little fearful tremor run through her, but she only replied:

"I am Katherine now. And you should call me 'Miss Brooke,' you know."

"Miss Brooke," he repeated, pleasantly. "Shall I take you back to the house?"

"No."

"As you wish."

"Ha," she said, as if she couldn't help it.

"I beg your pardon?"

"Nothing. Never mind."

Well, Hugo thought, this had turned out rather badly. Not that it wasn't refreshing to be around a woman who didn't fawn all over him, complimenting him about his looks until he heartily desired to be elsewhere, but it was obvious that Katherine Brooke found him unappealing.

His chances with her were plainly nil.

It was a setback, if not an outright blow, but at least he'd made the attempt.

Rapidly his mind moved across his alternatives. He'd need to immediately confer with their man of business and together try to reach an accommodation with their various creditors. Remembering his offer to Mama, at thirteen, to become a sailor, he wondered now if he might make good on that. He had always loved boats, had spent countless hours at the wharves looking at them. He'd hate to ship out and leave the family so soon, and the money would hardly make a dent in the enormity of their pressing needs, but it would be a start. And wouldn't it be jolly to climb a rigging at last?

"There it is," said Katherine.

They had come round another bend in the path, and before them loomed a high, massive, flat-topped structure made of artfully worn tan-colored bricks, featuring a long series of tall graceful archways; around it had been placed great tumbled blocks of the same tan material, conveying the impression that time had, across countless millennia, slowly and gently softened their hard geometrical lines. It was an extraordinary set-piece, intended to evoke an ancient Biblical era, the exotic Fertile Crescent, turbaned people in colorful robes and dusty hemp sandals, camel trains, a blazing sun, swaying palm trees, and so forth— and it had been placed in the middle of a sylvan English wood.

"Egad," said Hugo, having thoroughly looked it over, "that's not something you see every day."

"My parents just had it built," Katherine answered, but absently. A deep furrow had formed between her dark brows.

"What *is* it, exactly?"

"It's supposed to be the ruins of Babylon."

He wanted to laugh, but instead said, "It's certainly unusual," feeling himself to be on solid ground with this honest observation. As she did not reply, he went on: "Well, we've seen it; shall we go back?" He half-turned away, but then Katherine did speak.

"Wait. Let's go inside."

"Is that what you want?"

"Yes."

And so he followed her, among and past the huge artificial blocks and into the building itself, where the archways allowed cool gray light to flood the colorfully tiled interior. Against one wall was a low stone platform; on it were two high-backed marble thrones of an unpleasant ochre color reminiscent of dried blood, and, even worse, they were ringed by a threatening phalanx of large, carved wooden creatures that looked like a cross between an angry lion and a dyspeptic monkey. Katherine went to sit on one throne, and Hugo, reluctantly, sat on the other.

"One feels like King Solomon," he said. "Dispensing judgments and telling women to cut their infants in half. Not my cup of tea."

"Never mind that." Katherine swiveled around in her seat—he was damned if he'd keep thinking of them as thrones—and looked him straight in the eye.

"You asked if we met your Aunt Henrietta in London." He nodded.

"We didn't meet her, precisely. We saw her at the Royal Academy of Art, and my parents tried to introduce ourselves to her—to bring me to her attention." Katherine smiled without humor. "Hoping she'd choose me for her grandson. To have Gabriel Penhallow marry me."

Hugo pictured in his mind his elegant, slender, silvery-haired relative. Elderly she might be, but she was still sharp as a tack and with a posture as ramrod-straight as that of any soldier. Also she was the haughtiest, proudest, and, frequently, the most caustic person he knew. It wasn't hard to imagine what happened when she'd been approached by what she would doubtless pronounce a set of ghastly brazen *parvenus*. He said:

"Didn't go well, I expect."

"No."

"Snubbed you horribly?"

"Yes."

He nodded again. "I'm sorry."

"Don't be. We deserved it. My parents are desperate, you see, and that's stripped them of any subtlety they might ever have had."

"Desperate? About what?"

That humorless smile of hers was still there. "Well, I'm their only hope, I'm afraid, and I'm not exactly a *help,* am I."

Oh, damn, Hugo thought, this was just the sort of conversation he hated, filled with opacities as treacherous as any *fougasse,* the dreaded land mines which could suddenly blow the unwary to bits. Bluntly he replied, "Their only hope for what?"

"To establish themselves among the *beau monde.*"

"Ah." It seemed to him rather a trivial goal, but then again, he reminded himself, he was hardly in a position to judge; wasn't he here strategically deploying the Penhallow name, after all? Then something Katherine had said looped again in his brain, and he looked at her more closely. Her skin was very white and smooth, he noticed suddenly, and her lips the exact color of a ripe cherry. Delicious, tempting . . . but not for him, alas, to taste. He pulled himself together and went on, "They see you as their only hope? Puts rather a lot of pressure on you, doesn't it?"

Her big, dark eyes seemed to shimmer for a moment; but then she sat up a little straighter and said, "Oh, you should save your sympathy for my parents, Captain. It's been quite an arduous gamble for them, after all, especially since I'm of so little value—being, you know, a less than ideal commodity in their high-stakes game."

Well, here was another conversational land mine, especially given the reason for his visit today. Hugo wondered again how he might bring this awkward conversation to a close, and make a graceful exit. In the sudden silence that fell between them, he watched as her gaze traveled over him and abruptly she dropped her eyes; he saw her hands clenching tight in her lap. A minute ticked by, then another, and another. A red flush bloomed again on her face, spreading across the soft alabaster of her cheeks. Finally she said:

"Let's talk about something else."

"Certainly. What would you like to discuss?"

"You."

Katherine didn't dare look at Hugo Penhallow any longer, for fear she might actually do what she urgently wanted, what her traitorous body was yearning for her to do, which was to go over to him, put her hands on those broad shoulders, lean close and—oh, lick his face, rub her face against the dense gold of his hair, put her mouth hard on his, and more . . .

No.

No.

She took a deep, calming breath, could almost feel herself cooling down into that reassuring block of ice. Oh, better. She looked down at her feet, and registered with pleasure the fact that her slippers were indeed muddy and ruined, precisely as Céleste had warned her they'd be.

Back there in the Great Hall, she'd been just about to obediently change her slippers for the half-boots, but then she'd let herself glance up at Hugo—at that magnificent face, with its proud straight nose, perfect mouth, those extraordinary blue eyes filled with light—and inspiration had come to her, so fast and so dazzlingly it felt like there were fireworks inside her head.

She had an idea.

Sitting in this ridiculous building, on this absurd marble seat, it suddenly occurred to her that the young Katherine-that-was would have invited Hugo to play at being kings and queens. Would have pretended that those bizarre wood creatures surrounding them were their courtiers, or their servants, or their enemies, or their children, or—

She broke off this distracting train of thought, wrenched herself back into the present, and looked again at Hugo, pleased at how steady and firm she felt. She said:

"I heard Father talking as we left the drawing-room, Captain. Is it true that you're poor?"

"Yes," he said calmly.

"And were you telling Mother the truth, that you're not affianced elsewhere?"

"Yes."

Katherine nodded. Oh, damn, her heart was hammering hard within her, as if it were a caged animal trying to burst free. To combat it, to bring herself back into coolness, into her mind she summoned an image, a certain passage from one of her hidden history books, this one about the ancient Romans. Cornelius Tacitus had written in 97 A.D. about the Sitones, a tribe in northern Europe which was believed to be a matriarchal society. Among the Sitones, Tacitus said, the women were powerful; the women chose their mates.

It was a wild, a radical idea back then—disapprovingly had Tacitus commented upon its harmful effects—and it still was, of course, seventeen hundred years later. Even in this modern era, in which civilization had evolved with things like the printing press, steam engines, inoculations, gas lights, the *Encyclopædia Britannica,* and Herschel's great telescopes, women were still supposed to demurely sit around, waiting for some man to ask her to be his wife.

But an hour ago, Hugo Penhallow had unexpectedly strolled into her parents' drawing-room, and maybe, just maybe, they could effect a trade to their mutual benefit. It was not, to say the least, a romantic proposition, but it had been a long, long time since she had indulged in girlish dreams of love, a soulmate, happily ever after.

And here, right in front of her, was an opportunity to escape Brooke House.

So to Hugo she said, in a voice that was only a little bit breathless:

"Marry me."

She saw his blue eyes widen, and the look of surprise on his face. And then—and then—

He laughed.

And Katherine shrank back in her chair, almost as if he'd pushed on her chest with one large, strong hand. To her horror, it felt as if her face was crumpling, giving her away, showing too much, and quickly she brought her hands to cover it. Her fingers, she noticed distantly, were icy. *I should have worn my gloves, what a stupid girl I am. And what was I thinking, asking him such a thing? I deserve to be mocked.* Out loud she said in a low choked voice, "Go away."

"Kate," he said, not laughing now, "oh, Kate—"

"I'm *Katherine!*" It was a shriek, but muffled by the hands she still pressed hard against her face. "Go *away!*"

Then, startling her, his own hands were upon her bare wrists, and with enormous care he drew them away and onto her lap; he was kneeling before her, his expression one of deep contrition. "God, but I'm an oaf. I wasn't laughing at you, Miss Brooke, I swear it."

Pleasure at his touch, at his warm hands upon her cool flesh, shivered through her, and just as quickly came the old devastating fear. Misinterpreting that shiver, perhaps, he released her wrists, but remained on his knees before her. She said, rather roughly:

"What's so funny, then?"

"I laughed because you said the very thing I came here to say to you."

She stared at him. "Are you joking?"

"No."

"But—" She broke off. His admission made everything very easy, but why was it so painful to hear? At least he'd had the decency not to pretend he was madly in love with her. She took refuge in curtness. "Oh, do get up. You look foolish like that."

He only smiled, as if her words had no power to sting, then rose to his feet in a single lithe movement and sat again, with such easy self-assurance that despite herself she couldn't help but think how Penhallows and thrones just seemed to go together. She recalled that brief, humiliating encounter with Mrs. Henrietta Penhallow, an imperious and queenly dame, who, you could tell, moved through life with effortless grace, as one to the manor born, without ever having to question where she belonged.

Or *if* she belonged.

Those lucky, lucky Penhallows.

Then it blazed through Katherine's mind, like a comet lighting up the night sky: this marriage could not only set her free, it would make her a Penhallow, too.

Katherine Penhallow.

She could practically hear herself saying, with a confident little toss of her head, *Will I be going to Almack's this evening, you ask? Yes, of course, all of the Patronesses have called and presented me with vouchers. The Queen's Drawing-room? To be sure I am. The latest Carlton House fête? That also.*

Of course, her future in-laws would despise her, she was certain of that. She was no Ellena di Rosalba, the saintly, high-minded heroine of *The Italian*. She wasn't angelically and perfectly beautiful, nor was there royal blood running through *her* veins. She was just—a person.

But what did she care? To her came again an image of Henrietta Penhallow, this time one of her scandalized outrage when she received the news of Hugo's betrothal to that dreadfully common girl whose parents had shoved her forward at the Royal Academy. Katherine smiled, just a little. She couldn't blame Mrs. Penhallow for her reaction, but still, wouldn't it be enjoyable to meet her again one day as equals?

And wouldn't it be wonderful to have a very different Season next year? A chance to do it all over again?

How rarely in life did such an opportunity come along. Katherine's breath caught in her throat with a fierce, terrible joy. She said to Hugo:

"You need money."

"Yes."

"I've got plenty of it. Or, rather, my father does."

"So I've heard."

"Your name for Brooke money. That seems like a fair exchange."

He smiled ruefully. "I hope so. That's all I've got to give you."

Oh, but you're wrong, she very nearly blurted out, as helplessly her eyes traveled down the long length of him, then writhed as a hot, horrifying wave of shame flowed over her, much as she imagined lava might feel upon naked skin.

"Are you all right?"

Repressing the urge to frantically unbutton her pelisse, sorry she had left her fan behind in the house, Katherine gripped the marble arms of her seat, welcoming their hard inanimate coldness. "I'm fine."

"Are you? You reminded me of myself, when my leg's troubling me."

"What do you mean?" she asked defensively.

"I broke it a while back, and it hurts a little when I'm tired. You looked as if—"

"How did you break your leg?" she interrupted, wanting very much to change the subject.

"Oh, some mad American came leaping upon me with a bayonet, and after I clouted him with my musket I fell off my horse onto *another* American. Broke my leg, but it was a stroke of luck for sure."

"How was that a stroke of luck?"

"Why, that second fellow was creeping up behind me with a tomahawk." Hugo laughed. "I'm afraid he was rather done in after I fell on him. There's so *much* of me."

Katherine eyed him in surprise. How lightly he spoke. He wasn't bitter, nor was he boasting, as so many military men seemed to do. Among her parents' acquaintance, for example, was a relic of the Maratha wars fought against India in the previous century, and his single subject of conversation was his prowess on the battlefield, the terror he struck into the hearts of the enemy, the vast numbers of them he slaughtered, his expertise in every weapon known to man, and on and on, until she'd wondered if he had actually bored the poor Marathas to death by talking to them.

"A tomahawk is a type of axe, isn't it?" she said. "I've read about it."

"Egad, have you? Nasty things—frightfully effective. Not well-known here in England, though. Where'd you read about it?"

"Oh," she answered vaguely, "somewhere," and felt yet another awful flush coming over her. She had so much to hide from him. The books she read, the chocolates she ate, the kind of person she really was inside . . . Before Katherine could stop herself she said:

"You remember my grandfather the miner, don't you?"

She waited for his face to change, for the look of revulsion, whether open or masked, but Hugo only said, "Yes. Joseph Bugle, wasn't he? He used to terrify me when I was a boy. As I recall, he shouted more often than he spoke."

"That's about right. But—he was a *miner,* Captain."

"I know that."

"You're not worried about the taint to the Penhallow line?"

She saw that he was looking at her curiously. He said:

"Taint? Is that how you think of it?"

"Don't you?"

"No. I expect there was that sort of talk about blood-lines when my father married a vicar's daughter, but it's all rot in my opinion."

Coming from a Penhallow this was hard to believe, but still she gave him one last chance to easily withdraw. "Are you sure you want to marry me?"

"Very sure. You're helping my family, and I'm grateful to you."

"I hope you won't regret it, Captain."

"I won't."

"How can you know that?"

"I just do." In his deep, calm voice was obvious confidence, and Katherine envied him that. She, on the other hand, was still aflame with that hot revealing blush and her mind was skittering in a thousand different directions. She hardly knew what to say, or how to act. To her fevered imagination came a sound, the distinctive rasp of massive old gates swinging open, the noise Ellena di Rosalba might have heard as she was released from her lengthy confinement in the convent.

And then the sound shifted somehow, to the little scratches of a quill moving across a piece of paper. She needed, now, to be a Cardinal Wolsey or a Thomas Cromwell, those towering, fiendishly clever figures from Henry Tudor's time, writing their letters to kings and popes, to dukes and generals, masterfully negotiating pacts and orchestrating events. She wasn't about to surrender herself entirely to Hugo Penhallow. If her parents' marriage was anything to judge by, she needed to make certain of her sovereignty.

She must be hard and sure. Could, at least, *pretend* to be. Even if she felt like blancmange on the inside.

Katherine made her lips curve upward in a smile.

"Very well then," she told Hugo Penhallow. "I reiterate my offer. The bride takes a groom."

Chapter 4

It was done. It was really going to happen. Hugo felt a huge wave of relief wash over him, and he bounded to his feet, more than ready to leave the ruins of Babylon and return to the comforts of 1811. "I'm glad. Very glad. I'll do my best to make you happy, Ka—" He stopped himself, just in time. "Miss Brooke."

"It's nonsensical to talk of happiness in an exchange of commodities. A business arrangement. Where are you going?"

"Out. Aren't we done here?"

"Not yet. Before we seal our bargain, you must consent to my terms."

"Terms?"

"Of course. I just told you, this is a business arrangement."

He looked down at her curiously. He had spoken of happiness, she talked about business. "Go on."

"You're to make your own, completely separate financial arrangements with my father. I'll want my own money, to spend as I like."

"Agreed."

"You're not to tell me what to do."

"Of course not."

"That includes—" The line of her mouth tightened. "—that includes our intimate life."

By Jupiter, he hadn't even thought about such things—the delights of the marriage bed. But now that he was, it occurred to him how much he'd relish a stable arrangement. A wife, to have and to hold, someone with whom to give and receive pleasure across the decades. As a longtime soldier on the move, opportunities for sexual encounters had come to him all too erratically. Unlike the other men, he'd never actually had to pay a woman to lie with him—much to the envious derision of his fellow officers, but undoubtedly a benefit for one so perpetually purse-pinched as himself. However, given what Katherine had just said, it didn't seem that this aspect of their marriage was going to be at all simple.

A land mine of a different sort, evidently.

Well, in for a penny, in for a pound, and quite an apt metaphor under the circumstances, wasn't it? Affably, he said to Katherine:

"What do you mean precisely?"

"You must do as I say. I must be in control of—it. When it happens. *What* happens."

Her face, he saw, was as intense a red as her pelisse, and her big dark eyes had a fiery glitter in them. She reminded him of a pugilist against the ropes, on the verge of bursting out in a frantic rush of violence against a foe. He hoped—very much did he hope—that she didn't think of marriage as a boxing ring, with a husband and wife approaching each other with fists raised.

"Well, Captain? What do you say?"

"I accept your terms."

"Swear it."

"I swear it, Miss Brooke."

Her shoulders, which had been lifted tensely high, relaxed. "I suppose you think me shockingly crude, mentioning such things," she said, sounding defensive. "And to propose marriage in the first place."

"And I suppose," he answered, smiling a little, "you think I *should* consider it crude."

"Don't you?"

"I'm the wrong person to ask. As I said to Cousin Livia the other day, I'm barely fit to be around proper people. Been living the rough soldier's life for a long time."

"Livia? Oh—you mean the woman who's to marry your cousin Gabriel. You were with her recently?"

"Yes, at Surmont Hall. Stopped there on my way home."

"I know all about the Hall, thanks to my parents' obsessive interest in the *beau monde*. One of the country's most magnificent old homes, the Penhallow seat from time immemorial, fifteen thousand acres of the finest land in Somerset, and so on and so forth, *ad infinitum*."

"It's quite a place," he said. "Speaking of which, we'll need to decide where we're going to live."

"Anywhere but here. Anywhere else in England."

"Whatever you like. But I'll want to also spend time in Whitehaven, with my family."

"Ugh. I loathe Whitehaven."

"Do you? Quite fond of it myself. Well, you needn't come with me."

"Your place will be at my side, Captain." Her tone was imperious, her face set in hard, determined lines. He answered mildly:

"Then I hope you'll join me."

"If I don't want to go, then you shouldn't either."

"Miss Brooke, my family is important to me."

"But they're not to *me*. You agreed to my terms, remember?"

Hugo felt as if that pleasant, all-encompassing wave of relief was abruptly, and all too rapidly, receding. He looked down at her face, tense again and very pale, at those fiery dark eyes, and thought suddenly, strangely, of an actress upon a stage. And then his gaze went to the rich ermine-trimmed pelisse she wore, and that velvet hat adorned with so many silky artificial flowers, so much frilly lace, that it seemed as if somebody had for some perverse reason set out to cram it as full of decorations as humanly possible. Hugo thought of Gwendolyn, who probably hadn't had a new hat in quite some time. He doubted Mama had either.

Oh, Lord, they needed his help. They all did. But a man had his limits; it would be a terrible irony to make them secure financially but be exiled from them forever. He said:

"Then we may have a problem."

There was a new note in his voice, very subtle, but Katherine caught it at once and a terrible, creeping panic clutched at her. She had gone too far in playing her little Machiavellian game, had enjoyed too much the sudden and unusual feeling of power, and now he was going to change his mind. He was going to withdraw. And she'd be right back where she was. No, it would be worse, much worse, for she'd had an intoxicating glimpse of freedom. Oh, bother, why did he care so much about spending time with his family? An incomprehensible desire. Families meant nothing but arguments and demands, dissatisfaction and strife; she herself couldn't wait to be separated from her own family. In fact—

Katherine nearly gasped out loud.

An idea had sprung into her head, brilliant, fully formed, wonderful and ingenious. She tucked it away for further rumination, later, when she was alone, but in the meantime, it was of the utmost importance to solidify the agreement with Hugo. An occasional visit to Whitehaven wouldn't kill her.

She said to him, "There's no problem."

"You're sure?"

"Yes. And just so we're clear. I want to go to back to London next spring. For the Season."

"Fine." He smiled at her. "Anything else you'd like to discuss?"

It was all right again. Thank God. The creeping tension that had gripped her so tightly now began to fade away.

And something else came in its place. She tried to fight it down, but here it was. Something warm and exciting. Shivery and delightful. Shameful and wrong, just like those delicious secret meetings in the garden long ago. A pulsing, lovely heat seemed to fill up every empty corner of her being, and she was powerless against it. A little bit of driftwood swept along by the tide. "No," she said slowly to Hugo. "Not to discuss, Captain. But . . ."

"Yes?"

"I . . ."

"Yes?"

"I want you to kiss me."

He looked down at her, surprise in his handsome face.

Oh, what a forward girl she was, Katherine thought, her hands gone all clammy, what a bad, bad person. She could almost picture Lucifer writing in his book of sins—he would have one, wouldn't he? St. Peter, at the gates of heaven, had his Book of Life, so surely Lucifer would also want to keep track of his prospective flock. *22 October 1811. Katherine Brooke coarsely demands kiss from a man she hasn't seen in thirteen years. Another one of her episodes of lust. Thought she'd tamed it, but no. Am running out of space on her page already. Note to self: reserve special place for her.*

Suddenly it was as if all the light was blocked from her vision and her heart gave an odd frightened lurch within her breast.

Darkness already?

No, it was Hugo. So big, so very big he was. He'd come close to her, leaned down, and now his face was so close to hers—

His warm fingers cupping her chin—

Those incandescent blue eyes—

Katherine stopped breathing.

And then his lips were on hers, warm, firm, soft, gentle, utterly masculine, and her mind fell apart. *Oh God, oh God.* Her eyes closed of their own volition, she drew in an abrupt, audible breath of pleasure through her nostrils, her hands, which had been clenched, relaxed . . .

All too soon it was over.

So quick, so brief.

She opened her eyes.

Hugo was straightening, stepping away from her.

Was that the best he could do? And why was he smiling? Had he seen her vulnerability, was he glad he'd gained the upper hand over her?

Unable to stop herself, Katherine snapped:

"You call *that* a kiss?"

He looked surprised again. "I beg your pardon?"

"You *should.*"

"I should beg your pardon?" Now he looked perplexed. "For kissing you? I'm sorry, Miss Brooke. But I thought you wanted me to."

"I certainly didn't want to be kissed in that cursory way."

His face cleared. "Is that why you're upset?"

Already Katherine was sorry she'd been so frank. She slid down in her seat, ashamed all over again. "It's not important," she muttered.

"It's just that I thought—well, I assumed that's how one would kiss a lady. Under the circumstances, you know. Wanted to behave as a gentleman should." Now he looked rather mischievous. "I'd be glad to try again if you like."

His offer only deepened Katherine's chagrin. "You needn't patronize me, Captain," she said tartly, and got up, ignoring the ribbons of pain dancing up and down her back. "Now that everything's settled, let's go."

"As you wish." Hugo stepped aside with a courtly gesture, and offered her his arm which she also ignored, just as she had in the drawing-room. It was dangerous, dangerous, to be that close to him.

Together they went toward the long bank of archways where, in a silent moment of confusion about which way to go, it ended up that they each passed through their own separate arch, and so reentered a world gone grayer and wetter; the drizzle that had accompanied them on the way here had turned into a cold, steady rain.

"I say, Miss Brooke, you're going to be soaked," said Hugo, looking at her with concern. "Let me go on ahead, and come back with an umbrella."

Katherine shook her head. "There's no need," she answered, and began walking on the path that would lead them back to Brooke House.

Hugo caught up with her in a single stride of his long legs. "Your clothes may be ruined."

"I don't care." Actually, now that she thought about it, she *did* care, in the sense that she'd be thrilled if they were spoiled. The brim of her hat was already sodden and drooping around her face, and her gown's ruffled hem was getting just as muddy as her slippers. *Hurrah*.

They walked in silence, the air around them filled with the soft sounds of rain pattering on leaves. Finally, as they came round the bend that left the woods behind and brought Brooke House looming into view, Hugo said:

"Shall I come in, and speak with your parents?"

"No. I want to think about the settlements. Come again tomorrow, and be prepared to present your demands to my father. As long as they're not unreasonable, I'm sure he'll be willing to accept them." She laughed. "Actually, you could probably ask for anything you like—a chest of ancient Spanish doubloons, a dozen elephants, the Pope's mitre—and he'll say yes. To see his daughter wed to a Penhallow! The very pinnacle of his aspirations, and Mother's too. They may literally grovel. Can you be here around eleven?"

"Of course." He stopped then, and so did she. "Would you like me to escort you to your door, Miss Brooke?"

"There's no need. Besides, you'll want to go off toward the stables."

"Why?"

"To get your horse."

"I walked here."

She stared. "You walked? It's all of five miles."

"My horse needed a rest," he said easily, "and I like the exercise."

"I'm not," she said in a challenging way, "a great walker."

"To each his own."

"As long as you keep that in mind."

"I will."

"Why don't you take one of our horses? Or one of our carriages?"

"Thank you, but no. I'm looking forward to the walk home."

"The rain hasn't let up. If anything, it's raining harder."

"I'm used to it," he said, smiling a little.

"The rough soldier's life, et cetera?"

"Just so. Well, I'll take my leave of you then, Miss Brooke. Thank you again."

Katherine didn't answer, because with maddening irrationality, she was hoping that he would seize her hand, like a hero in one of Mrs. Radcliffe's silly novels, and raise it to his lips, or even just clasp it in that big warm hand of his, but he only smiled at her in that mystifyingly friendly way he had, and bowed slightly.

"I'll see you tomorrow. Goodbye, Miss Brooke."

"Goodbye," she echoed, but there came again a twist of fear, the eternal need for concealment, and she said:

"Captain?"

"Yes?"

She tried to make herself sound both authoritative and casual all at once, although she wasn't quite sure if she succeeded. "You won't tell anyone that *I* proposed to you, will you?"

One of Mrs. Radcliffe's characters would have said, with a sinister gleam in his eye, *Your secret is safe with me, miss,* but Hugo only replied, in a pleasant tone, "As you like, Miss Brooke," and instinctively Katherine knew he wouldn't betray her.

"Goodbye again," she said, reassured, and turned toward Brooke House, knowing she'd be pounced upon by her parents and exhaustively quizzed about what she and Hugo Penhallow had discussed. It would be easier to simply tell them about the betrothal, but instead she was going to hoard this extremely interesting little nugget of information, mention in an annoyingly vague way that Hugo might possibly be coming again sometime, and enjoy every single minute of her parents' ignorance. Ha! Who had the power now?

Katherine walked up the broad stone steps to Brooke House, a sudden fancy floating across her mind.

If Brooke House was a castle—and it certainly was big enough to be—and if she were a princess—doomed by an evil curse to sleep her life away—and if Hugo were a prince—and he *definitely* looked like one—who came to kiss the sleeping princess—and broke the spell—

Why, she'd just been awakened with a kiss.

Katherine smiled, then just as quickly assumed an expression of bored indifference as the front door swung open.

She turned around. A last look. There was Hugo, off in the distance. And there below her, on the steps, she saw it now. She had left behind her a trail of filthy, dirty, messy, muddy footsteps that were as dark as—as black as—sin.

Hugo walked on toward Whitehaven, within him an odd jumble of emotions. The intense relief was still there, yet it also felt a little like he'd just come through a battle. He'd survived, but not without cost. It was rather a silly thought—Katherine Brooke wasn't his enemy.

Was she?

He sidestepped an enormous mud puddle and recalled her saying in a surprisingly unemotional voice for someone who'd just agreed to be married, *This is a business arrangement.*

And he remembered how, on the way to Brooke House just a few hours earlier, he'd wondered if perhaps there was still an old bond of affection connecting himself and Katherine. A foundation on which to build genuine happiness together.

It had been an optimistic thought, but it was clear that no such foundation existed. The lively, laughing, sweet little Kate he'd known so long ago had grown up into an entirely different sort of person.

Well, that was life, wasn't it? Unpredictable, as Mr. Brooke had truly said. Nonetheless, he'd accomplished his mission, would save his family from ruin—that was the important thing. Soon, very soon, things were going to be different: Katherine's money was going to provide his mother and the children with a better, infinitely more secure future. He was tempted to immediately share his good news, but until he'd formally codified things with Mr. Brooke, it was better to keep it to himself.

Hugo continued on to Whitehaven and then home, where he found, to his pleased surprise, that Grandpapa—Mama's delightful father—was there, and Mama's older sisters Aunt Verena and Aunt Claudia too, the three of them having defied the elements to come from the parsonage on George Street. Also gathered in the big drawing-room was a middle-aged man he didn't know, introduced to him as their neighbor, Mr. Beck, along with his son Christopher, a sulky-looking young man of seventeen or so, and his daughter Diana who was just about Gwendolyn's age. Rather guiltily, Grandpapa admitted to having splurged and bought a crate of oranges and a pineapple to properly celebrate Hugo's safe return, even as Mr. Beck was loudly hailed by all the children for bringing with him from the confectioner's a veritable riot of marzipan, sugared almonds, sticky taffy, and licorice, and Mama said, apologetically, that despite the expense she simply *had* to have a nice fire lit so that everyone would be comfortable. Hugo laughed, swept her up into a hug, said blithely, "Of course you did, Mama," and helped himself to an orange.

Later, after their guests had gone home, and after supper, the six of them were cozily settled in the library, dispersed among the various chairs and sofas. The dogs lay in a sleepy mass on the hearthrug, and Gwendolyn conducted an affectionate, low-voiced conversation with Señor Rodrigo, who perched on her fine-boned wrist and seemed to find much of what she said vastly amusing, because he cackled a great deal. Hugo was leafing through an old volume of nautical illustrations, but looked up when Percy cleared his throat and said:

"I say, Hugo, we've got something we want to tell you."

Hugo closed his book and set it aside, noticing that all his siblings were now sitting up very straight, on their faces expressions of eager alertness. Even Señor Rodrigo had quieted, and was fixing him with a sharp, beady eye. To Percy Hugo said, "What is it, old chap?"

"We know how badly off the family is. Mama's done her best to keep it from us, but we all know it's true."

"Oh, Percy darling," said Mama in distress.

"It's all right, Mama," Percy said, "we're not little children, you know." He looked again to Hugo. "We couldn't be more glad that you're home, but it's our turn now. We want to help."

"We've been talking amongst ourselves," said Francis, "and we've decided that we boys can get jobs."

"I'm going to ask at the Globe Hotel if they need a

stableboy," said Percy, resolution in his voice. "I wouldn't mind that sort of work a bit. I could try the other inns as well, although the Globe's stables are the best in White-haven."

"I can do some tutoring," said Francis, and Bertram said:

"I'll try to get something at the salt works. I've been reading over Papa's papers, Hugo, did you know he left masses of them? He had some very interesting things to say about salt production."

"I want to help, too," Gwendolyn said. "I'd love to be a pirate, because I could get quite a lot of money very quickly, and also it would be delightful to be a dreaded scourge of the high seas. And Rodrigo would simply adore it, wouldn't you, darling?"

"Cleave 'em to the brisket," replied Señor Rodrigo agreeably.

"But," Gwendolyn went on with a sigh, "it's not a very practical plan, is it? I don't have a ship, or a crew, or even a single cutlass. So I've decided I can be most helpful by marrying someone who's already rich. I know I'm only fourteen, but I've asked Christopher Beck to marry me, and he says he will. The difficulty is that he won't come into his money for four more years, and by then it would be too late. So I thought perhaps I could somehow per-suade *Mr.* Beck to marry me, even though he's terribly old and a widower, which really, when you think about it, is a very troubling word, isn't it? I always think of spiders. But, of course, if Mr. Beck weren't a widower I couldn't marry him. Yes," Gwendolyn concluded, her tone surpris-ingly cheerful for one prepared to throw herself away on a man four decades her senior, "it would certainly be a sacrifice, and I daresay I wouldn't like it at all, but one shouldn't cavil at doing distasteful things when one's family needs one. Besides, I'd be just like a tragic heroine in a novel, and that would be consolation enough for me.

I'd wear black every day and droop, just a little, so that everyone would know how greatly I suffered." She demonstrated this by leaning her slender frame forward and lowering her head, thus creating a poignant suggestion of a tender spirit irreparably broken.

Hugo didn't know if he wanted to laugh or join Mama in a quiet bout of weeping, so touched was he, but he subdued both extremes of emotion and only said to the children:

"It's awfully nice of you. Thank you. We can talk about it more at another time, but for now, I'd love to know what you'd do if money weren't a question."

"You mean if we had a secret benefactor who died and left us his entire fortune?" Gwendolyn asked, straightening up. "I'd like that more than marrying Mr. Beck."

"Yes, that's what I mean," Hugo said, smiling at her.

"I'd go to Eton, like you, Hugo," said Percy without hesitation, "and get my commission in the Army when I'm eighteen."

"I'd go to Eton too," Francis said, "and then on to Oxford, so I could be a scholar and a clergyman like Grandpapa."

"School for me also," Bertram said, "and later I'd like to study in Frankfurt, as Papa did, as long as they're able to keep those odious French away. Then, of course, I'd become a scientist like he was."

"Duly noted," answered Hugo. "What about you, Gwennie?"

"Oh, Hugo, I don't know, really." Gwendolyn's exquisitely pretty face was thoughtful now. "On the one hand, I want to do something useful and important. But on the other hand, I'd like to have some adventures. *And* I'd want so much to have a London Season, and go to a different ball every night, and have a beautiful wardrobe with all the latest fashions, and meet my one true love."

"You could do all of this," Francis pointed out. "It doesn't have to be just the one thing."

Gwendolyn brightened. "That's true." And then all the light went out of her expression. "But it's only make-believe, Hugo, isn't it? We're just building our castles in the air."

Then Mama said in her soft voice:

"There may be a way, after all. Mr. Beck has asked me to marry him, and I believe he's quite well-off."

At this stunning pronouncement, everyone stared dumbly at her with open mouths.

"Shiver me timbers," said Señor Rodrigo, and began to preen the few bedraggled feathers with which his scrawny breast was adorned.

"Do you—do you *want* to marry him, Mama?" Hugo asked.

"Oh, dearest Hugo, not in the least! Mr. Beck is a very amiable gentleman, and he's been a wonderful neighbor to us for these past few years, but I often think that I buried my heart along with darling Anthony when he died. The *wifely* part of my heart, I mean. However," she added stoutly, "I'd do *anything* for my family."

"Oh, Mama, it would be dreadful to marry someone you didn't love," put in Gwendolyn earnestly. "*I'd* do it, but that's only because I haven't had my one true love as you have, so it wouldn't matter as much."

"I'd do it," said Bertram, "but only if the girl I married promised not to bother me, especially when I'm doing my work."

"I'll be busy in other countries, fighting and all that, so I suppose it wouldn't be a problem," Percy said. "I'd never have to see her, which would be good because she'd naturally be beastly. What about you, Frank?"

"Of course I'd do it," said his philosophical twin, "but that doesn't mean Mama should. We'll get by, Mama. Mr. Beck is awfully nice, but don't marry him unless you really and truly want to. It's better to eat tripe than to be unhappy."

The other children agreed in a chorus, and Mama's

troubled expression finally lightened. "Well, if you don't mind, darlings, I'd rather not, and just remain friends with Mr. Beck."

Hugo felt as if his heart would burst with love and gratitude for all of them. He was more tempted than ever to reveal his news; through a herculean act of will he refrained, although he was caught up short when Mama said:

"Dearest Hugo, you look exactly as you did when you'd pulled a great prank and were longing to tell everyone."

He tried to make his face bland. "What do you mean, Mama?"

"You look very mischievous, my darling."

"Oh, Hugo," said Percy eagerly, "have you done something ripping? Like the time you jumped off the roof into a water barrel?"

Hugo laughed. "How do you know about that dark incident from my past?"

"Hoyt told me about it ages ago, and I'd give anything to try it."

"Did he also tell you I twisted both my ankles so badly I had to stay in bed for a month?"

Percy's face fell. "No."

"Did you miscalculate the angle of your descent, Hugo?" said Bertram. "You'd have to factor in the pitch of the roof, of course, along with estimated velocity and the force of impact. People think water would make for a soft landing, but they're wrong."

"As I found to my dismay," said Hugo, laughing again. He leaned back on the worn, comfortable sofa and laced his fingers together behind his head. "I say, do you suppose we could have some tea? And is there any marzipan left?"

Too excited to sleep, Katherine lay awake all night, trying to read, ignoring the tossing about and irritable muttering from Céleste in her truckle bed, and wishing she had another stash of *diablotins*. When morning came at last, she was tired and rumpled, but so placid that Céleste looked at her suspiciously, and under her breath said something about informing *la chère maman* that Katherine had refused to get much-needed rest.

"Go ahead and tell her," said Katherine, "I don't care," and when Céleste as usual very roughly dragged the hairbrush through her tangled curls told her—for the very first time—to stop it.

As if hearing something new, something different, in Katherine's voice, Céleste did, looking at her—for the very first time—just a little bit uneasily.

Chapter 5

Having stopped in Whitehaven for a very helpful visit with Mr. Storridge, their man of business, Hugo arrived at Brooke House—promptly at eleven—with a very precise sense of his needs. As he went up the steps he smiled, thinking how Mr. Storridge had, in a very short time, gone from a mood that could only be described as gloomy pessimism into a state very nearly approaching cheerfulness.

The massive front door was swung open and he was with reverence ushered by the butler Turpin into a colossal library where, having refused an offer of refreshments, he was left to await the family's arrival.

Hugo took a turn about the room, marveling at the sheer quantity of books lining the mahogany shelves. There were several hundred, if not thousands. How Francis would love it, he thought, and paused before a shelf housing a magnificent array of tall, elegant tomes bound in soft burgundy calfskin. The complete works of William Shakespeare. He took *A Midsummer's Night's Dream*—wasn't that the one with all those weddings in it?—and opened it up, only to find that the pages were blank.

Odd.

He took out *Much Ado About Nothing*.

Its pages too were blank.

He went to another shelf, and opened up Chaucer's *Treatise on the Astrolabe*.

Also blank.

Another shelf: Homer's *Odyssey*. Blank. Machiavelli's *The Prince*. Blank. Yet another shelf: *Gulliver's Travels* by Jonathan Swift. Blank. *Beowulf*. Blank. Voltaire's *Candide*. Blank. Goethe's *Sorrows of Young Werther*. Blank.

What the devil?

He was still holding open *Sorrows of Young Werther* when the library's door was flung wide and in hurried Mr. and Mrs. Brooke, followed at a more leisurely pace by Katherine. At the sight of her, Hugo blinked. She was wearing a blindingly white, high-necked gown ornamented from throat to feet with a double column of large topaz buttons that glinted and twinkled; over this she wore a loose gold-colored robe fringed with silky tassels, and on each of her wrists jangled several gold filigree bracelets studded with topaz gemstones.

It did not seem to Hugo that yellow was a color particularly suited to Katherine's complexion, but then again, what did he know about fashion? He closed the book and restored it to its brethren on the shelf, and came forward to greet the Brookes, as he did so flashing an inquiring look to Katherine, on whose face was an expression that struck him as rather impish. Very slightly did she shake her head, which at once communicated to him that she hadn't told her parents why he was here.

He had to wait for half an hour until Mr. and Mrs. Brooke's flow of urbane small talk began to show signs of ebbing; and another fifteen minutes while the butler and four of his underlings solemnly paraded in and proceeded to lay out a quantity of food and drink sufficient for a small army; and then, at last, when they had gone, he made known to the Brookes his wish to marry their daughter Katherine.

The aftermath was protracted and deeply embarrassing to him. As Katherine had cynically predicted, her parents, in their extravagant effusions, seemed to him very nearly on the verge of sinking to the floor and prostrating themselves before him. Katherine, he saw, sitting at her ease in a high-backed chair upholstered in emerald-green velvet and in one hand a plate heaped high with macaroons, gave the strong impression of barely restraining a wild outburst of laughter.

Eventually the discussion proceeded to terms. Having established with Mr. Storridge an appropriate sum—encompassing his brothers' education, and the means by which to establish them in their careers; Gwendolyn's education, Season, and dowry; Mama's maintenance and comfort, including much-needed repairs to their house; and, finally, a modest amount which he could invest for his own sustenance—Hugo now named it, and made mention that Katherine—that is, Miss Brooke—wished to keep money matters separate. He glanced over at her, and saw that she was nodding, as well as jiggling her feet in their yellow kid slippers as if this was the only way to contain an intense impatience.

Mr. Brooke agreed at once to his terms, and began talking fluently of elite fiduciary instruments, capital enhancement, private partnership versus public ventures, joint-stock firms, and South Sea share flotation. "So you see, Captain," he concluded, "it would be much to your advantage to allow me to reinvest this sum, rather than merely placing it at your disposal. Naturally, as family, I'd be delighted to forego the customary three percent emolument for such services."

"That's very kind of you, sir," said Hugo, "but I'd prefer a cheque."

"Still, Captain—"

"Oh, Rowland, do stop, *mon cher,* it's all so tedious," intervened Mrs. Brooke, with a smile on her lips and venom in her eyes. "Enough prosing on about *les investissements!* Let's talk about the wedding, and about next year's Season. *Ma foi,* but it shall be a very different experience! We *must* lease a different house—with *une salle de bal* for four hundred at least—and hire a better sort of staff, and—"

"But my dear Hester," said Rowland, in an affectionate voice issuing from between visibly tightened lips, "what could be more important? First things first. And now, Katherine's financial situation must be dealt with."

He turned toward her and launched into another long speech peppered with so many arcane terms, as well as self-congratulatory allusions to his financial acumen, that after a minute or so Katherine stopped listening. A long and painful chapter in her life was closing, and she was about to wrap it up by delivering her *coup de grâce,* the revolutionary idea she'd had yesterday. Goodness, how Father could talk, talk, talk, and how obviously was he enjoying himself. Finally, about to explode with impatience, she interrupted him:

"Oh, do as you like, Father, just as long as the income is mine alone. How much will I receive each quarter?"

He disclosed a figure which, Katherine saw, had Hugo opening his eyes wide in astonishment. She only nodded, and responded:

"Very well. Is it all settled, then? Are the captain and I officially betrothed?"

"Yes," said Father quickly, as if forestalling any potential objections from Hugo Penhallow.

Mother clasped her hands together under her chin and exclaimed, *"Je suis ecstatic, absolument enchantée,* aren't you, Katherine *ma douce?"*

"Oh yes," answered Katherine, "I'm enchanted too." With a certain ostentatiousness she popped another macaroon into her mouth.

"Let me see," Mother went on, oblivious for once, "we

could make arrangements for a special license and have the wedding right away—but preparing a suitable trousseau will take a great deal of time, and—"

"I suppose, Captain," Father broke in, "you'll be inviting Mr. Gabriel Penhallow and Mrs. Henrietta Penhallow to the wedding, won't you?"

"Of course," said Hugo, "although—"

"If you sent an express today," Father went on, "they'd get it in four or five days—and it would be at least a week before we could expect a reply—and I daresay it would take a minimum of three weeks for them to get here—old ladies travel so deuced slowly—and then there's Christmas. So shall we set a date for the beginning of January?"

"That's fine with me, sir. I'll write to them today. However—"

"Merveilleux!" cried Mother. "Only think of it, a wedding with *la chère* Mrs. Penhallow in attendance! And Mr. Gabriel Penhallow, too! We'll be quite the talk of the *ton!* And then after the wedding, the four of us will travel to London, *en famille,* in plenty of time for the Little Season."

Here it was. Mother had unwittingly provided the perfect opening, and it took everything Katherine had to keep from grinning like a hyena. Struggling to keep her voice calm, she said:

"No, we won't."

These three simple words produced just as satisfying an impact as she had hoped. Her parents looked as if she'd just announced with irrefutable authority, *The world is ending tomorrow, the sky is falling, and pigs* can *fly.*

"I beg your pardon?" said Father, clearly unable to believe the evidence of his own ears.

"Captain Penhallow and I will be going to London, but you and Mother are to be elsewhere."

"Elsewhere?" Mother said sharply. "What does that mean?"

Ordinarily that tone in Mother's voice would have made Katherine's stomach clench, but today—oh, today was different. She thought of old Mrs. Penhallow, standing in the Royal Academy of Art as if she owned it, and how she had managed with superb aplomb to look down her nose at people who were taller than she was. Katherine did her best to mimic the old lady's haughtiness, and answered:

"It means, *ma chère maman,* that you're to stay out of London. It pains me to mention it," she went on mendaciously, "but you and Father will, I'm afraid, only hold me back. Do be logical. How often has Father rebuked you for your lowly birth? And how often have you told him, Mother, that he's merely the son of an obscure, pauperized baronet? So you see, it's really all for the best." She picked up the last macaroon from her plate, and as she bit into it, glanced at Hugo Penhallow whose expression was now quite blank. He probably thought she was the worst sort of harpy. If only he knew what her life had been like . . . Pride made her lift her chin, look away as if she didn't care.

"I'll withhold my consent to the marriage, you devious little baggage," said Father, his face a rather comical shade of red.

"You can't. I'm twenty-one. My birthday was last month, as perhaps has slipped your mind."

"You won't get a penny, then! And when Captain Penhallow asks to break off the engagement, I'll permit it! *And* cut off your pin-money!"

It was a clever gambit, Katherine had to admit, her nerves prickling in alarm. The slightest misstep could destroy everything. And if she was left without funds, how could she pay for her books, her sweets? Money was *such* a comfort when you had nothing else. *Stay the course, stay the course,* she warned herself, feeling a little sick with sudden tension as well as from eating all those macaroons, unable to resist the opportunity to brazenly do it right in front of Mother.

"I don't care," she said, making her voice cold. "It's not as if this is a love-match, and I'll wither away and die of a broken heart. Cut off my pin-money, lock me in my room. It doesn't matter to me."

There was a silence.

But not a peaceful, meditative one.

No, it was a silence filled with so much roiling hostility, so much enmity and malice and spite, that it was practically deafening.

Father looked as if he could happily throttle her, and Mother was wringing her hands in—had she but known it—a very effective imitation of Lady Macbeth's anguished "Out, damned spot" scene. Hugo Penhallow went without hurry to the window, turning his back as if to remove himself from what had become a ghastly little family confrontation. It also gave Katherine an excellent view of his broad shoulders, and the narrowing line of his athlete's torso showcased by his austere buff-colored tailcoat.

A very masculine, very appealing line.

Oh, she liked it.

And oh—here it came again, damn it, *damn* it—she wanted him.

For a few disorienting moments Katherine was just about to back down—tell her parents she'd changed her mind—do *anything* to keep Hugo Penhallow—but instead she dragged her gaze away, looked down, and began to turn one of the bracelets on her wrist as if it were the most fascinating activity in all the world, something she could do all day, into the night and, possibly, forever.

Turn, turn, turn, round and round . . . It occurred to her, abruptly, to wonder if what she had said was hurtful to Hugo. Surely not. Surely he knew she was playing a desperate game? Playing hard, and for keeps?

"Rowland, *mon petit chou,* I beg you to reconsider,"

said Mother, in an unusually soft, persuasive tone. "Katherine's success will be our success, *n'est-ce pas?* We can go to Bath—or Weymouth—or Tunbridge Wells."

"Those little watering-holes!" retorted Father with contempt.

"*C'est vrai,* they're not London, but they are very lively, very sophisticated, and keep in mind that no one, *absolument* no one, will be able to eclipse us! We'll be able to say 'our daughter, Mrs. Penhallow'—we'll be the cynosure of all eyes. That will be very agreeable, *oui?*"

"Yes," Father replied slowly. "Yes, it would. There is much in what you say."

Steeling herself to remain calm, Katherine glanced at him where he sat very still in his seat, one hand rubbing at his chin. Then at last he turned hard eyes on her. "Very well," he said in a curt voice. "The marriage can proceed under the terms to which we've agreed. Later we'll revisit the question of London for the year after next."

"To be sure, Father," Katherine said demurely, while thinking at the exact same time, *It will never happen, never! I'll find a way to ensure that, rest assured.*

And then it hit her.

I've won.

I've won.

I'm free.

An extraordinary feeling came to her then. It was a kind of buoyancy. Lightness. As one might feel, perhaps, having eaten not a handful of *diablotins,* but a thousand—

No, wait, interrupted her busy mind, that's not a good analogy, if you ate a thousand *diablotins* you'd be sick. And maybe die. I think what you mean is that you're—

"Well, isn't this *splendide!*" exclaimed Mother, but it was Hugo Penhallow at whom Katherine was looking, as slowly he turned around, on his handsome face that same expression of courteous, inscrutable blankness. Did he loathe all of them? Who wouldn't, really? But she—

she was different from her parents, wasn't she? Katherine couldn't help it, a curious, almost desperate impulse compelled her to stand up, to walk over to Hugo, to draw near him, and quietly say, over the awful jangling of her bracelets:

"You were wondering about that book you were holding, Captain, when we came in? It's a fake. They all are in this library."

"I see," said Hugo politely, pleasantly, but it seemed to Katherine that the light inside her drained away in a single beat of her heart, and that the sweet taste of triumph had all at once turned to ashes in her mouth.

Hugo's news about his sudden engagement was received by his family with reactions varying from blasé acceptance to astonishment.

"Katherine Brooke?" said Gwendolyn, eyes wide. "She used to live next door, didn't she, when I was little? And now she lives out in the country, in a house so big it's like a palace?"

"Yes, that's her," answered Hugo smilingly.

"Oh, Hugo, is Katherine your one true love? You've never stopped loving each other all these years, and Katherine's been waiting for you to come home so that you can claim her for your bride?"

Hugo was spared the necessity of thinking up a suitable reply when Cook, who had billowed into the library with a plate of her lemony Shrewsbury biscuits, remarked as if offhandedly on her way out, "Butcher's wife says those Brookes have more money than they know what to do with."

"Are we going to be rich then, Hugo?" asked Bertram. "Because if we are, Grandpapa and I could do a very interesting experiment on glass sintering."

"Not rich, Bertie, but comfortable. And yes, you and Grandpapa can sinter away. Whatever that is."

"Oh, good," said Bertram, as if this entirely wrapped up the conversation, and went back to his book.

"Hugo," Gwendolyn said, her voice trembling with excitement, "does this mean I'm going to have a Season?"

"To be sure. But not, you know, for a few more years."

"I can wait. I'll wait so very, very patiently now that I know it's going to be happening. *Thank* you, Hugo!"

He smiled at her, and took one of Cook's delicious-looking biscuits. "It's Miss Brooke you ought to be thanking."

"I will," Gwendolyn promised breathlessly. "Of course I will! Oh, Hugo, she must be the nicest, kindest person in all the world!"

Hugo hesitated, not quite sure how to reply as he was not at all certain if, in fact, his betrothed possessed either of those qualities in abundance. Thoughtfully, he wondered what he *could* say, and bit into the biscuit. By God, Cook had done it again. Somehow, on the tightest of budgets, she'd managed to produce the world's best Shrewsbury biscuits. He reached for another one.

"Heave ho, you bilge-sucking scallywag," said Señor Rodrigo, in such a darkly menacing manner that Hugo burst out laughing and offered him a piece of biscuit which Rodrigo, in a sudden turnabout, accepted in his outstretched claw with an air of gracious condescension.

And so the subject of Katherine's personal qualities was closed, although later that day, when Hugo went to the parsonage to further share the news with his grandfather and aunts, Grandpapa took Hugo into his study, shut the door, and said in his quiet way:

"My dear Hugo, are you quite certain about this plan of yours?"

"I am, Grandpapa."

"Indeed, I see your resolution. And how can I not appreciate the sacrifice you're making for the family? But—" His grandfather hesitated. "But yours is an affectionate heart, Hugo. I should have liked to see you marry for love, as I was fortunate to do, and as my own dear Elizabeth did with your father."

"It's a kind thought, Grandpapa, and I appreciate it. But I'm not repining. I've never fallen in love, nor had any particular expectations about it."

"Perhaps you haven't had the opportunity. Or you haven't yet met the right woman."

"That may be. Or perhaps I'm not cut out for it. At any rate, you needn't worry, though. I'm content."

"I can see that also," Grandpapa answered, and turned the talk to something else, though Hugo, in his turn, could see that his grandfather was not, himself, at all content.

————————

23 October 1811

Dear Coz,
 Trust this finds you all well. Things were rather topsy-turvy when I left Surmont Hall a few weeks ago but I hope everything's been satisfactorily re-solved. Am getting married on January 2nd here in Whitehaven, to Miss Katherine Brooke, and wonder if you, Livia, and Aunt Henrietta would like to attend? Unless I miss my guess it's to be a great elaborate affair—not how I'd have preferred it, but so it goes. I know it's a goodly distance to travel but of course it would be splendid to have you all here.
         Yours ever,
         Hugo

————————

In between sending announcements to all the really im-portant periodicals, writing gloatingly to everyone they knew, feverishly planning the wedding, and assembling a trousseau of a magnitude not unlike that which traveled with young Marie Antoinette to her marriage to the Dau-phin of France, Katherine's parents did manage to find the time to call upon Hugo's family, dragging along a reluctant Katherine in their train.

The visit was just as bad as she'd thought it would be.

First, there was something deeply intimidating about the sheer physical presence of those six Penhallows, each and every one of them tall and straight, with lustrous golden hair and vivid blue eyes, altogether surrounding her with so much dazzling human pulchritude that she found herself beating a mental retreat to a fascinating extract she had once read—it was about the genetic laws of nature—and pondering the mechanisms by which such consistently fine specimens had been produced.

Second, no sooner had she sat down than a pack of dogs had swarmed into the drawing-room, one of which was so big that it could look her in the eye. Which it did, and then tried to lick her face. And she had squeaked in a very loud and mortifying way. Those twin brothers of Hugo's—who looked exactly and unnervingly alike— had, at Hugo's command, ushered the dogs out of the room, but it was a little too late for her damaged dignity.

Third, Hugo's sister Gwendolyn had mortified her by drawing near and thanking her, with such sweet and obvious sincerity that all she could think to do was to nod, in a very lame, tongue-tied way.

Fourth, Mother had said to Hugo's mama in a kindly tone: "What a pity, *chère* Mrs. Penhallow, that your husband left you all so poorly provided. One wonders why he frittered away his time with his *petits efforts de la science* that brought in no reward."

In the hush that followed, Katherine noticed with a kind of detached amazement that one's blood could actually feel as if it was boiling within one. Maybe she really *would* die from shame which, although not her first choice, would still result in a tidy escape from Brooke House.

But then—fifthly—she herself provided the distraction to break the ghastly lull when a hideous bedraggled parrot had somehow, unnoticed, stumped toward her, climbed onto her nankeen half-boot, demanded, "Kiss me, you saucy wench!" and she had squawked in surprise, sounding not unlike a bird herself.

Gwendolyn hurried over and coaxed the bird onto her outstretched finger. "Oh, Miss Brooke, do forgive Señor Rodrigo! But he *likes* you, you know! He only wished to make friends."

"Who?" said Katherine, trying to conceal her embarrassment by ostentatiously resetting her skirts.

"This is Señor Rodrigo, el Duque de Almodóvar del Valle de Oro." Gwendolyn smiled at the ugly thing with an affection that Katherine found unfathomable. Who kept a bird as a pet? *I wanted to, once,* came the sudden thought, and in its wake, the memory of the injured seagull she'd found, long ago, on the shore. Mother's revulsion and Father's indifference, and nobody to help her at home; and then, to her infinite relief, Hugo taking the bird gently in his hands and bearing it off toward his house where, he had assured her, his mama would know just what to do . . .

Katherine blinked, fought her way back to the present, and said:

"That's quite a name for a bird with hardly any feathers."

"Oh, but Miss Brooke, I have so much hope that he *will!* Every day I tell Señor Rodrigo that he's perfect just as he is, but that someday, when he's ready, he'll grow the most beautiful green feathers in the world."

"He couldn't possibly understand what you're saying."

"He might," remarked Hugo's youngest brother Bertram. "I once read an article in the *Journal of Natural Philosophy* which said that animals may understand quite a large number of our words."

Katherine's interest was caught, but then Father put in with a patronizing chuckle, "Out of the mouths of babes," just as if Bertram was a freakish exhibit in a traveling-show, and Katherine could not have been more glad when Mother rose to her feet and said:

"Well! How *charmant* this has all been, and we've so enjoyed your delightful menagerie—animals everywhere, how quaint!—but I'm afraid we must hurry on home. Katherine has a fitting scheduled this afternoon for her new court-dress, as she will, *naturellement*, attend the Queen's Drawing-room. She was unable to go this past year due to an occasional, trifling indiscretion."

Katherine just barely repressed a snort. Yes, if you could call a complete absence of invitations a "trifling indiscretion."

Later, as she stood in Mother's enormous sitting-room encircled by the harried dressmaker and her half-dozen minions, looking—as she had no doubt—ludicrous in a set of hoops seemingly as wide as she was tall, Katherine glanced morosely at the rich lengths of pale-blue velvet and stark white satin, the tassels and lace, the elaborate turban and the white ostrich feathers, all of which would make *her* look like an eye-popping spectacle in a traveling-show.

Suddenly, inspiration struck.

And she said:

"Mother, I think this gown will need more diamond brilliants on it, don't you?"

As this was the first time during the lengthy fitting process that Katherine had offered a single comment that could in any way be construed as helpful, Mother looked a little startled, but then she agreed with alacrity.

And inside herself, secretly, Katherine smiled.

---

10 November 1811

Dear Hugo,

Apologies for my delay in replying; Livia and I have only recently returned to the Hall. We were both delighted to hear your news and we wish you very happy—as does Grandmama who is, I believe, writing to you also, tendering an invitation which may be of interest to you and Miss Brooke.

And speaking of invitations, although we would of course like very much to join you for your wedding, it is with regret that we must decline. Urgent matters keep us here: for one, I am deeply immersed in seeing that the workers' cottages are completed before the really bad weather sets in and that employment is found for anyone who needs it during the winter. Too, having been gone for so long, it feels especially important that, for the sake of the local folk, the family be here for the Christmas season.

And finally—it gives me great pleasure to inform you that Livia and I are to be married next week on the 15th. I am, I must confess, an impatient bridegroom, and especially having come far too close to losing Livia forever. (There's an odd little story about that, by the bye; I'll tell you about it when next I see you.) Suffice to say, I feel like the luckiest man on earth.

Wishing you every felicity, Hugo,
I remain, etc.,
Gabriel

———————

10 November 1811

Dear Hugo,
From Livia I have learned that you left Surmont Hall so abruptly because you were in pursuit of a likely heiress, and now Gabriel has informed us that you were successful. He mentioned also that prior to your departure you both reimbursed him for the cost of your commission and insisted that he stop your allowance.

It must be said that I had no idea you were experiencing such severe financial difficulties, else I would have of course stepped in to help. It grieves me to confess that for quite some time I have been far less perceptive than I would have wished.

It must also be said that it does you great credit to have sought an independent solution to your difficulties. As I have more than once declared, a Penhallow never fails to perform a necessary act, no matter how distasteful, and I am gratified to see that you are following the Penhallow Way.

If memory serves me correctly, I met the Brookes in London earlier in the year—although "met" is hardly the word to describe the encounter. The less said about the parents the better. Their daughter, at least, didn't look stupid, although it was difficult to ascertain this given the extraordinary number of artificial cherries with which her hat was embellished; they were permitted (in someone's mind no doubt artistically) to drape low across her forehead and I wonder she was able to see where she was going.

I cannot pretend, Hugo, to rejoice in my knowledge of the young lady's relations; it pains me to think of them even uttering the word "Penhallow" with any kind of claim to intimacy. Nor can I approve of someone who would venture out of doors wearing a hat so abominable. However, it is worth mentioning that I entertained the gloomiest sentiments about Livia when she and Gabriel were betrothed; and I am happy to say I was proved wrong.

Therefore, if you and your bride would like to stop over here at the Hall as part of your honeymoon, we should be glad to have you.

Affectionately yours,
Aunt Henrietta

P.S. In the interest of clarity, please note that this invitation does not, under any circumstances, encompass her unfortunate parents. One does have limits.

———————

"**G**o to Surmont Hall?" said Katherine to Hugo, who had come to Brooke House to relay Aunt Henrietta's offer. "She's invited us?"

"Yes."

"Why?"

In Katherine's voice was suspicion, but once again Hugo thought he detected within in a certain apprehension. He answered, "I believe she'd like to get to know you better."

"Oh, surely not," Katherine said low, almost as if to herself, then quickly added, as if to move the conversation beyond a remark she wished unsaid, "It's a signal honor, I daresay."

"That could be." He could almost hear the wheels and gears in her brain turning, and finally she said:

"Very well. Tell her yes."

"I'll write and let her know. There's one other thing, Miss Brooke. I know it's a lot to ask, but—"

"What is it?" she said, and he saw how her shoulders had gone up, tense, defensive. He went on:

"I've enrolled Francis and Percy at Eton for the winter term, and it would mean a great deal to me to bring them with us. My grandfather could take them, but it would be a wearying journey for him, and I'd prefer not to pay someone—a stranger—to escort them. We could drop them off at school, as it's more or less on the way, then go on to the Hall from there."

He was unable to decipher the differing expressions that flitted across her face, but she merely said, "If you like. Make the arrangements. We're to stay in the best inns, of course."

"We'll enjoy it vastly, the boys and I. Thank you."

Katherine only shrugged, and he watched as a crimson tide of color washed across her face. She looked down, fiddled with one of her rings, and added, "Oh, and Captain . . ."

"Yes?"

"I want separate bedchambers, if you please."

This, he mused, recalling their conversation in the ruins of Babylon, was not unexpected. And not particularly promising, either. But he thought of his family, and out loud he said, in a pleasant voice, "Certainly, Miss Brooke."

There was a tap on the door of the little saloon in which they'd been permitted a few minutes of privacy, and the butler Turpin came in to let Katherine know that the Bow Street Runners had arrived, and hoped she would be willing to oblige them with a few minutes of her time.

"The Runners?" said Hugo. "What the hell—I beg your pardon. What are the Runners doing here?"

"Last week my maid Céleste ran away with Father's valet," Katherine replied, "and she took one of my diamond aigrettes, several bracelets, and an emerald brooch. I suppose she realized I'd rather die a thousand deaths than bring her with me after the wedding, and decided to leave before Mother either demoted her or let her go. Or maybe she was really in love with that shifty-eyed, popinjay valet of my father's, though it's hard to imagine. My God! You should have seen Father when we realized they'd gone, and that Robert took several of his best rings also. I thought for sure he'd have an apoplexy on the spot."

Hugo took this in, then asked, curious, "Why would you rather die a thousand deaths than bring Céleste with you?"

"We didn't get along, that's all," Katherine said, vivid color mounting again to her cheeks. "At any rate, Father is still furious, which is why the Bow Street Runners are here. I doubt they'll find Céleste and Robert," she added, rising from her chair, "as Céleste is a very resourceful person. But if you find such activity amusing, Captain, Father's been taking bets with a great many of our house-guests as to the Runners' success. I'm sure you'd be welcome to join in."

Hugo stood up also. "Not a gambler myself, but thank you."

She gave him a small, cynical smile. "Aren't you? And yet here we are, betrothed."

He laughed, and left her, and went home, where he wrote a note to Aunt Henrietta. Then he spent several happy hours during which he fixed the hinge to the library door, put in new windows on the uppermost story where Bertram liked to conduct his experiments, chopped up a huge pile of wood for Cook's stove into neat rectangular lengths, and repaired a broken drawer in Gwendolyn's armoire which, she said, had been troubling her for a very long time.

As he worked, he thought about Aunt Henrietta's letter. Although he'd been acquainted with her for many years, he couldn't have said that he knew her very well, and this was the first time she'd ever written directly to him. It was surprising to see those patches of warmth and affection in her note. Gabriel's letter had surprised him a little, too. There'd always been something rather aloof about his older cousin, but in his letter there was a new warmth also, and a kind of openness.

It was a nice change, Hugo thought, and slid the drawer smoothly home.

———

21 November 1811

Dear Aunt Henrietta,

Miss Brooke and I are delighted to accept your kind invitation. Very many thanks. I expect we'll be arriving around January 16th; I'll write when we're en route to the Hall to confirm that date more precisely. If it's convenient for you, shall we plan to stay a week or so? We'll proceed to London thereafter.

With affection and gratitude,
Hugo

---

4 December 1811

Dear Hugo,
   Thank you for your letter. We look forward to seeing you next month.
   You mention going on to London in late January, which leads me to believe you intend to partake of the so-called Little Season. To this plan I strenuously object. Penhallows simply don't go to Town until March at the earliest. If you and Miss Brooke would care to linger at the Hall for a few more weeks, it may be that I would be willing to offer you the use of the family townhouse in Berkeley Square during the Season; it would add a decided luster to what I assume is Miss Brooke's ambition to assert her newly enhanced position in Society.
   As a side note, Miss Brooke may benefit from the very circumstance of additional time at the Hall. I do not say that osmosis in the metaphysical sense is a real thing. However, it couldn't hurt.

Affectionately yours,
Aunt Henrietta

"**S**he's dangling the notion of the family townhouse like a carrot," observed Katherine to Hugo, who'd again come to call. "As if I'm some kind of horse. Is it really so bad to go to London so early?"

He laughed. "You're asking the wrong person."

"Don't you care?"

"Not a bit, I'm afraid."

Katherine thought about it. The old lady could not have made a more tempting offer. There wasn't a more prestigious dwelling in all of London, excepting the residences of actual royalty. But—*weeks* at the Hall? Among all those Penhallows? She already knew what old Mrs. Penhallow was like. Hugo's cousin Gabriel was no doubt just as arrogant, and his new wife Livia was probably the same: one of those haughty, proud, supercilious Society ladies. How could she stand those long, long weeks?

An image of the magnificent Penhallow townhouse floated through Katherine's mind. While in London, several times had her parents directed the coachman to drive past it, and on their faces had been such naked, greedy longing that Katherine had averted her eyes, praying with all her heart that on *her* face was nothing but bland indifference.

And so, here was a chance—exclusively for her—to not only go inside the townhouse, but to *live* in it for a while.

Was she as bad as her parents? For a brief moment Katherine pictured herself as a Shetland pony, eagerly craning its neck toward a carrot.

She said to Hugo, once again, "Tell her yes."

Chapter 6

❧

Time passed, the marriage contracts were signed, and the wedding took place on a cold, frosty morning in January. The bride, her face as white as snow, wore a gown of amber silk bobbinet so heavily embroidered with metallic gold thread that she literally sparkled, as well as a long double-stranded necklace of pearls (rumored to have once belonged to Mary Queen of Scots) and a trailing manteau of rich, shimmering cloth-of-gold that extended behind her for some six or seven feet. The groom was dressed simply in dark gray trousers, a black jacket, and a slate-gray waistcoat, looking so handsome and serene that quite a few of the guests gathered in Whitehaven's largest church wept to see it.

After the ceremony, as the lavish wedding-breakfast at Brooke House was drawing to a close, Rowland Brooke took Hugo aside, and with an elaborate flourish presented him with a cheque. "Here you are, my dear fellow."

"Thank you, sir."

"You're certain you wouldn't like me to manage it for you?"

"I am. But thank you."

Mr. Brooke sighed, a gusty exhalation suggestive of regret and, perhaps, disapproval. Then he looked up at the gold-paneled ceiling, over at a potted palm, next at a large, glossy portrait of the King, and finally at Hugo. "One other item before you go, Captain."

"Sir?" said Hugo politely.

"My daughter . . ."

"Yes?"

Mr. Brooke cleared his throat. "My wife has, naturally, enlightened Katherine as to her—ah—conjugal obligations."

If there was a less appealing phrase for sex, Hugo thought, he'd yet to hear it. Poor Katherine. Also, he wondered what Mr. Brooke expected him to say. Somehow "Thank you, sir" seemed decidedly wrong. Luckily (or not), Mr. Brooke continued, in the same confidential tone:

"Thought you ought to know, Captain, that apparently Katherine was—er—less than grateful to receive my wife's advice. A difficult conversation, according to Hester. That's Katherine, I'm afraid. May as well tell you, now that the knot's all tied safe and secure, she's a thoroughly troublesome sort of girl. Well, that's the way it goes in business, eh? Full disclosure once the deal's struck." He chuckled. "The money we've spent on her over the years—daresay it'd shock you to hear the sum. I was beginning to think it an investment that wasn't going to pay off. And then you came along! Well, well, well. In any event, you're a great strong fellow, I'm sure you'll know what to do if she doesn't obey."

Hugo felt his face hardening. "That's not my way, sir. Trust it's never been your way with Katherine, or Mrs. Brooke's either." Something in his voice seemed to register with Mr. Brooke, who took a step back as if involuntarily.

"Of course not, Captain, I assure you. Words have always sufficed." He ran a manicured hand over his smoothly shaven jaw. "Powerful things, words."

The carriages—one for Katherine, the other three for her trousseau—stood ready in front of Brooke House, the horses for Hugo and his brothers were waiting, all the guests were dutifully assembled despite the chill, and everyone wondered where the bride and her parents were.

Now wearing her going-away gown and a pale blue pelisse embellished everywhere with black braid as well as with shiny jet buttons the size of small pancakes, Katherine was, in fact, placing in her father's hands her enormous jewelry-case.

"Here," she said.

"What's this for?" he asked, startled.

"I'm not bringing it with me."

"Don't be *stupide*," Mother said sharply. "You'll need your jewels."

Katherine said nothing, and began to pull on her gloves.

"You have only that dreadfully plain band Captain Penhallow gave you," Mother went on with a sniff. "Belonging to his grandmother. *Ma foi.*"

"Would have thought he'd go out and buy you a new one," Father rumbled in disapproval. "Bigger. Shinier."

"Your appearance is so *bare*," added Mother, her frown deepening. "*Si démodé*. Rowland, take out those diamond strands."

"I'm not your servant," Father said, and thrust the case rather forcefully at her. "*You* do it."

Katherine said, interrupting the quarrel which was just about to begin in earnest, "I'll choose my own jewels when I get to London," then added, airily, "Well—goodbye."

And without a backward glance, she made her way toward the front door.

To freedom.

Their cavalcade stopped for the night in the town of Keswick, pulling up into the capacious inn-yard of the large and luxurious White Lion. The roads had been rough and even in the beautifully sprung carriage Katherine had been jolted about; she winced as Hugo handed her out, for those flickers of pain in her back were more severe than usual.

"Are you all right?"

"Yes," she answered, flustered, taking a few stiff, awkward steps, then heard one of the twins laughing. For a brief, terrible moment she thought he was mocking her, but realized he was instead grinning at his brother, who was walking with long, wide, comically exaggerated strides, as if rendered bow-legged after his long hours in the saddle.

"What's so funny, Frank?" he said, with an air of oblivious innocence, then straightened up when Francis (she supposed) leaped upon him with a boisterous clinch-hold.

"Aren't you going to stop them?" she asked Hugo, watching, mystified, as the twins mock-wrestled with loud shouts of laughter.

"God, no."

"Doesn't it bother you?"

He laughed. "You're looking at them as if they're a pair of tigers escaped from a zoo. It's just the excitement of the trip, you know."

"If you say so."

"Better they get it out of their systems now, instead of at dinner. As long as they don't actually roll in the mud and dung, I'll be pleased."

"How strange boys are," she said, and he only smiled.

It wasn't long before Katherine was in her room, a handsomely appointed chamber which she surveyed with deep satisfaction. If there was a truckle bed, she didn't want to know about it. Ha. Didn't need to know about it.

Mother had had one of the other maidservants sleep in Katherine's room after Céleste had run away, and tried to force Katherine to bring on her honeymoon *someone* from Brooke House but she had adamantly refused. Not, perhaps, a practical response, but who cared?

As if on cue, there was just then a tap on her door, and Katherine admitted one of the inn's own servant girls to help her dress for dinner. She was eager to please, but not adept, and so when Katherine sat down at the table in their private parlor she wasn't surprised when one of the twins blurted out:

"I say, your hair's all sideways."

"Percy," said Hugo.

"He's right," Katherine said. "I look like the Leaning Tower of Pisa." Perhaps, she thought, a slight improvement over resembling a Shetland pony, and wasn't it a nice change to select for herself what she was going to wear? Katherine spread her napkin across her lap and looked across the table where Hugo sat, her eyes traveling from his strong, capable-looking hands, up the length of his arms, to the sturdy column of his neck and to his handsome face. He looked so cheerful, so calm. Not, she had to admit, as you would picture a groom on his wedding night. Not like someone who could barely wait for the evening to pass so that he could seize his willing bride and have her up against the wall of their room, so great was his violent passion—or maybe he'd lift her up in his strong arms and so sweep her off to the bed—would he fling her onto the bedcovers, or lay her down, gently as a feather? Which would be better? And by "her" who did she mean exactly? Was she imagining herself, or some other, made-up person?

"Katherine," Hugo said.

She jumped. "What?"

"Would you care for a little of this chicken?"

"Chicken?"

He smiled. "Yes. This roasted chicken."

"It's very good," put in one of the twins. "I've already had two servings."

"So have I," said the other one. "They had chicken at your house earlier on, Katherine, even though it was supposed to be a breakfast. I've never seen so much food in my life. It was *ripping*. Frank, how many servings did you have of the chicken?"

"Only two, but I had five slices of the ham and seven or eight potatoes."

"Is that all? I had that *and* some of the pheasant."

"There was pheasant? Damn—I mean, blast it. I missed that. Did you try the gooseberry pudding?"

"Yes, and the ices, too. Also some of the cakes." Looking very pleased with himself, Percy (she supposed it was him) took an enormous piece of the broiled salmon and resumed eating.

"Katherine," said Hugo, with unabated patience, "may I give you some of this chicken?"

"Yes, thank you," she answered, and so the meal proceeded, concluding when a chocolate roll was brought in. Hugo and his brothers each took a large slice, and oh, she would have liked to have one, too, but the very fact that she wanted it so much brought on an all too familiar wave of shame. So she refused it, then eyed the others resentfully and finally said, trying to keep her tone neutral:

"Aren't you worried you're going to burst from eating all that food?"

"No," answered Percy (if it *was* him), and had another slice.

"Cook says we have hollow legs," Francis (she guessed) said, doing the same. "Which always makes Bertram tell her about human anatomy—muscles and bones and blood vessels and so on. The dear old chap," and his twin added:

"It'll be splendid to bring him with us next year. He'll love it. It's all thanks to you, Katherine. We're awfully grateful." He smiled at her, and she flushed all over again, embarrassed, and changed the subject.

"How on earth do people tell you apart? You look completely alike."

"Oh, it's easy. Percy is the ugly one."

"And Francis is the stupid one."

Laughing, the twins began trying to hook their feet around the other's legs, and in a minute or two the table began to shimmy.

"That's enough," said Hugo affably, and they stopped it at once.

When they all went upstairs, Katherine was further embarrassed to see that Hugo's room was right next to hers. *Of course, you fool,* she chided herself, *why wouldn't it be?* Why, oh why, hadn't she realized ahead of time how difficult this was going to be? She'd been so busy daydreaming about freedom, picturing herself in the Season to come, making over in her mind all the unpleasant and painful events that had happened last year, that she hadn't focused on more imminent concerns.

"I get to be in Hugo's bed!" exclaimed one of the twins, "you get the truckle bed," and dove into the room, and the other one said, "Very well, blast you, but we switch tomorrow," and went inside in a more leisurely fashion. Hugo came to where she stood at her own doorway, and she noticed that she was feeling more than a little breathless, and that her heart was beating hard within her, so hard that it seemed to make her back sting and throb, and that she was suddenly very warm all over, and—

"Well, Katherine?"

"Well, what?" She folded her arms over her chest. To make herself seem confident. Also, to try and subdue that willful thumping heart of hers.

He said, "What would you like for me to do?"

Oh God, she didn't know, she didn't know. What did *he* think about all this? Had she wounded him by demanding separate bedchambers? How might she have felt if he'd done that? Rejected? Dejected? What *did* she want him to do? She had no idea. Wildly bargaining for time she said, "For one thing, not stand here in the hallway where anyone could see us. Come inside."

She whisked herself into her bedchamber, and quickly, stiffly, she sat down in a chair set near the fireplace. Hugo came near, but remained standing, on his face a quizzical expression.

"Are you going to sit down?" she said, making herself sound brusque, desperate to disguise the fact that she felt all soft and warm. Vulnerable. Confused. And deeply, deeply afraid.

"That depends on you, Katherine."

"Go ahead then," she said with deliberate rudeness. "Sit down."

Without hurry he complied, sitting on the chair opposite hers, and crossed one long booted leg over the other. He was looking steadily at her, calm, friendly, patient. She had a sudden image of herself with her gown on fire, her hands flapping at the flames in an urgent attempt to put them out, only the flames felt very good, which meant they were actually very bad and wrong—

Almost at random she said, "I never dreamed you'd share a room with your brothers."

"It seemed a logical choice under the circumstances."

"Yes, but it's all so—so awkward." In her voice was just the right touch of hauteur, she congratulated herself, and she pictured in her mind the flames all beaten away, her gown all black and charred, but no longer was she flaming hot. Good, good.

"Katherine," he said patiently, "tell me what you'd like me to do, and I'll do it."

A flame leaped up. She blurted out: "What if I were to ask you to stay with me?"

"I would."

"Do you want to?"

Hugo was silent, and Katherine watched with bemused fascination as a slow smile curved his mouth. It was an alluring smile. A warm and horribly seductive smile. Finally he said:

"Yes."

The charred gown of her imagination burst into flames again, but frantically, fearfully, she beat them down. Because she was in control. Because he had agreed to her terms. She said firmly, "Well, *I* don't want to."

Hugo said nothing. She saw his smile fade. But still he looked at her, calm and steady.

Hugo found himself thinking of the time he'd been marching with his men out of the Pocatière settlement, with orders to rejoin their regiment at Fort George. They'd gone about five miles or so, when scouts had returned with the unsettling news that to the east of them was a detachment of French foot soldiers; to the west was Mohawk territory and apparently the site of a recent and rather nasty massacre; and directly ahead was a large encampment of excitable—and hostile—Americans.

He'd turned them around and had them retreat to La Pocatière, where its disgruntled townsfolk, he knew, would not be pleased to see them, and might even try to keep them from reentering.

But that's the way things went sometimes.

Sometimes a situation was just plain bad.

And so here he was with his new bride, who gave every appearance of disliking him. Holy hell. He *would* have liked to stay and consummate the marriage, although not, of course, with someone who was glaring at him the whole time.

And yet—

And yet he had the oddest feeling, somehow, that once

again there was more going on here than what she was saying. More beneath that hard, brittle demeanor of hers.

Why was it, he wondered, that women were so hard to understand? Why were they so confoundedly complicated?

Men, on the whole, were simple creatures. She'd asked him if he wanted her and he said yes. And then been promptly rejected. Still, he wasn't sorry about being honest. Not only did he hate lying, he was bad at it and it was obvious when, on the rare occasion, he did prevaricate.

Hugo repressed a sigh. Just as returning to La Pocatière had been the lesser of the various evils, so too did discretion now seem to be the better part of valor: he had the distinct impression that no matter what he said, he would somehow make things worse. Perhaps if he had been one of those eloquent, articulate sort of fellows, who went about mesmerizing women with a rakish smoldering gaze and quoting epic poetry left and right—well, there was no use even contemplating it, because he wasn't. Regretfully, then, he relinquished his earlier anticipation of a night spent in connubial joy. Which was just as well, because Katherine said:

"I'm tired. I'm going to sleep. Good night."

She was pretending she was an empress—the indomitable Hatshepsut, for example, or the iron-willed Wu Zetian—dismissing a lowly subject.

A disloyal, maddening, horribly forthright subject.

With every evidence of an unruffled temper Hugo stood, said, "Good night, Katherine," and left the room. The moment he shut the door behind him she brought knuckled fists to her eyes, because she *wasn't* going to cry, because everything was fine, because she'd gotten everything she wanted. Because Hugo had kept his word and hadn't leapt upon her in a wild frenzy of unbridled lust and instead had behaved in a perfectly gentlemanlike manner.

Damn him.

Twenty minutes later, having sent downstairs to the kitchen for a large slice of chocolate roll and disrobed in a maelstrom of haste, Katherine was back in her chair near the crackling fire, clad in her ugliest cambric nightgown and with her plate in hand, her copy of *La Divina Commedia* (it having arrived, luckily, the day before Céleste had decamped for parts unknown) waiting on the little table set between the two chairs.

She cast a scorching glance at the empty chair which had recently housed Hugo's large delectable frame.

Was there, she mused, staring at the *Commedia,* Dante's equally scorching *Divine Comedy,* a suitable punishment for husbands who had the gall to abandon their wives on their wedding night? (That is, who had the gall to graciously accede to what was essentially an order to leave?)

Viciously she took a bite of chocolate roll.

And then another.

And another, and when it was all gone, she put the plate onto the little table and reached for her book. She could at least find some comfort there.

But instead, she got up and, moving with a surreptitiousness that was silly, given that she was alone in her sumptuous bedchamber, went to the wall which separated her from Hugo's room. She pressed herself against it, feeling all at once so lonely that she wished her atoms could disengage, penetrate the elegant flowery wallpaper and plaster and wood, and emerge on the other side, where she'd be reconstituted to her original form, and possibly even as a better version of herself.

Suddenly she heard a faint thumping sound issuing from the room next door. Somebody—it sounded like one of the twins—yelped. There was another thump, and then a crash, as if furniture had been knocked over, and one of the twins gave a high-pitched yip.

Katherine caught her breath in horror. Good God, was Hugo—

Was Hugo *beating* them?

Had he left the room so secretly infuriated by her rejection that he'd gone and taken it out on his brothers?

Was it *her fault?*

There was another thump, and Hugo's voice saying, "You're in for it now, lad," and Katherine waited no longer. She ran from her room and into the corridor, heedless of anybody who might see her only in her nightgown, and banged on Hugo's door.

She could hear one of the twins saying "Uh oh," and then the door was opened, and there was Hugo, in breeches and unlaced shirt, his feet bare and his hair rumpled, a pillow tucked under his arm. He looked down at her, surprise and concern in his expression.

"Everything all right?"

"Let me in." She shoved her way past him—even though he practically filled up the doorway—and into the room which looked like a storm had just roared through it. In the dim light of a single branch of candelabra set high atop an armoire, she could see that the bedclothes were in a wild tangle of comforters and sheets, pillows were scattered, a truckle bed was pushed higgledy-piggledy into a corner, an end table lay on its side . . . and there were the twins, one standing on a sofa and the other half-concealed behind a column of draperies, each holding a big, plump pillow and looking rather guilty.

The three of them had been having a *pillow fight.*

And obviously a rollicking one.

"Oh, hullo, Katherine," said the twin on the sofa, "sorry for all the noise, we were laughing like maniacs," and then the other one said, in tones of deep respect:

"I say, Katherine, your *hair*. You look just like a Valkyrie. All you need is a flaming sword."

"Or one of the Furies," said the first twin, getting into the spirit of things, "descending upon unwary mortals. It's simply ripping."

"Why do you keep it all scraped back during the day?" asked the other.

"You look better with it loose."

"Percy," said Hugo from behind her, "and Frank. That's enough."

Oh, her wretched hair. Katherine clutched at it. When she'd been getting ready for bed she hadn't even bothered trying to braid it, and here she was, with her untamed riot of curls, in all probability looking as if *she'd* been in a pillow fight.

Which she never had, of course. What, she now wondered, would that be like? She pictured herself swinging a pillow hard, with all her might, and landing it with a gratifying *thwack*—

"Did we say something wrong?" said Percy (she supposed), "I was *complimenting* Katherine," and his twin put in, "It's just that we were surprised, Hugo, she looks so different," and then Hugo said, from right behind her now, in his deep voice an urgency that startled her:

"Katherine, your back is bleeding. There's blood on your nightgown."

Had she been embarrassed before? It was as nothing to the raging torrent of mortification which subsumed her now. "It's nothing," she said quickly. "I'm fine. Well—good night." She turned, saw that Hugo had gone to one of the trunks—what was he doing? Avoiding looking at her?—and made her way to the door in a kind of blind confusion.

Then she realized that Hugo had caught up to her and was carrying a small wood box.

"I'll be right next door," he said to the twins.

"I say, is Katherine all right?" one of them (Francis?) said.

"Can we help?"

"Should we send for a doctor?"

"Maybe there's one in the common room."

"I'll go."

"We'll both go."

"Blast it, where are my shoes?"

"Oh, I kicked them under the bed."

"Rot you. I'll just put on Hugo's boots—by Jove, I'll look awfully grown up—"

"Thank you," said Hugo, "but for now I want you to stay put."

As soon as they were alone in her room, gently he steered her to the bed and had her sit. "Will you let me see?" he asked.

His touch on her arms had been light, impersonal, which should have pleased her, but it didn't. So Katherine said, "If I say no?"

"I won't press you. But I'd most certainly send for a doctor."

"And have him gawk at me?" She felt a little, horrified shudder ripple through her. "No, thank you. Go on, then, if you must."

Hugo drew aside the tangled spirals of Katherine's dark curling hair. He would have liked to let his fingers play upon the long silken strands, but he set aside this tempting distraction. Whatever had happened to her back had created an ugly lattice of dark red on the white fabric of her nightgown. "My God, Katherine."

"I'm all right," she said grudgingly. "It was only the carriage jostling me about."

"How could the carriage do that to you?"

With even greater reluctance she replied, "It's because of my—well, because of my corset."

"And how could a corset make you bleed?"

"It has steel bands. To keep my spine straight."

"Are you wearing it now?"

"No."

"You seem to be doing just fine without it."

"What do you mean?"

"You're sitting straight."

"What?"

"I said, you're sitting straight."

"I'm—straight?" Now she sounded dazed.

"Yes. Why do you wear it?"

"Oh, don't you remember? When I was small, and how my spine was crooked?"

"No."

"Well, it was, and so my mother had a special corset made for me."

"And you've been wearing it ever since?"

"Yes. Twelve years, eight months, and seventeen days. In various incarnations, of course, as I got bigger."

"Christ," he said, then, "It must hurt you like the devil. How did—how *do* you stand it?"

"I suppose I got used to it. Besides, my mother said I'd grow up into an awful hunchback if I didn't."

With an unusual burst of anger Hugo said, "I'd like to see her wear the damned thing."

"You would?"

"Well, not actually *see* her. But you know what I mean."

"I do know," Katherine breathed, as if she liked the image he'd conjured.

"Will you let me put something on those wounds?"

"I'll be all right."

"I wish you'd let me. You risk infection otherwise."

"Oh. Of course. You're right. But—how will you do it?" That fearful note had crept into her voice again.

"I'll cut open your gown. In the back."

"Oh."

"Are you worried I'll harm you? You needn't. Been doing this sort of thing for years."

"The rough soldier's life."

"Just so."

"Have you dealt with some really bad injuries?"

"Yes. I'm not a doctor, of course. Sometimes you only do what you can. So may I?"

"I—yes."

From his kit he took a small pair of shears. "If you could bend your head, so I can get at that ruffled collar thing round your neck? Thanks. There—it's done. I'm going to dab at those wounds with a cloth—sorry, Kate, I know it hurts—"

"Katherine."

"Katherine." He was silent for a while, methodically working his way down her lacerated back. The deep welts, the raw red marks on her otherwise smooth white skin made him furious. Holy hell, he'd like to do more than put her mother in the corset and cinch it extremely tight. As for that smug overfed father of hers . . . Deliberately Hugo took a breath and let it out, let the rage drain from him. In a voice that was a little rough he said, "You may have some scarring."

"A memento." She sounded steady. Calm. A bit more lightly he went on:

"Well, we'll be able to compare scars then."

"Do you have a lot?"

"Quite a few."

"From being a soldier."

"Some." He laughed. "Also some mementos from my misspent youth."

"Misspent how?"

"Have you forgotten? Ever one for a lark, that was me. I'm still surprised they didn't kick me out of Eton. I can only hope Francis and Percy aren't regaled with too many hair-raising stories of my exploits there."

"Like what?"

"Like the time I snuck a cow into my dormitory."

"A cow?"

"Yes."

"Really?"

"Yes."

"Why did you do that?"

"It seemed like a good idea at the time, I suppose. I had no idea it would start mooing at two o'clock in the morning. Or leave behind its own mementos. The entire dormitory smelt like a cow pasture." He laughed again.

"Did you like school?"

"Oh, I loved it, though I can't say I was the best student. Too restless to sit around with my nose in a book. I drove more than one master insane, I daresay. I'm nearly done here. You're being very brave. I'm just going to dab at this strand of hair—there's blood on it. If you don't mind my asking, why—" He broke off, but she said:

"Why what?"

Hastily Hugo said, "Never mind. A foolish question."

"Go ahead."

"I was just wondering why your fringe is so . . ." He trailed off, feeling very much like the proverbial bull lumbering around a china shop.

"Stiff?"

"Well, yes."

"Because it's straightened."

"How the hell—that is, how is *that* done?" he said.

"With hot irons."

"You're joking."

"No."

"Steel corsets and hot irons. All very medieval. And you think boys are strange. Why do females do such things to themselves? Could you lean forward? Excellent. Here's some basilicum powder. You do have another nightgown, don't you?"

"Yes."

"It's going to be mucked up also. These abrasions are raw. They're going to take some time to heal."

"I've got more than one."

He heard, for the first time this evening, the faintest note of amusement in Katherine's voice. "Of course you do. Would you like to put off our journey?"

"Why?"

"To give your back a chance to heal."

Her little smile fading, Katherine sat very still, with her hands at her chest to hold up the fabric of her nightgown. What a thoughtful question. She breathed in, deeply, and felt her rib cage expanding. For a moment—just a moment—it felt as if her soul was expanding, too. As if Hugo's gentle hands at her back, his kindness, had, in some strange and mysterious way, made it happen.

When, she wondered, had she last had a kind word, a soft touch, from anybody?

How sad that she couldn't even remember.

"Katherine."

"Yes?"

"Would you like to put off tomorrow's journey?"

She pulled herself back into the present and shook her head. "No. I don't."

"If you're sure?"

"Yes." She half-turned, and saw that Hugo had gathered up his things, including the bloodied cloths which he held without the slightest appearance of revulsion.

"Is there anything else I can do for you?"

"I—no."

"That's all, then," he said. "I'll be next door if you need anything. Good night," and he turned, and he left her room, and she was, once more, alone.

Good, she told herself. Just the way she liked it. In her very own version of heaven. Solitary. Peaceful.

So why did she feel so lonely *and* sad?

Was it because he had left her? (Again.) With such calm courtesy, too. (Again.) What was the *matter* with him? This had to be the strangest wedding night ever, and yet he seemed to be taking it all in stride. Ha. He was probably *glad* he didn't have to do the deed with her, didn't have to fulfill—what was that revolting term Mother had used before she had begun to pretend that Mother was a bug, a tiny little nasty talking bug with a voice so small it was impossible to hear? Oh yes, their *conjugal obligation*. The very phrase made her feel rather ill.

So off Hugo had gone, all too cheerfully, leaving her behind. With her stupid bloody back and her stupid bloody hair—and her stupid bloody personality—

Maybe her wounds *would* get infected, and the sepsis would spread with inexorable speed, and soon, very soon, there'd she be on her deathbed—with her hair somehow transformed into a pleasing golden shade, all straight and smooth, perhaps woven into neat plaits—with a celestial blue ribbon on each end—no, a white ribbon would be better, it would be more symbolic of saintly goodness—and she'd look so lovely and peaceful that everyone who'd ever hurt her would be sorry, so sorry—

Dwelling on this improbable image, she hardly knew whether she wanted to laugh or to cry. So instead she stood up, and went to the armoire. She stripped off the damaged nightgown, tossed it aside, and put on a clean one. Her glance then fell upon the discarded corset. She was tempted to put it into the fire, but the smell would be terrible. Instead she snatched it up—grimacing at the pain in her back—and rushed to one of her windows. Why not throw it out into the courtyard and let the horses trample on it?

She was just about to open the window and do just that, but then came a cold and unpleasant twist of fear.

What if she were to need the nasty thing again?

Out loud Katherine muttered to it a line from *Richard III*: "Bloody thou art, bloody will be thy end."

She contented herself with dropping the corset on the floor and giving it a vigorous kick.

Then she blew out the candles, gingerly got into bed, and lay on her side, listening to the deep silence all around her.

"Good night, Mrs. Penhallow," she said into the silence, into the darkness.

But, of course, there was no one there to answer her.

Chapter 7

They departed in good time the next morning, Hugo having somehow acquired several large, soft cushions to help Katherine ride more comfortably in her carriage. Their journey was uneventful for the next two days—aside from Percy once trying to ride standing up on his horse and falling (inevitably) into the mud—and on Saturday they arrived in the bustling market town of Kendal, where Katherine, having made inquiries of their innkeeper as to the poorest church in the vicinity, told Hugo that she wished to attend services there on Sunday.

"Fine," he said, looking at her curiously, but made no further response, and so there they were the next morning, sitting in a small, drafty chapel permeated with such a dank, musty odor that one of the twins (Francis?) was moved to whisper, approvingly and all too audibly:

"It smells like a dungeon in here."

The clergyman continued—as if unaware of this irreligious remark—with his sermon, a short, uncomplicated oration on the new year, new life, new hope, a topic that might, to some, be at odds with his dismal surroundings as well as the general tone of his rather shabby-looking parishioners. Mr. Stafford was a careworn, elderly man, who nonetheless received Katherine warmly when she approached him after the service and asked if she might speak with him.

"How can I help you, my dear?" he asked, with such a look of piercing compassion on his face that she was momentarily startled. But then she thought back to that moment in Mother's sitting-room, when she'd been encased in those hideous court-dress hoops, and answered:

"I have some things to give you, Mr. Stafford. You can sell them, or do whatever you like with them."

"What things, my dear?"

Another memory rose up. Or, rather, a whole array of them: Sunday after Sunday, year after year, watching her father place in the church collection-plate a few copper pennies, counting them out, one by one, plainly loath to part with them. She herself, little Kate, trying to add more to it, from her own pin-money, and being told, again and again, to stop wasting it. After a while, she had simply given up. It was strange, though, how she'd forgotten all about it until recently. She said to Mr. Stafford:

"Clothing, sir. And hats, shoes, fans, shawls, and so on. Twenty or thirty trunks' worth."

"Your trousseau, Katherine?" Hugo said. "What the devil? Oh—begging your pardon," he added to Mr. Stafford who, most luckily, seemed disinclined to take offense.

She lifted her chin. "Yes, my trousseau. I'm giving it away. Every gaudy dress, every garish bonnet, every tawdry shawl, every flamboyant, florid, ostentatious pair of shoes. Everything."

"I say, Katherine," said one of the twins admiringly, "you do use the best adjectives," and the other one added:

"Surely not everything, Katherine? Because then you wouldn't have anything left to wear."

The first twin said, enraptured, "You could be like Lady Godiva."

"Not riding in a carriage, you ass," pointed out the other.

"She could borrow my horse if she liked."

"Boys," said Hugo, and they subsided, and Katherine said, "They're right. I didn't mean literally everything. But *almost* everything." She looked to Mr. Stafford again. "Will you accept it, sir? So that it might be used to do a little good in the world?"

"You're sure, my dear?"

"I've never been more sure of anything in my life."

"Very well then," he said finally, "and thank you. Whatever you have to give will be a great benefit to our little parish. There's such need here. But—is there anything I can do for you?"

She knew a sudden, crazy impulse to say, very sincerely, *Bless me, please bless me, for I'm a wandering lamb,* but instead only said, softly, "Nothing," and so it was done. Mr. Stafford's struggling parish was soon to be enriched beyond the wildest dreams of many, with food, clothing, bedding, fuel, even a few precious books. For quite some time afterwards would his parishioners tell wondering tales of a mysterious dark-haired Lady Bountiful who had come and gone in a day, leaving behind all her earthly belongings. Many would speculate, in fact, if she were actually an angel who had briefly descended to earth before returning to her celestial abode.

The days wound themselves along as their travels continued taking them southeast. And Hugo found himself looking thoughtfully at Katherine. Curiously. She was still aloof. Brusque. Yet he had also noticed that she was unfailingly courteous to servants; generous in unobtrusively offering gratuities. She never passed a beggar in the street but that she reached into her reticule to press something into an outstretched hand. In Kendal's meanest parish she had given away a trousseau worth hundreds, perhaps thousands of pounds.

Gwendolyn had exclaimed, upon hearing the news of his engagement to Katherine, *Oh, Hugo, she must be the nicest, kindest person in all the world!*

He hadn't been sure of that. But he caught glimpses . . .

Still, in her intense self-containment she reminded him, a little, of—in his mind he searched for the image rising up to him. Yes: rather like a warrior, clad in protective armor.

But even the hardest soldier, inside, was just as vulnerable as any other person.

He wondered what *she* was like. Inside.

In due course the Penhallow party arrived in Eton, Francis and Percy were settled in at school, and now it was just herself and Hugo traveling on to Somerset. Unfailingly was Hugo polite, affable, pleasant, as each and every evening they went to their own separate rooms, and increasingly did Katherine feel that she was re-enacting that old story of Beauty and the Beast. Only it had gotten all twisted up somehow. It was the Beast who would ask Beauty, night after night, if she would marry him, and Beauty who would say no. Only Hugo—who was certainly no Beast—asked nothing of her. But wasn't she supposed to be the heroine, Beauty? Or was it *she* who was behaving beastfully? Yet what was wrong with wanting to be alone? Hadn't she earned the right to peaceful solitude after all those years of relentless surveillance?

These thoughts would whirl round and round her head until, inexorably, would come the dreadful sneaking suspicion: was Hugo *glad* to not be invited to her room? And on this dark dread she would ruminate, and brood, and gnaw upon her nails to the very quick.

Really, what was the matter with him? What kind of man was he? How could anybody remain so genial when he'd been barred from his wife's bedchamber? Maybe, just like in some of those novels she'd read, Hugo—the hero—had a dark secret. Maybe, she thought, that chaste peck in the ruins of Babylon was all that he was capable of. Perhaps—an awful possibility—an injury had somehow, well, incapacitated him. He'd mentioned scars, a broken leg, falling off his horse, having dealt with very bad injuries. Gory images formed, vivid and realistic, and the question stayed in her mind, built and grew, tormenting her, until finally, on the evening before they were to arrive at Surmont Hall, Katherine felt she had to say something or burst. They were alone in their private parlor, having dinner, and abruptly she said to Hugo:

"Is there something wrong with you?"

He paused in the act of lifting his fork, on which was embedded a juicy piece of rare roast beef. "I beg your pardon?"

"I have some questions. I want to know if there's something wrong with you."

"In what way?"

Almost was Katherine a little sorry she'd even raised the topic. Hugo's tone was so mild. But she blundered on. "Why are you so good-natured all the time?"

He put his fork down. "This troubles you?"

"It's not normal."

"I don't know about that. It's just how I am."

"I don't believe it."

"It's true. Have you forgotten? Been this way all my life. Feel free to ask my mother the next time we see her."

"Maybe I will."

"Do," he said cordially. He picked up his fork again and proceeded to eat his roast beef.

For a moment Katherine envisioned herself as an alpine climber, attempting without success to gain purchase on an icy slope. Although really it wasn't a very good analogy. Hugo *was* tall and big and therefore could be considered mountain-like, but as for being icy? No, no, he was warmth and life, fire and light— She veered away from this unhelpful train of thought and doggedly went on, "You're happy all the time. It can't be real."

"I'm not happy all the time."

"You act that way."

"I'm not acting at all."

"But you're so—so cheerful!" Katherine twisted the linen napkin in her lap as if it had suddenly come alive and she had to dispatch it. "I suppose," she added in a belligerent tone, "you wish I were more like you."

"I think you should be who you are."

In her frustration and confusion the words just came out. "Oh, no, you wouldn't want that, I assure you."

"Why not?"

Defiantly she reached for her wineglass and took a long swallow. "Because I'm not a good person."

"Really?" His voice was calm. "What have you done?"

Where to start, she thought, *where to start,* and had another drink of her wine. How curious on the tongue, tart and sweet all at once. She had never been allowed to drink anything other than lemonade at dinner. Metaphorically she thumbed her nose at those inane strictures and finished off her wine at a gulp, then looked at Hugo, waiting for him to remark upon her intemperate consumption of alcohol and try to make her stop.

But he only said, "More wine?"

She eyed him mistrustfully. Then: "Yes." Already she could feel her body getting a little bit of a floating feeling. Her brain getting a trifle soft around the edges. How intriguing. How pleasant. Because sometimes she got rather tired of how her mind ran, and ran, and ran. *What have you done?* Hugo had asked. Oh, but wasn't she supposed to be unmasking him, not talking about her fell deeds? She tried to hang onto this stern resolution, but found herself taking another big swallow of wine and saying, in a voice that seemed to be a little louder than was really necessary:

"Do you remember telling me about the cow you snuck into your dormitory at school?"

He smiled. "Yes."

"I went to school too, you know."

"Did you? Where?"

"In Coventry. At the Basingstoke Select Academy for Young Ladies."

"By Jove, what a ghastly name."

"A ghastly name for a ghastly place. And you weren't the only one to have exploits. I had some shocking ones too, you know." My, she thought, it was so interesting how the candle-flames seemed to be flickering in Hugo's eyes. How deep, and blue, and fascinating they were. She stared; it felt as if she were falling into them. Gliding, floating; pleasurably yielding to the forces of gravity, drifting downward like a feather. And maybe, maybe, she'd never come up again.

Katherine was looking rather adorably owlish.

Gazing at her across the table, Hugo thought of several things at once.

One—she had, apparently, given up on trying to coax the various inn maidservants to put her hair up in anything approaching what he supposed was the fashionable style, very high and smooth. Instead her dark curls were gathered into a loose sort of bunch at the nape of her neck, some of which trailed down alongside her bare throat, spilling onto the white skin above her gown's bodice, all in a simple, unfussy way he found very attractive.

Two—he was aware of a strong pull of desire, of wanting, strong and urgent. Which he doubted would be fulfilled anytime soon. One had to be thankful for all those years of military discipline, he supposed ruefully.

Three—she had said, *I want to know if there's something wrong with you,* which was followed by *I have some questions. . . .* This suggested the possibility of further interrogation, which made him wonder, half-amused, just what her fertile and inventive brain might produce.

Four—he thought, not for the first time, just how complicated she was. He remembered, suddenly, a set of gold and silver nesting boxes a school friend, whose father had been attached to the British Embassy in China, had once shown him.

You opened one box, only to find another box inside. You opened the next box, and there was another one. And so on.

And here was Katherine, who evidently had had some adventures of her own. Another box revealed. He said, "I'd love to hear about them."

She played for a moment with a curl that lay upon her collarbone. "Once," she said, leaning forward, "after someone said something nasty to me, I put worms in her bed."

He nodded. "I had that happen to me at school also. My cousin Thane did it."

"Were you angry?"

"Furious. I thrashed him right in front of a housemaster. My only consolation was that we both ended up being caned. Were you found out?"

"Yes. I was put in what they called the Reflection Room."

"That sounds bad."

"It was actually a closet off the dining-hall. The punishment was that I had to sit in there and reflect on my iniquitous behavior."

"Did you?"

"No."

"Good for you. How long did you have to stay there?"

"They locked me in for half a day."

"I'd have gone mad."

She nodded and took another swallow of wine. "I spent a lot of time in the Reflection Room."

"Due to further exploits?"

"Yes. Getting into arguments with the other girls. Speaking rudely to the teachers, and not doing my work. The only thing I liked to do were the compositions, but not the way we were told to do them." Katherine's smile was grim. "Oh, and they expected us to go to bed absurdly early, like babies. They sometimes caught me reading late at night, using candles which I'd—well, which I stole from the various parlors."

"Gad, it *does* sound like a ghastly place. I'm still not sure, though, why all this makes you not a good person. Murder anybody?"

"I'd have liked to murder the headmistress. Or at least thrashed her, like you did to your cousin. That in itself makes me not a good person." She fell silent, but looked at him with an odd expression on her face. It was as if she were longing to tell him something—of an earth-shattering nature—while at the same time she was struggling not to.

He waited. If she chose to tell him, he'd listen; if not, that was fine too, as he himself loathed it when people tried to force confidences. He took a sip from his wineglass. Good stuff, this: it was called Methuen, red and white Lisbon wines mixed, and very expensive. If someone had asked him ten years ago how he imagined his future, it certainly wouldn't have summoned an image of himself sitting in a luxurious inn, drinking costly wine, and in the company of a clever, fierce, strong-willed, intensely complex wife who, it seemed, found him quite unappealing. How strange life was. And—for better or for worse—how infinitely interesting. He took another drink of his wine.

Katherine said, "There was a music instructor at school. I—I was drawn to him. And we used to find places where we could be alone. So we could—we could kiss."

"Did you?" he said calmly.

Katherine seemed taken aback, as if expecting an entirely different reaction. "Yes, we *did*," she replied, looking more owlish than ever, and added, "Ask me why I did it."

"Why did you do it?"

"It seemed like a good idea at the time."

And then she laughed. It was something between a giggle and a chuckle, and the pleasing sound of it was like an echo from the long-ago past. It was as if he were hearing Kate—his friend Kate—laughing again. And he laughed too.

She said, "You don't mind my talking about it?"

"No."

"His name was Monsieur de la Motte. Germaine."

"A blasted Frenchman. Naturally. Did he quote poetry to you?"

"Yes. How did you guess that?"

"Seems inevitable."

"Does it? At any rate, he was so handsome and charming. So debonair. At least that's how he seemed to me. I knew it was wrong. So horribly wrong. But I did it anyway. May I have some more wine?"

He filled her glass again, and then his own. "Something tells me this all leads to the Reflection Room."

"Oh yes, we were discovered eventually. One of the servants saw us and told the headmistress, who—well, who caught us in the act."

"An awful scene, I daresay?"

"Yes." Katherine sipped at her wine, once, twice, and again, then looked at him with eyebrows raised. "Don't you think *I* was awful?"

He smiled. "No."

"No?"

"No. And I don't mean to be boastful, but I think I can top you with the time several of my friends and I decided we wanted to become—ah—more intimately acquainted with the fair sex. So money was pooled, and because I didn't have any to spare I was delegated to slip out very late at night, go into a certain part of town, and bring back with me two of the finest Impures I could find."

Her eyes were sparkling. "And?"

"We'd set up an elaborate communications chain which would let us bring our guests into the dormitory without being noticed. Unfortunately, our sentry in the second-story stairwell fell asleep and snored so loudly that one of the matrons heard him, and the jig was up. So when I came strolling up to the back entrance, arm in arm with a delightful pair of Impures, who do you suppose was waiting for me just inside?"

"Your headmaster."

"Yes. Never saw a sadder sight than those luscious women hurrying away back into the night."

"And what happened to you?"

"Whippings all round, though I got the worst of it, having been deemed the most enterprising one of the lot for having gone into town." He laughed. "It was worth it. I received some very satisfying—and educational—tokens of their esteem on the way toward school."

"How old were you?"

"Just fifteen."

"I was fourteen when it all began with de la Motte."

"Well, in that case you've topped me. You were far more enterprising than I."

"I've topped you?" She shook her head, as if trying to galvanize her brain into better processing what he'd said. "Haven't I shocked you even one little bit?" she demanded.

"No. That school of yours sounds so dreadful that had I been in your place I'd be looking for anything to make it a bit more bearable."

Katherine sat back in her chair, looking dazed. Then,

abruptly: "Do you remember asking why I'd never have brought my maid Céleste with me?"

He nodded. "It was the day I came to tell you about Aunt Henrietta's invitation."

"Yes, that's right. It was after the de la Motte incident that my parents, at the headmistress's request, sent a maid to sleep in my room. On a truckle bed."

"A spy?"

"Yes. The story was given out that she was there to look after my health, but it was a lie. It made everything even worse. And Céleste was so *mean*. I despised her."

"Understandably."

Katherine fell silent, and turned again to her wine. Hugo finished his roast beef, then moved on to the asparagus *en croute*.

"I remember now," she suddenly said.

"Remember what?"

"I've remembered something else I wanted to ask you."

"Yes?" he said, politely.

"Are you functional?"

"I beg your pardon?"

Her face was a vivid crimson and her gaze wavered a little as she looked at him. "I was just wondering if—you lost some of your—your vital parts in the war. If that's what's wrong with you."

He wanted to laugh, but managed to restrain himself. Another box revealed. How long, he wondered, had she been puzzling over this anatomical question? Gravely he replied, "No, I'm intact."

Just as gravely she asked, "And functional?"

"Yes."

She leaned forward again. "Prove it."

Don't laugh, don't laugh, he told himself. "And how would you like me to do that?"

"Let's go upstairs. You can—you can have me."

He assessed her with an experienced eye. Yes, it was a good time for them to leave. "I await your convenience."

"I'm ready." She finished off her wine at a gulp and off they went, up the stairs and along the corridor and into her bedchamber. Hugo closed the door behind them, then turned to see that his bride had sunk into a chair.

"Hugo."

"Yes, Katherine?"

"Oh, Hugo."

"Yes?"

"Oh, Hugo, I don't feel so well," she said, and Hugo, without surprise, moved quickly to take the ceramic basin from the washstand and make himself useful as Katherine retched and then—in the charming colloquial parlance of the soldiering corps—flashed the hash, and in spectacular style too.

Later, later, after he had mopped her face, given her a little water to drink, and helped her into bed, he pulled a chair up close and sat down. She was very white and wan. There was nothing left of the pugilist within her now.

Even as he thought this, Katherine's eyes opened to exhausted slits. One of her hands groped its way free from underneath the covers and weakly reached out to him. He took it in his own, noticing how white it was, the close-bitten nails, how the long tapering fingers seemed at once both delicate and strong. An interesting hand, and rather beautiful.

"Hugo." Her voice was a faint little thread.

"Yes, Katherine?"

"I'm sorry."

He smiled at her. "Don't be. Happens to the best of us."

"To you also?"

"My God, yes."

"Really? Oh, Hugo, I feel terrible."

"I know you do. You'll feel better tomorrow."

"Are you sure?"

"Yes."

"Oh, thank God."

Her eyelids drifted shut, and he waited, watching her.

He thought she'd fallen asleep, but she opened her eyes again and looked up at him.

"Hugo."

"Yes?"

"Thank you," she said, and then she did sleep.

He waited for a while before carefully disengaging his hand from her relaxed one, and stood up, blew out the candles, and went to his own room. Once in his large elegant bed, he lay awake for a while, thinking.

Boxes concealed, boxes revealed.

In his mind he heard again, as if in a pleasant echo from the past, the sound of her laughter tonight.

Her eyes—big, dark, and lovely—had lit up when she laughed.

In the darkness Hugo smiled a little, and turned onto his side, noticing as if for the first time just how much empty space there was. This bed, he thought, was far too big for just one person.

Then he, too, was asleep, and dreamed of the big, beloved house on the beach, the ocean's waves unfurling as they always did, one after the other, a welcome reminder that while some things changed, other things never did. Everyone inside the house was sleeping, safe, sound, content.

Chapter 8

Morning had come, and Katherine was back to sitting at the table in their private parlor, her eyes closed, leaning her throbbing forehead on her hands. Inside her skull, a gang of industrious little demons was, apparently, pounding away. With mallets, gavels, spiked mauls, flanged maces, quarterstaffs, and broadaxes. Oh yes, and with tomahawks, too.

She vaguely remembered Hugo saying last night, *You'll feel better tomorrow.* She supposed he was correct, in that she wasn't vomiting in a horribly sordid way anymore. Dear God, could there be anything more embarrassing— more unromantic—than that? Right in front of him! The immaculately beautiful Ellena di Rosalba, for example, would never have done something so low and vulgar. Nor would saintly Ellena have had too much wine; but if she *were* to feel unwell, she would only look interestingly pale, and perhaps press a white handkerchief to her lips, and her noble swain, Vincentio di Vivaldi, would keep a respectful distance and inquire, in the most delicate and flowery language, as to the state of her health.

Unlike Hugo, who had swung into action and deftly produced a basin exactly when she needed it, without a single word of reproach.

Would Vincentio have been so pragmatic? Or would he have wasted valuable time calling for a maidservant, or producing from somewhere on his person his own handkerchief which, in any case, would not have been very useful?

On the whole, she would rather have had Hugo nearby at such a moment.

Katherine heard the sound of the door opening, and with every fiber of her being she hoped it wasn't yet another maidservant popping into the room with a further offer of food, which only made her gorge threaten to rise again. If she could just sit very still, without moving, without thinking—she'd even try not *breathing* if it would help.

"Good morning. I've brought you something."

She opened her eyes. Here was Hugo, looking so cheerful and pleasant, so healthy and robust, so utterly in contrast to her own enervated state that she stared at him as one might view a visitor from another planet. Then she saw that he was carrying a silver pot, and to her nostrils came wafting the unmistakable aroma of freshly prepared coffee, slightly sweet, faintly bitter and woodsy. She waited for the nausea to swell up, but it didn't.

Normally she didn't drink coffee, but then again, neither did she normally consume alcoholic beverages until she was violently ill, so when Hugo poured some into a china cup and held it out to her, she reached out her hands to accept it.

"Thank you."

"You're welcome. It'll help your headache quite a bit."

"How did you know I have a headache?"

"Don't you?"

"Yes. A horrid one." Katherine sipped at the fragrant coffee, and as if by magic, the pounding in her head began to recede and her stomach settled. Too, her brain began to reanimate and all at once she remembered that not only had Hugo cleaned her up and put her to bed, just prior to that she had brazenly told him he could have her. What a ridiculous thing to say! And to have used such a melodramatic phrase!

She felt a hot blush coming over her, and, resisting the temptation to squirm like a snake under somebody's boot, looked across the table to see that Hugo had sat down, picked up a newspaper which a maidservant had left on the table, and was drinking his own cup of coffee. He glanced over at her then, and said:

"Feeling better?"

"Yes." And she added, in the tone of one being dragged to a miserable doom, "I can be ready to go in half an hour."

"Oh, you needn't hurry. I sent one of the carriages on to the Hall early this morning, with a note that we're probably going to be late. So take your time."

Katherine stared at him again, flummoxed. In her mind's eye she seemed to suddenly see a marquetry table, on which ivory alphabet tiles had been laid out in preparation for a game. She could form so many different words—different sentences—with the tiles. For example, she could create *Oh, thank you, how kind of you.*

Or: *No! I'm already worried about what your relations will think of me, and arriving late on our first day there will only make it worse.*

Or: *Let's just stay here forever. We could become innkeepers. And hide from the world.*

Or: *You should just go on without me. Maybe that would be better.*

Or: *How dare you make a unilateral decision that affects me?*

It was this last sentence that struck the deepest chord within her, its note of withering resentment entirely familiar to a person raised within the turbulent confines of Brooke House. How often we reflexively turn to what we know; and so Katherine said to Hugo:

"You ought to have asked me first."

"Well, I did poke my head into your room, but you were sleeping so soundly I didn't have the heart to disturb you."

The tiles reformed. *A few months ago, I was longing for a life in which nobody jerked me awake. Would have, in all probability, sold my soul for such a thing.*

Then: *I'm losing control. I'm losing control. I'm afraid.*

Her shoulders went up. "You should have woken me anyway."

Hugo looked across the table at Katherine. She was flushed, visibly tense, her dark eyes glittering. A very different Katherine from the one last night, who had reached out her hand for him to clasp. Who had shared with him a sweet moment of connection. But now she looked more likely to use that beautiful white hand to lash out at him with it.

Was this how it was going to be between them?

An unfamiliar feeling came over Hugo then—blazing through him, dark and bitter, like a shadow voraciously darkening the world.

It was regret.

Sorrow for what he had done. A glimpse of a future he didn't want.

The shadow swallowed him up.

Blackness, bitter and corrosive: serving up, as if maliciously, a memory. Standing in the so-called ruins with Katherine; they had come to their agreement. She had said, *I hope you won't regret it.* And without hesitation he had replied, *I won't.* How absolutely sure he had been. How laughably sure.

And then, with an intense effort, Hugo cast off the shadow. To regret was to live life backward, and that was not his way. He gave himself a little shake, resettled himself in his chair, but not before he realized that Katherine had seen on his face what he had been feeling. Reflected back in her expression was recognition, and a kind of horror.

The fire was crackling cheerfully in the capacious hearth, and the low bank of windows admitted into the room the soft gray light of a winter's day. She could hear from outside, in the inn-yard, the muted sounds of men's voices, horses, a dog barking, carriages rattling in and jangling away. Inside there was silence.

He's sorry, Katherine thought. *He's sorry he married me.*

The tiles reformed, to create a new word.

T.R.A.P.P.E.D.

Oh, who *wouldn't* be sorry he'd married such a hard, difficult person?

Shame and panic, unspeakable, whirling inside her like a storm, made her rise to her feet, to say to him:

"I'll be ready to leave within the hour."

"You needn't hurry," Hugo repeated, pleasantly.

"I will, though." She was already on her way, walking quickly, away from him and out of the private parlor, up the stairs, as if pursued. Perhaps by her own frightened thoughts.

An hour later, there they were, each in their own separate sphere: Hugo riding, Katherine in her carriage. On her lap was a book, a dog-eared copy of *Robinson Crusoe,* and a hat she had been too harried to put on. It was made of amber velvet and trimmed with a brilliant green feather. Which, strangely enough, reminded her of that poor bird back in Whitehaven. Señor Rodrigo. How he would have liked the feather, she thought with an aching sadness, how he would have liked it if it were his own.

A memory rose. Herself and Hugo—they were children then—standing near the column of bay trees, the boundary between their two houses. He had squeezed between two of the brushy trunks, come to show her a little bird he had constructed out of paper, which carefully he held in his hands. She had stared in fascinated admiration, and neither of them noticed that her grandfather had approached until he'd said over her shoulder, *What's that?*

I made it, sir, for my mama, answered Hugo. *For her birthday.*

Silly thing for a boy to do, Grandfather had said in his loud blustering way. His voice full of scorn. *Haven't you anything better to do, you great block?*

She had seen, instantly, the look of hurt on Hugo's face. He had gone away and later, as soon as she could, she crept between the trees. She found him sitting behind the stable, the paper bird still held cupped in his hands, and without a word went to sit next to him. It was some time before he spoke.

People think because I'm big I don't have feelings. That I'm stupid.

I don't think that, Hugo. She had leaned her head against his arm. *And I think your bird is beautiful.*

They had sat together behind the stable, and finally he said:

Thank you, Kate.

The carriage rolled smoothly on into Somerset. They passed vast hilly grasslands, winding rivers, towering woodlands. Katherine heard again Hugo's voice from long ago, not yet deepened by burgeoning maturity: *People think because I'm big I don't have feelings.*

Her fingers clenched, too hard, on the amber velvet hat. Crumpling it. Her own voice—Katherine, all grown up, and determined to take control of her life—seemed to ring shrilly in her ears:

You ought to have asked me first.
You should have woken me anyway.

I'm tired. I'm going to sleep. Good night.

I want separate bedchambers, if you please.

It's not as if this is a love-match, and I'll wither away and die of a broken heart. It doesn't matter to me.

It's nonsensical to talk of happiness in an exchange of commodities. A business arrangement.

Had she hurt him? And had that been her—*really* been her—talking like that?

———

15 January 1812

Dear Mama,

A quick billet before Katherine and I leave on the final stage of our journey to Surmont Hall. All's well here; trust the same is true for you—all of you? Storridge assured me that money would very soon be made available to you. Do use it. Also, I've had 50 pounds put on your account at the linen-drapers'—the clerk said some very nice new woolen fabric had just arrived, entirely suitable for winter gowns—and there will be a parcel arriving for Bertram shortly. Don't let him rattle it about. It's a microscope.

Love all round,
Hugo

P.S. I almost forgot. You know the milliner next to the linen-drapers, of course. I saw a hat in the window which rather reminded me of an admiral's bicorne and so I bought it for Gwennie. Send her to pick it up, will you? She'll look ripping in it.

———

Their cavalcade had turned off the road and stopped at a large stone and brick building of elaborate Gothic design, where they were greeted by the middle-aged lodgekeeper, a Mr. Allard, who hospitably waved them on.

Katherine sat up very straight and stared out her window as her carriage rolled forward. A dozen or so *diablotins* would come in very handy right now, she thought with a sudden intense craving. Or a big slice of chocolate roll. It seemed to take forever to wind their way among the woods to arrive at open land. It was like being in one of those eerie tales by the Brothers Grimm; you never knew what dreadful thing lay just around the bend.

A shuddery prickle ran down her spine and involuntarily her gaze went to Hugo, who was riding ahead. He was only some twenty feet away from her, but it might as well have been a million miles. He sat tall and straight in the saddle, easy and graceful, every inch a Penhallow.

A Penhallow, with more of them ahead. Together, one of the greatest families in England. What in heaven's name was *she* doing here?

And then Surmont Hall came into view. Katherine couldn't stop herself, she craned her neck to see it. Caught her breath at its grandeur. The Hall was enormous, with several wings added on in differing styles of architecture—telling the tale of a long and noble heritage—and all combining to somehow create a powerful impression of pleasing unity. It made Brooke House, very large also, but built on the strictest lines of symmetry, seem uninspired, raw, gauche.

The carriages pulled up on a wide gravel drive, Hugo swung himself down from his horse. Quick, quick, you, Katherine thought, pull yourself together. Lift your chin, arrange your face, don't rush your sentences. You may be a stranger in a strange land, but you're just as good as they are, so stop that stupid trembling *at once*.

Footmen had materialized as if out of thin air, her carriage door was opened and she was helped out. Be dignified, she told herself, be calm, stately, just like Livia Penhallow would be—

A fluttering movement, low on the ground, caught Katherine's eye and she half-turned to see that a large black chicken, with an immense spray of curling tail-feathers, had come pelting around the side of the Hall, its bright red comb wobbling madly. A few seconds after that, a pretty young woman followed behind, the white hem of her gown rippling and scarlet cloak streaming behind her as she ran after the chicken.

Oh, I hope the poor servant girl won't be in trouble for letting the chicken get loose. Impulsively Katherine stepped forward, as if to try and block the chicken's escape. The chicken, in turn, seemed to check for a moment, which enabled the girl to swoop it up in her arms.

"You miserable, wretched thing!" she said to the chicken, but with affection palpable in her voice, and the chicken clucked and settled against her, now as docile as any pet. Then her gaze shot up and her vivid green eyes went wide. "Oh! You're here!" she exclaimed, and Hugo said with a laugh:

"Hullo, Liv."

Liv? Livia Penhallow? thought Katherine, astonished. Could it be? This lively-looking girl, surely no older than herself, with her upswept auburn hair rather tumbled, her feet in sturdy, muddy boots, and holding a *chicken?*

"Oh dear, I'm so sorry, I lost track of time," said the girl, looking remorseful. A footman approached, offering to relieve her of her feathered burden, but she said, "No, thank you, James, nobody else should be forced to deal with this silly bird." She came forward then, smiling, and said, a little shyly, "You must be Katherine. I'm so glad to meet you! I'm Livia, you know. Won't you forgive me for being a bad hostess already?"

"How do you do," answered Katherine, still in such a state of amazement that the words came out sounding stiff. Stilted. The chicken eyed her with a malevolent gleam, as if she were an equally silly bird it would very much like to peck.

"And Hugo!" Livia went on, sounding considerably less shy. "It's wonderful to see you again."

"Likewise," warmly answered Hugo, and, coming around to Livia's side, hugged her, careful to avoid the chicken. "Gone in for poultry, have you, Liv?"

She nodded, laughing. "I'm obsessed. I promise not to bore you with longwinded stories about my Hamburgs and Blue Andalusians! Won't you both come inside? The wind is so sharp."

They followed Livia up the short flight of shallow stone steps to the porch and past the massive door of dark knotted wood which another footman held open, and into an immense hall, where Katherine caught jumbled glimpses of a huge fireplace flanked by gleaming suits of armor, an armament display, a coat of arms carved into the chimney piece with the words *Et honorem, et gloriam* featured upon it—*Honor and pride*—all throughout was gracious stateliness—and then abruptly realized that in the center of the Great Hall stood a tall, extremely good-looking man, with brown hair and piercing brown eyes, gazing with wintry sternness at another, shorter man clad in rusty black. Behind them ranged half a dozen brawny men dressed in rough, ragged clothing, on their less than clean faces expressions ranging from sullen defiance to outright fear.

The tall, handsome man said, in his deep cultured voice such hauteur that involuntarily Katherine took half a step back:

"I don't tolerate attempts to forcibly impress the men of my estate. If there are any who wish, of their own accord, to join His Majesty's Navy, then that, of course, would be a different matter."

The other man drew himself up to his full height. "Well, as to that, Mr. Penhallow, impressment's legal, don't you know."

Although Katherine would not have thought it possible,

Gabriel Penhallow—it *had* to be him—looked yet more regal and commanding. He said, icy cold, "Try coming again, sir. Come again and try to kidnap the men of my estate. You may trust me when I tell you won't enjoy what happens next."

"You're—you're threatening me?"

"Yes," said Gabriel Penhallow, his voice lethally soft.

The other man stared up at him, and Katherine could almost see the bravado collapsing. "Come on," he said roughly to his ragtag group of men, and they all hurried to the door, and out of the hall, with a scuttling sort of haste that struck her as more than a little comical.

The chicken in Livia's arms gave a squawk and Gabriel Penhallow turned to look at his wife. Katherine watched, fascinated, as into his brown eyes came a subtle, but unmistakable warmth, and the corners of his handsomely molded mouth quirked up, ever so slightly.

"My dear," he said, "must you bring that absurd creature into the house?"

She laughed. "Oh, Gabriel, I'm sorry, I only meant to bring Katherine and Hugo inside, and then dash away. I must say, you were *splendid* just now. I was very nearly shaking in my boots."

"You *were* splendid, Coz," said Hugo. "Those impressment fellows are a beastly lot. Wish I'd kicked them in their pants for good measure."

"Now that," Gabriel Penhallow said, "would have been an undignified spectacle, but not altogether displeasing." He came forward to where Katherine and Hugo stood, and Hugo said:

"Coz, may I introduce you to my wife, Katherine? Or ought I have to introduced Katherine to you? What an oaf I am! Katherine, here's Gabriel."

"How do you do," said Gabriel. His eyes no longer had that devastatingly attractive warmth, which perhaps he reserved only for his wife, but his tone was entirely civil.

"We're delighted you've come for a visit. I hope your journey here was a smooth one?"

Katherine wondered, rather wildly, if she should curtsy, then caught herself and said with all the composure she could muster, "Yes, thank you. I'm very pleased to meet you."

Gabriel and Hugo warmly shook hands, and as they did two servants came into the Great Hall from a side corridor—the butler and, Katherine thought, a housekeeper.

"Crenshaw," said Gabriel, "send a dozen or so men—armed—after the impressment gang, please, and tell them to make sure they go well past the boundaries of the estate. Mrs. Blake, would you take Captain and Mrs. Penhallow up to their room?"

"Oh, but Gabriel, I wanted to take them," put in Livia quickly. "I'm so proud of how nice it looks."

He looked at Livia again, and Katherine saw again that same subtle warmth, that same, small smile. "But perhaps," he suggested, "without the chicken?"

Livia returned his smile, and held his eyes with her own. It was only for a second, but it enabled Katherine to see, with a startling clarity, how deeply in love she was with her husband. And he with her.

Then the moment passed, and Livia turned again to her guests. "Would you mind very much waiting while I run to the poultry-yard, and return the wayward Hetty to my flock? I won't be but a few moments, I promise you."

"Not at all," said Katherine, still feeling bewildered. Gabriel Penhallow was everything she had expected, but Livia! She couldn't have been less of a haughty Society matron. How, she wondered, had Gabriel come to marry her? Surely his aristocratic grandmother would have fought against this unconventional union with every breath in her body!

And speaking of whom, Katherine glanced nervously around the Great Hall. This was an encounter which, she imagined, would go rather like a case presented before the ancient Greek jurist Draco. Whose famously harsh sentences produced the term "draconian." Her uneasy gaze collided with Gabriel's, who said, in his calm, reserved way:

"You are looking for something, perhaps?"

Flustered, she answered, "No—that is—well, I was wondering where your grandmother is."

"My grandmother routinely naps in the afternoon. However, she's looking forward to renewing her acquaintance with you at dinner this evening."

Katherine had to admire his tact. She managed to say, "I also," and was grateful that Livia soon reentered the hall, her red cloak exchanged for a simple wool shawl and her sturdy boots for a pair of delicate slippers.

"Please won't you come with me?" she said to Katherine and Hugo, and as they walked with her up a grand and curving staircase, she went on, "I feel dreadfully about not greeting you properly! When we got your note, Hugo, I thought I might just spend an extra hour or two in the kitchen garden and poultry-yard, and allowed myself to get distracted."

Kitchen garden? Poultry-yard? The mistress of Surmont Hall actually dealt in such things? Fuddled, Katherine blurted, "But—it's so cold out, Mrs. Penhallow. You didn't mind that?"

Livia flashed a smile at her. "Oh, please won't you call me 'Livia'? With three Mrs. Penhallows now in the Hall, it's bound to get confusing! As for the cold, no, I don't mind it a bit. I'm one of those people who have to get outdoors, no matter the weather. I grew up practically *living* in the woods."

Into Katherine's mind instantly came an image of Livia as a child, feral, wearing animal skins and being raised by a family of wolves. Which, she thought wryly, might have been better than growing up in Brooke House.

They made their way along a lengthy corridor, past several ancient galleries and through a vast, old-fashioned drawing-room, until finally they came to a beautifully paneled hallway with a high arched ceiling; they walked past another wide stairway, and came at last to a handsome, intricately carved oak door. Livia opened it and ushered them inside. "Here we are. I hope you'll be comfortable."

Katherine paused just past the threshold and in her memory suddenly heard again Gabriel Penhallow saying, *Would you take Captain and Mrs. Penhallow up to their room.*

Room.

Not *rooms.*

Panic overtook her and unthinkingly she looked up with a kind of desperation at Hugo. He met her glance and said at once, "Liv, I wonder if—"

No, no, no, she mustn't know about us, thought Katherine, and, quickly placing her hand on Hugo's arm, interjected:

"Thank you, Livia. It's a delightful room. I'm sure we'll be very comfortable."

"I'm so glad you like it," answered Livia smilingly. "I think it's the nicest of the guest bedchambers. Aren't those old wall-hangings beautiful? Supposedly they're a gift from Henry the Seventh, who was said to have stayed here in 1487, but Gabriel's grandmother says the resident Penhallows would never have allowed such an upstart to stay with them. At any rate—in the morning you'll have a spectacular view to the front. When we knew you were coming, we made sure all the work was done in plenty of time."

"Work?" repeated Katherine.

"Oh, we've been fixing and renovating everywhere around the Hall! Last week, for example, part of the roof in the Elizabethan wing collapsed, and yesterday Mrs.

Blake found more rats' nests in one of the saloons down-stairs."

"More?" Katherine was starting to feel like a parrot, dazedly echoing Livia. "Did—did you find any in here?"

Livia laughed, but kindly. "No, please don't worry about that! We *did* unearth an old packet of letters, written by someone named Anne. Granny says she has no idea who that is. Perhaps a guest who stayed here a long time ago and left them in a cupboard. Well, I won't keep you any longer. The servants should be here soon with your trunks. Do ask them for anything you need, of course. And won't you please come downstairs at five, to the Great Drawing-room? We'll all assemble there before going in to dinner."

"All," Katherine repeated hollowly—and parrot-like—and realized that she was still clutching Hugo's arm, as if he were ballast in a stormy sea. She released it, but didn't dare glance up at him this time, afraid, now, she might see again in his eyes that harrowing look of regret.

A footman placed before Henrietta Penhallow a shallow bowl of fragrant potato-leek soup, the surface of which had been dotted, with exquisite care, with fresh green chives. She thanked him, and marveled, not for the first time, at the circumstance of sitting along the side of the burnished mahogany table, rather than at her accustomed place at the foot. Change had come, as it would, she mused, whether one embraced it or not.

She let her gaze travel around the table. A small party this evening: Gabriel and Livia occupying, and rightly so, the head and the foot. Hugo's new wife Katherine sitting to Gabriel's right, and herself next to Katherine. Evange-line, her longtime companion, on Gabriel's left, and next to her Hugo. A flare of pain, remembering others who ought to have been here, her own dear Richard, and their children. Henrietta picked up her spoon with a steady hand. The pain would fade away, whenever it was ready.

She took a sip of her soup. It was delicious. She made a mental note to send a complimentary message to the kitchen. Or no: that ought, perhaps, to come from Livia now, not herself. How strange, after all these years, to let the reins of management begin to slip from her grasp. It wasn't as difficult as one would have thought. Perhaps she had gotten a little more tired than she had realized.

Henrietta's gaze went again, lightly and unobtrusively, to Hugo's wife, the granddaughter of a fabulously wealthy, extremely low-born miner and an unimportant, dissipated, bankrupt Yorkshire baronet. Not at all the sort of person whom she herself would have wished to join the family; her own parents would, if such a fanciful thing were possible, be rolling in their graves at the very idea. And yet so it was. Katherine, Henrietta observed gloomily, seemed to have very little conversation, her hair was pulled back so tightly it seemed to actually stretch her countenance, and also her gown was dreadfully *outré*. And yet—

Katherine wore no jewels, aside from the thin, elegant gold band on her left hand. That in itself was interesting. When she did speak, she gestured in an unconsciously graceful way that seemed to illuminate her words. Additionally, one couldn't help but notice that her large, dark eyes were brilliant and alive, alternatively dreamy and alert. The Brooke girl was a *thinker,* there was no doubt of that. And the world could certainly benefit from more of those in it.

Henrietta Penhallow, despite herself, was intrigued.

Livia Penhallow, as she ate her soup, hoped that everyone was having a good time. This was her first dinnerparty since becoming the official mistress of Surmont

Hall, and she wanted so much for it to be a success. The menu, which she had carefully planned with Granny's assistance, was both delectable and nicely varied. And people *were* talking, although Katherine, so far, hadn't said much. She would have liked to include Katherine in her conversations with Granny and Hugo, but—how annoying!—one wasn't supposed to talk across the table. At least she had managed to overset the usual modish rule of having enormous centerpieces cluttering up everything, so that you felt visually isolated from the people who weren't sitting right next to you. It was especially nice as she could look directly at Gabriel. How handsome he was. How distinguished in his dark evening-clothes. Her husband. Her *husband*. It was still sometimes hard to believe that they were really and truly married. There had been times, months ago, when that had seemed an achingly impossible prospect. Oh, she was lucky, *lucky*.

Livia looked again to Katherine, sitting between Gabriel and Granny. She hoped Katherine didn't feel intimidated. When *she* had had her first conversation with them, she'd felt very much as if it were two against one; they had, then, seemed to take up so much space, and she herself to occupy so little.

Tomorrow, Livia vowed, she'd make sure that she would claim a seat next to Katherine.

Hugo noticed with pleasure how happy, how blooming Livia looked. It was enjoyable, too, catching up with her news since he'd last been here at the Hall, during the autumn. They'd gotten on well together since they'd first met; very easy and unaffected she was. And Miss Evangeline Cott, on his right, was just as quiet and pleasant as he remembered. Just as self-effacing too; he'd had to draw her out on the subject of her forthcoming marriage to the local parson. It turned out, in a reminder of just how small a world it could be at times, that her Arthur Markson had actually gone to school with Grandpapa at Oxford.

As their soup bowls were removed, Hugo seized the opportunity to glance at Katherine, catercorner to him. She hadn't met his eyes once since sitting down for dinner and she seemed decidedly ill at ease. Not that he could blame her, placed as she was between Gabriel and Aunt Henrietta. They were veritable strangers to her, and that could, of course, make it difficult. That time he'd had to travel with Gabriel from school, in the aftermath of Father's death, he'd barely known him; and although Gabriel hadn't been hostile, neither had he been particularly friendly. He himself, still stricken with grief, hadn't bothered to try and drum up conversation between them, and so they had passed the journey from Eton to Surmont Hall pretty much in a silence that had grown more awkward by the mile. And Aunt Henrietta—he'd thought her rather a ghastly old dragon.

Katherine still didn't meet his eyes. Toward him she had been, since the morning's exchange, utterly remote, as if she were—or would have preferred to be—a million miles away from him.

A footman set before him a plate with two very thin-sliced *côtelettes de poulet* in a light, buttery *sauce blanche,* and Gabriel Penhallow nodded his thanks. He assumed that the cutlets did not have their origin in the renegade chicken which this afternoon Livia had brought into the Great Hall. No, Livia was too fond of her newly acquired brood, being, as she had only last week explained with delight and deep absorption, in the early stages of coaxing them to produce fresh eggs.

Gabriel smiled within himself. His unconventional bride. A year ago he would have been horrified at the idea that a Penhallow wife would sully her hands with such mundane matters (literally holding a chicken!), let alone take an interest in them. God, what a starchy fellow he had been. And still was, sometimes, he thought ruefully, but thanks to Livia he was trying hard to overcome it.

He looked down the table at his wife, just now talking animatedly with Hugo. She was, without doubt, the most beautiful woman he had ever seen in his life. So fiery and intelligent, and so infinitely fascinating. How lucky he was—lucky beyond words.

He could have dwelled on his miraculous good fortune for quite a while, but courtesy recalled him, and he turned again to Katherine Penhallow, wondering what additional topics he might introduce. He'd tried all the usual ones, the weather, the state of the roads, details of her journey here, the health of her family, and so on. Her responses had been short, verging on the curt, and he knew, briefly, a moment of instantly suppressed exasperation; and then he saw that her hands were trembling, just a little.

Damn it, had he done it again? How had Livia used to put it? Assumed the arrogant, aloof Penhallow mask? He said to Katherine, hearing in his voice the slightest edge of desperation:

"My wife has been trying to persuade me to take up Mrs. Brunton's new novel, *Self-Control,* which, she says, is unintentionally one of the funniest books she's ever come across. Have you by any chance read it?"

Katherine's eyes lit up, and Gabriel was startled at the change in her. It was like watching a statue come suddenly to life. She answered:

"Oh yes, and it *is* funny! There's a scene in which the heroine, having been spirited away to America, escapes the villain by lashing herself into a canoe and letting herself be carried away by the rapids."

Amused, Gabriel replied, "A plucky young lady, I perceive."

"Well, yes and no, and that's why it's so humorous.

Mrs. Brunton seems to view her heroine as a kind of blank slate, on which she can scrawl whatever she likes as the plot barrels along, rather than developing her in a credible fashion."

"An intriguing observation! And is the same true of the villain?"

Katherine laughed. "It's hard to say. He's a dastardly rake, you see, who offends the heroine initially with his coarse proposals, but then he spins about and offers to honorably marry her. She, however, refuses him, no matter how alluring his title and fortune, and—"

She broke off, looking abruptly and profoundly self-conscious, and Gabriel, in his heart, pitied her, and began to talk about a little tour through the Blue Gallery tomorrow which, he said, she might perhaps find of interest, as they contained some very fine works by Rembrandt, Bosch, the Brueghels, van Eyck, and the Limbourg brothers. Was Katherine familiar with Pieter Brueghel the Younger's *The Village Lawyer*? An excellent example of a remarkable workshop technique called pouncing; had she heard of it? There was also a charming little sketch by Rembrandt which was believed to have been drawn while he was a young student in Leiden. Gabriel went doggedly on. He feared, he very much feared, he was rambling, but he'd talk till midnight if necessary, if only to give Katherine the time to recover her composure.

Miss Evangeline Cott, who had for many years served as the companion, confidante, and general aide-de-camp to her longtime friend Henrietta Penhallow, partook in a limited way of the next course—rare white truffles in a red wine sauce—as it would not, she knew, agree with her tomorrow. She continued to make easy, pleasant conversation with her table-partners, Gabriel Penhallow and his cousin, Captain Hugo Penhallow, even as she pondered, as she had many times before, her curious position as one who was part of the family and yet outside of it at the same time. It enabled her to trace, with an interest that was both detached and kindly, the shifting lines of connection among them.

For example, Henrietta and her grandson Gabriel had, for many years, sustained a distressingly cursory relationship. Then Livia had unexpectedly come into their lives, bringing with her the bright sunshine of her personality, and had changed everything, in the best possible way. It was due to Livia, in fact, that she and her beloved Arthur had been reunited after decades apart, and were now soon to be wed.

An intense joy filled Evangeline at the thought, although she concealed it behind the usual calm placidity of her expression. She went on asking Hugo about his various family members. It was easy to see how much he loved them all, how deeply he cared about them.

Unfortunately, mused Evangeline, she could see very little in the way of connection between Hugo and his wife Katherine. She knew of course that Hugo had married to save his family, for pragmatic reasons, but still, one would have hoped that despite these inauspicious circumstances, such an unlikely couple would become more to each other than a means to an end.

And there was so much *potential* in each of them . . .

She repressed a faint, but heartfelt sigh, and without missing a beat said to Hugo, "How delightful to know that your twin brothers are now established in their educations. And your sister Gwendolyn? What are the plans for her?"

Evangeline listened with genuine attention to Hugo's reply, even as another part of her continued to observe, ponder, plan. For one thing, she had not yet mentioned to Henrietta her hope that she would soon engage another companion. Despite her new happiness here at the Hall, there was within Henrietta a deep and relentless loneliness, one which, perhaps, would never be remedied in this lifetime. But a sensitive, steadfast companion—such as she herself had been; Evangeline had no false modesty— might help, here and there, to at least partially assuage it. For another thing, she had noticed a change in Livia, a very promising one. Livia hadn't spoken about it, but perhaps even she wasn't aware of it. Also, Arthur had mentioned the idea of traveling to the Lake District for their honeymoon, and Evangeline wondered if it would be possible to take in the Wye Valley, as it was said to be a place of spectacular beauty. Indeed, the great poet Wordsworth had written most eloquently about it, saying, *all which we behold is full of blessings.* And this, Evangeline thought, is very true, though blessings are not always so easy to perceive.

For a brief and fleeting moment Katherine wished she were dead. Oh, would this wretched dinner never end? She had just embarrassed herself in the most ghastly way in front of Gabriel Penhallow. A hideous bookend to how she had started the evening by embarrassing herself in front of Henrietta Penhallow, who had sailed her way in a soft silvery-gray gown of such understated elegance that Katherine felt painfully dowdy, loathing her own dress with its lace and net and beads and bows, wishing she had removed all of them at some point along the way here, and just as quickly reminding herself that she hated sewing with a passion which had earned her more than one interval in the Reflection Room.

The old lady had said, in what seemed like a conspicuously neutral tone:

"Good evening. We meet again, I see."

Katherine had thought two things at once.

First, Mrs. Penhallow sounded exactly like a character in a Gothic novel, making a remark which on its face was harmless but which was practically vibrating with sinister implications that didn't bode well for the heroine.

Second, she had pictured herself answering, in an equally dramatic fashion and possibly in some kind of exotic accent, so that *she'd* sound like a character in a Gothic novel: *Yes, we certainly do meet again, madam, much to your dismay.* And she'd added in a sudden loud clap of thunder afterwards, for theatrical effect, and also brought in a butler in the background, very suave, but in actuality a scoundrel, who was scheming to . . .

And suddenly she had realized that she hadn't said anything in reply, the old lady was looking hard at her from beneath silvery eyebrows, and she had blushed an awful beet-red.

Which she was doing *again,* right now. Damn, damn, *damn.*

Chapter 9

As if taking cruel pleasure in Katherine's misery, time meandered its way along, loitering with almost unbearable slowness, but dinner did, eventually, end. Livia rose, and Katherine followed her, old Mrs. Penhallow, and Miss Cott to a large drawing-room furnished and decorated in the ornate, lively rococo style of the previous century. There, she paused just past the threshold, not quite knowing where she should sit.

As if sensing her uncertainty, Livia paused too, turned, gave her a warm smile. "Won't you join me, Katherine?"

Thankfully Katherine began to follow Livia into the room, but then old Mrs. Penhallow said:

"I should enjoy a little *tête-à-tête* with Katherine. That is, if you do not object, Katherine?"

"By no means, ma'am." *Smile, smile.* Trying to appear confident, she went to sit in a gilded, carved walnut chair upholstered in heavy embroidered silk that had her at a perpendicular angle to Mrs. Penhallow, who looked at her with silvery brows slightly knitted.

"You traveled here today from Bruton, I understand?"

"Yes, ma'am."

"Did you pass the night in the Pomfret Arms?"

"Yes, ma'am."

"I applaud your choice. By far the best inn in Bruton. I trust the sheets were properly aired?"

"Yes, ma'am, I believe so."

Mrs. Penhallow nodded, then began to turn upon the fourth finger of her left hand a singularly beautiful sapphire ring, of a simple yet exquisite design. "It has come to my attention," she said, "that you and Hugo are traveling with three carriages which are very nearly empty, and that you brought with you no maid or dresser. Naturally my curiosity is piqued. May I inquire as to the reason why?"

A little wildly, Katherine thought about making up a story of some kind—*We were waylaid by highwaymen, a rogue band of raccoons made off with everything during the night, I did bring a maid but she ran off to Mexico to join the fight for independence*—but it seemed impossible while being scrutinized by those sharp blue eyes. So she said:

"We left my house in Cumbria with those three carriages holding my trousseau, ma'am, but it didn't suit me. I gave it away on the way here."

Those silvery brows now arched high in evident surprise. "You gave it away because it didn't suit you?"

"Yes, ma'am."

"To whom did you give it?"

"A poor parish in Kendal."

"I see. A charitable gesture." Mrs. Penhallow nodded slowly. "Why did your trousseau not suit you?"

The clothing had itching powder in it. The shoes all squeaked when you walked in them. "Nothing in it was to my taste, ma'am."

"Indeed." Ruminatively Mrs. Penhallow added, "I recall a certain hat, strewn with artificial cherries."

Katherine grimaced. "Yes. It looked like I had a fruit bowl on my head."

There was a tap on the door and then it was swung open by a footman, who solemnly announced, "Here is Muffin, ma'am."

In shot a little white dog, with absurdly short legs and great pointy ears, who ran joyously to the old lady, then dashed over to Livia and Miss Cott, its curly tail thumping, and then to Katherine, as if wanting to make sure she was included in its exuberant greeting; after which it bounded back to Mrs. Penhallow and leaped up next to her on her elegant rococo chair. Her handsome face softening ever so slightly, the old lady gathered the little dog onto her lap. A further surprise for today: Katherine would have expected a graceful well-bred whippet, or a fashionable pug, not this charming, but rather motley-looking creature.

"The hat," pursued Mrs. Penhallow, with the air of one determined to get to the bottom of things. "Why?"

Because plums were out of season. I had a dreadful spot on my forehead I wished to conceal. They were actually real cherries, so I could eat them if I got hungry. Katherine blurted out:

"Oh, ma'am, how can I explain it to you? It was easier to wear it than to fight about it. I gave up years ago. You don't know my mother, but . . ."

"A domineering sort?"

Already regretting her impulsive frankness, Katherine only nodded, and saw, to her surprise, an expression of—why, it looked like sorrow flitting across Mrs. Penhallow's face. Somehow it galvanized her to go on. "My mother—my parents—believe that one's wealth should be clearly signified by what one wears. And so they allowed themselves to be guided by what I believe were unscrupulous modistes, who indulged in all the worst—and most expensive—excesses of fashion. They wanted to make sure that everyone in the *beau monde* knew that I was very wealthy."

"A miscalculation. Such displays are garish and vulgar, and deceive no one. If anything, they make things worse. You had a Season last year, then?"

"Hardly deserving of the term, ma'am."

"A failure."

"Yes."

"And you hope for a better one this year?"

"More than hope, ma'am. It *must* be better. It has to be."

"You want this very much, I perceive."

"Yes."

The old lady was silent for a few moments. "You remind me of someone," she said, in her eyes now a faraway look. "A strong-willed young woman bent on taking the *ton* by storm."

"Who was that, ma'am? And was she successful?"

The tiniest of smiles played about the old lady's lips. "It was me. And yes, I *was* successful, though not in the way I originally planned."

To Katherine came a sudden vision of Mrs. Penhallow as she might have been when young: slim, upright, graceful, dazzlingly lovely. She would have worn those elaborate gowns with the very wide, full skirts and ruffled sleeves, and the high-dressed, powdered hair. Oh, a diamond of the first water, without doubt. It was easy to believe the young Henrietta Penhallow would have conquered Society in a heartbeat.

It came to her, too, that here was, perhaps, a commonality between herself and Mrs. Penhallow, as different as they were. Katherine leaned forward. "Ma'am, might you be willing to offer me your guidance? I'll need to replace my trousseau, and you're renowned throughout London for your *sens de la mode*."

"Only throughout London? Dear me, how the mighty have fallen." Mrs. Penhallow's voice was serious, but in her eyes there was a faint little twinkle, encouraging Katherine to say:

"Perhaps everywhere, ma'am. Will you help me? Is there a seamstress nearby whom you patronize?"

"I do. But she's engaged in work for Miss Cott, for her

wedding-gown. However, I may be able to persuade a certain modiste I know in Town to travel here, along with her assistants. But she's very expensive."

"That wouldn't be a concern for me, ma'am."

"I didn't think so. You'll require everything? Gowns, shoes, hats, gloves, shawls, and so on?"

"Yes."

"I'll let Madame Hébert know, and that she's to bring along some colleagues, whose names I shall also suggest." Mrs. Penhallow looked at Katherine with an exacting kind of deliberation, and Katherine felt—not with rancor, but with hope—as if she were a lump of clay being assessed by an artist.

I saw the angel in the marble and carved until I set him free.

The great Michelangelo had once said that. Though, of course, she herself was no angel—

"Jewel-tones," said Mrs. Penhallow decisively. "White cannot be avoided, of course, for day-wear, but *you* will do better in a softer white tending toward cream or ivory. No pastels, ever! As for your hair . . ."

"I know it's a horrid mess, ma'am. At school they called me Medusa." Oh, God, she hadn't meant to reveal this hurtful memory, ever! But somehow it had just slipped out. Katherine felt herself blushing hotly.

The old lady, however, only said, "Girls can be so cruel, can't they? I daresay they may have been envious, for it's quite arduous to transform straight hair into curls."

Envious? Of *her?* Katherine's mouth dropped open. She stared at Mrs. Penhallow, who, for her part, continued gazing back in that same pensive manner. Finally she said:

"As someone with curly hair myself, I may be biased, but I must say I think curls very attractive. My suggestion to you is that you stop fighting them. It doesn't suit you to pull your hair so tightly onto the crown of your head, or to pin it behind your ears. Better, perhaps, to have a loose arrangement across your forehead and framing your face—and a simple, unadorned coil in the back, with tendrils allowed to trail at the nape of your neck and a few brought forward, as if an ornament to the collarbone. Yes, that would be a great deal more flattering. What you need is a competent *friseur* who understands curly hair."

"I like your suggestion very much, ma'am," said Katherine in a voice in which sincerity, and a kind of awe, were blended. "Do you have a particular *friseur* in mind?"

"I do. I'll send for him as well. Would you like me also to engage the services of a dresser?"

"Yes, but . . ." Katherine trailed off, embarrassed all over again.

"But what?"

"Oh, ma'am, I'd like to have someone *pleasant*."

Those silvery brows went up a little. "There is an employment agency I patronize while in London, and I'll write to the proprietress tomorrow. Your request is not unreasonable."

"Thank you, Mrs. Penhallow." For a crazy few seconds she felt like leaping to her feet and hugging the old lady.

Henrietta Penhallow didn't immediately reply; she had that faraway air again, as if she hadn't heard, as if her thoughts had drifted elsewhere. "We know what we are," she murmured, "but know not what we may be."

"Hamlet," said Katherine, and the old lady's look sharpened again.

"You know your Shakespeare?"

"Well, I like reading it, ma'am," she answered, and then, to her surprise, she and Mrs. Penhallow plunged into an amiable debate about the plays—the old lady plumping for *The Tempest* as the Bard's best, and she herself arguing for *Macbeth*. It proved to be a pleasant distraction, but fell away when the gentlemen joined them again.

Because soon it would be bedtime.

Hugo looked around the capacious room that was his and Katherine's bedchamber. There was a reasonably big bench, padded with dark blue fabric, over by one of the windows. That would do, although he'd have to prop his feet up on the armrest, or wedge himself between the two armrests, and hope he didn't roll off in the middle of the night. Or, worse, get stuck there.

"Hugo."

"Yes, Katherine?"

"Thank you for not saying anything to Livia—or anybody—about our—arrangement. About the bedrooms."

He looked down into her face. She was pale and tense; strained. Visibly exhausted. He exerted himself to say, pleasantly, "It's all right. I'll just take a blanket and a pillow, then."

"What? Why?" Her glance flashed around the room, to the bench, then to the bed and lingered there: it was quite a bed, very high and old-fashioned, and draped with crimson bedcovers. It was set on an equally old-fashioned platform, formed from carved oak, and above it was a canopy with long silken hangings in the same vivid red. "Oh. I see." Her face worked; she brought one of her hands to her mouth, worried at a fingernail. Finally: "There's no need for that. We can share the bed. It's big enough for two people. Will you keep to your word?"

"Yes."

"I'll undress behind that screen. If—if you could undo my gown for me?"

Oh, damn. Damn, damn, *damn*. Help her undress. It was not unlike asking a starving man to hold a delicious loaf of bread and refrain from eating it while you just stepped outside for a while. He said, "Certainly."

Katherine turned, and he began—with an efficiency that was, under the circumstances, remarkable—to unfasten the long column of buttoned loops at the back of her gown. He wondered if she had any idea how hard this was for him. Standing so close, performing such an intimate task. He caught a subtle scent from her, sweet and faint. Delectable. It took him a few moments to identify it as chocolate.

Then her gown slid apart, revealing the delicate white linen of her shift. It was all that stood between him and warm, soft flesh. Between him and Katherine.

Speaking of hard, *he* was hard now, and breathing rather audibly.

Damn it to hell.

Last night she had accused him, *You're happy all the time.*

He definitely wasn't happy right now.

No, he was in agony.

Because he wanted quite a lot to topple her and take her right there on the wide, ancient oak floorboards upon which Henry the Seventh may or may not have trod. Ho. Unmanned in the war? He'd show her unmanned. Until she screamed with pleasure.

Sweating, he gritted his teeth.

Will you keep to your word?

Yes.

Then, with effort, he relaxed his jaw.

"Well," he said, "that's done."

"Thank you," she answered, and quickly went behind a tall three-paneled screen set in a corner of the room. Her voice, a little steadier now, came floating to him from behind the screen:

"Will you let me know when you're in bed? And could you blow out the candles?"

"Certainly," Hugo repeated, rather heavily, aware that before him loomed again the dark, dangerous, fatal slough of regret. Christ, what had he done?

He turned away and rapidly began to undress.

They lay in the dim flickering light of the waning fire. Katherine was on her back, safe under the bedclothes, hands folded over her middle. It was strange, but she wasn't tired anymore. She was, in fact, wide awake, her mind looping, over and over again, to those moments during which Hugo had unbuttoned her gown. She had felt his warmth, his solidity, his bewitching maleness, from behind her and an electrifying thrill had shimmied everywhere within her. These were circumstances, had they been related in a naughty novel, which would have had her eagerly turning the pages to see what would happen next.

But this was not a novel, this was real life, with all its uncertainties. Its mystifying twists and turns. The unknowable future. Looming large . . . frighteningly large.

When she'd taken off her shift and put on her nightgown, she had very nearly kissed the screen for being there. Because she could hide behind it. At least for a little while.

Oh, God, how awkward this all was, sharing a bedchamber.

Sharing a bed.

But *anything* was better than having people know the truth.

Luckily, she was in control.

Completely and fully in control.

That was the saving grace of this difficult situation—her self-control. And into her mind, with immediate irony, popped an image of that hapless, silly heroine in Mrs. Brunton's *Self-Control*. Tumbling along a raging river. Lashed to her canoe.

It came to Katherine that *she* felt a little like that heroine right now. Tumbling, hapless, helpless . . .

Go to sleep, go to sleep, she told herself sternly. She made herself picture sheep, identical white fluffy sheep, jumping over a stile. That would work for sure. *Count them, damn you.*

One.

Two.

Three.

Four—

Was Hugo sleeping? she wondered. The sheep vanished and she noticed, out of the tail of her eye, his big body next to hers. She could just make out that he had one long muscled arm, bare, above the covers.

His shoulder was bare, too.

Was he . . .

Was it possible he was naked?

Her fingers flattened out on the cambric material of her nightgown.

She was properly attired.

But Hugo?

An image came to her: Hugo, so tall, big, broad-shouldered. Lean-hipped, long-legged. Utterly naked. Completely male. Her mind projected it in two dimensions, as if it were a lifeless portrait on a wall, something from which you could stand apart and objectively view. An image you could coolly walk away from.

But—as incendiary as it was—it was just in her imagination.

Hugo himself, three-dimensional, living and breathing and solid and *real,* was right next to her. Just a few feet away. Her nostrils flared, like a deer scenting danger. And—oh God, oh dear God—her body was reacting to his presence. Between her legs, in that secret place, a slow delicious swirl of energy, of subtle pleasure; in her breasts, a warm, lovely, tingly sort of feeling, as if that same illicit energy was flowing throughout her, unquenchable, unstoppable, a river broken free from a dam.

Treacherous.

But, undeniably, delightful. That is to say, full of delight. Her arms and legs felt heavy, languid, in the most wonderful way, she was melting, spreading across the bed, hot, like wax from a burning candle.

Oh yes, she *was* awake, as wide awake, Katherine was certain, as she had ever been in her whole entire life.

Then came a torrent, urgent, from deep within her brain, repeating old, scathing, familiar words from the past. No, no, no, you mustn't, you sordid sneaking criminal girl, this is shameful, this is wrong, *this is bad,* and continued with increasing panic as desire nonetheless built, grew, overtook her. No, no, *don't,* but still her hand drifted up, to slide around the cambric-covered curve of a breast, to feel a hard and sensitive tip beneath the fabric; her fingers slid up, up, to wonderingly stroke lips that felt swollen, hungry. Needful. That is to say, full of need.

A wave of lust lifted her, rising high above her brain's chatter, and recklessly she rode it.

No, no, stay the course, don't, *don't,* be careful, be safe, be good . . .

But it was as if every cell in her body combined to shout out a loud and defiant response:

No.

Out loud Katherine said:

"Hugo."

Perhaps he had been awake also, because right away he answered, in his deep, calm voice. "Yes, Katherine?"

How to begin, she wondered, how to frame it? Hunger, impatience, rose up. Roaring. And before she could stop herself she said it. Again.

"You can have me."

There was dead silence.

Finally: "I beg your pardon?"

Recklessly she rode the wave. "You can have me. If you want to. *Do* you want to?"

Silence again. Then: "Yes. Do *you* want to?"

"Yes." Katherine watched, a little breathless, as Hugo lifted himself up on one elbow, facing her. She could see that the bedclothes had slipped down quite a lot. And that his chest was bare. Oh, delicious. Saliva began to pool in her mouth and she swallowed convulsively.

"Are you sure, Katherine?"

"Yes."

"What do you want to happen?"

She blurted it out. "Surprise me." And in the dimness she saw a slow, slow smile come to Hugo's perfect mouth.

"I'll do my best."

He slid close to her then, brought his long self against her. Oh my goodness, he *was* naked. And his—what was the right word for *that?*—his—well—*manhood* was pressing against her thighs, hard, hard, utterly foreign, incredibly exciting, but her nightgown was in the way. The damned thing. But she had a feeling that somehow they would fix that annoying little problem. She felt herself arching up, as if involuntarily, and her mind seemed to be fizzling away like a spent firework. O joy. She said, in a soft, silky voice she hardly recognized as her own:

"There's just one thing."

He paused. His face was so close to her own, and she fancied she could see fire kindling again in the sapphire of his eyes. "Yes, Katherine?"

Reckless. "Are you going to kiss me like you did in the ruins of Babylon?"

"Do you want me to?"

"No."

He laughed. "Good."

"Hurry up then."

"As you wish," he said, and brought his mouth to hers.

In a heartbeat she could tell that it wasn't at all like that brief salute from before. No, it was delightful: full of delight. Brimming with delight. Hugo's mouth was hard, sure, persuasive, entrancing—all of this, and all at once.

She felt her own lips parting, eagerly yielding, welcoming with a low guttural sound in her throat the warmth, the wetness of his tongue. In her mouth. In her.

My, she thought in a dim, dreamy sort of way, he knows exactly what he's doing. He's very sure. This is good. *He's* good.

Very, very good . . .

One of her hands lifted, groping, found Hugo's muscled shoulder and slid up to the sturdy column of his neck and then around to his nape, and up, into his thick short hair, gripping it, gripping him, to bring him yet closer as she kissed him back, her own tongue meeting his in wet, warm, intimate collusion.

Had she really believed that she and Germaine de la Motte had reached the height of passion with their furtive kisses?

She would have laughed but there was no time for that. "Do come here," she muttered against his mouth, her hand sliding down, urgently, to his shoulder again, tugging at him, and obligingly he brought himself full upon her. Chest to chest. His body heavy upon hers. His—well— manhood hard against her thigh. Sublime.

"Am I crushing you?" Hugo's voice was muffled, as he was speaking into the fat, untidy, half-loosened plait of her hair.

"No."

"Good." He licked at her neck, from the base of her throat up toward her jaw in a long, slow stroke, wet and sensuous, making her shiver.

"You're cold?" he asked her.

"My God, no."

"Good," he repeated, and found her mouth again with his own, kissed her hard and deeply, kissed her until she was a hot puddle of wax, melting, spreading. Languorous. But still so hungry. Greedy. She could have gone on like this for much longer, perhaps an hour, perhaps all night, maybe forever, but then Hugo, without hurry, shifted again, so that he lay on his side, his body close to hers. "So, Katherine?"

Dazedly she replied, "So what?"

"Better than before?"

Now she did laugh. "Much better."

"Excellent. And now . . ."

"Yes?" she said, breathless.

"Could you sit up for a moment?"

"Yes." She did, and Hugo did too, and took hold of the rumpled hem of her nightgown. Politely he asked:

"May I?"

"By all means," she answered, just as politely. She helped him by tugging the fabric from underneath her, and helped him when it got tangled up in her hair, and laughed again when finally she was rid of it and he tossed it aside without a second glance. Now she was naked, too, and felt with a galvanic, exciting shock cool air everywhere upon her bare skin. Now she was free. Her hair, she realized, had come unbound and tumbled about her face and over her shoulders in a mad nimbus of curls. She shoved them back and lay down again, turning her head to look up at Hugo with eager expectancy. She said:

"Well?"

He was silent, and in the dark intimacy of the crimson bed she watched him looking at her, saw his eyes travel from her face to her breasts, to her hips and legs and in between them. "Lovely," Hugo said at last, his voice a little ragged. "Katherine, you're so lovely. I can see you now."

"See me now?" she echoed. "What do you mean?"

"I couldn't, before. All those *things* on you," was all he said, then he lay down too, he sent himself lower, trailed his tongue around the soft yielding flesh of her breast, circled the hard tip of it, and she jerked as a kind of willing thrill shot through her, voluptuous, here, there, everywhere. And then his mouth was fully upon her breast, suckling hard, even as his hand found the other, cupped and caressed it with such assurance, such cunning, that a wild flutter of pleasure sparked in the very core of her and she groaned out loud in a way Hugo seemed to like a great deal, for he gave a little laugh, and brought his hand away from her breast, let it slide in a slow deliberate movement down to her belly, playing along its gentle rounded rise, sweeping along the flaring curve of her hip and slowly, slowly, with a tantalizing lack of speed, into the soft hair, the tender, sensitive flesh between her legs, where he stroked her, suckling her still with his mouth as his fingers continued to stroke, to find the places that lit her up with fiery sensation:

"Here?" he said, his deep voice sounding softly against her ear, almost like a caress itself.

"Yes," she gasped.

A little later: "And here?"

"Yes. But . . . oh, higher. A bit higher. Can you?"

"Yes. Like this?"

"Y-yes."

"More?" he said softly.

"Oh, Hugo, yes . . ."

"Yes," he said, "yes." And then, a little later, "What about this?"

She jerked, and gasped again. "*Yes*. Oh, Hugo, yes." Her breath came faster, she panted, muttered, "Oh, Hugo, please," and he seemed to know, now, precisely what she meant, and went on stroking her and touching her, without pause, as if effortlessly, as if there was nothing else in the world he would rather be doing. And so Katherine gave herself up to the light, the joy in her body illuminating her, in every part of her; deepening, intensifying, until—just when it seemed she couldn't contain this wild, overflowing goodness for a single second more—an ecstatic convulsion took hold of her.

Her limbs went taut, she flung back her head, and she cried out.

Chapter 10

Katherine's eyes were closed, her lips parted. Her face framed by dark curls in what seemed to Hugo the most glorious disarray. She looked so . . .

He stared.

She looked so *happy*.

Seeing it made him happy also. He said, still softly: "Well?"

She opened her eyes, deep, dark, shining, and looked up into his own. She smiled; he caught a glimpse of white teeth, pearl-like. "Well what?"

"Did I surprise you?"

"Oh, yes. But . . ."

"But?"

Katherine ran the tip of her tongue over her lower lip, pink against red, and Hugo remembered how he had once hungered, hopelessly, to taste her cherry-red mouth. And now he had. And would, he thought, again. He felt in himself a slow roll of pleasure and lust.

She said, "But we're not done, are we, Hugo?"

And then he smiled too. "I hope not."

"So now what?"

"This, if you like." Hugo lifted himself up and over her; he was hard, and achingly ready, and gave a groan of his own when Katherine murmured, "Yes, I *do* like," slid silky, fleshy thighs up and along his own legs, opening herself to him. He had just enough presence of mind to say:

"There may be some pain for you. I'm sorry."

"A lot?"

"I don't know. I've never been with a virgin before."

"I'm your first?" She seemed pleased to hear it, and gripped him more firmly with her legs. He groaned again. Christ, but he was so close, he was nearly there, inside her . . . "Yes," he managed to reply between clenched teeth, managing, somehow, to keep himself in check.

Katherine was looking up at him, rather wonderingly, he thought. "A first time for us both, each in our own way," she said, and he saw how onto her face came again that same look of wanting, of wildness. Rapture. Her eyes were shining like stars on a dark night. She said:

"I'm ready."

"Thank God," he said, with genuine reverence, and brought himself into her, within her, at last.

There was, at first, a resistance within her, unpleasant, sharp, a last and literal remnant of a girlhood she was glad to leave behind. Hugo was inside her now, taking her with him to a new place; filling her, moving with gentleness, carefulness, until finally the barrier was gone. Katherine shuddered, and he paused. She sensed how difficult it was for him to do that, the extraordinary self-control it required.

"Are you all right, Katherine?"

"Yes."

"Shall I go on?"

"Oh, God, yes."

And he began to move again.

A ribbon of thought danced across her mind. This, this, was better than any daydream, infinitely better than a

fantasy. Far better than orchestrating—commandeering—
the scene in her head, for here she yielded up that absolute
control, here she gave herself over to Hugo, and together
they were creating this . . . oh, it had to be called *magic*.

And then the thought was gone, just as the pain, too,
went away, and there was only sensation. All newness.
Hugo: she was moving in concert with Hugo, her arms
around him, her breasts pressed roughly against the warm
skin, the hard muscled expanse of his chest, the difference
between their bodies profound—shocking—wonderful.

With a little laugh she lifted herself up to receive him
yet more fully; fiercely she gripped him with her arms,
with her legs. *Wonderful.*

Hugo was moving more quickly now. "Yes," he said,
in his deep voice a kind of beautiful harshness, the side
of his face pressed hard against her, as intimate as a kiss,
"oh Christ, yes—"

A thrust—a final thrust—another groan seemed
wrenched from his throat. And then—he was done, he
slowly withdrew from her, but only a little ways. He slid
his arm underneath her shoulders and pulled her close.
Willingly did she lie against him, her head just below his
collarbone, both of them damp with sweat.

"Christ," Hugo said again, still breathing rather hard,
his expression, she saw, quite beatific.

She smiled. Thought, said, nothing for a little while,
simply lay there. Simply being. Listening mindlessly to
the steady beat of his heart. Then: "Hugo."

"Yes, Katherine?"

"May I ask you a question?"

"Of course."

"Did you like it?"

"Need you ask?"

"I was just wondering."

He drew aside a clump of long tangled curls and kissed
her forehead. "Yes. I liked it. Quite a lot. But—did you?"

"Couldn't you tell?" she asked in surprise.

"Well, I *thought* so. Hoped so. But I don't believe you came?"

"Came? What does that mean?"

"You know—when I was touching you, before. You came."

"Came," Katherine repeated dreamily. "Such a plain little word for such a—such a *large* event. 'Explosion' might be better, but it hardly seems poetic enough." She trailed her fingers across his shoulder and down along the hard masculine line of his sternum. Oh, the *feel* of him. She went on:

"On the other hand, perhaps 'came'—'to come'—*does* work, because it's a verb, which signifies action, and also in the sense that one is transported to another plane. One comes somewhere else. Attains another state of being. Which reminds me." She slid her hand further down, along his flat stomach, taut with muscle, then below, and heard with pleasure his indrawn breath. "Different now," she remarked, stroking him, felt it stir. "Even though the term 'vital parts' is a euphemism, I must say it's a good one."

"Thank you. I think."

"Oh yes, it's a compliment. *So* vital. What do you call it?"

"Call it?" He sounded a little startled.

"I mean what is it called, this part of you?"

"Well, the technical term is 'penis,' but we men tend to use more colorful language. And by 'colorful' I mean vulgar."

"Like what?"

Hugo laughed. Never in his experience with women had he lain with them afterwards and talked about the vocabulary of sexual experience. Another box, a little more of Katherine, so sweetly, charmingly, revealed. "Oh, cock, prick, roger, flute, sugar stick, to name just a few."

She laughed too. "Very colorful indeed." And then her hand slid lower. "And these?"

A distraction, a fine one, but he was able to answer: "Testicles if you're feeling technical. Otherwise, ballocks. Tallywags. Baubles."

"Also colorful. Shakespeare," Katherine said, moving her hand back up, to slide along his penis, cock, flute, whatever, "made a lot of jokes about such things."

"Oh?" said Hugo politely, though his thoughts were, in fact, drifting elsewhere. "Like what?"

"Oh, 'dying' for 'coming,' 'my tongue in your tail,' 'arise, arise,' which, incidentally, is what you're doing right now. Can you do it again so soon?"

"By God, yes," he answered, turning to her. "But can you? Do you want to?"

"Yes." Katherine slid a warm, plump thigh over his hip and brought them groin to groin. "And—" She gave a little, pleased-sounding hiss as he, in turn, ran his hand down her back and around the curves of a gloriously full bottom. "And what are some of your colorful terms for it? For the act?"

"Screw," he promptly said, "tup, knock, dock, hump, grind, shag, wap."

She laughed again. "That actually sounds a little poetic."

"If you say so," Hugo replied, and brought his mouth to hers, lightly, very lightly, nipping with his teeth at that full, tempting lower lip, that made him think of sweet juice, succulent flesh, and everything that was delicious and good in this world. She made a noise, a hum, a sigh, tightening her leg over his hip to snug him closer, said, then, in a throaty little voice, "Knock, dock, tup, hump."

He grinned. "Now I hear the poetry."

"The words just needed a little rearranging, that's all. Hugo," Katherine went on, whispering, her hand going down between them to take hold of his roger, flute, sugar stick, that was now so very hard again, "what you said before. A woman can come when a man's inside her?"

"Yes."

"Let's do that."

"Yes," he said, "let's," and then there were no more words, just movement, a primal rhythm, a deep understanding between their bodies, a dance: and later, rather later, Katherine, beneath him, her hair around her in that wonderful, wanton froth of curls, said on a gasp:

"Oh, Hugo, you were right."

"I'm glad, Kate," he said, and kissed her hard, and then he, too, came, came with such an intense rush of pleasure that after, when he was able to think again, it occurred to him that Shakespeare might have been correct, that maybe it *was* a little like dying, to feel oneself all shattered to bits, albeit in a very good way, and that maybe Katherine was onto something, too, by calling it an explosion.

Interesting things, words.

He laughed, wrapped his arms around her, and fell asleep.

She dreamed. Who *was* that beautifully dressed, gorgeously coiffed woman, ascending with stunning grace the white marble steps to the Penhallow townhouse? She looked familiar, with her dark eyes and curly dark hair. But why did she look so worried? Why did she look so sad?

I've forgotten something. I've lost something I need.

She was flanked on both sides by admiring crowds of people, bowing and curtsying as she went past. Some even prostrated themselves before her. But she didn't care about that, it wasn't real.

She knocked on the townhouse door, which was made, apparently, of solid gold. The sunlight glittering on it hurt her eyes.

The door swung open, and old Mrs. Penhallow stood on the threshold.

I've forgotten something, but I don't remember what it is. It's something very important.

You've got to find it yourself, the old lady said, *you won't find it here,* then shut the door in the young woman's face.

Morning: a new day, filled with possibility. Hugo looked at Katherine, who slept still, curled up on her side, long dark lashes shielding her eyes, the bedclothes drawn up to her chin. He wanted to wake her, wanted to—how had she so charmingly said it?—yes: he wanted to have her again. He thought, also, that she might want to have *him* again. Knock, dock, tup, hump . . . By God, but last night had been—

A good word for it would be "amazing."

He saw, however, looking at her, the dark shadows beneath her eyes. Recalled how strained, how tired she had appeared all yesterday. Let her sleep, he thought, it was very early.

Quietly Hugo got out of bed, dressed, and left their bedchamber. He was hungry. Whistling a little under his breath, he went lightly downstairs and toward the breakfast-parlor, confident that there he would find a nice, hearty meal awaiting him. He passed a servant in a hallway, said, "Good morning," and reflected, cheerfully, that it really was. Maybe even a great one.

A gentle tapping on the door woke her, and at first Katherine had no idea where she was. Oh God, had Céleste come to wake her already? Make her go downstairs and be bored to death?

But it couldn't be—Céleste always hung over her,

saying in that sour way of hers, *Wake up, mademoiselle, wake up.*

So who was at the door? What bad thing had she done now?

Tap tap tap.

Katherine's eyes flew open. Crimson bed-hangings. The high, old-fashioned bed. Not Brooke House, but Surmont Hall. Alarmed, still groggy, she called out, "What is it?"

The door opened, a maidservant came in, bobbed a curtsy. "Please, ma'am, I'm to tell you that breakfast is ready."

Breakfast? Quickly Katherine looked over at Hugo's side of the bed. He wasn't there. He'd probably been gone for hours. And he'd let her sleep . . .

A warm feeling came over her then, like a wave advancing on the shore. Last night, oh, last night . . . it had been heavenly . . . And Hugo had told her she was lovely . . . and here she was, with no idea where her dowdy nightgown had gone . . . how wonderful . . .

"Ma'am?" came the voice of the maidservant, who was still standing by the door, and Katherine realized she hadn't answered. How late was it? Was she already making herself conspicuous among the Penhallows by being a bad guest and making them all wait for her at table? Quickly she sat up, clutching the bedclothes to her chest, and said to the maidservant:

"Breakfast. Yes. Can you help me get dressed, please?"

"I'd be glad to, ma'am, but I'm no lady's maid."

"That's all right. We must hurry, though."

"I'll do my best, ma'am."

Half an hour later, Katherine was following the maidservant along a mystifying warren of corridors and galleries, and found herself worrying at a fingernail. She dropped her hand, resisted the urge to firmly smooth a few wayward curls behind her ears, to press them flat.

A memory surfaced.

Her first breakfast at the Basingstoke Academy. How nervous she'd been. How badly she had hoped to make friends. She'd been a little late, having had a difficult time scrambling into her clothes, and so entered the gloomy, crowded dining-room only to see everyone already seated, only to see the look of glee on the other girls' faces when she earned a black mark on her very first morning at school. *Tardiness, Miss Brooke,* said Miss Wolfe, staring at Katherine through her pince-nez, *is evidence of an inferior character.* There had been sniggers, quiet but unmistakable, and Katherine could still remember the red flush of shame which heated up her face.

And so when finally she was ushered into a sunny, spacious room, wallpapered in cheerful yellow, Katherine had to admit to a certain relief when she saw that Livia was its only occupant.

Smiling, Livia looked up at once and put aside her fork and knife. "Good morning, Katherine! Did you sleep well?"

"Good morning," she replied, nervousness making her sound rather stiff. "I'm afraid I'm very late. I'm so sorry."

"Oh, don't be, please! Breakfast is very informal. Gabriel and Hugo have had theirs and gone out riding, and Granny and Miss Cott have too. They've gone to the hothouse to look at flowers."

Katherine took this in, then said, still awkwardly, "But am I keeping *you* from other things?"

"Not at all. I was hoping to have a nice talk together." A little shyly Livia added, "I've never had a cousin, you see, and now I have you and Hugo, which makes me so glad. I expect you have several? Most people seem to have a lot of them."

"I suppose I do, but I don't know them. Both my parents are estranged from their families."

A shadow crossed Livia's pretty face. "Families can be

so complicated, can't they? Oh, but please forgive me—I'm being a dreadful hostess *again*. Please help yourself to anything you like from the sideboard. And won't you come sit next to me?"

A few minutes later, Katherine was settled in her place near Livia. She said, still a little stiff and uncertain, "What a charming room this is."

"Isn't it? It's one of the few rooms in the Hall that doesn't need much fixing or renovation."

"The Hall needs a lot of repairs?"

Livia nodded. "It was neglected, you know, for a long time."

"I didn't know. Why?"

"Neither Gabriel nor Granny lived here for many years, and—well, we're here now, and determined to make things right. Not just in the Hall, of course, but all across the estate and for its people as well."

"It sounds like a great deal of work."

"It is."

Katherine looked more closely at Livia. "You don't seem as if you mind it."

Livia laughed. "I don't. I enjoy it. For one thing, we're all working together as a family. And I love having a home—a real home—at last."

"A real home? What do you mean?"

"I grew up in an old, ramshackle house that was also neglected."

"But—why was *it* neglected?"

The shadow had returned, a little, to Livia's face. "Indifference. And money frittered away on other things. I was virtually penniless."

"How did you receive your education, then? And make your *début* in Town? Did you have relations to help you?"

"No. And I didn't have a proper *début,* either. Or any real education until recently."

"But . . ." Katherine trailed off, embarrassed, having

suddenly recalled her mother asking Hugo about Livia, in an awful prying way, *Yes, but who is she? No one's ever heard of her.*

Livia brightened and then laughed. "I daresay you're wondering how a little nobody like myself ended up married to one of the *ton*'s most eligible men."

Guiltily, flushing, Katherine said, "I'm sorry, I shouldn't have plagued you with so many questions. It was very wrong of me."

"Oh, I don't mind. It *is* an improbable story. With a very strange beginning. But what about you and Hugo? How did the two of you meet?"

"We've known each other since childhood."

"How romantic! And now you've found each other again."

Romantic? The truth flew at Katherine with merciless force. It wasn't romantic at all. Hugo had married her for her money, and she had married him for his surname. It was a *transaction,* and just about as *un*romantic as you could get. How had she let herself forget it, how could she have drifted so far from the cold hard facts? She and Hugo were using each other, that's all.

The warmth of the morning dissipated and a painful flood of emotions swamped her. Drowning her with sadness. The horror of seeing Hugo's regret. And anger—at herself, at Hugo. What a mess of things, what a mockery, they had made. Had willingly created. And last night had only muddied the already murky waters.

Well, he could have the money, but that was all. Nothing else was included in the deal. *The deal.* O God. Here in the bright sharp light of day, she needed to be an island again, a locked box, a closed book. The images flashed through her mind in quick succession, and despite herself she felt a cold, unsettling shiver run down her spine.

Think, think, say something, before the silence becomes horribly obvious. "Yes," Katherine managed to say to Livia, "we've found each other again," and quickly she reached for the coffee-pot, and ate a roll, and remarked on the freshness of the butter, and admired the pretty floral wallpaper, and talked about the weather, and altogether created such a flow of inane small-talk that she could see Livia looking a little puzzled. Oh no, thank you, she wasn't really up for a walk outside, or a tour through the Hall, she really was rather tired, actually, and would Livia mind if she went back upstairs to her room and rested a little? *After all, even a big pile of money gets tired and wants to go lie down,* she thought, but of course didn't say out loud, because it was important to pretend that she was all right. That everything was all right.

"Of course I don't mind," said Livia. "Is there anything I can do for you?"

"No. Thank you." And Katherine stood up, and went away. It took all she had not to run.

It was late afternoon when Hugo opened the door to their bedchamber and went inside. To his surprise Katherine was there, in bed and propped up on pillows. In the cool sliver of wintry light coming in through only partially opened curtains, he saw her start and press something against her chest. A book. He smiled, thinking of last night, and said:

"Hullo."

"Hullo," she said, but without returning his smile, and his own began to fade.

"Are you unwell, Katherine?"

"No."

"Been reading?"

"Yes."

"What's the name of your book?"

"Oh—well—it's *Pamela*—"

"I don't know that one. Enjoying it?"

"I suppose so," she muttered, and he noticed her quick, darting look to the tray set next to her on the bed. A teapot and cup; a large plate half-filled with confectionaries; a crumpled napkin. That faint scent of chocolate, sweet, pleasing, came to him.

"Had tea sent up, then?"

"Yes," she said coldly, lifting her chin, reminding him, oddly, of a cornered animal. Reminding him, too, of their stilted conversation in the drawing-room at Brooke House that rainy day last fall, when she gave the distinct impression of heartily wishing him elsewhere. Had they come full circle? Gone back to the beginning, where all was obscure and unpromising?

"Katherine," he said, "what's the matter?"

"Nothing."

Boxes revealed, boxes concealed. "You're sure?"

"Very sure." She opened her book, bent her head, and simply went away.

That night, alone again in their bedchamber, together in the bed and in the darkness, Hugo tried again. He said, "Katherine."

"Yes?"

"Are you all right?"

"Yes."

"Would you—can we—" He felt the pull of his desire for her, raw and powerful. He wanted to find her mouth with his own, to hungrily splay his fingers against the small of her back, urging her against him, so she could feel how much he wanted her. So she could know how much he wished to please her. *Knock, dock, tup, hump . . .*

But those playful words from last night seemed wrong, painfully wrong right now. Last night seemed like years ago. "May I—could we—" Damn it, he sounded like an idiot. Maybe he *was* an idiot.

"No."

"What's wrong?" he said to her, "what have I done?"

"There's nothing wrong." Her voice was cool. Firm. "You've gotten what you wanted, and so have I. Let's just leave it at that."

Hugo lifted himself, leaned on an elbow, peering at her. She was only a foot or two away from him, but he didn't know what to do next. Or what to say. She was as opaque to him as a sheet of iron; no light could get through. *Nothing, nothing, nothing,* she had said. He ground his teeth and wished, not for the first time, that he was one of those men who could easily serve up an elegant phrase, a man from whose lips tumbled paragraphs, pages, speeches, fine orations, that could cleave through the knots of this impasse.

But he wasn't.

He was—himself.

Silence lay upon them, heavy, dark. In the end, finally, he did nothing. Sleep, finally, claimed him. And when he woke the next day, once again very early, he saw that at some point in the night, Katherine had crept from the high bed and gone over to the blue bench by the window, where she lay, eyes closed, very still, beneath one of her shawls.

Nothing.

He left the room, favoring, ever so slightly, his left leg.

Katherine heard him go. Once the door was safely closed behind him, the tears began to fall. Oh God, what had she done? What kind of person would marry for a surname? She wrapped herself more tightly in her shawl, her mind restless—maybe even desperate—searching, hunting for relief, like a bird hoping for a friendly branch on which to alight. Then: *London.* Yes, that was it. She could look forward to London. Everything would be better there. She'd make a new start. She'd be a different person. And everything would be wonderful.

24 January 1812

Dearest Hugo,
Thank you so much for your note letting us know of your safe arrival at Surmont Hall. Forgive my brevity, but your Aunt Claudia is just now getting over an ague and I've promised to spend the day with her. Bertram comes with me for his lessons with Papa, and Gwendolyn has begged for a morning's reprieve as she wants to go next door to Diana's where, she says, they are going to pretend they are sailors, and has vowed to keep on all day long that splendid hat you gave her. Please send my warmest regards to everyone at the Hall. I'm sure you and Katherine are having the most marvelous time there.

With much love,
Mama

P.S. Cook says the butcher's wife told her that Brooke House has emptied out very nearly overnight, and that her husband regrets the loss of orders but not the erratic manner of payment. Also Cook wants me to thank you again for fixing the handle on her favorite pot.

It was strange how even though you were completely estranged from your husband, you still got up, still walked and talked and acted as if everything were normal.

Katherine sat at her dressing-table while Mary, the maidservant who had been helping her, carefully brushed her hair. In the mirror Katherine could see that from time to time Mary looked rather wistfully at a bottle of scent which was set out on the dressing-table, a gift from someone at the wedding—one of Father's cronies—which she had never used. The little porcelain bottle was rounded at its base, with a long, narrowing neck, and painted all over with flowers in a fashionable chinoiserie style.

"Mary," she said, "may I give you that scent-bottle? Would you like to have it?"

Mary's face lit up. "Oh, ma'am, really?"

"Yes. Let me find the box it came in, too. It's very pretty." Katherine pulled open a drawer of the dressing-table, then another, and found it in the next drawer she opened. "Here it is." She held it in her hand, paused for a moment. It was a tin box, decorated on its lid with more chinoiserie flowers. You could put more in it than just a scent-bottle, couldn't you? She remembered, suddenly, her dream from two nights ago.

I've forgotten something, but I don't remember what it is. It's something very important.

You've got to find it yourself, old Mrs. Penhallow had said in her dream, *you won't find it here,* then shut the door to the London townhouse.

Puzzled, Katherine stared at the tin box.

Then she gave herself a shake. Took one of her largest handkerchiefs, wrapped the scent-bottle in it, and carefully put it into the tin which she placed on her dressing-table. She turned to look up at Mary. "For you," she said, and Mary's obvious pleasure in the little gift made tears once again threaten to fall.

Chapter 11

~~~~~~~~~~∞∩∪∩∽~~~~~~~~~~

Sooner than Katherine could have possibly expected—
was old Mrs. Penhallow a sorceress, with supernatural
powers?—to Surmont Hall came Madame Hébert and
her cadre of helpers, as well as a milliner, a shoemaker,
a *friseur, and* her new dresser, a soft-spoken, agreeable
woman named Ellery, as different from Céleste as night
from day.

The new gowns began, in rapid succession, to appear.
Without hesitation Katherine said yes to them all, they
were as elegant, as ravishing as those worn by the other
Penhallow ladies, and in the deep strong colors that
seemed to make her complexion glow. She said yes, yes,
to the shoes, the hats, the pelisses, the reticules. Yes.
Everything. She would be a new, different, better person
in them.

The days passed.

Her trunks filled up again.

She spent a great deal of time reading as if her life
depended upon it. How lucky that the magnificent library
here was filled with books—actual books, as opposed to
the ones at Brooke House. *Candide. Les Liaisons Dan-
gereuses. The History of Sir Charles Grandison. The
Seasons. Sense and Sensibility* (written "By a lady," and

Katherine wondered exactly who that was). *Philosophie Zoologique. The Vision of Don Roderick.*

And all around her, the busy life of Surmont Hall went on.

Henrietta Penhallow was absorbed in the preparations for Miss Cott's wedding, and with the recently formed village school for which she was serving as benefactress. If she was considering the idea of a new companion, she made no mention of it.

Livia oversaw the renovations within the Hall, went daily to visit the tenant-farmers' families, flitted back and forth from the library and the kitchen to the garden and her poultry-yard, and continued her lessons with the head groom who was teaching her how to drive a pony-trap—though, as she was the first one to admit, her progress was slow for she was still rather nervous around horses.

Hugo spent his days riding out with Gabriel, making himself useful and getting spectacularly dirty in water-logged fields, ditches, and drainage trenches, inspiring Gabriel to admiringly remark upon Hugo's uncanny ability to perceive and solve mechanical problems. Hugo merely shrugged and said, *It's just a way of seeing things, coz, that's all.*

Miss Cott, as always, made herself useful, helped anyone who needed it, watched and listened, and, as ever, kept her observations to herself.

It was well into the fourth week of the bridal visit, when, on a cold February evening, with the entire party gathered in the rococo drawing-room, Mrs. Penhallow announced without preamble, looking between Katherine and Hugo:

"Regarding the family townhouse, I am willing to offer it to you as of April first. That would be an appropriate time for Penhallows to arrive for the Season. You'll wish to engage servants, of course, so I recommend you contact the Dauntrey Agency as soon as possible. Also, you will benefit immeasurably from the sponsorship of a—shall we say—a seasoned campaigner?"

"Oh, ma'am, are you coming with us?" exclaimed Katherine. She was surprised to find that she welcomed the idea, wished for it very badly, in fact.

But the old lady was shaking her silvery head. "I've far too much to do here, and I must, of course, attend Miss Cott's wedding. However, I've written to a relation of mine, the Duchess of Egremont, on your behalf. It's quite convenient as she and the Duke will soon be arriving in Grosvenor Square."

"Great-aunt Judith is going to London?" said Gabriel. "Didn't I hear you once say that both she and the Duke heartily dislike Town life?"

"That is so. But Thane is causing such difficulties that, according to Judith, they feel obliged to personally attempt to rein him in."

"Thane's there?" said Hugo. "Damn—I mean, blast it."

"Who is Thane?" Livia asked, glancing up from her needlework.

"Oh, he's a cousin, Liv, and a nuisance. We were at school together."

"Not," put in Mrs. Penhallow, "a true cousin, strictly speaking. Judith is my sister-in-law," she explained to Livia and Katherine, "the sister of my late husband Richard. She married the Duke of Egremont not long after Richard and I were wed. They had only one son who, in due course, married—despite their objections—a widowed lady, Almira Thane, who had a young son of her own. This is the Thane to whom I refer—Philip Thane, who for half a dozen years now has made for himself an unfortunate name with his rackety, dissolute habits, scandalizing anyone with even a modicum of decency."

"I saw him at one of Mrs. Drummond-Burrell's parties last year in Town," Gabriel said, accepting from Miss

Cott a cup of tea. He thanked her and went on, "She's a notoriously high stickler, as you know, so I was more than a little surprised that he was there."

Mrs. Penhallow sniffed. "Thane is notorious for his ability to exert a peculiar fascination upon women—the susceptible ones, that is—who *will* invite him everywhere."

"Cannot his stepfather provide a—well, a calming influence, Granny?" Livia said. "Or his mother?"

"His stepfather is dead, I'm sorry to say, and Almira Thane is a pretty, empty-headed woman without a particle of commonsense. It's Judith and the Duke who have undertaken to help raise the two children Almira bore after she married their son, as well as, naturally, Thane. They did their best with him, but he proved himself unmanageable from an early age."

"Well do I know it," remarked Hugo. "An unholy terror, loathed by the entire school."

"What happened to Almira's other children?" Livia said. She had set aside her sewing, and was holding, thanks to the quiet efficiency of Miss Cott, a plate which held a thick slice of seedcake, dotted with caraway seeds and fragrant with cinnamon.

"The boy, I believe, is presently at Eton," replied Mrs. Penhallow, "and the girl is being educated at home."

This boy, Katherine thought, was the heir to the dukedom, not Philip Thane. She found herself thinking, imagining: *young Philip, having lost his father, is swept by his mother's remarriage into a great aristocratic family. One of them, and yet not one of them. Outsiderness.* Was that even a word? Maybe if you used it often enough, they'd put it in the dictionary. It was a word she herself knew very well. Oh, all too well . . .

"Judith," Mrs. Penhallow said, abruptly recalling Katherine to the conversation, "has agreed to act as your guide, as it were—to take you about, ensure that you're introduced to the right people, and so on."

"Given that Aunt Judith dislikes Town life," said Gabriel shrewdly, "it's rather interesting she agreed to your request."

Everyone watched in fascination as a slow, secretive smile curved the old lady's lips. "I once did Judith a great favor. Now she is returning it."

"What favor, Granny?" asked Livia.

But Mrs. Penhallow only shook her head and would say no more on the subject.

Hugo, watching her, thought how that faintly mischievous expression made her appear years younger. There was no doubt in his mind that Gabriel's marriage to Livia had benefited not just them as a couple, but Aunt Henrietta also. She had softened somehow, had become—well, more human. It was as if some good fairy had waved a wand over the three of them.

Which reminded him. He looked now to Gabriel. "When you wrote to me last November, coz, you mentioned an odd little story concerning Livia and yourself."

Gabriel, on his face a small, subtle smile, exchanged glances with Livia. He said:

"In October, when Livia had gone, and I didn't know where she was, I ended up relying on the advice of a local woman, who evidently believes she has mystical abilities. She'd seen something in her tea leaves, she told me, which indicated that I should go toward the ocean. I was desperate—and so off I went. It seems that she was right. I found Livia in Bristol."

"And you believe this was more than just coincidence?" asked Katherine, glancing, as if unknowingly, into her own half-full teacup.

Gabriel didn't immediately answer. He was looking again at Livia, and for a moment Hugo felt as if he was seeing something so powerful, so private, that he ought to turn away his own gaze. Finally Gabriel said to Katherine:

"I don't know. I'm not one to ordinarily place credence

in such things. I only know that I found Livia, and that it seemed like a miracle."

Slowly Katherine answered, "Forgive me, but we live in rational times now. Modern times. Those things—those beliefs—well, our scientists say they're the product of a disordered mind."

Gabriel laughed. "That may be so. I was definitely disordered at the time."

"Oh, I was too," exclaimed Livia. "I had run off, determined to take my fate into my own hands, then ended up, in a stupidly anticlimactic way, falling ill with the most horrible fever."

"Thank God you did," Gabriel told her. "Not that I'm glad you were ill, of course, but what you did—well, it woke me up."

There was a brief silence. Abruptly Katherine said:

"Why did you run off, Livia?"

"It seems so silly now, but at the time, it was dreadful," Livia answered. "Gabriel and I had had the most ferocious quarrel, and we broke off our engagement. Or I should say, rather, that *he* broke it off. In a very high-handed way."

"I was never so shocked in my life as when I found out," said Aunt Henrietta. "Pretty behavior for a Penhallow indeed!"

"You weren't wrong to criticize me, Grandmama. In my defense, I was half-crazed." Gabriel gave Katherine a little quizzical smile. "You're looking at me as if I have three heads."

She blinked and looked rather flustered. "I'm very sorry."

"There's no need to apologize," he replied, pleasantly, and turned his attention to the efficient Miss Cott who was passing round further slices of seedcake. Hugo accepted a second serving, Katherine refused with a quick shake of her head and a word of thanks, and then rather dreamily Livia said:

"That local woman, Mrs. Roger, told me—" She paused, her eyes going to Gabriel, in their green depths a sweet glow, then added to the room at large, "What I mean is—well, it may be that there's more to life than what we believe we know. Or perhaps there's more inside *us* than we can know."

Hugo found himself watching Katherine, upon whose face came again a look of deep abstraction. Very different she'd become in these past weeks, in her new gowns and so forth, with her hair done in a simple, elegant way that revealed the extraordinary beauty of her dark, gleaming curls, which in turn highlighted the dark brilliance of her eyes, the beguiling curves of her cherry lips. All of which he might look upon, but not touch.

He was staring, Hugo suddenly realized, like a lovesick boy.

"Speaking of pretty behavior," said Aunt Henrietta, "our relation Alasdair Penhallow, up in the wilds of Scotland, has apparently been conducting a shocking courtship ritual. I'm told that he summoned to his castle the eligible highborn maidens of the Eight Clans of Killaly, in order that they might engage in a competition for his favor."

"Like the one for Gabriel last year?" said Livia, with a saucy glance at her husband.

"One hardly cares to imagine," replied Aunt Henrietta, "the astonishing reports of Alasdair's disgraceful mode of life being what they are. Dear me! I do pity the poor woman who becomes his wife."

---

2 March 1812

Dear Hugo,
    Thanks very much for your letter and the five-pound notes for Frank and me. I spent mine on

some maps and a new cricket bat as I cracked my old one swinging it round in the dormitory (I may have hit the foot of my bed rather hard), and Frank bought a great fat book, Spinoza's Ethics. We're getting on splendidly here, although Greek is dashed annoying (for me, not so much for Frank). Last week I kicked two goals in wall game and so we won. About the Lent Half holiday—Owen FitzClarence has invited us to go home with him to Northamptonshire. He's a cousin of sorts, which makes it all right, doesn't it? A capital fellow, I assure you, and wants me to tell you he's not at all like his half-brother Philip Thane who he says is a rotter. Also Owen's grandparents have quite a lot of horses and he says he'll teach me how to jump. He is the heir to a dukedom which seems rather funny as he is only thirteen, like Frank and me, and exceedingly short.

Owen also wants me to let you know his old tutor, Mr. Dawkins, is coming to get him and will be with us the whole time. Do say yes.

Faithfully yours,
Percy

P.S. One of the older boys told us a ripping story he'd heard about you stuffing a drain with a hand-kerchief and causing a tremendous flood in the maths classroom. Is it true?

———

13 March 1812

Dear Hugo,

Thank you for your letter. Yes, Owen did write to the Duke and myself, and I think it's a lovely idea for your brothers to accompany him home for the *holiday. Owen will enjoy it so much. Mr. Dawkins is a thoroughly conscientious young man and will take good care of the boys.*

We look forward to seeing you and Katherine in Town very soon.

Cordially,
Cousin Judith

---

22 March 1812

Dear Hugo,

Percy and I were very pleased to receive your letter. Yes, of course we'll behave ourselves at Owen's. Or I suppose I should say, more realistically, that we'll try hard to. Thank you for those ten-pound notes. One feels very grown-up having money for traveling expenses.

By the way, Percy wants me to add that you never answered about that flood in the maths classroom. I asked one of the prefects about it and he only grinned and didn't answer. Qui tacet consentire videtur, as the Latin proverb goes—'he who is silent, when he ought to have spoken and was able to, is taken to agree.' Would a single handkerchief have been sufficient to entirely stop a drain? One wonders.

Yours most faithfully,
Francis

On a bright, frosty day, in which the barest hint of spring was in the air, Katherine stood on the porch to Surmont Hall with old Mrs. Penhallow, Livia, and Miss Cott. The last of her trunks had been loaded into the carriages; her dresser Ellery had already taken her seat in the carriage they were to share. Katherine had said goodbye to Livia and Miss Cott, and now she turned to Mrs. Penhallow.

"Thank you again for your hospitality, ma'am, and all your guidance. I'm very grateful to you."

"I hope you enjoyed your time here."

"I did indeed, ma'am."

The old lady looked keenly at her, but only said, "Give Judith and the Duke my warmest regards."

"I will, ma'am. Well—goodbye." Katherine started to turn away, but Mrs. Penhallow said:

"Wait."

"Ma'am?"

"A few words of advice," said the old lady. "Not that I've always followed them myself, I'm sorry to say. But for whatever it's worth: to thine own self be true."

"Hamlet," said Katherine, trying to summon a smile.

"Yes. Goodbye. And—good luck."

Katherine nodded, suppressing once again a mad, possibly desperate impulse to hug Mrs. Penhallow, then went down the steps to the graveled carriage-sweep. Gabriel had gone with Hugo to where his horse stood ready, and they were saying their farewells. A footman helped her up into her carriage, Hugo swung up on his horse, and so began the long-awaited journey to London.

They sat at dinner at a luxurious inn in Newbury. Without speaking. Wordless. Hugo looked at Katherine in her elegant gown of vivid blue, seeming very cool and composed to him. Like a sculpture you might see in a museum or, for that matter, in Surmont Hall—all gorgeously composed and still. Remote and untouchable.

There came to him a memory. The two of them were on the beach. It was early morning, the sky was filled with great hurrying clouds, and the wind had whipped around them, ruffling her blue dress with insistent force. It was the day he was to leave for Eton and on her face had been such grief—even he, a lanky, gawky boy of twelve, could see it—that in a way it was worse than if she had openly wept.

Well—goodbye then, Kate, he had said, hating his own inarticulateness.

Goodbye, Hugo, she managed to say in a small voice, though he could barely hear it over the whipping wind.

He had hesitated. He went a step closer and clumsily put his arms around her. She'd reached her own arms, just as clumsy, around his neck, and awkwardly they had embraced, just for a moment, and then stepped apart.

Well, Father's waiting for me, he'd said. *Goodbye again.*

Goodbye.

He ran back toward his house, stopping once to look back and lift a hand in farewell. How small she looked on the shore—how tiny against the vast backdrop of the ocean and sky. Her blue dress looked just like a piece of the sky. She lifted her hand, he turned away, and was gone.

How strange, he now thought, to have remembered that moment from so long ago. How long had she stood there before trudging back to her house next door? The waiter came with the roast pheasant, and he accepted some, and began to eat it, but the image of Kate, on the beach, very small, stayed fixed in his mind.

Four days later, as Katherine walked up the steps to the Penhallow townhouse, she found herself strangely relieved to see that the front door *wasn't* made of solid gold. Her dream had been wrong—though she continued to be dogged by that faint ghostlike sense of something missing, no matter that Ellery assured her that nothing had been lost along the way.

The door opened, a butler greeted them, and they went inside. Here were other members of the hired staff, all very pleasant and competent-seeming; next, the house-keeper took her around. It was no surprise to see that it was a magnificent dwelling, furnished and decorated in a spare, elegant, neoclassical style, with the first floor featuring a morning-room, a dining-room, a library, and various other saloons. Upstairs were the bedrooms, and in the bustle of arrival, with Hugo seeing to the horses and the carriages over at the mews, and the many trunks being ferried up the stairs, and maidservants coming and going, it was easy to discreetly communicate to the housekeeper about the need for two separate bedchambers. Shortly she was ushered into a spacious, high-ceilinged room, very handsome and comfortable, with a door that—she learned a little later, when she was alone—connected it to Hugo's bedchamber.

She knew because she tried the knob, as stealthy as any spy bent on dark deeds, and peeked into it. And she searched her own room until she found the key, slung on a green silk ribbon, in a drawer of the table next to her bed, after which she quietly locked the door.

Still later she told herself, *Well, everything is going splendidly.* She had looked over the heap of correspondence already awaiting her, including a note from the Duchess of Egremont, who indicated her desire to call tomorrow, and together they would craft a plan for the week. Would Katherine and Hugo care to attend an evening-party at Lady Jersey's house? And what about a ball on Saturday, at the Hedleys'? Also—

Katherine put down the note and looked around the sumptuous bedchamber. Yes, everything *was* going splendidly. She had dreamed of this moment for quite some time. Everything was working out just as she had hoped. She wondered, a little, why she didn't feel happier. Maybe she was just tired from the journey. Tomorrow, tomorrow would be better; the Duchess was coming, for one thing, and also she was going to Rundell & Bridge, to purchase new jewelry for herself.

But, oddly, as it turned out, it didn't seem better, even though she had had a pleasant time with the Duchess, a tall, thin, elderly lady, vigorous, blunt-spoken, weather-beaten and horse-obsessed; an undemanding conversationalist with a slightly distracted air, which Katherine attributed to her concern over her quasi-grandson, the notorious Thane. His mother Almira Thane had accompanied the Duchess. She was, as old Mrs. Penhallow rightly said, a pretty, middle-aged woman, tremulous, chattery, easily moved to tears and just as easily cheered.

And now, here Katherine stood before a counter at London's premier jewelers, waited upon by not only two attentive clerks but also by Mr. Bridge himself. When the Brookes, last year, sallied into the store, occasionally a second clerk joined the first, in order to help with the Brookes' many purchases; but never did Mr. Bridge join them. For Mrs. Hugo Penhallow, however? Why, that was a very different thing, Katherine knew.

She looked at the glittering necklaces, the pretty ai-grettes; the sparkling rings, bracelets, brooches, and ear-bobs. She could choose anything she wanted. Nobody to tell her she must have this or that. Now was her chance. She thought about all those new gowns at the townhouse, carefully unpacked and stowed away by Ellery. One wore jewelry with such gowns. It was expected. Everyone did it. Father had provided her with a great deal of money; she could afford to buy half the store if she wished.

Katherine lowered shoulders which she realized had been held rather high. "Yes," she said, pointing to this and that. "Yes," and again, and again.

Lady Jersey's crowded, brightly lit drawing-room. Noisy. Cheerful. Even a little raucous. The scents of perfumes, sweat, tobacco, intermingling. Servants everywhere, bearing trays of champagne and lemonade, nimbly making their way among the guests, who gathered together in clusters large and small. Hugo watched as Katherine, striking in her crimson gown and rubies, stood in the center of a group of people, talking. Laughing. He watched until his own attention was claimed, and he turned away.

She was pretending to be a former schoolmate of hers, Lydia St. John, all sleek, well-dressed confidence she had been at the Basingstoke Academy; a great many girls, hoping to please her, went to her with secrets, gossip, the latest *on-dits,* all of which she would receive with a hard gleam in her eye, judging, evaluating, and, if sufficiently interesting or damaging, she would laugh, then ruthlessly pass them along.

"Oh, my dear Mrs. Penhallow," someone said, "have you heard about Colonel Mackinnon? At Covent Garden last week he circled the entire theater by running along the boxes and knocking off as many of the ladies' hats as he could. A *most* diverting feat! Quite acrobatic!"

"Yes, and don't forget that banquet at the Lord Mayor's!" somebody else put in, in a voice unstable with laughter. "Colonel Mackinnon stuck his head in a bowl of punch and kicked his feet into the air. He insisted on having the punch served after, too."

"How very droll," Katherine answered, adding a lilting note into her own voice, pretending to be amused, and suppressing the thought, *What an ass.*

The Hedleys' ball. Herself in a gown of fine, soft violet silk. With more partners for the dances than she could possibly accept. Here she was, moving through the intricate steps of the quadrille with Mr. Hedley himself, one of the *ton*'s leading lights, a close friend of the King, and, as he himself had earlier confessed, an ardent devotee of paleontology.

He said, as the dance brought them together again, "You've heard, perhaps, that a complete skull of some lizard-like creature was found last year in Lyme Regis by a twelve-year-old girl? Thought to be thousands of years old. Most impressive. William Bullock's displaying it on Picadilly Street and refuses to sell it."

Under other circumstances, Katherine would have been interested. An ancient lizard skull; the remarkable little girl who had discovered it. But tonight she was pretending to be Countess Lieven, that incredibly haughty patroness of Almack's, and so she only gave a single nod of her head and looked away.

And saw that Hugo was dancing with the beautiful Mrs. Waring, who wore a daringly low-cut dress of diaphanous yellow silk.

It was not, somehow, a particularly agreeable sight.

A strange, twisty feeling stirred within her.

It took her a few moments to realize that it was jealousy.

"**H**ow superbly you dance, Captain Penhallow," said Mrs. Waring. "Particularly for such a . . . such a *large* man." In her voice was insinuation. An invitation too, perhaps, confirmed when she added, "We must get to know each other better. I'm sure my husband would love nothing more himself, but unfortunately he's in Sussex for the Season, there's some problem with his cattle. The blackleg disease, or some other nasty thing. Cattle-breeding is positively a mania with my dear Samuel. He's very . . . passionate about it." Mrs. Waring smiled up into his face. "I'm at home on Thursday afternoon. All alone, I daresay."

Hugo felt himself—felt his body—respond. What man

wouldn't? Mrs. Waring was an attractive woman. Willing. Eager.

He glanced across the gleaming hardwood floor. There was Katherine, chin lifted proudly, dancing with Laurence Hedley as though she hadn't a care in the world. It seemed difficult—impossible—to remember the Katherine who lay in her bed at that inn, exhausted and ill, stretching out a hand to be clasped, or the Katherine who had, at Surmont Hall, given herself to him with such sweet abandon.

The black, sorrowful sough threatened once more. A siren's song now tempted.

Quite a few men of the *beau monde,* in his position, would have accepted Mrs. Waring's invitation without a second thought. Here again, if he were a different sort of person, if he were to change himself into another kind of man, with a more loosely held set of morals, he would say yes. And go to her house on Thursday. And, very probably, as often as he liked. No one need ever know . . .

Hugo looked down again at Mrs. Waring.

"Thank you," he said, "but I've another engagement that afternoon."

And luckily, it was true. Cousin Judith was considering the purchase of a pair of carriage horses, matched bays, and wanted to consult with him about it. So at least— some sort of small consolation—he didn't have to lie.

Chapter 12

28 May 1812

Ma chère Katherine,

According to the newspapers, the Court announcements, and the reports of our wide and illustrious acquaintance here in Bath (so extraordinarily well informed they are), you and le plus cher Hugo have been in London nearly two months—and in the Penhallow townhouse, no less! Félicitations à vous! Naturally I should have liked to hear from you directly but I daresay you are très occupée with countless engagements. We are told that you're seen everywhere under the aegis of the Duke and Duchess of Egremont—at Almack's—at Carlton House—at the most exclusive dinner-parties, assemblies, breakfasts, and balls. Bien joué!

Your father and I are, naturellement, extremely busy ourselves, as we receive more invitations than we could possibly accept. We too are seen everywhere, at the assemblies, concerts, lectures, fashionable excursions, et comme ça. I declare I am all awhirl. And next year, pour être sûr, London!

I remain, etc.,
Mother

P.S. Your father wishes me to inform you that last week he received a cheque for 4,300 pounds from the Batavia–Jakarta Joint Stock company—its annual dividend for a 500-pound investment. He thinks you and cher Hugo ought to invest also, before the initial-sum requirement is raised.

Slowly Katherine put down Mother's letter, on top of an untidy sheaf of other correspondence, circulars, and a great many invitations. She pulled open a drawer of the dressing-table at which she sat, taking from it a box from Fessler's Confectionaries that Ellery had just brought earlier this afternoon. She opened it; it was filled with rich, thick chocolate conserves. She ate one. It was delicious.

Then she ate another one, her gaze sweeping around her bedchamber as to her came again that vague, niggling sensation of having lost something—forgotten something.

She ate another conserve.

Her gaze fell on a stack of books on a small table next to her bed. They were new; she'd purchased dozens and dozens of them, and there were similar stacks all around the room, novels, poetry, travelogues, plays, and more, each and every one lovingly added to its own growing tower. How enticing they looked. But, ironically, she'd had no time to read; virtually all her waking hours were devoted to the demands of her new life, her new self. Being dressed; her hair being done, the *friseur* coming and going. Changing this gown for that one, and changing *that* for the next one: you couldn't wear the dress you wore on morning-calls when you went out for a carriage ride, and of course you had to wear something else for a dinner-party or a ball, and everything required different shoes, different stockings, different wraps, different hats.

A sigh escaped her, and she took up from her correspondence pile a large, gold-edged card of invitation. Tonight she and Hugo were to dine with a select party of guests at Lord and Lady DeWitt's, and attend the ball there that was to follow. Everyone said it was going to be the biggest, most important event of the Season; Lady DeWitt herself had come to call, bringing the invitation and expressing her hope that the Penhallows would deign to come.

Katherine ate two more conserves, and put the box back in the drawer. Who, she wondered, was she going to pretend to be tonight? At those parties and balls, breakfasts and picnics, about which Mother had written so approvingly, she had already tried being Queen Charlotte (calm, civil, a little distant), Esther from the Bible (supremely tactful and courageous), Lady Caroline Lamb (high-spirited and vivacious), Portia in *The Merchant of Venice* (brilliant and high-minded), she had even tried to be the Prince Regent (good-natured, courteous, full of expansive bonhomie). Occasionally, dangerously, she had let the mask slip—in a bookshop, wandering through an art gallery, a quiet moment of conversation here and there—but tonight, she told herself, she was going to hold firm.

Who would she be?

The DeWitts' dinner-party. A massive table, crowded with intricate centerpieces of spun sugar, tall dripping candles, flowers in Venetian blown-glass vases, dozens of glasses, silver flatware, rich and heavy in the hand. Another lavish meal. Elaborate courses almost beyond counting; you could eat until your stomach swelled, drink wine until you quite literally sloshed. Hugo looked at his gold-rimmed plate, and found himself wishing, with a startling intensity, for something to do. Something real. A sluice to fix, a jammed musket to repair, a ship's rigging to climb; he'd almost be willing to jump off a roof into a rain barrel.

"Oh, Captain Penhallow," said the lady to his left, smiling and dimpling, the feathers in her headdress fluttering wildly, "when I realized I was to sit next to *you*—a *Penhallow!*—I nearly went into palpitations! Such a privilege! I had no idea you'd be so *tall!* So *regal!* Has anyone ever told you that you look just like a Greek god?"

"Yes," Hugo said baldly, then instantly regretted it. Luckily the lady to his left didn't even seem to notice, her eyes were roving over him with a kind of greedy awe that made him want to either laugh, or fling over the entire table with a roar. A damned good clatter it would make, too.

Katherine was standing in the DeWitts' magnificent ballroom, conscious that she was looking her best in an exquisite gown of deep forest-green, around her neck and wrists tasteful, elegant chains of sparkling emeralds. She stood as part of a large and jovial crowd, talking and laughing, laughing and talking. How happy she was, she told herself, how very, very happy—*extremely* happy—no one in the entire history of the world had ever been happier than she—

She was jostled, then, by someone passing by, and reflexively she turned to see a young woman all in white who said:

"I do beg your pardon, it's such a squeeze," and then, "Why—Katherine! Katherine Brooke!"

The voice was familiar, and with a shock that seemed to rattle her bones Katherine recognized at once the Honorable Lydia St. John, in whose bed at the Basingstoke Select Academy for Young Ladies, she had, on that fatal day, placed a large handful of wiggling, dirt-incrusted worms, instigating a scene—and a punishment—of epic proportions. Lydia St. John, so popular and self-assured, who in a soft sweet voice continually teased her about her grandfather the miner; who, one day, took her handkerchief and rubbed it on Katherine's cheek, and said so that everyone in the room could hear, *Oh dear, Miss Brooke, you've got coal dust on your cheek. But I'm afraid, dear Miss Brooke, it will never come clean.* And that was when, in a scarlet haze of fury, Katherine had stalked into the garden and begun digging her fingers into damp earth, in a single-minded quest for revenge.

Well, well, well.

Putting worms in someone's bed was one thing, but this . . .

This was a gift laid at her feet.

A singular moment in which it all came together; a moment when she, at last, need no longer feel inferior to the girl who had tormented her, year after year, whose sweet voice had made her, sometimes, sit in her room with her hands pressed over her ears in a futile attempt to drown out what Lydia had that day said.

Katherine felt a smile curl her lips. She answered, "You are mistaken, Miss St. John. I am Mrs. Penhallow now."

"Mrs. *Penhallow.*" Lydia St. John stared, her eyes gone as round as buttons. "I—I didn't know. I've been in the West Indies, you see, with my brother and his family. We've only just returned."

"The West Indies?" Katherine said, casually. "It's very sunny there, I believe."

"Sunny? Yes. Very."

Katherine nodded. Within her was such giddy anticipation that she almost felt as if she were vibrating with it, as if, from above, mapping out the scene, she could see herself reaching with perfect nonchalance into her deep-green satin reticule, pulling from it a fine linen handkerchief which—in front of everybody—she gently, oh so gently, brushed against the smooth cheek of Lydia St. John, not quite the alabaster shade it had been three years ago, and Lydia blanching—and then she would turn her back on Lydia in a cut direct—and Lydia would melt away in shame and humiliation, as if she never was and never had been—

It was, in fact, just the sort of thing a villainous character in a novel would do.

Hurtful, and unkind.

Was that really who she was? She, herself—not Ellena di Rosalba, or Lady Caroline Lamb or Queen Charlotte; not Hatshepsut, or Esther, or Thomas Cromwell, or Richard III, or Wu Zetian.

Who *was* she?

Her hand, Katherine noticed as if from afar, was sliding into her reticule. Even with gloves on she could feel how cool and smooth was the satin. There: there was her handkerchief, soft, delicate, on it, she knew, embroidered in silken thread the letters KP.

She pulled it out.

Looked at it as if never, ever in her life had she seen a handkerchief.

Who was she?

Was she *really* like a nasty character in a novel? A character about whom you'd be glad when bad things happened to her? And if so, what sort of sorry heroine would that be?

Not a heroine at all.

Katherine looked up and over at the Honorable Lydia St. John, abruptly aware of the lights and the music, the chatter and the laughter all around them. Too bright, too loud. She felt shaky—weak—desperate to get away, to go sit down somewhere quiet. Where she could think. Reflect. Breathe.

But there was something she had to do first.

So she put her handkerchief back into her reticule, and she said to Lydia St. John, "Sunny. Yes. How delightful. I do hope you had a nice stay there."

There. She had done it. She had been civil; polite. *Not* villainous. That was not who she was.

She could go now.

But a tall, beefy man, with a big ruddy face, had borne down upon them and taken Lydia's upper arm in a firm grip, and was saying to her with a heartiness that somehow grated in Katherine's ears:

"Been holding out on me, hey? Didn't know you were friendly with Mrs. Penhallow—*the* Mrs. Penhallow."

"Yes," said Lydia, looking rather smaller all at once. "We were at school together. Mrs. Penhallow, may I introduce to you my brother, Denis St. John?"

"An honor, ma'am," said Denis St. John, looking very much as if he wanted to seize Katherine's hand and press it hard, or—worse—kiss it. Katherine clenched her fingers on the silken strings of her reticule which, perhaps, deterred him, but still he went on, undaunted:

"Yes indeed, quite the honor to meet you! Well! Isn't this cozy, you knowing little Lydia here! Speaking of honor, you know *I'm* an 'honorable,' of course. My father's a baron, not that that's anything to a Penhallow, naturally, but still, it's not nothing! Been in Jamaica, you know, overseeing the family plantation. Brought Lydia along—a planter friend of mine—had expected—well, that's neither here nor there. Daresay the two of you will be wanting to renew your friendship, hey? Go for drives in Hyde Park, strolls through Richmond, that sort of thing? Let the world know and all that." He gave Lydia's arm a squeeze, and she opened her mouth to reply, but was interrupted yet again when the Earl of Westenbury came to Katherine's side, reminded her that she was promised to him for the country-dance which had begun to form, and she was swept away, leaving the St. Johns behind.

She and the Earl had nearly joined the set, and Katherine saw Hugo escorting his partner, Lady de Courcey, onto the floor; her ladyship looked up at him, smiling, her arm intimately through his. Katherine's heart gave a hard thump and she put her hand to her chest, as if to subdue a painful twisty ache. For a wild, rash moment she wanted to dart over there, shove pretty Lady de Courcey aside, and take her place in the dance with Hugo. But even if she really intended to do such a deranged thing, she didn't know if she had the strength for it, as her legs still had that odd trembly feeling, the noise of the ballroom seemed almost to be hurting her ears. She paused and said—not as Shakespeare's Portia, or Ellena di Rosalba, or Cardinal Wolsey, but as someone who ached for a moment of quiet—she said to the Earl:

"My lord, would you excuse me? I'm afraid I'm a little tired and must sit down."

"Of course, Mrs. Penhallow," said the Earl at once. "May I bring you some ratafia? Or lemonade?"

"No," she answered, trying to smile, "thank you, my lord, I'm just going to—if you'll excuse me—"

And she slipped away, to the open French doors, out onto the terrace. Oh, it was cooler here. Blessedly quieter. But there were still other people about. So she went down the shallow, broad steps onto a graveled path, went past the ornamental garden with its beautifully tended shrubs and large plashing fountain, then alongside the lengthy narrow kitchen-garden, and finally, her steps slowing, she came to the DeWitt stables. It was quiet, calm. Deserted. A horse nickered, another horse answered, and then there was blessed silence. Toward the end of the building was a wooden bench, and gratefully Katherine sank down upon it, propped elbows in her lap, let her forehead sink onto open palms.

Her mind was whirling with images, coming at her faster than she could process them.

Hugo dancing with Lady de Courcey. Dancing with Mrs. Waring. And so many others, in other dances, at other balls. So many of them these past weeks in London. Attractive, charming women, looking up into Hugo's face with an eager willingness. She, Katherine, had observed it, time and time again, as if watching a play from the

very top tier, very far from the stage. As if it didn't matter
to her.

She had looked, but she had not seen.

Katherine repressed a groan, her forehead drooping
heavily onto her palms.

Our very eyes, said Shakespeare, *are sometimes, like
our judgments, blind.*

Yes, she had been blind. Willfully, stubbornly blind—

"Oh, Philip," came a woman's voice from around the
corner of the stable, followed by low breathy laugh, and
Katherine, startled, lifted her head. She had been sure she
was alone. The woman went on:

"Do hurry up, my husband will notice I'm gone."

"It's just this curst slip of yours getting in the way,
Letitia."

"I'm Lucretia!"

"Whatever you say, my dear. Ah—here we go—"

"You're tearing it!"

"Must you caterwaul, Letitia? You spoil my concentration."

"It's Lucretia!" The woman's voice rose to a muffled
shriek, then subsided into a gratified moan, and Katherine belatedly realized what was happening just around the
corner. Rapidly she stood up and the bench gave a rather
loud and piercing creak; she froze.

"Philip, stop," came the woman's voice, urgent now.
"Did you hear that? There's someone near."

"So what? I don't mind an audience."

"I do! Stop it."

"Very well. What a bore you are, Letitia. I wish I could
remember why I took up with you in the first place."

"You—you *cad!* And it's *Lucretia!*"

A few moments later the woman, skirts more or less
in place, flounced around the stable's corner, checked
for a moment when she saw Katherine, then hurried past
her, head down, toward the DeWitt mansion, even as her

partner sauntered into view, calling, "Sorry about the slip," before stopping and—rather than scurrying away in embarrassment—looking Katherine up and down, with a lazy, brazen lack of hurry. He was a tall, loose-limbed man, dark-haired and dark-eyed, seeming to be in his late twenties: not conventionally handsome, but there was something about his sublime confidence that caught the eye—as if *he* was so pleased with himself, he was sure you would be, too.

"Oh, hullo," he said. "Like to eavesdrop on other people's naughty activities, do you?"

Katherine was so taken aback by his entire attitude, so suddenly annoyed, that instead of prudently retreating she instead answered, rather snappishly, "As a matter of fact, I don't."

"Really? Still, it wasn't very nice of you to hang about like that."

"It wasn't very nice of *you* to pursue a married woman."

He came closer. "You're straitlaced, eh?"

"I'm none of your business, that's what I am."

"I think you ought to be." He was closer now—closer than he should be—and Katherine could almost feel his rakish charm, smooth, oleaginous, rolling over her as he again swept his dark gaze over her in a highly improper manner.

"You're like a ripe little pear," he remarked. "Juicy and delicious. Of course, the green of your gown doesn't quite work with the metaphor."

"It's a simile."

"Whatever you say, my dear. I'm glad you're not wearing yellow—you'd look more pear-like, but also, I fear, jaundiced. Really, the only solution is to take your gown off."

"Take my gown off." She didn't know whether to laugh or to spit in his eye.

"Do you need some help? Chivalry is not yet dead, you know. Allow me."

He was actually crouching down, reaching for the hem of her dress, and Katherine was so surprised by his casual audacity that even though her brain was saying, *Kick him, and hard,* her body was still a few beats behind. She felt his hand on her ankle and in a rather muddled way managed to say:

"Stop it."

"Surely you don't mean that," he said with the same smooth confidence, and just as his hand began to slide up her leg, he was whisked up and away from her and set on his feet as easily as an adult might remove a small troublesome child from a place where he ought not to be.

Hugo had done it. Hugo. He was here. He had found her, and she was safe. With Hugo she always felt safe. Always. He said to the other man, "She told you to stop," and his deep voice was very calm, but within it was a distinctive timbre that made Katherine's eyes go wide.

The other man resettled his coat and nodded in the most amicable way at Hugo. "Oh, hullo, I haven't seen you in ages. Didn't you go off to our benighted former Colonies? Meet any interesting women there? I hear those American ladies are quite an armful."

"What," said Hugo, "is going on here?"

"What's going on," replied the other man with unimpaired sangfroid, "is that I was in the midst of an intimate encounter, and you're getting in my way."

"An intimate encounter? Why, you—you nasty, despicable *marmot!*" Katherine exclaimed, gathering her scattered wits. "He's lying, Hugo, I assure you!"

"Oh, you know each other? Is this an assignation? Hugo, I extend to you my felicitations. She's charming. A little too fierce for my tastes, to own the truth, but still, a prime article."

Hugo's jaw was now visibly clenched. "I don't care to hear my wife described like that, Thane."

"Your wife?" echoed the other man, even as Katherine gaped and said:

"You're *Thane?*"

He executed a low bow with an extravagant sweep of his arm, as would a gallant of the old French court. "Philip Thane at your service, my dear Mrs. Penhallow."

"Ha," she said rudely, adding in a severe tone, "Your grandparents have been looking for you, you know."

"I do know, and that's why I've been laying low for the past several weeks. I don't care to be scolded or, in the case of my mama, wept over. But when the wealthy and willing Letitia summoned me here, how could I resist her wiles?"

"It's Lucretia."

"Whatever you say, my dear. It's coming to me, by the way, that you look a little familiar. Weren't you at a party last year hosted by the rather common Mrs. Spindlow? If I recall correctly, you wore diamonds, rubies, *and* pearls. Frankly, it was too much. I *was* going to talk to you, thinking you might benefit from a little kindly advice about your *ensemble,* but then I heard who you were. Rowland Brooke's daughter, aren't you?"

She scowled. "Yes."

"I took nearly a hundred pounds off him that night at piquet. He fancies himself quite the Captain Sharp. If I were you I'd tell him to leave off the cards."

"When I desire your counsel, Mr. Thane," Katherine said coldly, "I'll be sure to inform you."

"Oh, do call me Philip, we're more or less cousins, after all." He swung around to Hugo. "So you caught yourself an heiress, eh? That's very well done of you. Speaking of heiresses, I've got my eye on a promising one myself, only her curst parents have carried her off to Tunbridge Wells and I'm a trifle low on travel funds at the moment. Any chance you could lend me a small sum, now you're rolling in the stuff? A few hundred pounds would set me up nicely."

Hugo gave him a level look. "As it's well-known that

you never pay back a loan, Thane, I'm more likely to give you a good drubbing."

Philip Thane raised his hands, as if appeasing an armed opponent. "Never mind, my dear Hugo, never mind! It was merely a request. Well, I'll leave you two love-birds alone to enjoy the moonlight. Do try to avoid creating a scandal. That's *my* purview, after all." He smiled breezily. "It was a pleasure to meet you, Mrs. Penhallow, and may I compliment you on your greatly improved appearance? Good night."

And with that he loped past Hugo and away toward the house, the sound of his shoes, crunching on gravel, rapidly fading away.

Katherine said quickly, "Oh, Hugo, you know he was lying, don't you? With his ridiculous story of an assignation?"

Hugo didn't answer for a moment; he was hearing again Thane's insouciant congratulations. *So you caught yourself an heiress, eh? That's very well done of you.* The words were a stiletto, worming their way inside him, sharp and wounding. Now he wished he *had* given Thane a drubbing, if only for the sake of relieving his own feelings. If only to forget for a moment that he was on a lonely dark road, going nowhere. He said to Katherine, "Yes, I believe you. Shall we go in?"

She remained very still, her brilliant eyes huge in her face as she looked up at him. "Would you—would you like to stay here for a little while? And we could talk?"

More talking, more words. What good could words possibly do? "I think not," said Hugo. "Westenbury told me you were tired. Are you feeling more refreshed? Allow me to take you in."

He spoke to her with kind courtesy, the sort of politeness he would extend to—well, anyone really.

And so they went in.

Chapter 13

Katherine was in her room, Hugo was in his. In the hallway, a little earlier, having returned from the DeWitts' ball, they had parted as they always did; he had said good night to her with that same civil, distant tone that seemed to turn her blood to ice. Why had he begun talking to her in that way? She hated it.

Still in her beautiful green gown, Katherine was sitting on the floor, next to one of her tall stacks of books, from which she had carefully extracted a certain volume, very large and heavy; set it on her thighs, opened it. Shakespeare. The complete plays. That line about blindness—where had it appeared? Was it *Titus Andronicus*? *Julius Caesar*? *Cymbeline*?

She began scanning the pages by the flickering light of a single candle.

Searching, searching: *Our very eyes are sometimes, like our judgments, blind.*

When she reached page 28, Katherine realized just how absurd a task she had set before herself, given how small the type was. And that there were some six hundred pages to go.

She pressed on.

When she got to page 43, she realized that she *was* tired. Oh so tired.

When she got to page 47, she realized that for the last thirty pages or so she hadn't really even read anything. Because the truth was that she didn't want to be sitting here on the cold floor flipping pointlessly—hopelessly—through a book of Shakespeare's plays. The truth was that there was some other place she wanted to be.

Wanted it more badly than she had ever wanted anything in her life.

So she set the book aside and stood up, and went to the table next to her bed, where she found the key on its green ribbon—noticing without surprise, as if it were meant to be, how precisely it matched the green of her gown—and then, quietly, she went to the door that separated her room from Hugo's and quietly, carefully, she unlocked it.

She pushed the door open a little and peeked inside. It was dark in Hugo's room; she could just barely see him in his bed. He was there, thank God, he *was* there. Katherine blew out her candle and softly, padding on stockinged feet, went into his room, went to the unoccupied side of the bed, and very quietly crawled underneath the covers.

Her heart was beating hard, hard, within her, so loud in her own ears that she was surprised the noise of it didn't wake Hugo. Now that her eyes had adjusted to the darkness, she could see that he slept on his side, facing her, one bare arm flung over the bedclothes. She looked, as if for the very first time, at him, at the strong lines of his face, that perfect straight nose, the firm jaw, his hair, slightly rumpled, which in the light would shine like gold.

Katherine looked, and this time, she hoped, she saw.

She didn't know what the morning would bring—if Hugo even wanted her there—if there would be an uncomfortable, painful, possibly devastating scene—but for now, at this moment, in this time and in this place, she was exactly where she needed to be.

He was dreaming of chocolate. The sweet, tantalizing scent of it in his nostrils, teasing him, filling him with desire. Hugo stirred, brushed aside a great handful of curly hair from his face, snugged his arm over a plump silken hip. Vaguely was he aware of a feeling of contentment. Rightness. Of being alone no longer. He smiled a little, and let himself drift back into a deep untroubled sleep.

It was only a tapping—knuckles on a wood door— that brought him awake, that made him realize that he lay body to body with Katherine, who, sleeping on her side with her back pressed against him, still wore her green dress from last night. Surprise came first, and then desire flamed again, the quick rush of lust, but there was nothing to be done as, standing on the threshold to their connecting rooms, was a maidservant with a tray which she balanced on her forearm, using her other arm to tap again on the open door, her eyes very wide with the surprise, Hugo supposed, of finding her mistress in bed with her husband. Who could blame her? It was an unprecedented event.

"I brought the chocolate, sir," the maidservant said. "Like I do every morning. Where shall I put it, sir?"

"On the table next to me, please," he answered, and she complied, then bobbed a curtsy and went back to the connecting door, closing it so slowly, and with her eyes fixed upon them with such fascination, that he wanted to laugh. He sat up, and poured chocolate from its little silver pitcher into the delicate china cup.

"Katherine," he said, and he watched as she stirred, sighed, and then turned onto her back and looked up at him. Her hair, still with its green silk ribbons and jeweled ornaments, was in a wild, tangled tumble, and he could see that she had on her emerald necklace from last night, lying twisted on her collarbone. Her mouth curved in a

dreamy smile and she said, as if it was the most natural
thing in all the world:

"Hullo."

"Hullo," he answered, just as easily, as if this was
something they said to each other every morning in bed,
and added, "Here's your chocolate."

She looked at the cup, then back at him. "You first."

"Are you sure?"

"Yes."

"Thanks, then." He took a sip. Warm, sweet, wonderful. "It reminds me of you."

"What does?"

"Chocolate. The scent of it. Here." He held out the cup,
and Katherine sat up to accept it. Her green ball-gown
was rumpled, the neckline was askew, and one puffed
sleeve had slid haphazardly down to reveal the soft white
skin of her shoulder. She looked, he thought, wonderful.

She sipped at the chocolate, then held the cup out to
him. "Your turn."

"But it's yours."

"Let's share it." She was sitting very straight, and he
saw that her expression was no longer sleepy, dreamy, but
alert. Determined. He took the cup.

"Thanks."

"You're welcome. Hugo, I have something I want to
tell you."

She reminded him, suddenly, of how she'd been that
night at the inn. Words wanting to spill out: about that
ghastly school of hers. The music instructor. The so-
called Reflection Room.

Boxes concealed, boxes revealed.

He said, "What is it, Katherine?"

She had flushed a vivid red. "Hugo, sometimes I have
a scent of chocolate about me because—well, I like to
eat it."

"Oh, is that why?"

"Yes."

Her face was even redder, her lips compressed, and so in the spirit of helpfulness it seemed only decent of him to add:

"I like chocolate also."

"Yes, but . . . I like it very much."

"I too."

"No, I mean I like it *a lot*."

So might a shamed penitent in the confessional admit to criminal acts. He said, "Is there anything wrong with that? I've been known to eat spring lamb till I was ready to burst."

"Yes, but I—love chocolate."

"And so?" He handed her back the cup. She stared into it, then up at him, and hurriedly said, as if afraid her nerve would fail her:

"My mother told me I couldn't have it. I've been sneaking it for years."

It seemed, on the face of it, rather a small thing, but then again, you couldn't know unless you walked in another person's shoes. "If you expected I'd be shocked, I'm not."

She was silent. Then: "Have you ever done anything like that?"

He smiled, just a little. "Surely you've not forgotten the time I tried to sneak a pair of Impures into my dormitory."

"Oh!" She knit her brows. "Yes, I remember. You told me about it the night before we arrived at Surmont Hall. I was a trifle drunk, as I recall."

"You were well on the way. Hope you won't feel bad about that either."

"There's so much to feel bad about." Katherine gave another sigh, on her face now an expression of such sadness that he seemed to feel it within himself, heavy and dark. She went on: "Do you want to hear about my books?"

"Your books? You feel bad about them also?"

"I've been sneaking them for years, too. You remember my maid Céleste?"

"Yes, of course."

"We had our own little smuggling scheme. Books and chocolates. I paid her, and somehow she got them for me. Whatever I wanted. From all over the country. Even from abroad."

Hugo couldn't help it, he laughed. "Katherine, I'm impressed."

She was staring at him. "Impressed?"

"Very. How delightfully clever of you. Wish I'd been as practical, instead of smuggling in cows and ladies of the night. Should've been sneaking in portable things, like spirits. And cheroots, just to try them. Now drink your chocolate before it gets cold."

Looking a little dazed, Katherine obeyed. He took the cup and put it back on the tray, then tugged up a pillow so that she could lean back against it and did the same for himself. "Comfortable?"

"Yes."

"Good. Is there anything else you want to tell me?"

"Last night . . ." she said, then stopped.

"What about last night? Still worrying about our awful cousin Thane?"

"No. He *is* awful, isn't he? But last night—you didn't want to talk."

"Last night," he said, "was a long time ago."

She took this in, and slowly nodded her head. "Hugo, I want to thank you for coming when you did. You were very heroic, lifting Thane up like that."

"Heroic?" He laughed. "Hardly. A bit of brute strength, that's all."

"It seemed heroic to me. So—thank you."

"You're welcome."

"And—you don't mind my being here?"

"No. I'm glad you came."

Hugo was smiling at her, and Katherine felt her spirits lifting, in a giddy rushing swoop upwards. Physiologically impossible, of course, but the sensation seemed very real. Wonderfully real.

Yesterday evening, she had been afraid that Hugo would never smile at her again. It would be like living in a world in which the sun had been blotted out. Desolate. Hopeless. *Last night was a long time ago.* And today was a new day, filled with possibility.

Katherine pushed back the bedclothes and scrambled out of bed, went with eager steps to the windows and flung back one of the curtains. Bright sunlight flooded the room. She turned back around. Yes. Hugo's hair illuminated to gold. The blue of his eyes like a Grecian sea. He was naked to the waist, and probably everywhere. *I'm glad you came.* The word *came,* Katherine thought, feeling warm all over, had multiple meanings, some of them more immediate than others.

Hugo said, "You're getting up, then?"

"No. I'm coming back to bed." Which is what she did. She knelt next to Hugo, her gown splayed about her. *Coming. To come.* "Is that all right with you?"

He looked at her for a long moment. "Yes. What do you want to do?"

The answer—the idea—bloomed inside Katherine, as beautiful as a flower in spring. "This." She brought herself closer, put a hand on his shoulder, lowered her face to his. Lightly, lightly, she touched her lips to his mouth. Connected the two of them in this powerful, intimate way. And without hesitation she tilted her head to allow the kiss to deepen, into something that was urgent and needful, and hot and wet, and tongues and teeth, and Hugo making a delicious growling sound in his throat redolent of both satisfaction and hunger, and his hands coming up to slide around her, and everything that was simple, honest, real, *good.*

When at last they broke the kiss, she was breathless and smiling. And oh, how happy Hugo looked. That beautiful flower bloomed and opened wide within her. She said:

"Second, I want to do this." She sat up. With unhurried deliberation she touched him: in a long caress slid her hands from his shoulders down the warm muscled length of his arms; up again, then down along the broad, hard planes of his chest, the sculpted lines of his torso, his flat stomach. It was as if her palms and fingers, sensitive, alive, weren't just feeling him, they were seeing, *knowing* him. And knowing he liked what she was doing. Maybe as much as she liked it, too.

Her hands came to the bedclothes where they lay against his waist. He was hard, hard, beneath them, and a new idea came to her.

"Third," she said to Hugo, "I want to do this."

She drew the bedclothes down and away. Such magnificent . . . maleness. *What a piece of work is man,* Shakespeare had written, although not, perhaps, as she was interpreting it now, with earthy awe and appreciation for this very particular aspect of a man. Of Hugo. She thought of Sonnet 128. *Me thy lips to kiss.* She revised it in her mind: *you my lips to kiss.*

She leaned down and—shyly at first, then with more boldness—she tasted him. Explored him, with her lips and tongue and fingers and mouth. Heard with her own deep delight his ragged groan. She received even as she gave, and rapidly did she lose herself in the hot mindless joy of it.

It was only when Hugo gently pushed her away that Katherine came to, a little, and straightened. "What is it?"

He raked his fingers through his hair. "You'll have me toppling off the bed in a moment."

"In a good way?"

"In a very good way. What do you want to do now?"

She thought. Then: "This. Fourth thing." She pulled from over her head the emerald necklace, let it spill like water on the far side of the bed, then her bracelets, too. "My gown. Will you unlace it?"

"Yes." Hugo sat up, and she twisted around, marveling, in some distant part of her, at the miracle of how easily she did it, how the pain had entirely gone. She could feel her gown loosening, and when he said, "It's done," she turned back around, hitched up the hem, and tugged her gown up and over her head; and then her shift, too. She was rewarded by his smile, the fire in his eyes, by every taut line in his body.

He said, "What's the fifth thing?"

"This." She lay back with catlike indolence upon the rumpled bedcovers.

"Lying sideways on the bed? Now you *are* shocking me."

"Somehow I doubt that."

He laughed. "And now what?"

"Sixth thing." She opened her legs wide for him, and smiled when his body told her exactly how he felt about that. He came to her then, brought himself sliding above her and against her, kissed her long and deeply. All the while—and how was it even possible to *feel* so much? With, seemingly, every atom, every particle of her, everywhere?—all the while she was aware of, delighting in, the contrast between his hard chest, flecked with golden hair, and her own chest, her breasts so smooth and soft; the contrast between his iron-hard legs and her soft fleshy ones; the contrast between him, all hard and erect and utterly male, and herself, all soft and yielding, and so very ready.

Male and female.

He and she.

Hugo and Katherine.

Us, together, she thought, and said out loud: "Seventh thing," sliding her hand down between them, reaching for him, eagerly guiding him closer, closer, and into her at last.

Later, much later, when they had done, and their bodies were slick with sweat, and the room was quiet again, Hugo rolled onto his back. He unhooked a long spiral of Katherine's hair from around his ear and took a moment to orient himself. Somehow they had ended up with their heads at the foot of the bed; his feet were on Katherine's pillows.

"I say," he said, in a tone of deep appreciation, "that was something like."

Katherine turned onto her side and brought herself closer, sliding a warm, soft arm over his chest. "Yes, it was." She gave a happy-sounding sigh. "Thank you."

He laid his hand over her forearm where it rested atop the scar from the sharpshooter's bullet. All nicely healed. "If it comes to that, I should be thanking *you*. I'm glad you don't find me unappealing anymore."

"You? Unappealing?" She lifted her head to stare at him. "What do you mean?"

"I've had that impression quite a lot these past months."

"Oh. No. It's not true. At all. I'm sorry you've thought so." Katherine raised herself up, so that she could reach his mouth with her own, and kissed him with such ardor that he had no doubt that she meant it. This, Hugo thought, returning her kiss, was a new and promising box revealed. He brought his hands down along the length of her back, and to the fulsome, exquisitely feminine curves of her waist and hips and thighs.

Suddenly she pulled away. "Hugo, this can't be bad."

"Bad?" he echoed in surprise. "What can't be bad?"

"This." Her glance encompassed him, herself, the rumpled bed. "What was explained to me as the 'conjugal obligation.' It was about *duty,* Hugo, not pleasure, or fun. And after my little—ah—*contretemps* with the music instructor, and I was told how low and bad I was to want such a thing—well, I believed it for a long time. But now . . ." Katherine took a deep, deep breath, and let it out on a slow exhalation. "But now I think they were wrong. I think this is good. I *know* it is."

"I agree," Hugo said, smiling, and lazily he stretched. Speaking of good, he hadn't felt this good in a long time. Maybe he'd never felt this good before, in fact. He laced his fingers together and put them behind his head. "Well, Katherine?"

"Well what?"

"What do you want to do now?"

She looked thoughtful. And then she smiled. "I'll be right back." She got off the bed, and he watched as she went to the door between their rooms and, opening it, went inside. God in heaven, that bottom of hers. Sweet, sweet lust was running rampant through him again. And she could tell, too, when—returning with a green-and-yellow-striped pasteboard box—she looked down the length of him and smiled again. She got back onto the bed, drew close to sit near him, and said:

"Seventeenth thing."

"We're up to seventeen already?"

"Yes."

"Quite the morning, Katherine."

"Yes. And it's not over yet." She put the box on the bed next to her. Opening the lid, she took from it a dark square.

"Is that a conserve?" he said. "I haven't had one in ages." And then it hit him: Katherine wasn't secretively indulging in her affection for chocolate. Here she was, quite literally revealing to him a box.

"Yes. Would you like one, Hugo?"

"I would, thanks."

He reached for it but instead she brought the chocolate square to his lips while with her other hand she lightly caressed his cock. He groaned, but with pleasure. Sweet chocolate in his mouth; fire everywhere else.

After a while it occurred to him that two could play at that game. He sat up. To her he said, "Lie down."

"Why?" Her eyes were sparkling.

"You'll see."

"If you insist." She lay back, with such languorous slowness that he almost shoved the green and yellow box off the bed and had her then and there. But he reminded himself that patience is a virtue. He took a conserve from the box and offered it to her. She looked at it, and up at him: and then she bit into it, smiling with such devastating sensuousness that again he had to restrain himself. Patience . . .

"It's good, isn't it?" she said.

"Very good," he answered. He took a small bite of the conserve, allowed his saliva to moisten the rest of it, and with the same languid slowness she'd displaying in lying down, he rubbed the conserve around the pretty pink areolae of her breasts. She quivered.

"Oh, Hugo."

He didn't stop. "Yes, Katherine?"

"Oh, Hugo."

"Yes?"

But, apparently, that was all she had to say at the moment, and he saw with gladness how her arms and legs went taut and her face very flushed. He continued for a little while longer, then, slowly, he ate the conserve and with the taste of it still lingering on his tongue, he stretched himself out next to her on his side, leaned close, and licked wet, leisurely circles round her areolae.

"Oh, Hugo."

"Yes?"

"Eighteenth thing."

He laughed softly, then took a sweet luscious nipple into his mouth and suckled it, enjoying a great deal the breathy little noises she was making, and even as he sucked harder he slid a hand down between her legs.

She gasped, "Nineteenth thing," and arched herself up to meet his fingers.

"It's remarkable how you haven't lost track of your numbers," Hugo said admiringly, then brought his mouth to her other nipple and sucked hard at it, too. And then he moved down, down, until his head was between her warm fragrant thighs, and another taste, musky and feminine, was there for him to savor.

"My God, you delicious armful, you beauty," said Hugo, his voice a little rough, "you're better than chocolate," and slid his palms beneath her, to bring her yet closer to him.

"Am I really?" she answered, rather jerkily.

"Infinitely better."

"Oh, good. Oh, Hugo, that's good . . ."

"Twentieth thing?"

"Yes. Oh my God, yes."

After, they had breakfast in bed, and after that Katherine entertained them by reading out loud from her new copy of the *Canterbury Tales,* which made them both laugh quite a bit, and then they made love again, and then they took a nap.

It was early afternoon when Katherine, lying close to Hugo, drifted slowly up into consciousness. Fragments played in her mind's eye, something between dreams and memories. Last night: the DeWitts' ballroom. Crowds of people. Being jostled. Lydia St. John, her tawny good looks seeming surprisingly faded for one so young. A big hand around her slim upper arm, a loud hearty voice and a big red face. Who? Oh, yes, her brother Denis.

Daresay the two of you will be wanting to renew your friendship, hey? Let the world know and all that. The big hand, squeezing hard.

Revulsion rippled through Katherine, and she remembered, now, the look of helplessness in Lydia's light brown eyes.

She sat up suddenly, pushing her hair off her face, and Hugo woke up.

"What is it, Katherine?"

"Hugo, I want to call on someone. And I'd like it if you came with me. Would you?"

"Of course. When?"

"Now."

Chapter 14

The St. Johns were staying in Upper Wimpole Street—what a wonder a good butler was, thought Katherine, what an astonishing fount of knowledge—and by four o'clock she and Hugo, having quickly bathed and dressed, arrived in their carriage. It was a genteel neighborhood, but was by no means considered one of the better addresses among the *ton*. So when the butler obsequiously ushered them into the empty drawing-room, Katherine was surprised to see how elegantly furnished it was.

She and Hugo had been seated for only a little while before Denis St. John hurried in, in his wake both an angular, fashionably dressed woman and his sister Lydia, who looked at Katherine with a kind of cringing expression so very, very different from the one she had habitually worn at school. Katherine recognized the expression at once—it was one she knew all too well.

It was shame.

"Well, well, if this isn't an *honor*," exclaimed Denis St. John, bringing the angular woman forward and introducing her as his wife. He glanced around the empty room and said, with the heartiness that Katherine disliked more and more: "Can't think where everyone is! Usually we're mobbed with visitors, aren't we, Mrs. St. John?"

His wife simpered. "Oh yes, *mobbed.* And constantly! All sorts of important people! The *best* people!"

Denis St. John directed a glowering look of reproof at his wife before breaking again into a wide smile and saying to Katherine and Hugo, "No one as important as *you,* of course. Penhallows are better than dukes, everyone says so. Well, well, and so you've called on us! *Quite* the honor! You there, Lydia—don't just stand there like a ninny, ring for some refreshments, hey?"

Listlessly Lydia did as she was told, and Katherine had seen enough. She rose to her feet and said, "Miss St. John, it's been so long since we've seen each other, and I should enjoy a little *tête-à-tête* with you. Perhaps we might go to your bedchamber?"

That look of shame intensified, but before Lydia could answer, Denis St. John hastily put in:

"Oh, there's no need to do that, Mrs. Penhallow! You and Lydia can enjoy a comfortable coze right here! Reminiscences from the good old days, plans to make, bosom companions, isn't that right, Lydia? There's a window-seat over there which would be just the thing!"

"No," said Katherine, as imperious as Henrietta Penhallow in her haughtiest mood, "I would prefer to go upstairs with Miss St. John." She went to Lydia, put her arm through hers, at the same time flashing a quick glance at Hugo which she hoped communicated *Hold the fort here, please,* and was glad to see the look of instant comprehension in his eyes, and the slight, martial nod of his head.

Plainly flummoxed, Denis St. John shot an angry look at his hapless wife, then went to the bell-pull and yanked hard upon it, muttering under his breath, "Where's that butler, damn his mangy hide?"

Katherine, satisfied, swept Lydia out of the drawing-room, then followed her lagging steps up a flight of stairs onto a landing, sunless and not very clean. About halfway down the corridor Lydia opened a door and stepped aside to let Katherine in.

It was a mean little room, cheaply furnished with a narrow iron bedstead, a small armoire, a rickety-looking dressing-table and a single chair. The contrast between the drawing-room below and this dismal bedchamber caught Katherine off-guard and she frankly stared. At school Lydia St. John was known to be the daughter of a very wealthy baron, long established on the vast family estate in Kent, a fact which Lydia herself had frequently mentioned.

"Well, have you seen enough, Mrs. Penhallow? Or would you like to stay and gloat some more?" Lydia's voice was bitter.

"Gloat? No!" Quickly Katherine turned to her. "It's just that—" There was no tactful way to say it, but Lydia stepped in.

"Yes, there's quite a difference between the public rooms and the private ones." Lydia smiled without humor. "The St. Johns have fallen on hard times, Mrs. Penhallow, but my brother Denis is doing everything he can to conceal it." She pulled out the chair, and gestured to it. "Would you like to sit down? I promise you it won't break. I know because Denis has sat on it many times when he comes to lecture me—and he's quite a substantial man, isn't he?"

Katherine sat down and waited until Lydia had sat on her bed opposite her. "I'm sorry to hear about your—your financial reversals. I had thought your father's fortune to be secure."

"It might have been, had he not passed into his dotage a hateful drunkard and allowed Denis to take over its management. Denis has lost everything—most of the estate, my dowry, the family's plantation in the West Indies." Lydia added, with a terrible casualness, "He tried to marry me off to one of his rich so-called friends in Jamaica. The only way I managed to avoid it was by spreading rumors that I was mad. His friend became worried that any children we'd have would inherit the taint, and withdrew. Denis was—furious."

"Oh, Lydia, I'm so sorry," exclaimed Katherine.

Thin shoulders went up in a hopeless shrug. "That's why we're here for the Season, you know. A last chance to salvage the family fortunes. Denis intends for me to wed, and as soon as possible. Which explains why he was thrilled that you and I knew each other. He's hoping you'll help me—take me under your wing." Bitterly, Lydia went on, "He doesn't know that we're not friends at all, and I'm afraid to tell him. I was dreadful toward you, wasn't I, all those years? I was so jealous of you. So beautiful, so brilliant."

"*Jealous?* Of me?" Katherine could hardly believe what she was hearing.

"Yes. Very. And I took it out on you in any way I could think of. My God, but I was awful. You'll be pleased to know, Mrs. Penhallow, that life has humbled me."

"I'm not pleased at all. And I *do* want to help you."

Lydia was silent. Then, finally, suspiciously, she said: "Why?"

"Because I know what it's like to be a pawn in someone else's game."

Silence again. Then: "Now that you're a Penhallow, once it's known I'm your *protégée* it will make all the difference in the world."

"I'll do my best. Is there someone you want to marry?" Katherine asked, then saw how a shudder rippled through Lydia's slender frame.

"God, no! And put myself under the control of someone else?"

"Not all men are like that," said Katherine, thinking of Hugo, thinking with a rush of gratitude of him downstairs, steady, calm, strong.

"I don't *want* to be married," Lydia said with suppressed violence, hands clenched tight in her lap. "And I *hate* living with Denis. And my nasty sister-in-law."

"Then being here is pointless," said Katherine. "Being made to attend the Season. Is there someplace else you'd rather be?"

"Yes! I want to go to Bath. I have an elderly aunt—she's rather lame—she lives there for her health, she's got a small income and has rooms by the baths, and she's written to say I could live with her. Before Denis started reading all my mail, that is. She's very kind—I could be happy there—living very quietly—" Lydia was leaning forward now, looking at Katherine with a kind of desperate intensity. "But I haven't any money to get away. Nothing. I'm trapped here, Mrs. Penhallow."

"Does Denis have any legal hold over you? Are you of age?"

"I'm twenty-two, and no, he's not my guardian. His hold over me derives from—well, you know the Scottish saying, don't you? 'Possession is eleven points in the law, and they say there are but twelve.'"

Katherine nodded. "Then let's get you to Bath. We can send you there in one of our carriages. Nothing could be easier." She watched as slowly into Lydia's tired face came a heartbreaking look of relief. But then it faded and she said:

"Oh, but how, Mrs. Penhallow? Denis will do everything in his power to stop me. And you've seen how—forceful he is."

Katherine glanced around the shabby room. There was so little here. "Pack your trunk now, Lydia. Hugo will carry it down. We'll take you with us to the Penhallow townhouse, and you can sleep there tonight. Tomorrow we'll send you off to Bath."

Lydia's tawny brown eyes were wide. "You would do that for me? After all the hateful things I did to you?"

Hugo had said, *Last night was a long time ago.* And so now Katherine said to Lydia St. John, "That was a long time ago." Briskly she stood up. "Come on, I'll help you pack."

The scene that followed was, as Katherine had expected, unpleasant. Upon hearing the news of his sister's immediate departure, Denis St. John was flabbergasted, then hostile, blustery, vituperative toward his sister, and began to issue some very ugly threats, but Hugo, with a few blunt, well-chosen words, rapidly reduced St. John to a cowering silence. He then shouldered Lydia's trunk and escorted Katherine and Lydia downstairs and into the street, where they cheerfully crammed themselves and the trunk into the carriage and bowled away.

Later, when Lydia, exhausted, had gone to bed in one of the guest bedchambers, and Katherine and Hugo were alone in his room, she reached out to squeeze his hand and said, "Oh, Hugo, you were marvelous! I know it's very wrong to feel this way, but there was something so satisfying about seeing the dreadful Denis vanquished like that."

"Yes, very heroic of me," said Hugo complacently.

Katherine laughed. "Well, it *was.*"

He raised her hand to his lips and kissed it. "You were rather heroic yourself, you know. Or should I say 'heroine-ish'? 'Heroine-ic'? Is there a word for it?"

"If there's not, there should be," Katherine answered. She leaned back in her chair, looking thoughtfully at Hugo. Their seats drawn close together, they were sitting near the fireplace, where a small fire danced and leaped, and they each were holding a crystal glass of deep red burgundy wine. "Hugo, are you sorry we didn't go to Almack's tonight as we had planned?"

"Not particularly. Are you?"

"Well, Mr. Brummel had sent me a note hoping I'd be there, and that nice Lady Mainwaring said the same thing at Countess Lieven's dinner-party, but . . . Am I sorry?

Yes—no—I'm not sure. I just know I'm not sorry to be here with you."

"Likewise," said Hugo, and smiled, and Katherine thought that although their bedchamber was all lovely and dim, it was, at the same time, very bright.

They walked with Lydia to the mews early the next morning, accompanied by a footman and a maidservant who were to travel with Lydia to Bath. Her battered trunk had already been strapped atop the carriage, and the maidservant got inside; Hugo went to talk to the coachman. Katherine turned to Lydia, reaching into the side-pocket of her pelisse, and pulled out a small purse which she pressed into Lydia's gloved hand. "Something for your journey," she said. "For your expenses."

"Oh, Mrs. Penhallow, I couldn't accept it." Lydia's eyes were shimmering with tears. "You've done so much already."

"You can and you must. And please, please, call me Katherine."

"Katherine, then," said Lydia, and slipped the little purse into her reticule. "Thank you. For everything." She looped her reticule over her wrist, held out her hands, and Katherine took them in her own. She said:

"Safe travels, Lydia. And—won't you write to me sometime, and let me know how you're doing?"

"I will," promised Lydia, and then Hugo had said his farewells and helped her into the carriage, and the carriage rolled away. When it had gone from their sight, Hugo said:

"Well, Katherine? What would you like to do now?"

Katherine raised up the hem of her gown, just enough to show Hugo her jean half-boots. "I thought perhaps we could go for a walk."

"A walk, really?" said Hugo in surprise. Then, recovering, gallantly he held out his arm. Katherine laughed and took it, and so they went for a long stroll, uncaring that the sky was a sullen, lowering gray, all too typical for an early summer day in London.

When they returned to the townhouse, the butler inquired as to whether they cared for refreshments—to which Hugo said, "By Jove, yes"—and also made mention of some newly arrived correspondence which awaited them at their convenience.

Half an hour later, they were sitting in a spacious saloon which overlooked a charming walled garden, sharing a sofa. Katherine was perched at one end, sorting through her invitations, letters, circulars, calling cards, and so on. Hugo sat on the other end of the sofa, a plate of savory quiche tarts set next to him. He ate one of the tarts, thinking how sometimes, there was nothing nicer than a companionable silence. He picked up one of his letters.

29 May 1812

Dear Hugo,
  Thanks awfully for your letter. Percy and I are coming along nicely. He's been elected captain of the cricket team and I won a prize for my essay on Seneca the Younger—all six volumes of The History of the Decline and Fall of the Roman Empire which I am enjoying immensely. Owen has invited us back to Northamptonshire for the summer holiday and we'd love to go. Would you mind very much if we did? The only bad thing is that Owen's sister Helen will probably be hanging about bothering us as she did the last time we were there. Owen says he'd like to kick her in the seat of her gown but as she outweighs him by three stone he doesn't dare. Percy says she's a good fellow and a bruising rider but I must say I find her rather obnoxious.

Still, difficulties strengthen the mind, as Seneca the Younger says, so I daresay association with Helen will at least confer some kind of moral benefit.

Yours most faithfully,
Francis

Hugo smiled, and opened the next letter.

26 May 1812

Dearest Hugo,
Thank you so very much for the beautiful fan you sent me! It is just right for pretending that I am a captivating lady of Society. I've been practicing fan gestures for days. So far my favorites are when you cover your left ear with the fan opened up, which means 'Do not betray our secret,' and when you slide the fan across your forehead, which means 'You have changed.' Diana says her favorite is when you twirl the fan in your left hand, which means 'We are being watched.' Bertram came upon us while we were practicing, took my fan and opened it, and beat it violently over the top of his head to create a great breeze, which he said means 'I am thinking hard.' I tried not to laugh but of course I did. He also says, by the way, that he very much appreciates those long-handled tongs you sent, which have proved very useful in his sintering experiments. He wrote to thank you but it was only this morning that he realized he forgot to mail it.
Are you dreadfully sad the Season is coming to a close? How romantic it must be! When are you coming home? We all miss you so much. You will be pleased to see how nice things are looking. Mama

has had several rooms painted, for example, and Cook adores her new stove. Also, the roof has been fixed.

Love always,
Gwendolyn

P.S. I do believe Señor Rodrigo misses you also. He has lost some more feathers, the poor darling.

P.P.S. But I will never give up hope, and so I tell him at least twice a day now.

P.P.P.S. I almost forgot. Please give Katherine my regards.

Hugo smiled again as he reread the postscripts, rendered in Gwendolyn's looping, still childish hand. He reached for another tart. "Gwennie sends her regards."

There was no reply from Katherine, so after Hugo had taken a bite of his tart and swallowed it he looked over at her. "Gwennie sends her—" He broke off. Katherine was sitting bolt upright and clutching in one hand an opened letter, at which she was staring as if turned to stone. "Katherine, what's the matter? What is it?"

Still she said nothing. Quickly he set aside the tart, moved to sit next to her on the sofa. "Katherine, what's wrong?"

Her mouth opened and then closed, as if she wouldn't—couldn't—speak. She only thrust the letter at him.

28 May 1812

Katherine,
    Your father is ruined. I do not fully understand it, but it has something to do with various bubble companies in which he has for the past several years

vested as partner. The lawyers came yesterday and
he was closeted with them till well after midnight.
All is lost. His debts are extreme and he must sell
or relinquish every asset we own in order to avoid
being sent to debtors' prison, or worse. That includes Brooke House and all its contents including
furnishings, artwork, carriages, and so on, as well
as the jewelry you (foolishly) left behind. Your father
has agreed to all that the lawyers demanded, but
vows he'll not stay in a country where one cannot
pursue enterprising business practices without being
harassed. Therefore, tomorrow we travel for Bristol,
where in a fortnight we shall set sail for Porto de
Galinhas—your father being confident that in Brazil
he'll be able to avoid the embarrassment of further
legal prosecution as well as enjoy a more congenial
environment in which to rebuild our fortunes.

Speaking of which, it was quite lucky that at the
very last moment we were able to have your next
(and, obviously, last) quarterly allowance diverted
to us, as while we wait to commence our journey—at
the Royal Arms Inn, Bristol's best accommodations,
of course—we must hurry to purchase clothing more
suitable for a sea voyage as well as for the climate in
Porto de Galinhas. They say it is quite agreeable—
nearly always warm and mild. However, I shall have
to guard my complexion most carefully.

No more now, as I must oversee the packing of
my trunks. Really, all things considered, it may
well prove to be a delightful new adventure for us.
Your father and I are bound to be greeted among
the expatriate community there with acclaim, he
being the son of a baronet and I of course an accomplished Society hostess. It is, after all, an ill
wind that blows no good.

I remain, etc.,
Mother

"Good God," said Hugo, and Katherine, her face gone very white, said in an even voice:

"Did you notice anything peculiar about the letter?"

"I should say I do. Not a word of concern for you."

"Oh, not that, I wouldn't have expected anything different." Katherine's eyes were glittering, bright and fierce. "You didn't notice a distinct lack of French terminology? I did. It's quite amusing, don't you think? Mother, stripped of her Continental pretensions for once."

She laughed, but there was no humor in it.

"And there's something else, Hugo, which is very funny. Do you remember the Greek myth of King Midas?"

"Of course. The chap whose daughter was turned to gold."

"Yes, that's right. The god Dionysus granted him a wish, and he asked for the ability to turn anything he touched into gold. He was warned to be careful in his wish, but he ignored it."

"And so?"

"And so, when you had the good sense to refuse my father's offer to handle your financial affairs, I was too busy enjoying the idea that I finally had a wedge to keep my parents at bay—to insist they not come to London with us—when I should have paid more attention to my father's nonsense. And after I agreed to allow him to manage my money, when they made mention of joining us for *next* year's Season, all I could think was how it would never, ever happen." She gave that same humorless laugh. "My income is gone. We'll never be able to come back. So now, like King Midas, I've gotten what I wished for."

"Katherine, none of this is your fault."

"And yet here I am." She jumped to her feet and began pacing around the room, her fingers clenched into fists, eyebrows drawn tight together, and rather irrelevantly Hugo found himself recalling Gwendolyn's remark about Bertram waving her fan above his head to indicate *I am thinking hard.* But of course he didn't say anything about that. He simply sat and watched as Katherine stalked back and forth; he waited. Waited until he had a better understanding of how he might help her.

Katherine went on pacing, silent, fierce, abstracted, until abruptly she came to a halt. She remained like that, motionless, for what seemed like hours to Hugo but could only in reality have been a few minutes. Then she came back to the sofa, snatched up the letter, and crumpled it into a tiny ball.

"Hugo," she said in a hard flat voice, "I want to do something."

"What is it, Katherine?" he answered calmly.

"I want to sell all the jewelry I bought, back to Rundell and Bridge. I want to sell the extra carriages. I want you to sell the horses we won't need anymore. Can you find good owners for them?"

"Between Cousin Judith and myself, I'm sure we can."

"Good. Lady Mainwaring—how funny that I was mentioning her only last night—has started a charity for war widows, and I want to donate most of my clothing and shoes, and all those other things—the hats and shawls and so forth—to it."

"As you like, Katherine." This was leading to an obvious conclusion about their time here in London, but it would be cruel for him to thrust it upon her. So he would wait for her to voice it; for her to own it when she was able.

"I want to release all the servants back to the Dauntrey Agency as soon as possible."

"Yes."

"Then I'm going to sell back all the books I've bought in London."

He knew how much that sacrifice in particular had to hurt her, but he only nodded.

"And then, when all of it is done, I want to take whatever money I have, Hugo, and I want to send it all to my parents. I *hate* their money. I want to get rid of it forever. It's like a sickness, and it's been killing me for years. And now I want them to have it all back."

"Fine."

"Oh, Hugo, it's not fine. It's not fine at all."

An image came to her. A blank page. And then a hand, a pot of ink, a quill moving across the white expanse:

What is a story without unexpected occurrences? Our heroine really ought to have anticipated them. Things had been going so well for her; it was, perhaps, inevitable. So now, in a sudden twist, she's been stripped of—is letting go of—her wealth. The money which, for many years, has defined her. "The Brooke heiress" no more. Who is she, then? Who is she now? She recalls yet another grim tale from Greek mythology. Icarus, who in wings of wax and feathers had recklessly flown too close to the sun. Then—inevitably—plunged to his death. Our heroine is not dead. Far from it. But her circumstances have most certainly been altered. What will she do in this new chapter of hers?

Calmly Hugo said, breaking into her thoughts, "Why isn't it fine, Katherine?"

"Oh my God, don't you see?" she answered, hearing in her own ears how harsh her voice was. "I'll be poor." Even as she said the words a deep and blinding grief barreled at her like a storm. Katherine looked down into his handsome face, and made herself say, in a torrent of brutally honest words:

"Oh, Hugo, I'm sorry. I know you only married me for my money, and soon it will all be gone. I should never have asked you to marry me. You should have come to

London and found someone else, someone better. I'm sure your Aunt Henrietta would have helped you, or Cousin Judith. I'm so sorry. I know you wish you hadn't married me."

"I don't wish that at all."

"What?"

"I'm glad I married you." Hugo reached up, took her hands in a warm clasp, and drew her down to sit next to him on the sofa.

"But—" She was staring at him. The grief seemed to whistle through her, like a cold wind filling up an empty ravine. "But the money. Once it's gone, there will be no more."

"I understand that."

Katherine gave her head a little, baffled shake. "What will I do with myself then? The Brookes are all about money, Hugo, that's what we do. Make it, spend it, think about it, want more of it."

"But you're not a Brooke anymore, are you."

Not a Brooke? A Brooke no more? *What will our heroine do in this new chapter of hers?* Katherine looked down at Hugo's hands holding hers, then back up into his eyes. It seemed impossible to believe that he wasn't sorry; that he was glad. It was like saying, "Up is down, white is black, fish can walk, and pigs *can* fly." But there was no time to think about it, she had to set her plan in motion, and right away, she couldn't rest until the damned money was gone. Fiercely she gripped his wrists. "No matter what happens, you're not to touch your mother's funds. Or the children's. Promise me that."

"I promise," he said, and that, at least, she could believe. She nodded, and at last said the other words that had to be spoken:

"We must leave London."

"Yes."

"Where will we go?" But even as she said it, the answer

came to her. It was pragmatic. It was inevitable. Once she had said to Hugo, *I loathe Whitehaven.* Here again was a case in which her words had come back to haunt her. But there was no time to think about that, either. "Is there room for us in your house?"

"Yes. Plenty."

"You're sure?"

"Yes."

"Then that's where we'll go." *To Whitehaven. There's nothing for me there. Nothing.* She pulled her hands free to cover her face with them. To hide her expression. To conceal her grief. Her agony.

"Katherine."

She didn't lift her head. "Yes?"

"We'll get through this."

"Will we?" She felt her mouth curving in a smile that wasn't a smile. "Will we indeed?"

Chapter 15

Mrs. Serena Dauntrey, of the prestigious Dauntrey Employment Agency on Harley Street, looked across her desk at Mrs. Katherine Penhallow. She had previously only corresponded with Mrs. Penhallow, the newest relation of the redoubtable Mrs. Henrietta Penhallow, whose townhouse in Berkeley Square she'd had the honor of staffing the previous Season. Of course Serena knew all about Mrs. Katherine Penhallow's remarkable second Season, and also she was aware that there had been some kind of mysterious alteration in Mrs. Penhallow's financial affairs; she made it her business to keep abreast of the happenings in the *haut ton*. Not that she would mention it, of course. Discretion, in her line of work, was paramount. She said:

"How may I be of service to you, Mrs. Penhallow?"

"I must release by the end of the week all the servants I engaged in April. They've been given three months' severance pay as well as letters of recommendation. I've written out copies of the letters, which you may wish to keep for your files."

Mrs. Penhallow extended a soft leather document folder which Serena accepted with a surprise she hoped didn't show. Not every employer was as generous under such circumstances. She looked a little more closely at Mrs. Penhallow, observing the pallor of her complexion, the dark circles beneath her eyes, which perhaps suggested the strain under which she labored. Yet Mrs. Penhallow was dignified and civil. She was wearing a simple pelisse of deep plum, and over her dark curls, an equally unfussy hat of the same rich color which complemented her vivid looks. The reports Serena had heard described her—quite accurately, it turned out—as a very striking young lady, something not in the common way at all.

Serena put the document folder onto the tidy surface of the desk at which she sat. "Thank you, Mrs. Penhallow. It's very kind of you. Is there anything else I might do for you?"

"A reassurance that you'll be able to find congenial new positions for the staff would be most welcome."

"I have no doubt of it, ma'am. It's something upon which I pride myself."

"Excellent." Mrs. Penhallow rose to her feet. "Thank you, Mrs. Dauntrey."

"Thank *you*, ma'am," Serena said, standing also, and added, with an impulsiveness which was unusual for her, "I do hope to work with you again."

A shadow seemed to come over Mrs. Penhallow's face, but she only said, with the same civility, "Thank you. Good day to you," and then she was gone.

Within a matter of days, their life in London was taken apart—disassembled with the speed and efficiency of a child's puzzle. Naturally Katherine was not the first person whose financial issues were resolved by a rapid sell-off of assets, and it all turned out to be very easy. Harder, perhaps, had been receiving the influx of visitors to the townhouse. A few had come, she knew, to gawk and to carry away gossip, but quite a few others had come to say goodbye and to wish them well. She had, Katherine learned to her surprise, more friends in London than she had realized. Cousin Judith, the Duchess of Egremont, had even hugged her, said, in her kind, abrupt way, "You're a good girl," adding, "Don't worry about the horses, they'll be grand," and had gone off with her customary long strides, quite possibly in search of her maddening and erratic grandson Philip Thane, whose whereabouts—following his brief, scandalous appearance at the DeWitts' ball—were at present unknown.

---

13 June 1812

Mother,
    I enclose herewith a cheque. It's all that I have; there's nothing left.
    Adieu.

                                    Katherine

The night before they were to leave London, they lay in the bed where they had shared so much pleasure, so much joy. Hugo turned to Katherine in the darkness; her face was a pale ghostly oval.

She said, "Hugo, are you there?"

A question, he knew, that meant far more than was he simply in the bed next to her.

"Yes. Is there anything I can do for you?"

"No. Hugo, that time back in Canada, when you were shot, what did it feel like?"

"There was a pain, very sharp, in my chest."

"Did you feel as if you were coming apart?"

"No. Not then. Later, though, when the fever took me, I remember feeling as if I'd somehow been detached from the universe. Separated from myself."

"Yes."

"Is that how you feel now, Katherine?"

"Yes, Hugo."

"I'm sorry. But I'm here."

"I know that. Thank you," and he heard the little wobble in her voice, but did not comment upon it, and so the long night wound its slow, slow way along.

It took them a week, traveling to the north and to the west. Past Oxford, past Stratford-on-Avon, through Coventry and Birmingham; past the Peak District, through Manchester, then through the Forest of Bowland and the Lake District. Katherine made no complaint, submitted to the long hours in the carriage, did not remark upon the modest nature of the inns at which they stayed, quietly ate her meals and promptly made herself ready each day. She did not read, Hugo observed, only sat straight as an arrow in the carriage, looking out the window, day by day growing more and more silent. More remote. Her lovely face, Hugo thought, like a graven mask. He knew she was hurting, he ached for her in his soul. But sometimes, he knew, words could do nothing. Sometimes you simply had to wait, and watch, and hope.

The carriage wheels turned, as if without end. Idly Katherine pictured them going round and round, and imagined that in their monotonous rumble she could hear them mocking her, saying—echoing what Gabriel Penhallow had said that evening at Surmont Hall—*to the ocean, to the ocean.* Toward nothing. Inside her was nothing, too. A kind of vast white expanse.

A blank page.

On the sixth day they came into Cumbria, and Hugo fancied he could already catch the familiar tang of salt air.

He found himself listening for the sounds of the waves; he wanted to hurry their horses along.

But he didn't. Because patience, he knew, is a virtue.

It was on the seventh day that they came at last into Whitehaven, and to the big old house on the beach—its windows now clean and sparkling, Hugo noticed with pleasure, the crumbling reddish clay bricks replaced with new ones, and the roof, as Gwendolyn had mentioned, now solid and sturdy. Altogether, he thought, the dear old place looked wonderfully well-kept. It had always been loved, but now it looked it. As he and Katherine walked toward the portico, the front door opened and out tumbled Gwendolyn, joyfully calling his name and wearing, he could see at a glance, a pretty new gown; she was followed at a slightly more decorous pace by Mama and Bertram. Here, he thought, smiling at them, glancing at Katherine, thinking of Francis and Percy, Grandpapa and the aunts—here was everything he needed. Here was everything.

Nothing, nothing, nothing. "Thank you for your hospitality, ma'am," said Katherine to Hugo's mother, doing her best to keep her voice from sounding wooden. "It's kind of you to have us."

"It's not kind at all," said Hugo's mama, smiling. "It's an entirely selfish happiness. I'm so glad you're both here! Oh, welcome home, both of you," and she turned to Hugo and enveloped him, as best as she could given his great height, in a comprehensive hug. He hugged her back, and then Gwendolyn said, "Oh, Hugo!" and threw herself into his arms. "We missed you *terribly.*"

Standing a little aside, Katherine watched, feeling, perhaps, as lonely as she ever had in her life. Maybe even lonelier. Outsiderness. The same old story.

They lay in their bed. The long bank of windows, facing the shore, had been left open to admit a pleasant evening breeze, and Hugo could just see the white curtains fluttering a little. To his ears came the old, familiar, primeval rumble of the ocean; his blood seemed almost to sing with it.

Home. He was home again.

Then: the mattress shifted, bedclothes rustled.

"Are you there, Hugo?"

"Yes. Is there something you need?"

"No. Thank you." And then Katherine fell silent again.

---

17 June 1812

Dear Hugo,

Thank you for your letter regarding your departure from the townhouse. You didn't elaborate on the circumstances surrounding the removal, but rumors have reached me from London regarding the re-sale of jewels, carriages sold, and so on. Have you and Katherine suffered some kind of catastrophic financial setback? And if that is the case, what can I do to help? If you require assistance—pecuniary or otherwise—please do not hesitate to ask.

Affectionately yours,
Aunt Henrietta

P.S. A report has also reached me as to Katherine's magnanimous gift to Lady Mainwaring's war-widow charity. Here I must observe that Katherine seems to be developing a habit of discarding entire wardrobes at a stroke. Nonetheless, as by so doing she is assisting a great many of those in need, such gestures, however eccentric, can only be lauded. Indeed, Katherine may not know it, but apparently she has launched a trend in London—almost an avalanche one might say. So many women of the haut ton have donated to Lady Mainwaring such vast quantities of clothing and the various accouterments that she has had to scramble mightily to find extra storage space to accommodate it all.

---

17 June 1812

Dear Katherine,

Granny mentioned that you and Hugo encountered some unforeseen circumstances in London and are now reestablished in Whitehaven. She didn't go into detail but I must confess to feeling concerned. Are you both all right? Is there anything I can do?

I hope that my other letters, sent to you while you were in London, arrived safely? Please do write back if you have the time. It would be lovely to hear from you.

Yours most sincerely,
Livia

---

5 July 1812

Dear Aunt Henrietta,

Thanks very much for your letter. It's awfully kind of you to offer to help. Please be assured that we're all right in the way of money—not just Katherine and myself, but also my mother and my sister and brothers. As you might guess, the whole thing's been wretchedly difficult for Katherine, but she soldiers on. Pluck to the backbone.

Trust all's well at the Hall.

With affection and gratitude,
Hugo

---

19 July 1812

Dearest Percy and darling Francis,

We all enjoyed your latest letters. We miss you dreadfully but are also glad you're having a splendid time in Northamptonshire. Owen sounds so nice. I'm sorry you find his sister Helen such a nuisance, Francis. I wonder why she trails after you and pesters you so?

It is lovely to have Hugo home again. I'm not quite sure what to say about Katherine. I had been looking forward to having a sister, but now . . . Please, please, don't tell anyone else, but now I'm not so sure. Hugo belongs to her now, doesn't he? I hadn't thought of this before. It makes me feel, well, rather like an outsider.

It must be dreadful to be rich and then suddenly not, don't you think? Hugo doesn't seem to mind it, but of course he was only like that for six months or so. He has been over at Grandpapa's church quite a bit lately, helping the laborers fit in the new stained-glass windows which Mr. Beck has so kindly donated, and Grandpapa says if it weren't for Hugo he's sure several of them would already have been broken. Also Hugo goes over to the wharves as he used to do when he was a boy, just to look he says, but Mama has made him solemnly promise not to sign on as a sailor. He agreed, although Mama said afterwards that there was something in his eyes that made her so nervous she actually brought out our Bible and had him swear upon it, which made Hugo laugh.

Speaking of the wharves, Hugo told me I'm not to wander alone there anymore, which is annoying as they are terribly fascinating. They simply reek of adventure.

Love always,
Gwendolyn

P.S. Bertram blew up one of the attics again. But most luckily he didn't lose any more fingers. His hair was completely black for an entire week and Mama had to wash it ELEVEN TIMES until it was back to normal.

P.P.S. Diana has just come over and I shared this letter with her. She says that Helen probably likes you, Francis. I find that difficult to believe. If she likes you, why is she always trying to pinch you?

Hugo looked around the table. Grandpapa, Aunt Verena, and Aunt Claudia had come for dinner, as they did at least once a week, and his enjoyment would have been complete had it not been for the still, set expression on Katherine's face. Not that it was new. She'd had it for weeks now. Quiet, polite, detached, she moved restlessly around the house—on the beach—as if she were here and yet not-here. It was painful to see.

"Kiss me, you saucy wench," suddenly uttered Señor Rodrigo from his perch near the fireplace, and Aunt Claudia put down her knife and fork to turn and look at him.

"I'd love to sketch him," she said in her dreamy way.

"Good gracious, why?" retorted Aunt Verena. "It would hardly be decent, given his scandalous lack of plumage."

"Oh, but he has such *personality,* Verena dear." Aunt Claudia was undeterred. "Only see what a lively look he has."

"No doubt he's still enjoying the fact that he almost took my finger off an hour ago," answered Aunt Verena sourly.

Señor Rodrigo giggled, and Gwendolyn put in from across the table:

"Oh, Aunt, it's quite possible you offended poor Rodrigo when you called him 'a great ugly thing.' He's very sensitive, you know."

"Sensitive?" Aunt Verena gave a sardonic laugh. "If that animal is sensitive, then I'm the Empress of France."

"Speaking of animals," said Bertram, seated to her right, "I read a very interesting article last year in the Royal Society's *Philosophical Transactions* which argued that humans' place in the Great Chain of Being should be on par with both wild and domesticated animals, rather than claiming a more elevated status."

Aunt Verena frowned. "It sounds highly irreligious."

Grandpapa, a vicar for nearly all of his adult life, gently cleared his throat. "I lent Bertram my copy of the journal."

"Francis read the article also," Bertram said, "and so did Mama."

Aunt Verena's frown deepened, and from his perch Señor Rodrigo remarked, "Ho, bilged on her anchor," and reached up a sharp prehensile claw to scratch at his head.

"I'd love to sketch Katherine, too," pursued Aunt Claudia, turning her dreamy gaze to the foot of the table where Katherine sat looking at her plate, on which reposed a generous slice of Cook's excellent roasted chicken, small boiled potatoes in a tangy mustard sauce, and a wedge of spinach pie. She was looking, though Hugo was fairly certain she wasn't seeing it. She gave the impression, rather, that she was listening intently to something, but not necessarily the conversation at the table.

"A sketch first," Aunt Claudia went on, "and then I should like to paint Katherine. In oils. Not watercolors. Only oils could do justice to her personality."

"As you are interested in personality," said Aunt Verena, "perhaps you could paint both Katherine *and* the bird."

The suggestion was obviously a sarcastic one, but Aunt Claudia slowly nodded, without taking her eyes from Katherine. "The brilliant green of Rodrigo's feathers, contrasted with Katherine's dark, dark hair . . . How beautifully it gleams. What a marvelous idea. Would Rodrigo sit for me, I wonder? How clever of you to propose it, Verena dear."

"If he *had* any feathers."

"You must envision what could be," said Aunt Claudia to her sister, still thoughtfully studying Katherine. "The possibility of things. Perhaps after dinner you might permit me to begin a sketch, Katherine? There will still be plenty of light."

It came to Katherine at last. That image of the blank page—empty, frightening—had gradually given way to something else. She imagined that inside her was a swarm of bees, stinging bees, buzzing, swirling, colliding, as if creating a low dreadful hum to which one would have to listen all day long.

"Would you let me do that, Katherine dear?"

She jumped at the sound of her name and quickly she looked down the table at Hugo's aunt who was smiling at her. Which one was it, Verena or Claudia? Why did they have to be identical twins? (How curious, just like Percy and Francis.) These two here, the aunts—older sisters to Hugo's mama, both of them unwed and living with their father Mr. Mantel in the parsonage—seemed to be strikingly different in nature, one very soft and vague, the other alert and rather crisp. Katherine answered, "Would I let you do what, ma'am?"

"Sketch you, dear, after dinner. I'd like that ever so much."

So one of the aunts—it had to be Claudia—wanted to sketch her. Why? Was she good at drawing bees? Katherine knew that her mouth was curving in a small, bitter smile, but before she could answer there was a sudden hush in the dining-parlor, one of those odd, awkward conversational lulls that occur seemingly at random, and then Bertram said, as if unaware of it, or that he was coming to Katherine's rescue:

"There was also a very good article in that issue of *Philosophical Transactions* which discussed Molyneux's Problem. Did you read it, Grandpapa? Or you, Mama?"

Mr. Mantel replied that he had, and enjoyed it, and Hugo's mama said she had too, although there was a reference to John Locke which she had thought not quite correct, and Gwendolyn turned to Hugo, to ask if they could go riding tomorrow, and Aunt Claudia was now gazing at that poor scrawny parrot, who was chuckling under his breath, and the maid Eliza came into the room, to clear away the plates, and Bertram said, having agreed with his mother about the John Locke reference:

"The text should have read 'No innate principles,' but perhaps it was a typographer's error. Hugo, shall we go for a swim once we've had our dessert?"

"A dreadful idea," said Aunt Verena, who wore an old-fashioned lawn fichu and over her graying blonde hair a lace cap of severe design which only accentuated the stern handsomeness of her face. "Don't you remember that custom officer's child who nearly drowned last fall?"

"Yes, Aunt, but the waves were rough and Tom had

been warned to stay away, only he didn't listen. They're not like that today."

"It's dreadfully unfair that girls aren't supposed to swim in the ocean." This from Gwendolyn, her pretty face gone sulky.

"There are bathing machines," remarked Aunt Claudia, whose slender hands showed faint splotches of color as she gestured in the air, as if outlining the shape of those famously bulky conveyances. "In places like Brighton and Margate."

"Oh, I'd love to try that," said Mrs. Penhallow. "Cook says the butcher's wife told her they're hoping to bring some to Seascale."

"That's fifteen miles away," objected Gwendolyn. "And it doesn't help me *today*. Hugo, mayn't I come with you and Bertram?"

"Oh, but dearest, you promised to go with Aunt Verena to visit Mrs. Quent," Mrs. Penhallow said. "Poor old soul, laid up like that with a summer's ague. She's had a terrible time of it."

"Aunt Verena won't mind if I go to the beach with Hugo and Bertram." Gwendolyn looked appealingly across the table. "Will you, Aunt?"

"Yes, I will. A promise is a promise."

"Oh, but I want so much to try swimming." Gwendolyn clasped her fingers together at her breast and somehow managed to make her blue eyes twice as big. "Please, Aunt? I'll go with you another day."

"You needn't try your wiles on me, missy." Verena was unmoved. "I told Mrs. Quent yesterday you were coming with me next time, and she said how much she was looking forward to it."

Gwendolyn looked between her mother and Hugo, but getting no response from either of them, dropped her clasped fingers and replied rather sullenly, "Very well then, I'll go. But I still say it isn't fair."

Just then Señor Rodrigo squawked and said, "Thar she blows," as if to herald Eliza's return with dessert, big bowls of strawberries and raspberries, a pitcher of cream, walnuts and raisins, and a platter of light, delicate rolled wafers.

Mr. Mantel exclaimed over the bounty, and Claudia said, bringing together her delicate, paint-splotched hands, to make a little temple of them on which she rested her chin: "Summer agues are dreadful, aren't they? I had one last August, and I do believe that's why the influenza laid me so low in November."

"That may be, but if you'll recall, I told you not to go wandering about when the wind changed in October," responded her sister with a frown. "Yet you insisted on taking your easel to the shore."

"The light on the water was so beautiful. The waves were shimmering . . ." Absently Claudia accepted from Verena a bowl of fruit and cream. "The colors, my dear. The greens and grays! I had to try and capture them."

"Eat your dessert," Verena said. "Every drop of the cream, mind you."

Obediently Claudia picked up her spoon, and the talk drifted on, shifting into a discussion of modern medicine and thence to some of the really interesting diseases Hugo had seen while abroad as well as Mr. Mantel mentioning his theories about bodily manifestations of what he termed soul-sickness, a complicated metaphysical topic which evoked a veritable storm of questions from Gwendolyn and Bertram, and it occurred to Katherine that she might well have had some of her own, if only it weren't for the bees inside her, which roiled and stormed, swarmed and raged, and she clenched her fingers on the napkin in her lap, half-wondering if emanating from her very pores was a low, revealing buzzing sound.

It seemed to take a long time until dinner was over. "Well, Gwendolyn," said Verena briskly, standing up, "get your bonnet and let's be on our way," and Aunt Claudia meandered over to talk to Señor Rodrigo, and Mr. Mantel was telling Hugo about a subscription to a relief fund he was organizing, and Hugo's mama was looking anxiously at the dessert Katherine had been unable to eat (so full as she was already with bees), and then an idea flashed into Katherine's head. Abruptly she pushed back her chair, put her napkin on the table, said "Excuse me, please," and left the room. In the passageway the dogs were patiently ranged and they all got to their feet as she came in. But she didn't stop, she went on to the stairs and up them, to the wide landing, and down the long private corridor that led to the room she shared with Hugo.

She went inside, shut the door, and went to a trunk that she had yet to unpack. She crouched down and flung open the lid.

Chapter 16

Hugo had watched Katherine leave the dining-parlor, looking so determined, so fierce, that he stood up and took a long step after her, pausing but briefly when Bertram said, "Hugo, shall we go to the beach?" He replied, "Perhaps a bit later, Bertie," clapped him on the shoulder, and continued on his way.

At the closed door to their bedchamber, he paused again and knocked upon it.

"Who is it?"

"It's me."

"What do you want?"

"May I come in?"

A silence. "Are you sure you want to?"

"Yes."

Another silence. Then: "Very well."

Hugo opened the door and went in. Katherine was sitting on the floor, in her hands her old steel-framed corset and a small pair of scissors. Here and there, between the metal ribs, the fabric had been cut apart. She looked up at him defiantly; he said curiously, "What are you doing?"

"I'm destroying this ghastly thing."

"I didn't know you still had it."

"I forgot all about it till just now."

"Ah. May I sit down with you?"

"Do you want to?"

"Yes."

Katherine pushed aside a little box to make room for him, and he sat next to her on the wood floor. "What's in that box?"

"It's a sewing kit my mother must have had packed before I left Brooke House. Even though I hate sewing almost more than I hate this corset." She jabbed at the fabric and cut another jagged wedge between the ribs. "Oh, Hugo, I'm so *angry*."

"About what?"

"About everything, it feels like."

"Well, you have plenty to be angry about."

She cut another wedge, then looked up at him. "Do you think so? Really?"

"My God, yes."

She studied him intently. Her dark eyes were brilliant, alive, in her white face. "The funny thing is," she said, very slowly and deliberately, "it's not about the money being gone. It's a relief, it really and truly is. I was at the beach the other day, it was sunny out and I could see the fools' gold glittering in the water. And I thought, that's all it was, the Brooke money—fools' gold. Goodbye and good riddance." She drew a deep, deep breath. "But it's just that—oh, God, Hugo, that letter from my mother—I still feel that what I did was right, to get rid of all the money, but I'm also still angry. *So* angry. I feel like—oh, as if a rug's been jerked out from under my feet. Have you ever felt that way?"

"Of course. After Father died, I was grieving, but I was angry, too. Furious at the world. A common reaction, I daresay, when things happen beyond our control."

"How did you get through it?"

"For a while I simply shut down. Wouldn't even look at a book, or write papers or whatever. Once I stole a horse and tried to run away. It got bad enough that eventually the headmaster wrote home about it. Then Grandpapa wrote me a letter that helped."

"What did he say?"

"For one thing, he and Mama both agreed I could leave school if I wanted to. It gave me a choice, you see. For another thing, he said that it's his firm belief that we're never given more than we can handle. And that he had faith in me. That's all. He's never one to force his views. But it was enough to help shift me—help me climb out of the hole, bit by bit."

Katherine was silent for a while. She looked down at the corset and then back up at him. In a low, small voice she said, "Do you have faith in me, Hugo?"

"Yes."

"Why?"

"Because you're one of the strongest people I've ever known."

"Really?"

"Yes."

"You think I'm strong?"

"Yes, I do. Life's been hard to you in a lot of ways. But it hasn't broken you. And it's made you who are you are today."

Katherine had been looking at him with that same intentness, and now she lowered her gaze again to the corset. "Do you think it's stupid of me to destroy this?"

"No."

She cut another wedge of fabric, but with less violence now. Then she paused. "Hugo."

"Yes, Katherine?"

"On a more practical note, I can see how these steel bands are going to be a problem."

"Yes."

"Do you have any suggestions?"

Hugo thought for a few moments. He said, "Do you remember my tin soldiers?" He watched as her dark brows drew together and then cleared as she answered, and with just the tiniest lilt of humor in her voice:

"Oh, Hugo, I *do* remember! We pretended they were Vikings, and gave them a burial at sea."

"That's right. I made a little raft for them, you made a fire out of yellow and red paper, and we let them sail away."

"Let's do that. Can we? Right now?"

"By all means."

Katherine scrambled to her feet. "Let's go."

Ten minutes later, they stood side by side on the broad sandy shore. The sun, a great orange ball in the sky, was slowly making its way down toward the horizon and a little breeze played around them, rippling the hem of Katherine's gown and sending her curls softly aflutter. Never had she looked so lovely as she did now, Hugo thought, in her simple cream-colored dress, and her big dark eyes sparkling. In one hand she held the old steel corset.

"Are you ready, Hugo?"

"I am."

She lifted it up. "Goodbye, you dreadful thing," she said, and with a tremendous heave she sent the corset flying into the ocean. It splashed, then bobbed gently in a receding wave. With satisfaction Katherine said, "The tide's going out."

"Yes. Shall we sit?" He had brought with them an old blanket which he'd spread on the sand, and together they went to it and sat down, Katherine keeping her eyes fixed on the corset as it drifted away. The sun sank a little lower and sent its warm orange-gold radiance more fully upon the ever-shifting sea.

"What are you doing?" It was Bertram, standing next to him. "What are you looking at?"

Hugo hesitated, not wishing to intrude upon Katherine's privacy. But she said calmly:

"It's an old corset of mine, Bertram, which I wanted to get rid of. Do you see it there? All gray and sodden?"

Bertram stared. Then he nodded. "I see it. Why didn't you put it in the rubbish heap? Wouldn't that have been more efficient?"

"Because I wanted the ocean to swallow it up. I'm symbolically doing away with my old life. The cage of my old life."

"Do you mean that although the end result is the same, this method is more pleasing to you?"

"Yes, that's it."

Bertram nodded again, and Katherine added, "Would you like to join us?"

"Is there room for me?"

"Absolutely," she said, and moved aside, toward the edge of the blanket. Hugo brought himself closer to her and Bertram sat down next to him, folding his long thin legs underneath him as might a Buddhist monk. The three of them sat in companionable silence for a while, shoulder to shoulder. Dreamily Katherine said:

"I wonder where it will end up. Do you think it might make it all the way to Australia, or Japan?"

"If it doesn't sink," said Bertram, "the Gulf Stream is more likely to carry it to Iceland or Norway."

"Yes, of course," answered Katherine. "The North Atlantic Drift. I should have thought of that."

"There was a very interesting article in the *Popular Journal of Knowledge* which describes Juan Ponce de León's sixteenth-century discovery of oceanic circular currents," Bertram said, and soon he and Katherine were discussing wind patterns, the Gulf of Mexico, gyres, and hurricanes. Hugo said nothing, only listened, and faintly, very faintly, he smiled.

Late that night, into the darkness came her voice, softly. "Hugo."

He stirred at once. Drowsily: "Yes, Katherine?"

"Do you remember once telling me—no, *suggesting* to me—that I should be who I am?"

"Yes, at that inn. The night before Surmont Hall."

"That's right. And as we were leaving the Hall, your Aunt Henrietta said to me, 'To thine own self be true.' How curious—like bookends to our visit there." She gave a long sigh. "I'd like to be who I am, Hugo, but I don't know how to."

"You'll find out."

"Do you really think so?"

"Yes."

She was silent for a while. Then: "I hope you're right. Can you do something for me?"

"Yes. What is it?"

"Would you mind opening the windows very wide? I want to hear the ocean."

"Of course." Hugo got up, did as she asked. Into their room wended a silken breeze, cool but not unpleasant, and the sounds of the sea, too, rumbling, murmuring, lapping at the shore, steady and rhythmic, eternal and unchanging. "Is this what you want, Katherine?"

"Yes. Will you come back to bed?"

He did. And she said:

"Will you make love to me?"

"You want me to?"

"Yes. I'm sad right now, and also scared. But that doesn't stop me from wanting you. If you know what I mean?"

"I think I do," Hugo said, and then Katherine drew close to him. Gently he kissed her, gently he touched her here, there, everywhere, and wordlessly she opened herself up to him. In turn he gave himself to her, quietly, tenderly, without hurry, with a passion that for them both rose and built and crested; afterwards they slept close together, sheltered underneath the warm bedclothes as the cool breeze of night swirled into their room, and the eternal sounds of the ocean played on.

He was deeply asleep when this time she said into his ear: "Hugo." He opened his eyes to see, in the soft gray light of dawn, Katherine sitting on the side of the bed, already dressed and a warm shawl around her shoulders. He smiled, stretched, said, still sleepily, "You're up early."

"Yes. I'm going down to the beach. I want to make sure the corset is really and truly gone. Would you like to come with me?"

"Of course."

And in a few minutes they were back on the shore. Hugo had let the dogs come with them, and all six of them—another one had recently joined the household, a puppy Gwendolyn had found, half-starved, on her way back from Mrs. Quent's house, and brought home with her—all six of the dogs, despite their various infirmities, romped together on the sand.

"Do you see it, Katherine?"

"No. It's gone forever. On its way to Iceland."

Hugo laughed. "Or Norway."

"Yes. Oh, Hugo, look." Katherine stooped, picked something up. She held it out to him. A piece of sea-glass, cornflower-blue, rounded and translucent in the morning light. "I used to love collecting these."

"I remember. This is a rare piece, too. This blue color."

"Yes. It's like the color of your eyes. I'm going to keep it. Are you ready for breakfast?"

"Very. Shall we go in?"

"Yes."

And together they went inside, the dogs frisking happily at their heels.

Shyly Katherine stood at the entrance to the sunny little parlor where Hugo's mama was often to be found in the mornings. And there she was, sitting in a chair drawn close to an open window, her hair, still golden, shining brightly underneath its little frilly wisp of a lace cap; her head was bent over a large piece of dark blue fabric and her needle flashed in and out of a long seam she was sewing.

"Ma'am?" said Katherine, and Hugo's mama looked up, saying in her soft, pleasant way:

"Come in, Katherine. Is there something I can do for you?"

"Actually, ma'am, I was wondering if there was something I can do for *you*."

"For me?" Mrs. Penhallow smiled. "Thank you, my dear, how very kind. There's nothing, really. Although— I've been sewing these gowns for the girls at the charity home. So many are needed! Would you like to help with that?"

Katherine repressed a sigh. Of course it would have to be sewing. She said, "I'll be glad to, ma'am."

"Oh, that would be lovely! Do come in, please, and sit next to me here."

An hour later, having wrestled with two big rectangular lengths of heavy cotton, unpicked half a dozen irregular seams, twice sewn two armholes backwards, and several times pricked her fingers till they were bloody, Katherine did sigh, looking at the wrinkled mass in her lap and then over at Mrs. Penhallow.

"Ma'am," she said, "do you suppose there's anything else I might do to be helpful?"

Mrs. Penhallow glanced up, her gaze going to the mangled would-be gown which Katherine ruefully held up for her inspection. "I'm afraid I'm not much of a seamstress."

"Oh, my dear, I'm sorry, I should never have asked you."

"Rather, I should never have said yes."

Mrs. Penhallow laughed. "We're not all born to embrace the needle. I like it, but that doesn't mean you must."

"Thank you, ma'am. Is there anything else I can do?"

"Let me think." Mrs. Penhallow was silent for a few moments, then said, a little doubtfully, "There *is* something. I'm so busy with these gowns! But I wonder if it might be tedious for you. Papa—my father—has written several letters of appeal to potential benefactors, and as he often does, has asked me to look over his drafts. He says his mind moves more quickly than his quill, and so quite often his writing isn't as polished as he would wish."

"I'd be happy to do that," said Katherine, and it was true. How infinitely better a task than sewing!

"They're on my little escritoire—do you see them? Please feel free to mark up any phrases or sentences you think aren't quite up to snuff. Papa won't mind. In fact, I'm sure he'll be grateful to you."

At once Katherine rose and set aside the wad of fabric, and went to sit at Mrs. Penhallow's escritoire. She heard, from outside, birds singing. The far-off voice of old Hoyt talking affectionately to one of the horses. Eliza, in the corridor, softly humming as she went. Katherine picked up the first letter. She began to read. A little later she lifted up the lid of the inkpot and into it she dipped a quill. Carefully, in the margins, she began to write.

Hugo walked along Duke Street toward the harbor, whistling a little. His left leg, he noticed cheerfully, hurt him not at all these days. It was a bright, clear day and the wharves were busy and noisy, the sounds of human voices intercut with the loud, distinctive cries of the gulls.

He stepped onto the old stone quay where two collier-boats lay at anchor, a dozen or so brawny men loading them with coal. Beyond the colliers, further out in the harbor, were several long, low smacks, back from a fishing run, and a successful one: the wells were crowded with mackerel. A flat-bottomed ketch was maneuvering its way out toward the open sea, and alongside the quay beyond that, two low hay-boats lay ready for departure, the tall stacks of baled hay well-covered with tarps.

He looked over to the next quay, where a dry-dock floated. A new ship was in the process of being constructed, long, triple-masted, with a deep and capacious hold. He was eyeing it thoughtfully when someone said:

"A beauty, isn't she?"

A stout middle-aged man had come to stand next to him, a little rumpled in his old-fashioned jacket and breeches, but his eyes keen and alert in his sun-browned face.

"It is," answered Hugo, "but there's a problem with the rigging."

The other man's look sharpened. "How so?"

"Do you see how the spars aren't precisely perpendicular to the keel and the masts? It'll slow her down."

"By God, you're right," said the other man, frowning. "They're not square."

"Which means the primary driving sails won't function properly."

"Well, I'll be damned. You're a Navy man? You've the look of the military about you."

"Army," said Hugo, holding out his hand. "Eight years in the Americas. Captain Hugo Penhallow, sir, at your service."

The other man shook his hand with a firm grip. "Will Studdart. Newly arrived, formerly of Liverpool. I've seen you around here quite a bit, Captain. Looking at the ships. Fond of 'em?"

Hugo nodded. "Very."

"You live here, then?"

"Yes. Whitehaven born and bred."

"Know the winds and tides?"

Hugo nodded again. "I spent so much time here as a boy it's in my blood, seems like."

"Looking to buy a sailboat, are you? For the summer months?"

"That's a grand idea, but no." He smiled. "To own the truth, sir, I come here to daydream, I suppose. There were times, back then, when I'd have sold my very eyeteeth to become a sailor."

Will Studdart looked at him consideringly. Then he said, his voice casual: "So how would you fix those spars?"

Hugo thought about it. "It would be tempting to try and leave them in and adjust them by the pin connections only, but you'd risk an inexact fix. I'd take them off and start over again. It would take longer, but it's bound to produce a better result."

"I agree. What would you do if the keel started to over-balance once the masts were all in place?"

"I'd take a hard look at its central timber and its rela-tionship to the hull."

"And if it was faulty?"

"Well, you could try to set it correctly again, using blocks, but if it's not completely right you should dis-mantle it."

Will Studdart nodded, and continued to fire questions at him. How would he adjust the mainsail if the winds sent a ship toward the shallows? What would he do if the hull-to-deck joint began leaking? How many crew would he hire for a three-masted ship?

Amused, Hugo answered to the best of his ability, feel-ing as if he was back at school again, but as a student being examined on a subject he loved rather than loathed.

Finally Will Studdart said, "Come have a drink with me," and Hugo agreed. Together they made their way to the Blue Dolphin where, seated at a table near a window, open wide to admit the summer breeze, Hugo and Will each had a tankard of ale. Hugo wondered if his new friend could afford to stand him a drink and said:

"Let me pay for it, sir."

"Nonsense. You've pointed out a problem which will prevent me from making a costly mistake."

"You, sir?"

Will Studdart smiled. "Yes. She's my ship. The *Arcadia*. A fast merchant clipper, fourteen hundred tons when complete. We've lost so many ships to the war, and trade's been suffering. Liverpool's all for naval vessels these days, which is why I came here to build my ships."

"Utilizing also, unless I miss my guess, the proximity of the brickworks, coal mines, and salt works," Hugo said, nodding. "And the raw wool. All needing to be shipped out."

"Yes, that's right." Will finished off his ale, and set down his tankard with a thump. "I've asked you a lot of questions, Captain. Now I have just one more."

"**M**y dear Katherine, this is wonderful," exclaimed Mr. Mantel, looking up from the letters which she had annotated with care. He sat at his desk in his study at the parsonage, an unpretentious, cluttered room in which Katherine at once felt at home, no doubt in part, she thought, to simply being around all those shelves and shelves of books. But also because of how warmly Mr. Mantel had greeted her, and ushered her to a seat across from him.

"My notes are helpful to you, sir? I was worried that I overstepped myself."

"Not at all! It's brilliant work. You're right about that second paragraph in this letter to Felix Cobb, for one thing, its constructions were quite awkward, and how nicely you've altered the closing. And in this letter to Lady Denniston, you've reworked the opening paragraph to much better effect. The appeal for their support is much clearer now."

A glow came over Katherine then, and into her mind floated up a little snippet from her conversation with Livia that day at breakfast at Surmont Hall. Livia had been talking about her busy life there. *I enjoy it. For one thing, we're all working together as a family.* Then, it had been an unfathomable concept. But here, now, was something she had enjoyed very much indeed. For what was better than words and sentences, paper and ink? And she and Mr. Mantel were working together; she had been helpful to him. Katherine looked at her hands—on the fingers an ink-stain here and there, the nails still short but not quite as gnawed-upon as they had been—and she found herself admiring their strength, their capableness. She said:

"I'm so glad, sir. Would you like me to write out clean copies of the letters for you?"

"That would be marvelous, my dear! But only if you include all your changes, alter 'I' to 'we' throughout, and sign the letters also. You are truly my coauthor."

"You're—you're certain?"

"Yes indeed! You've helped me immeasurably."

"Then I will. It's an honor, sir." Katherine smiled back at him. "I'll get started right away."

After dinner, the family gathered, as it always did, in the library. As she crossed the threshold Katherine looked around as if seeing it for the first time, as if her vision had been dulled during her first weeks here, so consumed had she been by the anger roiling within her. What a pleasant room it was, with its books and paintings and comfortable chairs and sofas, a big soft rug underfoot, and heavy drapes left open to admit the still-bright summer sun.

The dogs, in their own now-familiar ritual, had gathered on the hearthrug, and Gwendolyn knelt there too, playing with the puppy which was noticeably less thin thanks to her tender ministrations. Hugo was sitting on one of the sofas, his long legs stretched out on an ottoman, and nearby was Mrs. Penhallow, sewing yet another blue gown for the charity home; Bertram was here, too, curled up in an armchair and deep into a great thick book about metallurgy.

A book.

What a good idea.

It seemed like forever since she'd last held one in her hands.

Katherine turned to look at the shelves crowded with volumes of all sizes. Why, there were hundreds of them. And she was sure that Mr. Mantel would let her borrow from his extensive library too. That lingering ache at having to relinquish so many of her books when in London, that abiding sorrow, vanished. She went closer to the shelves.

Oh, so many friends, and strangers, delightful strangers, here! Walter Scott's *The Lady of the Lake.* Jane Porter's *The Scottish Chiefs.* Immanuel Kant's *Logik.* Anne Louise Germaine de Staël's *De l'Allemagne.* Mary Wollstonecraft's *A Vindication of the Rights of Woman.* William Wordsworth's *Guide to the Lakes.* Percy Bysshe Shelley's *Zastrozzi.* The complete works of Shakespeare, unedited, how marvelous, and here was *La Divina Commedia,* in the original Italian, and even one of Maria Edgeworth's famous novels. She pulled it from the shelf and lovingly ran her fingers across the worn burgundy binding. "The delicious *Castle Rackrent*! With that horrid Sir Kit! I haven't read this in ages. I must reread it."

Quickly Gwendolyn looked up. "I was going to do that."

"Oh, were you? Never mind then. Here's *The Lay of the Last Minstrel.* I'll read that instead."

"That was a gift to me from Grandpapa," said Gwendolyn. "I was going to bring it up to my room."

"Gwennie darling," Mrs. Penhallow said, but Katherine moved away from the shelves, saying pleasantly, "I've changed my mind. Bertram, may I read your *Journal of Natural Philosophy*?"

"Certainly," said Bertram, not looking up from his book, and Katherine picked it up from a side table and went to sit next to Hugo, noticing, as she did so, the little frowning sideways glance which Gwendolyn gave her. Why was she doing that?

Hugo said, "I stopped at the parsonage on the way home and Grandpapa was full of praise for how you helped him."

"What did she do?" asked Gwendolyn.

"Katherine made emendations to letters Grandpapa had written to some philanthropists he's hoping will help support the charity home. And she's going to help him with an essay he's writing for the *Eclectic Review*."

"I could do that," Gwendolyn said. "Grandpapa says I write beautifully."

Hugo looked a little fixedly at her but said nothing. She lifted her chin and went on:

"You promised to go riding with me today, Hugo, and you didn't."

"He didn't promise," said Bertram without raising his head. "You asked him, but then I started talking about John Locke, and Eliza came in to take away the plates, and Aunt Verena didn't want us to go swimming in the ocean."

"Which reminds me." Gwendolyn gave him a belligerent look. "I saw you at the beach last night with Hugo and Katherine."

"Yes, and what of it?"

"Nobody invited *me*."

"Nobody invited me, either, but I just went. You could have come too, you know. Katherine and I had the most ripping conversation about the Gulf Stream."

"Of *course* you did," said Gwendolyn, then abruptly burst into tears. She moved the puppy from her lap onto the floor, shot to her feet, and fled the room.

"Oh dear," Mrs. Penhallow said, her hands stilled at her sewing. "Katherine, my dear, I'm so sorry. Fourteen is such an awkward age, isn't it? I remember how I used to blurt out the most dreadful things and feel so awful afterwards."

"There's no need to apologize, ma'am," Katherine answered. "I only hope I haven't offended Gwendolyn in some way."

Mrs. Penhallow looked rather startled. "How could you have?"

Cook came in then, through the door Gwendolyn had left open, advancing with her usual magisterial bearing and in her hands a platter of her delectable almond biscuits, redolent of cinnamon and mace. "Miss Gwendolyn's run off next door, madam, to the Becks' house," she remarked to Mrs. Penhallow. "Thought you ought to know." She set the platter on a low table near the sofa on which Katherine and Hugo sat, surveyed her handiwork with a kind of doleful satisfaction, added, as if at random, "Butcher's wife says Brooke House has been sold," and left the library.

There was a brief silence.

"Almond biscuits," said Bertram, "how jolly," and took three.

"Oh, Katherine dear," Mrs. Penhallow said, "I *am* so sorry."

"Don't be, ma'am." Katherine leaned forward to pick up the platter which she held out to her and then to Hugo. They each took a biscuit, she took one for herself, and put the platter back on the table. "It was a ghastly place. I don't miss it in the least. If you could have seen my bedchamber! It was like being trapped in a mausoleum." She leaned back against the sofa and nibbled on her biscuit, then jumped when a little, sharp voice said from below:

"Bring the spring upon 'er, matey."

It was Señor Rodrigo, staring up at her with his beady black eyes.

Katherine looked back at him. Then at her biscuit. She broke off a piece and with extreme caution, recalling Aunt Verena's comment about how Rodrigo had almost taken off her finger, held it out to him. Visibly mellowing, Señor Rodrigo accepted it in one of his sharp claws and greedily ate it. Then he climbed onto the toe of her slipper and demanded:

"Kiss me, you saucy wench."

Katherine smiled. "I won't. But you can have some more of my biscuit." She gave him another piece, and when he had finished that, bravely held out her finger to him near his claws. He chuckled and stepped onto her finger, allowing himself to be borne upwards and established on her lap. They looked at each other.

"I once had a hat that was trimmed with a green feather," she told him. "It reminded me of you. Why don't you have more feathers, *pequeño amigo?*"

Señor Rodrigo only chuckled again, and so the subject was dropped. They shared another biscuit, the dogs lay huddled in a drowsy mass on the hearthrug, Bertram turned a page in his book, Hugo smiled at her, looking more handsome than ever, and it occurred to Katherine, then, that the bees were gone.

My God, she thought in wonderment.

Gone, gone, gone.

Inside her was, instead, a kind of . . .

It took her a little while to come up with a word for it.

Peacefulness.

Inside her she felt . . . peaceful.

Bertram said, "How fascinating. The earliest known use of copper smelting is at a site called Belovode, in

Russia. They found a copper axe that's believed to be six thousand years old."

He turned another page.

"Dearest Hugo," said Mrs. Penhallow, "you seem great with news."

He looked at her, smiling. "I am. I've got a job."

Chapter 17

"**A** job?" his mother echoed in surprise, and Hugo nodded.

"Why are you taking on a job, Hugo?" Bertram said. "I thought you had an income thanks to your marriage settlements."

"Oh, Hugo, is there not enough money?" exclaimed Katherine, looking anxious.

"We're fine. An offer came my way today rather unexpectedly, and it sounds like such a lark I had to say yes."

"What kind of job is it, Hugo dearest?" Mama asked.

"I'm going to be helping build some merchant ships."

"Helping?" repeated Katherine. "How, Hugo? And where?"

"Here in Whitehaven. There's a fellow come from Liverpool, and I'm to oversee the work." He laughed. "I may climb a rigging yet and fulfill an old ambition."

"Blimey," said Señor Rodrigo, and looked at Hugo with such bright-eyed alertness that he laughed again.

"You're going to enjoy it, Hugo, do you think?" asked Katherine.

"A great deal, I believe. I can't sit about, as you know.

And it's not about the money, either—I asked for stock in Will Studdart's firm rather than payment. Oh, and I've invited Will to supper on Thursday, if that will suit you, Mama."

"Of course it does. Has he any family to bring as well?"

"No, none. He lost his wife several years ago, and they'd no children."

"Poor man! We'll do our best to make him welcome."

"I know you will," he said, and Katherine asked:

"When do you begin, Hugo?"

"Whenever I wish."

"There's something I'd like to do tomorrow, if you're able to join me."

"Of course. What is it?"

"I want to go see Brooke House. Not to go inside, naturally, but just to look at it." Katherine's voice was calm, even casual, and so Hugo merely nodded, as if this was but a routine, everyday request, and said:

"Shall we ride there?"

"Oh, is it too long a walk for you?" In her voice was now a teasing note.

Hugo grinned. "A great walker, are you?"

"I believe I am. I find I do some very good thinking while I'm walking."

"Aristotle," said Bertram, "was apparently such a proponent of walking that he used to lecture his students while strolling around the Athens Lyceum. That's how his school of philosophy got its name, you know—the Peripatetic School, derived from *peripatêtikos*, which is Greek for 'given to walking about.'" He took two more biscuits. "I say, these *are* good, aren't they?" And then he went back to his metallurgy book.

They stood in front of Brooke House which had about it the still, forlorn look of an abandoned building. No smoke issued from its chimneys, and curtains had been drawn across its many windows. There was no one going up and down its front steps, no carriages arriving, no carts from the grocer and the butcher pulling round to the back, no distant sounds of hunters' guns.

Katherine stared at the vast empty façade. On the third story, toward the right, was what had once been her bedchamber. Empty now also. "I wonder who bought it?" she said to Hugo.

"You don't mind, Katherine?"

"Oh, no. Not a bit of it. I suppose I wanted to come here to—well, I suppose to say goodbye. Oh, Hugo, what if an *interesting* family moves in? A great nabob from India, say, with a dozen lovely children?"

"Or a legendary warlord from Timbuktu, having retired from the life. Who brings his herd of yaks."

"A rich, kind spinster, who turns Brooke House into an orphanage. A *happy* one."

"A kite factory."

"A *chocolate* factory."

They laughed together, and Katherine slipped her arm through his. "Shall we go back? What a nice day it is. I'm just sorry Gwendolyn didn't want to join us. Another time, perhaps."

"Yes," Hugo said, "when we come to pay our respects to the warlord, who's married the spinster, adopted all the orphans, and opened his chocolate factory."

They laughed again, and began the walk toward home.

"Hugo," said Katherine, "will you tell me more about your job? What exactly *is* a merchant ship? How big are they? How do you build one? What is Mr. Studdart like? Is it hard to climb a rigging?"

He looked curiously down at her. "You really want to know?"

"Oh, yes, please. If you don't mind telling me."

"No, of course not," and as they walked, Hugo did.

————————

10 August 1812

Dear Katherine,
  I write this to you sitting at my little desk, look-
ing out at the tiny, sweet garden which is now my
responsibility—my pleasure—to tend. My aunt is
very fond of flowers and I am trying my hand at
azaleas, delphiniums, and lilacs. I find, to my sur-
prise, that I seem to have some talent for it.
  We lead a very peaceful life, my aunt and I. We
go to the Pump Room to drink the waters; we visit
the Circulating Library; I escort her to the baths.
We read, we talk, I play her little pianoforte; and
on the days she is feeling better, we go to the Sydney
Gardens, or to a lecture, or to a concert in the
Upper Rooms. I am happy.
  I think of you, and your kind husband, every day,
and with infinite gratitude. Thank you for giving me
my life back.

  Yours very truly,
  Lydia St. John

————————

12 August 1812

Dear Mama and everyone,
  Frank, Owen, and I are back at school. The
holiday at Owen's was splendid. I can jump like
anything now and Owen says I ought to take up
steeplechasing which, I must say, I think I would
enjoy quite a lot. In the meantime I am playing foot-
ball and Frank has joined the Classical Society.
  Owen has invited us to go back to Northamp-

*tonshire after the Michaelmas Half but we want to
come home. Even though we don't talk about it we
miss you all quite a lot.*

Most faithfully,
Percy

---

17 August 1812

Dear Livia,

*Please forgive my long silence. I'm so sorry
for not writing you back while Hugo and I were in
London, but I will be a better correspondent now, I
promise. Yes, we are in Whitehaven. And thank you
for your thoughtful words of concern. We are all
well. Hugo has been working at the harbor, helping
in the construction of an enormous boat, the first
in a fleet of merchant ships, and is hoping to take
it out on its maiden voyage in a few months. He's
having the time of his life, and comes home dirty,
oily, muddy, greasy, and ravenously hungry. Our
Cook says he will eat us out of house and home, but
you can tell she loves nothing better than serving
up the most massive and delicious meals I've ever
seen.*

*I hope you are all well and thriving at the Hall.
How are your chickens coming along?*

Sincerely yours,
Katherine

*P.S. Have you ever had a feeling that you're forget-
ting something? A vague, strange sort of sense that
it's right there in front of you all the time?*

---

22 August 1812

My darling boys,
We all enjoyed your letter so much. Thank you for writing. I'm so glad you had a lovely time at Owen's. He sounds a delightful boy.
We're so pleased that you're coming home for Christmas. Your room has been repainted and the fireplace repaired and I think you will like it all very much.
It will soon be fall. I do hope you both will wear your jackets.

With much love,
Mama

23 August 1812

Dear Lydia,
I was so pleased to receive your letter. Thank you for writing. And I'm so glad that you are happy in Bath. I've never been there, but you make it sound like quite a nice place to be. I like picturing you among your flowers. Have you found some interesting books at your Circulating Library?

Sincerely yours,
Katherine

The work came to him, was understood by him, as naturally as breathing air. To be sure, he had a lot to learn, but Will Studdart, long a master-builder, was generous in sharing his knowledge, and in implementing it, in overseeing the men, Hugo's abilities found true and rapid expression. He was here and there, all day long, on the ship and back and forth to their office, the joiners' shop, the sawpits, the blacksmith's, the storage sheds, the cook-house, the so-called steam-box where planking was rendered pliable. Day by day, week by week, the *Arcadia* was coming to life.

Katherine had preceded Hugo upstairs, and was tucked into bed with *The Scottish Chiefs* when a little while later he came into their room. The windows had been closed against a cooler, brisker breeze and Katherine had laid on top of her an extra wool blanket.

"Oh, Hugo, listen to this," she said, and read out loud: "'Looking up, I beheld a young chieftain, with a bow in his hand, leaping from cliff to cliff, till, springing from a high projection on the right, he alighted at once at the head of a wounded deer.' It makes me think of your Scottish cousin Alasdair. He's a chieftain, isn't he?"

"I've never met him, but I believe so."

"Well, this is the very picture of romance! I'm going to think of Alasdair just like that, jumping nimbly over the cliffs in his kilt and sporran."

Hugo laughed, and took off his jacket.

Katherine closed her book and set it on the little table next to the bed, on which stood a small candelabra. In its flickering golden light she watched as Hugo continued to undress.

"Hugo," she said, "I do like to look at you."

He stood, naked. "Likewise."

"Do you really?"

"Yes."

"Oh, good." She slid to the edge of the bed and got out.

"No nightgown, Katherine?"

"No. I was waiting for you."

He smiled, a slow, slow smile that made her feel as if her blood, her bones, her spirit had caught on fire. And he looked at her, from head to toe and everywhere in between, and he said, "You're beautiful, so beautiful," his deep voice filled with such awe and sincerity that she believed him, believed him absolutely, and moved to meet him where he stood. He brought her against him, flesh to flesh, and kissed her, mouth against mouth, hard, hungry, sure and sinuous. Katherine made a low, urgent noise in her throat, brought her arms around him, slid one of her legs up high around his rock-hard thigh.

Hugo lifted her then, effortlessly, turned them both until her back was against the wall, and, with her thighs around him, opened to him, he slid himself home within her.

"Yes," she gasped, and as Hugo moved, as steady and rhythmic as the waves outside their windows, and as pleasure and delight filled her, she was glad she had said the word. Just that one word signaling a welcome, a desire, light, brightness, joy as together they moved and rocked, joined, connected, giving and receiving, receiving and giving. *Yes.*

It was only later, when they lay in their bed, replete, that it occurred to Katherine. That there were other words she could say. Soft, sweet words. Tender. Truthful. Deep, immense, beautiful words, as big as the sky, the sea, the universe.

She hesitated.

Opened her mouth to speak.

Closed it.

Brought the covers a little higher up over her shoulders.

Adjusted her pillows.

Brushed a long spiral of hair away from her face.

Opened her mouth, closed it again.

Hugo said, "Good night, Katherine, sleep well," kissed her, and within moments was fast asleep.

"**Y**esterday was Katherine's birthday," said Gwendolyn to Diana Beck. The two girls were in the long yard to the back of Diana's house. Gwendolyn swung her little wood racket hard and sent her cork-and-feather shuttlecock high into the air.

"And?" Diana held out her own racket and caught the shuttlecock as it descended.

"Oh, Hugo gave her a pair of seed-pearl ear-bobs, and Mama a shawl she knitted. Aunt Claudia gave her a little watercolor of a cherry-blossom tree, and—" Gwendolyn broke off. "Oh, I don't want to talk about it anymore! But then Grandpapa told everybody how successful were the letters that he and Katherine wrote, and today Bertram actually took her up into the attic and let her look through his microscope, and—oh, Diana, it's dreadful of me, but I feel so *alone* inside my own family!"

Diana was flicking her racket, making the shuttlecock bob up and down. "Yes, but Gwennie, *your* birthday was last month, and everyone made a great fuss over *you*. You said so yourself."

Gwendolyn frowned. "That's true, but—"

"*I* know what it is," said Diana. "Katherine's mean to you, isn't she?"

"No, she's not mean, but—"

"Does she keep you out of the conversations, then?"

"No, but—"

"Ignores you?"

"No, she's very nice to me, but—" Gwendolyn paused, then burst out, "I don't know what it is! I'm just unhappy, Diana, that's what it is!"

"You won't be unhappy when Hugo lets you climb the rigging on his new boat."

Gwendolyn's face cleared. "Oh yes, I'm *so* looking forward to that! Hugo says we can all go next week and look it over. I'm going to wear that marvelous hat he gave me, and put Señor Rodrigo on my shoulder, too! The bad news is," she added, a note of discontent creeping once more into her voice, "Hugo says I can only go up six of the ratlines and not all the way to the top."

"Still," Diana replied, rather enviously. "Climbing the rigging! You're so lucky to have a brother like Hugo. Christopher is the greatest beast in nature. Nothing ever pleases him. He can't go back to university till the Lent term, and Papa's told him he'll be very disappointed if he gets sent down again." Diana bounced the shuttlecock over to Gwendolyn, who caught it on her racket and said:

"Did you ever find out what happened?"

Diana shook her head. "No, which makes me think it was something splendidly bad."

Gwendolyn brightened again, and then the two girls leaned close together, whispering, speculating as to what, exactly, Christopher's bad, splendid, and wholly fascinating crime might have been.

It was a lazy Saturday afternoon, and Katherine was lying on a sofa in the library with the big white and brown Great Dane, Ruby, dozing on the carpet, snugged up against the sofa, snoring ever so gently. Katherine had one hand on Ruby's soft furry side, and in the other held a letter from Livia which she read, smiling.

—and the baby is due sometime in November. Everyone is coddling me outrageously, which is silly given that I feel so well, but I must admit I'm rather enjoying it. I get fatter by the day and to own the truth I couldn't be more pleased, especially when Gabriel says I look like some kind of pagan goddess, a compliment I like very much.

As for the chickens—how kind of you to ask!— they are coming along nicely, particularly my Hamburgs, although the Blue Andalusians, I have found, are temperamental creatures and only seem to lay when I go into the hen-yard and talk with them for half an hour at a time. Gabriel finds this very amusing, but it really does seem to make a difference. He came out with me the other day and despite himself had a little conversation with the hen Hetty—do you remember her? the renegade I was chasing the day we met?—who took a great fancy to him. The next day she gave us the biggest, nicest egg she has ever produced, which only made us laugh the more.

You asked in your letter about a curious sense of forgetting something. Have you found what you were looking for? I hope so.

With love from all of us at the Hall—

A tap on the door had Katherine looking up. It was Eliza, who poked her head in and said:

"Oh, ma'am, Mr. Studdart is here, looking for Mr. Hugo, but I couldn't tell him where he is. Will you see him, ma'am?"

"Of course, Eliza, bring him in, please." Katherine sat up and set her feet on the floor, even as Ruby lumbered upright on her crooked front legs and went to greet Will Studdart, who came into the library holding a battered leather portfolio under his arm. He smiled, petted Ruby's great head, and gave Katherine a courtly little bow, saying:

"How d'you do, Mrs. P.? Beautiful afternoon, isn't it?"

"Indeed it is, Mr. Studdart. May I offer you some tea?"

"No, ma'am, thank you, I wanted to show Hugo something, that's all."

"He's over at the parsonage. A pipe burst in the scullery, and he's helping fix it."

Will Studdart laughed. "Of course he is. Never knew anyone more clever than Hugo at fixing things."

"It's true," Katherine agreed. "Do you want to leave something for him?"

Will paused, looking so eager and bright-eyed that she couldn't keep from adding:

"Is it anything I can see also?"

At once he whipped open the portfolio, and with such enthusiasm that its contents—a large notebook—fell to the floor, big yellowed pages splaying everywhere.

"Damn! That is to say—begging your pardon, Mrs. P.—"

Katherine crouched down to help Will gather up the pages. On them were illustrations of ships, rather crudely rendered albeit with great verve and detail, with hand-written text underneath describing them. And then she noticed, below each illustration, very small, the words *William Studdart*.

"Mr. Studdart, this is *your* work?"

They rose to their feet, Will replying, with unmistakable pride in his voice:

"Indeed yes, Mrs. P.! It's an old sketchbook of mine. I wanted to show Hugo what inspired the *Arcadia*." He held out one of the pages for her inspection. "This old clipper, the *Starling*. Only two masts, but fast and sturdy."

"What a handsome ship! And how many pages you have in your sketchbook! May I see more of them?"

With equal care Will spread out the yellowed sheets on the low table set near the sofa. Katherine sat and looked at them admiringly. "Mr. Studdart, this is remarkable. Your expertise—your love for these ships—is so clear."

"That's it, Mrs. P., it's been a labor of love," answered Will, pleased. "I'm no artist, nor a writer, either, but I've been keeping these little notes for more than thirty years now. Don't mean to be boastful, but back in Liverpool I had all kinds of offers to sell my sketchbook. Why, Lord Barham—First Lord of the Admiralty as he was then—begged me to let him have it back in oh-five, and a few years after that I got a note from the Duke of Clarence—a Navy man, you know—offering me a hundred pounds for it."

"The Duke himself! But you said no?"

"I'd be lying if I said I wasn't flattered, Mrs. P., or that I wouldn't have welcomed the money, but there was something that stopped me." Will began to collect the pages. "I suppose it was the idea of me not having my drawings anymore. Almost as if my sketchbook was going to disappear into thin air."

Katherine nodded. "Yes, I see what you mean." Then she added, "I met the Duke a few months ago. When Hugo and I were in London."

"Did you now!"

"Yes, at the Queen's Drawing-room. He told me how he joined the Royal Navy when he was thirteen and that it was the best decision of his life. He got to help with the cooking, he said, and get into drunken brawls, and it all made him feel like he was just another sailor. Oh, Mr. Studdart, he actually began to cry."

"Good God, Mrs. P., what did you do?"

"I was so taken aback that all I could think to do was to offer him my handkerchief."

"And?"

"He took it, blew his nose, and gave it back to me." Katherine laughed. "Luckily the Queen called him away and I could escape with my dignity intact. That is, if one could be said to escape wearing a gown that weighs twenty pounds."

Will slid the pages into his portfolio. "Quite the metropolis, London. You must have had a grand time there. Whitehaven's a very different place—seems a bit drab to you, I reckon?"

Katherine sat very still, arrested. "No," she answered thoughtfully. "No, it doesn't."

"That's nice to hear. Well, Mrs. P.," Will said, his portfolio tucked once more under his arm, "I'll be off then. I'll show Hugo the *Starling* some other time."

"I'll tell him you came by," replied Katherine. And

when Will was gone, she stretched out again on the sofa. Thoughtful still, and more than a little surprised. No, Whitehaven didn't seem at all drab to her.

"**O**h, Hugo, *please* let me go higher!" begged Gwendolyn, radiant, her golden hair flying loose about her face. She'd been upset about not being allowed to bring Señor Rodrigo—Mama having said, compassionately, *Dearest Gwennie, I know you believe he would enjoy it, but only think, darling, how cold he would get*—but she *was* wearing the hat he'd given her, and had leaped up the six ratlines with such nimbleness that Will had laughed and exclaimed:

"She'd make a right proper sailor, she would!"

With one hand on the halyard Hugo now looked up at Gwendolyn and shook his head. "That's high enough, Gwennie."

"*Please,* Hugo, just up to the—what did you call it?— the futtock shroud?"

"No."

"But it's so easy, only watch me, Hugo!" Gwendolyn reached up to the ratline above her head but before she could proceed Hugo stepped onto a lower ratline, wrapped an arm around her waist, and brought them both onto the deck.

"I said no."

Sulkily Gwendolyn pulled away from him, and walked over to the ship's railing, where with a certain ostentatiousness she peered into the harbor below. Mama said:

"Oh, Hugo, I'm glad you did that! Really, I don't think anyone who's not wearing trousers should go up any higher than she was."

"Aside from the modesty issue, Mama, I wouldn't have let her. Not without some kind of harness to keep her safe, and we don't have any."

His mother nodded, and went on, "I've enjoyed our tour so much! How *small* your sleeping quarters are! And I had no idea the hold would be so vast, with so many compartments. I was afraid I might get lost in one of them."

"Nonsense, ma'am, we'd never let that happen," said Will gallantly.

Mama smiled. "Thank you, Mr. Studdart. But if I ever decide to become a stowaway, I'd know where to go! Are you still planning to make your maiden voyage in a few weeks?"

"Yes, ma'am. But first we've got to go over every joint and sail, every timber and beam. If we look sharp, we'll be just in time to avoid the storm season. If all goes well, and we expect it will, we'll put the *Arcadia* on the market and hope for our first buyer."

"It's such a delightful boat; how could it not sell very quickly?"

"Actually," said Bertram, "you should call it a ship, Mama. The term 'boat' refers to a smaller craft. Although sometimes fishing vessels are quite large, and yet you never hear them called 'fishing ships.' Why is that, Mr. Studdart?"

"No idea, lad," said Will good-naturedly, and Mama added:

"It's a very delightful *ship*." She turned to him. "Hugo dearest, you and Mr. Studdart have done a magnificent job. I'm so *terribly* proud of you."

He smiled back at her, then looked to Katherine where she stood gripping the railing of the short flight of stairs that led belowdecks. "Well, Katherine?" he said. "Are you getting your sea-legs?"

"Not yet," she said. "Hugo, it really *is* a delightful ship, and I know it's still at anchor, but it does *roll* so."

Her face, he noticed, was unusually pale, and she had begun to look a trifle peaky. "Would you like to get back on land?"

She smiled faintly. "I would. And if you don't mind, I'm going to cling to your arm in a very missish way."

"I don't mind a bit," he said, and went to her at once. Their party made their way off the *Arcadia,* Gwendolyn the last to disembark, saying, to no one in particular, that she, herself, had never felt better than while on board and would have liked it if the waves were quite a bit stronger, but as Will Studdart was busy guiding Hugo's mama around a large neat coil of rope, and Bertram occupying himself by calculating the total volume of the ship's hold, and Hugo both eyeing Katherine's slightly greenish pallor with concern as well as enjoying how she did, in fact, cling tightly to his arm, nobody really paid much attention to her remarks, which were issued in a rather defiant undertone and promptly carried away by the wind.

Chapter 18

It was on the next morning that Katherine woke early to the sound of rain pattering against their windows. Hugo, she saw, was already gone. She smiled a little, reaching out a hand to smooth the indentation on his pillow where his golden head had been. Then she yawned, turned onto her back, closed her eyes again. How cozy it was, to snuggle underneath the warm bedcovers and listen to the rain.

Her thoughts drifted here and there, easily, without direction or purpose.

She was hungry. It was nice to look forward to another one of Cook's delectable breakfasts. Maybe there would be oatmeal, with cream and currants. Or perhaps hot muffins, fresh from the griddle, and lavishly spread with strawberry jam. And coffee. Today she was going to finish her work on Mr. Mantel's essay. Too, Will Studdart had asked if she would help him compose a notice of sale for the *Arcadia*. It occurred to her to wonder if a drawing might increase the notice's attractiveness. She herself had no skills in that regard, but . . . Aunt Claudia did.

Katherine was pondering this idea, which struck her as an excellent one, and also considering some phrases for the notice. *Modern design. Superior construction.*

All-English materials. Hold equipped with sturdy hatch covers to keep merchandise dry. Oh, she wanted to write these phrases down, before they slipped away. Maybe she should start keeping a little notebook and pencil on the table next to the bed.

She opened her eyes and looked at the simple wood table, with its square top and painted a cheerful yellow. Yes, what a good notion. There was plenty of room. Right now it held only her small candelabra, a stack of books, and the piece of blue sea-glass she had found that morning on the beach with Hugo.

Something stirred at the back of her mind, very deep. Obscure. Buried, as it were.

Sea-glass.

A little notebook; paper.

An image formed, hazy. Dirt. A trowel she had borrowed from Hoyt, who had seemed very large to her own small self. The shelter of the bay trees . . .

She tried hard to grasp at the image, but it was as if the very act of focusing her attention made it dissolve, disappear. She lay very still, but the wispy image was gone, although a bit of its essence—something wonderful, something important—somehow remained.

Her stomach growled. Breakfast. She wanted breakfast right away.

Katherine got out of bed and as she started to get dressed, a line from Edmund Spenser's *Fairie Queene* came to her.

For there is nothing lost, that may be found, if sought . . .

Later that afternoon, walking home from the parsonage on George Street and glad that the sun had come out again, that wispy, hazy, intriguing image from the morning surfaced again in Katherine's mind. Her steps slowed as she came to the Penhallow property. She passed the stable, looked to the house, and then to the line of tall bay trees separating it from the house where she used to live as a little girl, now the Becks' home.

Paper.

Sea-glass.

Buried.

A trowel from Hoyt.

Katherine almost gasped out loud.

Was it possible it was still there—?

Quickly she turned and went to the stable, where Hoyt, crouching, was examining one of the shoes of Hugo's horse.

"Hoyt," she said, rather breathless, "have you a trowel I could use?"

"Aye, missus," he answered, straightening, and found one for her. Quite possibly the same one she had borrowed when she was eleven years old, not long after her grandfather had died, after her parents had inherited his enormous fortune, and they were to leave behind their house on the beach and move into the newly constructed Brooke House five long miles away.

Her heart beating hard, Katherine went to the bay trees, but not on the Brooke side of things, here on the Penhallow property. Where . . . ? She paced up and down, then stopped at a place where the trees grew closely together, obscuring the view of her old house. Yes. Here.

She kneeled down and began to dig.

A few minutes later she came upon something besides dirt and stones. She dug harder. There it was. She used the trowel's tip to maneuver it free, then picked it up, held it in hands that were grimy now. Grimy, reverent hands.

A tin box.

On its lid, a scarred and faded picture, a bouquet of pink roses.

She had buried the box here, afraid that it would somehow be discovered on the journey between here and Brooke House. She had hated to part with it, but it was better than risking having it be found, and perhaps taken away from her.

Katherine sank back onto her heels and opened the lid.

Papers, folded; paper scraps; paper rolled into little cylinders and tied with pieces of yarn; and, here, a little book she had made by gluing together the pages at their margins. A dozen bits of sea-glass, green, amber, white, blue. A nub of a pencil, its tip all blunted from use.

Gently, one by one, she unfolded the papers.

Here were the little stories she had written. Brief accounts of her day. Her opinions of the books she had read. Descriptions of her dolls; the flowers, the clouds, the ocean. A little story about a seal carcass that magically came back to life. A short tale about a fairy she had named Bérénice, who liked to ride horses and fight battles and go fishing. All in her immature vocabulary, the sentence construction rather charmingly simplistic; all in her childish handwriting, but even so very neat and straight.

At the very bottom of the tin was a piece of paper which she had folded into a tiny, tiny square and sealed with a bit of wax.

Carefully she unfolded it.

In small, even letters she had written:

Tomorrow we have to leave here. Hugo is gone away to school. I don't know when I will see him again. Or how. But someday I will. I hope for it so much that it MUST happen.

It was strange, but Katherine felt as if she wanted to both laugh and cry at the same time.

Strange, but in a good way.

It came again to her, like a whisper from the past: *For there is nothing lost, that may be found, if sought . . .*

Something bumped her on the side of her face, soft and cold and damp. It was the nose of Ruby the Great Dane, who had wandered over from somewhere and seemed to be looking at her inquisitively. With her kneeling, and Ruby standing, they were precisely eye to eye.

"Hullo," Katherine said, "I've just found an old box I'd forgotten about, Ruby. It's been here for ten years. Waiting for me, perhaps."

Ruby seemed so interested that she added:

"I was a writer, you see. And I hoped with all my heart to see Hugo again one day. And I have, and I've *married* him, Ruby. Aren't I lucky?"

Suddenly Katherine thought about the scent-bottle she had given to Mary, the maidservant at Surmont Hall, and how holding its tin—which was decorated with chinoiserie flowers—had somehow made her pause. And made her remember, too, the dream she'd had, in which she said to old Mrs. Penhallow, *I've forgotten something, but I don't remember what it is. It's something very important.*

In her dream old Mrs. Penhallow had said, *You've got to find it yourself, you won't find it here,* then shut the door to the London townhouse.

Katherine thought as well about Livia's letter, in which she had written, *You asked in your letter about a curious sense of forgetting something. Have you found what you were looking for? I hope so.*

Yet another memory floated up. Mother's letter: *It's an ill wind that blows no good.*

Katherine laughed, part giggle, part chuckle. This time it really *was* funny, because Mother was—for once—right.

Leaving London so abruptly, feeling forced to come to Whitehaven: it had seemed so dreadful. Like the end of the world. But if she and Hugo hadn't come here, maybe she would never have found her little tin box again.

And that really *would* have been dreadful.

Just holding the box in her hand, feeling its weight, looking at what it held, filled Katherine with joy.

As she looked, and laughed, an idea burst into her mind, big and wonderful and so exciting that she leaned over and kissed Ruby's big soft nose. She didn't quite know how she would execute it—it was rather complicated—maybe even impossible—but still, it had a lovely sort of coherence to it. And she could *see* it, fully formed, in her mind's eye.

Just then Ruby lifted her head, ears pricked high, and looking toward the street beyond the stable she gave a sharp bark.

Katherine put the lid back on her box and stood up. She followed Ruby who was walking toward the street, ears still high and on alert. Coming around the stable she saw a slender woman, clad in dark clothes, limping, one arm bandaged and in a crude sling—carrying a small, worn-looking bag; she was dark-haired, narrow of face—

Good God, it was *Céleste.*

Even as Katherine stared in astonishment, Céleste staggered and dropped the bag onto the ground, seeming so imminently in danger of collapsing altogether that Katherine flew to her and wrapped an arm around her to help keep her upright. She noticed with fresh horror that Céleste's left eye was blackened. "My God, what's happened to you?" she exclaimed.

"*Mademoiselle,*" Céleste murmured, sounding rather dazed. "Or I should say *madame, non?* My . . . my *cher ami* Robert was not so kind to me. As you see."

"Oh, Céleste, I'm so sorry."

Céleste's head lolled back a little. "He took everything, *madame.* Luckily I had a bit of money sewn into one of my gowns, just enough to let me return here. Your old house, *madame,* is a . . . *maison des fantômes* . . . how do you say . . . a house of ghosts now. I am *défait, madame,* I am well-served for my treachery to you."

"Nonsense! He shouldn't have treated you like this."

"And yet he did." Céleste grimaced. "I have no right to ask it of you, but . . . *voulez-vous m'aider, s'il vous plaît?*"

"Of course I will! Hoyt! Hoyt!" Katherine called,

as Céleste closed her eyes and her knees buckled. "Help me!"

Hoyt hurried to her, and together they managed to convey the half-fainting Céleste into the house and lay her down on the bench in the entry hall. Hugo's mama came, as did Cook and Eliza; it was Cook who grimly produced a little brace of chicken feathers which she set alight and waved underneath Céleste's nose, bringing her up into a confused sentience. Dr. Wilson was sent for, and after briefly examining Céleste, he and Hoyt carried her to a bedroom upstairs. Katherine followed, carrying Céleste's little bag which Eliza had fetched and her own tin box which she put on her bedside table before continuing on to the room where Céleste lay limply on the bed.

"What can I do, Doctor?" Katherine asked.

"Not a great deal at present, ma'am," said Dr. Wilson, unwrapping the makeshift bandage around Céleste's arm, "but as you know this unfortunate young woman you might stay near, talk to her a little, let her hear the voice of someone she knows. This will not be pleasant for her. Her arm is badly broken."

Her stomach quivering in apprehension, Katherine obeyed, sitting on the edge of the bed and taking Céleste's uninjured hand in hers. What followed was just as difficult as Dr. Wilson predicted, and it seemed like a very long time until, having been given a generous dose of laudanum, Céleste fell into a drugged sleep. Katherine tucked the blankets around her, then wearily got up and went out into the hallway where a scared-looking Eliza stood, hands over her mouth.

"Oh, Mrs. Katherine, the poor thing *screamed* so! Is she—is she going to die?"

"No, Eliza, she'll be all right. But she'll need a lot of care over the next couple of days. Will you help me?"

"Of course, ma'am! But—but she won't scream no more, will she?"

"I don't think so. Will you sit with her for an hour or so, while I go get my supper? And make up that truckle bed for me? I'll stay with her tonight."

Later, Hugo walked with her to Céleste's room. "You'll be all right? Is there anything I can do?"

"I don't think so, but thank you."

"It's good of you to do this, Katherine. I know you never liked her."

"Oh, Hugo, that seems so long ago. I feel so dreadfully sorry for her. Besides, it's the Penhallow way, isn't it? Taking in misfits and the vulnerable, just like I was when I lived next door."

He smiled. "Come wake me if you need anything."

"I will."

Although Céleste slept soundly, Katherine passed a restless night. For much of it she lay awake, thinking over the idea she'd had earlier in the day. In the morning, Eliza came to relieve her and, still deep in thought, Katherine made her way downstairs and to the dining-parlor where the family sat at breakfast. It was only Bertram saying very loudly, *"Katherine,"* that brought her out of her abstraction.

"I'm sorry, Bertram, what did you say?"

"I was wondering if you saw the bone poking out of her arm."

"Bertram dearest," said Mrs. Penhallow, "perhaps not at breakfast."

"I didn't ask Katherine to describe it, Mama. I only asked if she saw it."

"Bertie," said Hugo, and with the air of one cruelly disappointed in a modest request, Bertram turned back to his eggs.

"I'll tell you all about it later, Bertram," Katherine said, "but first I want to walk to the harbor with Hugo. If that's all right, Hugo? There's something I'd like to talk to Will about, if he has the time."

"Of course," Hugo said. "Whenever you're ready."

"**Y**ou want to write a *book,* Mrs. P.? Out of my old sketches and notes?"

They were in the little office Hugo shared with Will Studdart, with Katherine sitting in the only extra chair, Will at the desk, and Hugo standing. Will was gazing at her amazed.

"Yes. Together," Katherine said, leaning forward. "I'll rework the text, with your approval, and Hugo's aunt Claudia can recreate the illustrations. I'll have to ask her, of course, but she'd be perfect! And we'll all share in the profits."

"But—you think it would make a good book, Mrs. P., that people will want to read? And buy?"

"I *know* it. You've documented a wonderful piece of maritime history. In fact, I think the title could be something about the English maritime heritage. 'Heritage' is an evocative word, and there's such strong sentiment about such things. Not just in our time, of course, but stretching all the way back to the Tudor era, with the building of our first navy and Queen Elizabeth's famous pirate fleet, too. And I had another idea, quite marvelous, I think—"

She told them what it was, and wide-eyed, Will said, "The book'd sell like cakes at a fair!"

"Well, we'll see. First we have to create a manuscript. And secure a publisher."

"Do you know any, Mrs. P.?"

Katherine shook her head. "But we'll find a way. I'm sure of it." She sat back in her chair. "What do you say, Will?"

"I say yes. It's a way of letting me keep what I've done, but also sharing it with the world. I'm grateful to you, Mrs. P."

She smiled, then looked up at Hugo. "What say *you,* Mr. P.?"

He smiled back at her. "I say bravo."

"You have no objection to your wife writing a book?"

His brows went up. "Why would I?"

"Oh, I suppose some people would think it unladylike, even scandalous."

"I don't."

"I'm glad." Katherine got up. "I'm off to see Aunt Claudia. Good day to you, gentlemen," she said, and stood on her tiptoes to brush her cheek against Hugo's, his skin warm and slightly, deliciously, rough; and then with brisk, eager steps she went to the parsonage, where, sitting together in Claudia's light-filled studio, she told her about her idea. Claudia listened intently, her big blue eyes unwaveringly on Katherine's face.

"—and altogether I envision about seventy-five pen-and-ink illustrations, Aunt Claudia, for a finished book of perhaps a hundred and eighty pages. And, as I told Will Studdart, we'll all share the profits. What do you think?"

"Oh, my dear, I do like drawing boats and ships, and I did enjoy doing that little illustration of the *Arcadia* you asked for, but . . . I've never *exhibited* my work before. To the public, you know. Am I really and truly good enough?"

"Yes, you are."

"You seem so sure of this, my dear."

"I *am* sure. I've been in London and to all the important galleries. You're more than good enough."

Claudia said, rather dreamily now, "I can hear it in your voice. I can *see* your surety. My dear, you've changed since the summer. I can't explain it exactly, but this is something *I'm* sure of. How is that poor parrot of Gwendolyn's doing? Has he gotten any feathers yet?"

"No, poor Señor Rodrigo is still the same. And to own the truth, Aunt Claudia, I think he's a little lonely since Gwendolyn's been spending so much time next door with her friend Diana."

"Such a sweet bird, Señor Rodrigo. I like him, so very much. About the book idea . . . I'll make you a bargain, Katherine dear."

Katherine smiled. "What sort of bargain?"

"I'll do the illustrations if, when I've completed them, you and Señor Rodrigo will sit for me. For a portrait."

"Done," said Katherine, and they two shook hands, and then Claudia sneezed, and five minutes later Aunt Verena sailed into the room with a tisane which she pressed upon her sister, and then she sneezed too.

"God bless you," said Claudia, and, setting aside her cup and saucer, stood up.

"Where are you going?" demanded Verena.

"To make *you* a tisane, dear," Claudia answered, drifting off, and as she reached the doorway they heard another sneeze, tremendously loud, issuing from Mr. Mantel's study, and Claudia added, "And one for Papa also. I do hope we aren't all succumbing to an ague. Goodbye, Katherine dear. Bring Mr. Studdart's sketches over whenever you like, and I'll begin."

Katherine drew open the curtains in Céleste's bedchamber and mellow autumnal sunlight, soft and cheerful, illuminated the room. "There," she said. "Now that you're well enough to sit up again, you can see the ocean from your window." Then she went to the table next to the bed, where a cup of Cook's warm beef tea was set on a saucer. She held out the cup to Céleste, who lay propped up on pillows, her dark hair, lank, in a plait trailing over one shoulder, and her left arm cradled in Dr. Wilson's professional-looking sling. The bruise around her eye was healing, but it was an ugly yellow and green now. Still, she looked considerably better than she had a few days ago.

Céleste took the cup. She said, looking up at Katherine, "*Merci, madame.* But there is something I must first say to you."

Katherine sat in the chair next to the bed. "What is it, Céleste?"

"I must apologize for my *malade*—my ill will—toward you all those years. I came to your parents' employ an orphan, destitute. I did whatever they told me to do. But this ought not to excuse *mon attitude désagré-able*."

"It does, though, I think. When one's circumstances are hard, one can, perhaps, behave in ways one might not like." Even as she said this Katherine knew she was referring to herself as well as to Céleste. She wondered, then, if people were shaped as much by how they grew up as by their intrinsic natures. A question to write down in her little notebook, and perhaps to mention for discussion at a family dinner.

Céleste was nodding. "*C'est vrai, madame,* it is all too true. Looking back, it seems to me there was—forgive me—*le poison* in the house. *Une essence noire,* overcoming me."

"I know what you mean," Katherine answered thoughtfully. "A dark essence. Well, that's all over now. Won't you drink your tea?"

Céleste obediently took a sip from her cup. "*Madame,* what is going to happen to me? I cannot work at present, I have no money, I am dependent on *votre charité,* and—" She inhaled a deep, shuddering breath. "I am afraid that *la police*—your Bow Street Runners—*me conduira à la prison*. For the theft of your jewelry, which I so deeply regret."

"Oh, they won't," Katherine said. "Father changed his mind, Céleste. Mother persuaded him that it would be socially embarrassing to pursue criminal charges against you and his valet. Although," she added, "I must say I do wish *something* bad would happen to Robert."

"We shall never know, *madame*. He has sailed off to Brazil."

"Brazil? Well, maybe he'll meet up with my parents then."

"*Votre parents* are there also?"

"Yes. Oh, wouldn't it be funny to see it? I'd give anything to be a fly on that wall. I can just imagine them going into business together and cheating each other blind." Katherine laughed, then said, "As for yourself, Céleste, please don't worry. Your only task is to get better again."

"I will try, *madame*. But I do not think I shall ever earn enough money to repay you for the jewelry."

"Oh, please forget about that. It wasn't even mine, really. Please do drink your tea, or Cook will scold *me*."

Céleste sipped again, then looked up, in her eyes wonderment and gratitude. "*Madame,* you are very good to me. I hope to repay you, someday, in another way."

Katherine smiled at her. "You needn't worry about that, either. Is there anything else you need before I go? I've promised to carry more of Cook's tea to the parsonage. Both of my aunts and my grandfather-in-law are feeling poorly."

"There is one small thing, *madame*. I—I have sometimes fancied that there is *le marin*—a sailor—in the house. *Est-ce vrai?* My late father was one, you see."

"A sailor? Oh—it must be Gwendolyn's bird you're hearing, Céleste! I'm sorry if he's been troubling you. He can be rather loud at times."

"It doesn't trouble me, *madame*. But . . ."

Céleste was looking so wistful that impulsively Katherine said, "Would you like to meet Señor Rodrigo? I can bring him up here if you like."

For the first time since she had arrived, Céleste smiled. "His name is Señor Rodrigo? *Oui, madame,* I should like that very much, if it does not incommode you."

"I'll do it as soon as I'm back from the parsonage," Katherine promised, and she was as good as her word, a few hours later returning to Céleste's bedchamber bearing Señor Rodrigo on her index finger.

"Ah, *le pauvre oiseau*, but he has no feathers! *Quelle dommage!*" exclaimed Céleste.

"*Bonjour, ma chérie*," said Señor Rodrigo. "*Comment vas-tu aujourd'hui?*"

"You speak French," Katherine said to him in surprise.

Señor Rodrigo giggled in a distinctly coy manner.

"We had no idea," Katherine said to Céleste, and laughed. "Señor Rodrigo, you clearly have had a very interesting past. May I introduce you to Céleste?" She sat on the edge of the bed and extended her finger, with Rodrigo upon it, toward Céleste, who in turn stretched out her own hand. Katherine held her breath, a little anxious as to how Señor Rodrigo would respond, but with total insouciance he stepped from her finger onto Céleste's.

"*Tu es très beau, monsieur,*" Céleste murmured, "so very handsome."

"*Voulez-vous danser, ma jolie?*" replied Señor Rodrigo, and began to climb up Céleste's arm where, reaching out to the end of her plait, he began to nibble on a strand of her hair.

Céleste watched him, smiling. "I cannot dance, *señor,* but perhaps we can talk?"

Rodrigo cackled agreeably, and Céleste looked up. "*Madame,* might you leave him here for a little while? If he is not missed downstairs? It would be *un grand plaisir* for me."

"I think that's a lovely idea," answered Katherine. "For both of you."

Later, at supper, when she explained where Señor Rodrigo was, she thought for a moment that Gwendolyn would object, for her expression darkened, but she only shrugged and looked to Hugo, saying:

"Are you still going on your first voyage on Friday? What is it that you call it? The shake cruise?"

"The shakedown cruise," he answered, and accepted from Bertram the platter of pork chops he was passing.

"Thanks, Bertie. Yes, early on Friday morning. I know you wanted to go, Gwennie, but it's not the sort of voyage for bringing along a guest. It's to make sure she's truly seaworthy."

"Oh, that's all right," she answered airily. "I don't mind anymore. Mama," she went on, "will you play cribbage with me after supper?"

"I'd love to, darling, but I'm going to stop by the parsonage to see how Papa and your aunts are doing. They were all a trifle worse today. It's only an ague, but . . ."

"I'll go with you," said Hugo, and Mrs. Penhallow replied gratefully:

"Oh, thank you, dearest Hugo. If you don't mind?"

"Not at all. Katherine, how's your writing coming along?"

She smiled at him. "Today I finished a section about a little ship called the *Kingfisher*. It had a fascinating history over a decade ago, when it was secretly fitted out as a military vessel and sent to the Strait of Gibraltar."

"In one of Papa's notes," said Bertram, "he theorizes that if the two land masses divided by the Strait were to be connected, the water in the Mediterranean basin would evaporate and a tremendous layer of salt would be laid down."

"Your papa was so *brilliant*," Mrs. Penhallow said, her eyes bright and soft. Then she rose to her feet. "Hugo darling, might we go sooner rather than later?"

"Of course, Mama," answered Hugo at once, standing up also.

"If you like, Gwendolyn," Katherine said, "I'll play cribbage with you. Bertram, will you join us?"

"I've changed my mind." Gwendolyn got up. "Mama, may I go over to Diana's house?"

"Just for a little while, darling."

"Katherine," Bertram said, "I'll play with you. Would you like to see my faro shuffle? I've been practicing it.

Mathematicians, you know, use it in an attempt to achieve the perfect shuffle, so that it can be classified as an element of the symmetric group."

"Bertram," said Katherine with absolute truth, "I would love to see your faro shuffle."

Chapter 19

Hugo and Will stood on the old stone quay where the *Arcadia* lay at rest in her moorings, completed, scrubbed, shiningly new, her clean white sails rippling in the breeze.

"Beautiful, isn't she?" said Will, pride in his voice, and Hugo nodded, just as proud. He'd loved being a soldier, but this—by God, this was even better. How lucky he was, to have moved so swiftly into another profession which suited him so well and also, as a side benefit, reduced to a great degree his chances of being shot, stabbed, captured, or hung.

"And thanks to Mrs. P.'s clever notice of sale," Will went on, "we've got those three offers already, waiting only on the results of tomorrow's cruise to proceed, and the fellow from Bristol's preemptively upped his offer by a third."

Hugo felt a glow of pride in Katherine, too. "Well, all's ready," he said to Will.

"Excited?"

He laughed. "Very."

Will laughed too, and clapped him on the shoulder. "So am I. There's nothing like a ship's first voyage. See you tomorrow morning, bright and early."

When Hugo got home he found a discombobulated household.

"Oh, Hugo," said his mother anxiously, "both Cook and Eliza have come down with the ague, and Claudia's a little worse today. One of the dogs ate something it shouldn't, and nobody can find the puppy. Bertram's out looking for it, and Katherine kindly offered to clean the mess in the drawing-room. Papa's cook is making some more broth and so I'm going now to the butcher's to bring her fresh bones. Dr. Wilson promised to come by and see Cook and Eliza, and also to look in on Céleste, who insisted on getting up to help and then almost passed out on the stairs." Mama pressed her palms against her face for a moment. "Oh, Hugo, and I did want to have a special supper before your voyage!"

"We'll have it when I get back," he told her. "Is Hoyt feeling all right?" At her nod, he went on, "Send him to get the bones, and you go straight on to the parsonage. Where's Gwennie?"

"She's gone over to Diana's, where she's to spend the night."

"She ought to be helping here."

"Oh, darling Hugo, she's been so dreadfully out of sorts lately, there's no need to trouble her." Mama had already put on her pelisse and was tying the ribbons of her bonnet. "Do you think you can scramble something together for your supper?"

"After eight years in the Army? Gad, I should hope so. Don't worry about us, Mama. Go tell Hoyt what you want him to get, and I'll see what else needs to be done around here."

His mother's expression brightened. "Hugo darling, you're such a *comfort*. Thank you! Oh, I do hope Bertram finds the puppy."

With that, she was gone. Hugo checked on Cook and Eliza, and then on Céleste, and went to help Katherine in the drawing-room, and Dr. Wilson arrived, and when, a little later, Bertram triumphantly returned with the puppy, he put him in charge of feeding all the dogs and went into the kitchen to make cold beef sandwiches and a potato salad which he offered to anyone who felt like eating. His supper was pronounced entirely delicious, even Cook, who was persuaded to sit up and have half of a sandwich, allowing as how it was passable.

"Which," Hugo later told Katherine, when they had gone up to their room, "was such a compliment that I very nearly blushed."

She laughed. "Unlike myself, I don't think I've ever even seen you turn red."

"That's because I'm shameless."

Katherine laughed again, and Hugo went on to finish packing his small canvas bag. He set it near the door, then turned to see that Katherine, in her white nightgown, was sitting on the bed, her knees drawn up and her arms clasped round them. Her mood had shifted; she was now looking at him gravely.

"Hugo," she said, "you'll be careful, won't you?"

"Of course I will."

"You've thoroughly inspected the *Arcadia*?"

"From stem to stern."

"There are no leaks?"

"Not a one."

"You trust your crew?"

"Absolutely."

"The weather looks auspicious?"

"Yes."

"And you'll only be gone for three days?"

"Yes."

Katherine's dark eyes were fixed on his own, intently, and to Hugo it seemed as if there were something else she wanted to say. Another box she wished to reveal. He stood there patiently, waiting for whatever it was. Then she said:

"Hugo, is it bad luck to make love before a maiden voyage?"

For a fleeting moment, it seemed to him that this wasn't what she had been struggling to say, but the thought vanished as he felt the warmth of desire begin and build within him.

"No, by Jove, it's not," he said, and went over to the bed. He got onto it, sat with his back against the headboard, and reached out for her; she came willingly, straddled him, and he slid up the hem of her nightgown so that he could stroke her legs, slowly and without hurry. She shivered a little, with pleasure, he knew, but still looked grave.

"You're sure?" she asked.

"Very. If anything, it's good luck. In fact, we'll have to be sure to make love before all my ships launch."

He saw the smile begin to form on her sweet cherry lips.

She said, "Do you mean to have a great many ships?"

"Yes. Which means we'll have to make love quite a lot."

"Do you promise, Hugo?"

"Yes."

"Well then," she said, and began to tug up the hem of his shirt.

It was still dark when Hugo left the house. She wanted to go with him to the harbor, but to this he would not agree. So Katherine walked him just to the street, inside her words she longed to share, words from her heart, but all jumbled and raw, unpolished, disorganized, and by the time she thought how she might put them into proper order, Hugo had kissed her goodbye, and all she could think to do then was to cling to him rather tightly, smile, and say:

"Three days?"

"Yes. *Au revoir,* as those beastly French say."

Katherine stood watching him walk away. It was cold this morning, with a sharp wind that seemed to take perverse delight in finding its way down the collar of her pelisse and go slithering up her sleeves, sending her skirts aflutter and her curls blowing every which way. But she waited, unmoving, until she could see Hugo no longer. It was only then that she went back into the house.

It was quiet and dark inside. The dogs came to meet her in the entry hall and softly she greeted them, then went back upstairs where she got into bed again. But not to fall asleep once more. No, she was wide awake. She lit her candles and took up her manuscript. Scattered throughout Will's notebook were a dozen or so sketches of various types of anchors, which she thought would make a very interesting section all to itself.

On her little table was her inkpot and quill. She dipped her quill into the ink and began to write, and in her deep concentration the shadowy hours before sunrise passed quickly away. When she looked up again, it was a new day.

Katherine blew out her candles and gave a last satisfied glance at what she had written, then got up and went to the windows. She looked out at the vast white-capped ocean. Somewhere out there was Hugo. She wasn't afraid for him precisely. He was so capable, so clever. It was just that—

It was just that she wished she had said to him what she wanted to say.

The three days until he came home seemed, all at once, to stretch ahead into eternity.

But then she gave herself a little shake, sent a last lingering glance upon the sea, and went downstairs to help with breakfast.

The *Arcadia* sailed smoothly west, out into the open waters of the Solway Firth. The winds had picked up, of course, and the ship rolled more noticeably, but the sky overhead was a bright blue, practically cloudless, benignant.

Oblivious to the sea-spray being dashed against him, Will stood next to Hugo on the quarterdeck, feet braced wide apart and his fluid stance easily accommodating the ship's rolls and lurches. "Couldn't have asked for better weather," he said to Hugo. "If we're lucky, we'll get a glimpse of the Isle of Man before we turn about."

Hugo nodded, smiling. Everything about the day seemed lucky to him. Everything about his *life* seemed lucky.

It was late in the afternoon of that same day, and Katherine was coming downstairs with a bowl that had been in Céleste's room, but paused on her way to the kitchen when somebody banged hard on the front door's old iron knocker. As she put the bowl onto the entry hall's console table, the dogs came tearing in, barking ferociously.

"Quiet," she said to them, and was gratified to see how quickly they obeyed her. Smiling, she opened the door. There on the porch stood Christopher Beck, holding the arm of his sister Diana in a firm and possibly painful grip. Diana, for her part, was so white that her freckles stood out in sharp relief and she looked extremely scared.

Katherine felt her smile fading and she said, "Are you all right? Has something happened to your father? Please come in." She opened the door to them, and Christopher shoved Diana in ahead of himself. He said, his brusque, rough way of speaking more in evidence than usual:

"Father's fine. He's in Blackpool on business, else he'd be here too. Diana has something to tell you."

"Oh, Christopher, must I?" faltered Diana. "I swore on my *life* I wouldn't say anything to anyone."

He scowled with such savagery that Diana flinched away from him. "You've already told me, you silly little fool," he said harshly. "I knew something was wrong just by looking at you. And now you're to tell Mrs. Penhallow if I have to thrash it out of you."

Diana swallowed, and fearfully raised her eyes to Katherine, who waited, trying to control her own ripple of fear. Christopher gave Diana a push, and finally Diana said, in a small and trembling voice:

"Oh, ma'am, it was only for a lark—"

On the second morning of their voyage, Hugo was woken up by a hand on his shoulder. It was young Dombley, one of the sailors who had taken the night-watch, his face seeming pale, blanched, in the light of earliest dawn coming in through the small porthole of Hugo's little cabin.

"Sir," he said, his voice urgent and rather frightened, and Hugo sat bolt upright.

"What is it, Dombley, what's amiss?"

"Bent and me, we—we didn't know what to do, sir, and Bent said—Bent said to go and get you."

"What is it?"

But Dombley only shook his head, as if robbed of his full powers of speech. "Come see, sir," he said, still stammering. "Hurry, sir."

Rapidly Hugo dressed, his mind racing. Had the *Arcadia* struck something, or was there a leak after all? He'd have sworn on his life there wasn't. He took the companionway steps four at a time and emerged onto a deck damp with sea-spray and into a soft blue cloudless morning. The green and gray-white waves all around them were higher today, with deeper troughs, and the ship rocked more strongly from side to side.

"Well, Dombley?" he said, scanning the decks for any irregularity. But there was only Bent, who stood clutching the halyard, looking just as scared as Dombley.

"Look up, sir," Bent said, and Hugo did.

And there was Gwendolyn, high above him in the rigging, nearly up to the topmast. She was dressed like a sailor in wide canvas trousers and rough linen shirt, her hair in a golden braid that flapped wildly in the wind.

For a single beat of his heart, Hugo felt a rush of admiration for his adventurous little sister, recalling Mama's remark about the hold, its many compartments, and being a stowaway. Just as quickly, after that, came such a deluge of fury at Gwendolyn's recklessness that everything seemed to be blotted out in a crimson haze. But then, as he stared up at her, he saw that she was terrified. And she had to be freezing. If she'd been up there for any length of time her hands would be stiff with the cold. How long could she maintain her grip, with her soft small hands, on those painfully rough ropes?

Just then the *Arcadia* slipped into a deep trough and tilted hard to leeward.

Gwendolyn screamed his name.

Hugo leaped up onto the ratlines, shouting over his shoulder, "One of you get Will, the other keep your eyes on my sister," and began to haul himself upward. "Hold on, Gwennie," he shouted up as he reached the futtock shroud—he was halfway there now—and then the *Arcadia* tilted herself upright and just as promptly lurched into another trough and swung even more sharply leeward—

And Hugo watched as Gwendolyn fell—

Fell, like a little wounded bird, and plummeted into the ocean.

In some lightning-quick, analytical part of his mind he knew that it was only by the grace of God that she'd let go of the ropes as the ship rolled, for if she'd fallen onto the mercilessly hard wood of the deck she'd have snapped her neck and died.

But now she was in the cold, roiling, gray-white waters below, and there was no certainty at all that she would survive *that*.

He remembered her saying, once, in a sulky voice, *It's dreadfully unfair that girls aren't supposed to swim in the ocean.*

It took the merest pulse of time for these thoughts to flash through Hugo's brain and then without hesitation he leaped after Gwendolyn into the sea.

The shock of being submerged in the frigid waters paralyzed him for a moment, but with three, four, five strong kicks of his legs, with forceful sweeps of his arms, he brought himself up to the surface, gasped for air, looked around for Gwennie. There. Fifteen feet away, there she was, flailing her arms, on her face such a look of abject terror that Hugo had to school himself not to think about that, but only about reaching her.

He swam, hating how the ocean seemed to fight him.

Christ in heaven, but the water was cold.

Faster, go faster. Hurry—

Vaguely to his ears came shouts from high above him, from the ship.

He got to Gwendolyn just as her head was sinking under the surface. He grabbed her shirt and shoved her up so she could take in a sobbing, choking breath, then wrapped an arm around her, kicking hard to keep them both above the water. She clutched at him, shrieking as a cold wave crashed over their heads.

"Don't let go, oh, Hugo, don't let go," she pleaded in a jerky little voice, gasping, her lips blue and her bright hair plastered, sodden, about her face.

"I won't." He kicked hard with his legs, used his free arm, too, to keep them afloat, pushing against the roiling water, and looked up to the ship, searching with his eyes for the rope that would save them.

Another shout. He saw Dombley, then—thanks be to God—Will Studdart, still in his nightshirt, and then Bent and some of the others. It was Will, he hoped—he trusted—who was knotting the rope, quickly but carefully, with the strong unerring skill born of years of experience—

Another wave hit them. They both swallowed water and Gwendolyn gave a keening cry of despair. He could feel her grip on him loosening and he tightened his arm around her slim frame, trying to ignore how his own limbs were weakening in the churning, icy-cold sea, how his teeth had begun to chatter, too.

"Hugo," he heard Will shout, and then he saw the rope that Will flung out to him. Its knotted end splashed into the water only a few feet away, but it seemed like miles to Hugo as ploddingly he brought himself and Gwendolyn to it. Damn, *damn,* he was weak, he could barely feel his arms or legs now, but with every particle of his being—his strength, his will, his absolute determination—he fixed his mind on the rope.

He kicked again.

And again.

And got to the rope, which danced in the rough water almost as if it were alive.

With his free hand Hugo grabbed it, just above one of the knots. Felt with his feet for the knots at the bottom. God *damn* it, where were they? Yet another wave sent Gwendolyn and himself bobbing helplessly. No—not helplessly, for he didn't let go of the rope. Would *never* let go of the rope, no matter what.

At last his feet connected with the knots below him. They gave him a little, much-needed purchase. He looked up at Will, shouted, "Now," and with a gratitude more intense than he'd ever felt in his life he registered the upward movement of the rope.

"Hang on, Gwennie," he said in her ear, "just a little longer," and saw with relief that she managed to weakly nod.

The men above hauled them up.

Hugo concentrated. The rope. His hand on the rope. His arm around Gwendolyn. Never mind the cold, the numbness everywhere. His hand on the rope, that was all that mattered, his arm around Gwennie. The *rope.*

Bit by bit, they were drawn upwards at a speed that felt to Hugo like tortuous slowness. He fixed his mind. The important thing was that they were going up. The rope, the rope, the rope—

They must have been nine or ten feet short of the ship's railing when the *Arcadia* slid into a trough and rolled. Hugo and Gwendolyn swung wide, in a dreadful mockery of that giddy sensation children feel when playing on a swing, and as they flew back toward the hull Hugo had just enough presence of mind left to jerk his body in a way that brought him, and not Gwendolyn, against the inflexible hull.

He slammed hard. His body felt as if it exploded with pain, most acutely in his head and the whole left side of him. Everything started to go black. But grimly he hung onto the rope, hung onto Gwendolyn—only five feet now, only four feet now—

Then: hands grabbing at them, hauling them over the railing and onto the deck. Voices. Will Studdart: "Thank *God*."

Pain exploding everywhere within him.

He managed to say, "Gwennie?" in a voice so weak and ragged he hardly recognized it as his own.

"Alive, Hugo, alive," said Will, and Hugo, satisfied that he had kept his promise, let himself sink into darkness.

Katherine was afraid to tell Mrs. Penhallow where Gwendolyn was, but of course it had to be done. But first she went to Bertram in his attic. He listened without comment, said, "I'll go get Mama's smelling-salts, just in case," and together they made their way to the sunny little parlor where Mrs. Penhallow, exhausted from her long hours at the parsonage, had sat down for a moment and ended up falling asleep.

They woke her, and when she heard the news her face went so white that Bertram held out to her the little vinaigrette, but gently she waved it aside. "Thank you, darling Bertram, but I don't need it," she said. "Oh, my poor, brave, foolish little Gwendolyn. Will Hugo be very angry when he finds her, do you think, Katherine?"

"Oh, Mama, I don't know," said Katherine, then blushed furiously. "I'm sorry—I have no right to call you that, ma'am."

Mrs. Penhallow reached out her hand, and drew Katherine down next to her on the little sofa. She gripped Katherine's fingers tightly in her own. "But you do, you do, my dear," she said. "You're my own dear daughter, too." Her big blue eyes were shining with tears. "And now, what's to be done?"

"There's nothing," said Katherine. "Nothing to do but wait. Bertram, could you bring Mrs.—Mama a cup of tea, please?"

"Of course," said Bertram, and went away to the kitchen. But it was Cook who came following after him when he returned, carrying a tray with three cups and a plate heaped with little iced cakes. She put the tray down on a table and stood looking gloomily at Mrs. Penhallow.

"Mr. Bertram's told me, madam. What was Miss Gwendolyn thinking? Oh, madam, do you remember poor Tom, the custom officer's son, who—"

"Cook," said Katherine, with the tiniest shake of her head, "would you give Mrs. Penhallow her tea, please?"

For a moment Cook looked startled, then comprehension came into her big round face and she picked up one of the cups.

"Here, madam, it's nice and hot," she said. "Fresh-made. I've put a cake on the saucer, too. With my good butter icing on it, there was fresh vanilla at the grocer. Here, Mrs. Katherine, here's your cup, and yours, Mr. Bertram. Madam, *do* drink your tea, it'll do you good."

Obediently Mrs. Penhallow brought her cup to her lips, and sipped at it, but Katherine could see that her mind was elsewhere, stretching out toward the distant, dangerous ocean. Toward those two of her children, much loved, and so far away.

"Three days, Mama," Katherine said. "Hugo said they'll be back in three days. Which is tomorrow."

"Tomorrow," echoed Mrs. Penhallow, but her voice lacked conviction.

"Hugo will keep his promise," Katherine said firmly. "He always keeps his promises."

The day dragged on, and night came, and in the morning no one looked as if they had slept very well, if at all. Cook, whose health was markedly improved, prepared a breakfast more suitable for a crowd of twenty, but it was tacitly understood that it was a product of her own nervous energy and nobody remarked upon it.

Katherine drank her coffee and ate a muffin, then said to Mrs. Penhallow and Bertram:

"I'm going to the harbor."

"I'll come with you," said Bertram.

"I'd like to go, too, but I'm needed at the parsonage." Mrs. Penhallow looked between the two of them. "You'll send word if—when the *Arcadia* arrives?"

"Of course," Katherine said. "We'll be in the Blue Dolphin, if that's all right, Mama? It's a tavern, but we'll be able to keep warm and dry."

Mrs. Penhallow smiled faintly. "Under ordinary circumstances I might be a little concerned, but . . ."

Half an hour later Katherine and Bertram were seated at table by a window which commanded a good view of the harbor. They had both brought their books, and Katherine her manuscript and Bertram an essay he was drafting on copper-extraction techniques. The hours ticked by. They went for a walk up and down the quays. They ate a nuncheon. They read their books; they wrote;

they walked some more, occasionally glancing up at a lowering sky which had filled with heavy gray clouds. The afternoon light began to dim. They had dinner. Christopher Beck came, and sat with them. Once or twice a couple of men, a little drunk, approached them, but Christopher stood up and faced them with such ferocity that they backed away. Other than that, nobody said much. Twilight gave way to evening, and massing clouds obscured the stars. Silently they paced together along the quays.

Finally Bertram said, "Do you think they'll come tonight?"

"Hugo said three days." Katherine stared out into the *Arcadia*'s empty slip, and hugged herself against the chill.

"Things happen," said Christopher in his rough way.

"Hugo promised," Katherine said, simply, and then they fell silent again, waiting, watching, walking, waiting.

It was a quarter to nine when they first caught sight of the *Arcadia*.

"There she is," said Bertram, and Katherine couldn't help it, she took hold of his hand and gripped it hard.

"Does it bother you, Katherine?"

"Does what bother me?"

"That you're holding the hand that had some of the bits amputated."

"No," she said honestly, then added with concern, "Am I hurting you?"

"No. It's rather comforting, holding hands."

"I think so too." For a moment Katherine wondered if she should reach out for Christopher's hand also, but as if sensing her thought he twitched his whole self, like a restless horse, and took half a step away from her, and so she refrained, though she fancied that his profile showed him to be both sullen and deeply sad.

The three of them watched and waited, as slowly the *Arcadia* sailed into the harbor.

At exactly eleven-fifteen she inched her way into her slip. Hugo, bless him, had kept his promise. Katherine stared up at the deck, her eyes straining in the darkness. There was Will Studdart, she could hear his voice; there were some of the crew. Where was Hugo, where was Gwendolyn?

"Will!" she shouted.

She could, just barely, see him turn and look at her, then say something to his men. The anchor was lowered, and some crewmen jumped onto the quay and began to help secure the ship with their ropes. The gangplank came out. A deep, dark dread filled Katherine.

"Oh, Bertram," she whispered, and convulsively gripped his hand yet harder.

Then she saw it. Saw them. Crewmen carrying two rough canvas stretchers, on them two blanket-swathed forms. The words were torn from her: "Oh God, oh *God*—"

They ran to the gangplank. After that, it was a living nightmare. Hugo, eyes closed and unmoving; Gwendolyn, weak, so weak she could only just turn her head. Will, explaining what had happened; Christopher, bolting for Dr. Wilson's house, to send him on to the Penhallow home, and then to go tell Elizabeth Penhallow that her children had returned. That her children would be borne home as quickly as possible. They were alive, but not well. Oh, not well at all.

Chapter 20

He was floating somewhere, in the ether perhaps, far from the realm in which his body could hurt him anymore. There was no pain, no fear. He had brought Gwendolyn out of the ocean. He had brought his family out of ruin. He had brought Katherine out of Brooke House. Even though he was sorry to go, he knew they would be all right.

He floated.

Peaceful and free.

No pain, no fear.

He let himself drift further and further into the noiseless, comfortable embrace of the ether.

Katherine stared down at Hugo's face, ghostly pale in the wan moonlight spilling between curtains she had forgotten to close. He lay in their bed as still as death itself. Dr. Wilson, brisk, efficient, kind, had come and gone. Gwendolyn had said a few words, to everyone's relief; Mrs. Penhallow was with her now, in her bedchamber. Bertram had wanted to stay here, with Hugo, standing as stiffly as a soldier on sentry duty, but after a while had literally fallen asleep on his feet and she had told him, gently, to go to bed. Groggily he'd complied, and she was now alone with Hugo. The quiet seemed to press heavily upon her, with almost a physical force, and Katherine could feel herself breathing rapidly, shallowly.

Could feel her heart beating too fast.

A great black abyss seemed to open up before her, and she knew it was the place of despair. The point of no return; the dark night of the soul.

How was she going to get through this? How could she help Hugo—help his family?

Katherine looked at Hugo, the heavy weight of anguish hard upon her, and slowly sank down onto her knees. She was weak, weak. What use could she possibly be? She brought her hands up onto the side of the bed, and it was some time later that she realized she had clasped them, as if in prayer.

Into her mind came something Mr. Mantel had said during his sermon the very first Sunday after she and Hugo had arrived in Whitehaven. The church's simple, pleasing interior had been flooded with colorful light streaming through its stained-glass windows. Mr. Mantel had talked about the turbulence of the world, the earthquake in Caracas, the Luddite riots here in England, the siege in Badajoz, and how one might strive to find peace amidst it all. He had quoted from the book of Hebrews:

Now faith is the substance of things hoped for, the evidence of things not seen.

She had been too angry, then, to really listen. To truly hear. But now his words came back to her, and it was as if she reached out to grab at them. To take them in and hold on tight.

Faith is the substance of things hoped for.

Hugo's voice came into her head:

Then Grandpapa wrote me a letter that helped. He said it's his firm belief that we're never given more than we can handle.

She had said, *Do you have faith in me, Hugo?*

And he had answered in his calm, steady way:

Yes. You're one of the strongest people I've ever known.

Faith. Hope. Strength.

Powerful words.

Beacons of light.

Guiding her away from the abyss. Illuminating her path.

She knew, now, what to do.

Faith, hope, strength.

Katherine realized that she'd bowed her head over her clasped hands, as if in prayer. She lifted her head. Stood. Looked down at Hugo, and *believed*.

With astonishing rapidity Gwendolyn rebounded from her ordeal, but as the days passed Hugo remained silent, still, deeply and utterly unconscious. He had broken his left leg again, Dr. Wilson informed them, and hit his head with such force that it was unclear—well, it was unclear if he would ever wake up, or even survive his injuries.

Pale and drawn, Mrs. Penhallow moved between the house and the parsonage, where, at last, Grandpapa and the aunts were recovering from the ague that had stricken them. It was only once, when she and Katherine were alone, that she broke down and cried. They sat on the little sofa in her parlor and Katherine held her hand, and finally Mrs. Penhallow said in a low voice:

"Oh, my dear Katherine, what if—what if my darling boy doesn't—doesn't get better?"

"He will, Mama."

Mrs. Penhallow wiped her eyes with her little wisp of a handkerchief. "I know it's a terrible thing to say, but I feel so—so *hopeless*."

"I have enough hope for both of us, then."

"*How* do you, Katherine dear? Of course I'm so thankful that Gwendolyn is better, and my sisters and Papa also, and I'm very grateful for all of Mr. Studdart's offers to help, but with Dr. Wilson so guarded, and Cook so despondent I can hardly bear to look at her, I feel my own spirits sinking very low. I *try* to keep my face brave, but . . . How do you do it?"

"It may sound strange, Mama, but have you looked at Señor Rodrigo lately?"

Mrs. Penhallow shook her head. "I've been so distracted. Why do you ask?"

"Come with me."

Together they went to the open door of the library where Gwendolyn lay on a sofa, napping, her cheeks flushed a healthy pink and a book tucked in next to her, slid upright against the sofa-back. And Mrs. Penhallow looked at Rodrigo, who perched on the book's spine, his dark eyes bright and unfathomable. She looked at Señor Rodrigo, el Duque de Almodóvar del Valle de Oro, whose brilliant green feathers had, for some unknown and mysterious reason, started to grow again.

"My goodness," Mrs. Penhallow whispered in amazement, and Katherine whispered back:

"Hope, Mama. Hope, and feathers."

They walked together back down the hallway and stopped at the foot of the stairs. Katherine said, "When Hugo first came home that night, I felt like you did. So frightened and hopeless. But . . . I thought of some things your father said, and Hugo, too. And then, the next day, I saw the very beginning of Rodrigo's new feathers. Do you remember my once making a rather unhelpful comment to Gwendolyn about how he didn't have any feathers at all? She said to me, 'I have so much hope that he *will*. Every day I tell Señor Rodrigo that he's perfect just as he is, but that someday, when he's ready, he'll grow the most beautiful green feathers in the world.' I'm not sure why, but I remember so clearly what she said that day. And—" Katherine smiled, just a little. "I'm a little mad, perhaps, but somehow Señor Rodrigo is giving me hope. I'm going back upstairs now, to Hugo." She hugged Mrs. Penhallow, and so they parted, Mrs. Penhallow looking, perhaps, just a tiny bit brighter.

Gradually, gradually, he realized that a voice was talking to him. Had been talking to him for quite a while, softly, steadily. And even though the voice felt a little like a tether, keeping him from floating away, keeping him too close to the racking pain, despite himself he found he wanted to hear what the voice was saying. Curiosity had always been one of his abiding sins.

He listened.

Hugo, I have something to tell you. It's that I love you. I've been wanting to tell you for a long time, but I've been afraid. And I didn't know how to say it properly. Elegantly. As if that mattered! But now I know—with a certainty that takes my breath away—that what truly matters is those three simple words.

I love you.

I love you just as you are, now and forever. For better or for worse. For richer or for poorer. Come what may, now and always.

I know you'll come back and be with me. With us. We can't do without you, Hugo, we love you so dearly.

Oh, Hugo, I believe I've loved you all my life.

We have so much to look forward to, you and I.

I know you'll come back someday.

The voice went on and on, steadily, quietly.

It was a voice that sounded rather familiar.

He listened.

"Katherine," said Gwendolyn. Supper was over, but she stayed sitting at her place at the table.

"Yes, Gwendolyn?" Katherine had already gotten up. She paused by her chair. "Is there something I can do for you?"

"I know you want to go back upstairs, but if you could stay for just a minute?"

"Of course." Katherine sat down again, and Mrs. Penhallow said:

"Would you like for Bertram and me to leave, dearest?"

"No. I want you to hear, too." Gwendolyn fiddled with her fork and spoon for a few moments, then looked up and to Katherine. "I'm very sorry for how I've behaved toward you. I've been beastly. It's because—well, I've felt so outside of things. And afraid."

"Afraid how?" said Katherine gently.

"Afraid that Hugo wouldn't love me as much, now that you're here. I waited so many years for Hugo to come home, but—then you came, too. I didn't want to share him, you see."

Outsiderness. Fear. Katherine made no attempt to hide the emotion in her voice as she answered, "I know what it's like to be afraid. And to feel outside of things. I know it all too well. But I haven't come here to displace you, Gwendolyn. And I know—oh, I know for sure that Hugo loves you just as much as ever."

"*Do* you, Katherine? How can you know that?"

Katherine smiled at her. "I've learned, Gwendolyn, being here among all of you, that the human heart is a very capacious thing. That it can expand to hold more and more love, freely and generously. I used to know it, when I was a little girl living next door—I learned it here, in this house, long ago—but then I went away and forgot. I'm so glad to have remembered it all over again."

"I believe," said Bertram, "you're speaking metaphorically, Katherine. Although the heart does expand, it immediately contracts in a pumping motion, thereby sending freshly oxygenated blood through the aorta which is, of course, the main artery of the body and extends down to the abdomen, where it splits into two smaller arteries."

"Just so, Bertram," Katherine said, with perfect gravity.

"*Je t'aime passionnément, ma chérie,*" said Señor Rodrigo on his perch near the fireplace, in which a cheerful fire crackled. "*Rapprochez-vous un peu, s'il vous plaît.*" He added, as if in an afterthought, "Yo ho ho."

"So you forgive me then, Katherine?" asked Gwendolyn.

"There's nothing to forgive. Truly." She smiled, and Gwendolyn smiled back, and Katherine felt her heart expand still more, pausing for a moment before she stood again, to watch as Gwendolyn got up to go over to Rodrigo and give him the little end piece of bread she'd been saving for him as, she had earlier disclosed to the family, it was quite his favorite part of the loaf.

Oh, Hugo, I've been reading Shakespeare again. Your grandpapa has a beautiful edition of the Sonnets. Today I read Sonnet 116. Do you know it, darling Hugo? There's this bit of it which almost made me cry. But in a good way.

'Let me not to the marriage of true minds / Admit impediments. Love is not love / Which alters when it alteration finds, / Or bends with the remover to remove. / O no! it is an ever-fixed mark / That looks on tempests and is never shaken; / It is the star to every wand'ring bark . . .'

Hugo, dearest Hugo, never once have you tried to make me into something I'm not. You've accepted me as I am, with all my faults and flaws, and you've shown me how to be that way with others, too. I love you so much. You're my ever-fixed mark, you're my star which never fades or falters.

I know you'll come back when you're ready.

I know you'll come home when the time is right.

I'm waiting, and watching over you, and hoping.

I love you, Hugo.

The mighty storms of autumn rolled into Whitehaven, bringing with them fierce winds and cold rain, and, at the beach, tall curling waves that crashed, magnificent, onto the sand. Inside the house they were warm and snug, thanks, Katherine knew, to the money which she had brought to them, a thought which gave her a great deal of pleasure.

Eliza was well again, and Céleste, too, who had come downstairs determined to help however she could with an arm still in its sling. Will Studdart had received five competing offers for the *Arcadia*, but was waiting, he told the brokers, until his partner was well enough to participate in the decision; in the meantime he busied himself looking for a house to buy and also reading Katherine's manuscript, a full first draft which she had copied out neatly and given to him. Claudia resumed her work on the illustrations, and Bertram finished his essay on copper extraction. The puppy Gwendolyn had brought home, plump now, had become great friends with Señor Rodrigo, whose feathers continued to grow, daily rendering him more handsome and regal, a fact of which he seemed to be keenly aware, for he spent a good deal of time complacently preening himself.

And day by day, Katherine sat by the bed which she shared with Hugo, talking to him. Spooning into his mouth the light, nourishing broth which Cook made with the finest bones—the best bones—which the butcher's wife set aside for him.

Katherine talked to him, easily, softly, naturally, holding Hugo's hand, tenderly brushing the golden hair, longer now, off his forehead. Told him about what everyone was doing, and about the *Arcadia*. Read out loud to him from her manuscript. And she spoke her words of love, and need, and hope, words which sprang from a well that would always, she knew, be full.

And then, on a cold, foggy day in November, Hugo opened his eyes. Katherine had gone to look out the windows, admiring the beauty of the ocean in all its many moods, and when she came back to the bed she saw that Hugo had woken up. He smiled at her and he said:

"Hullo, Kate."

Carefully, so as not to jostle him, she sat down next to him on the bed and took his big hand in hers. Joy, sweetest joy, flooded her, and in a flash of memory she remembered how, a year ago, she had imagined that heaven was a place where she could be alone. That there was no greater happiness than to be by herself. But slowly and gradually, week after week, she had changed her mind. And now— oh, now, here, with Hugo, here was her heaven. In a voice that surprised her with its calmness she answered, softly: "Hullo."

"Gwennie all right?"

"Yes, she's fine."

"Everyone else well, too?"

"Yes."

"Including you?"

"Oh, yes."

"Well, that's excellent news."

"Yes, it is. Can I get you anything? I've a cup of mulled cider right here, or I can go get you anything you like."

"Don't go away, Kate."

She smiled. "I won't. A little cider, then?"

"Yes, please."

Tenderly she helped bring him upright on his pillows, hating to see how he grimaced. "Your leg, Hugo?"

"Yes. Did I break it again?"

"I'm afraid so."

"Damn it to hell."

"I know. I'm sorry." She held the cup of cider to his lips, and he drank.

"Thanks. Kate, I'm as weak as a damned cat."

"It's understandable. Does your head hurt you, or anything else?"

"No, it's just my leg."

"You'll be better soon. I'm going to take very good care of you."

He was looking at her, and even with the pallor of illness on his now-gaunt face, the dark circles underneath his eyes, the scruffy golden beard, he was so handsome to her, so familiar and so beloved, that Katherine had to keep herself from kissing him with the fervor—all the relief and the happiness, the hope and the optimism—that made her feel that she could float up like a feather on the breeze.

"I think," Hugo said, "you *have* been taking good care of me. You've been talking to me, haven't you, Kate?"

She nodded, and he said:

"You saved me."

She smiled. "It was Will and your men who did that."

"Yes, they saved me from the ocean. But it was you who brought me back."

"Well, if we're to talk of saving," Katherine answered, stroking his hand, "you saved me too, my darling Hugo. Which means we're even."

He looked at her, in his blue eyes a dawning glow. "*Am* I your darling, Kate?"

"Yes. Oh, yes."

He took this in. And he smiled, too. "I'm glad. Very glad. Will you tell me again those things you said to me, while I was elsewhere?"

"Of course. But a little later, perhaps? Right now, there are so many other people who need to know that you're awake. Will you excuse me for just a few moments?"

"To be sure."

When she was at the door he added:

"Kate."

She stopped, and turned. "Yes, Hugo?"

"I love you, you know."

And she said, easily and naturally: "I'm glad. I love you, too." Yes indeed, the heart certainly was an ever-expanding organ. Katherine smiled back at Hugo, then went to gather her family and bring them upstairs, so that they could all share, together, in the joy of Hugo's awakening.

---

14 November 1812

Dear Francis and Percy,

A very quick note to let you know that Hugo regained consciousness today. He spoke with all of us, had some of Cook's delicious chicken soup, and went back to sleep. Your mama has gone to the parsonage to share the wonderful news with your grandpapa and aunts and I will shortly send this to you by express.

I hope this finds you both well.

More soon.

Love,
Katherine

"**B**reakfast in bed," said Hugo the next morning, eyeing with satisfaction the tray which Eliza had brought up. "Excellent. I'm hungry as a bear. Thanks very much." Smilingly Eliza dipped a little curtsy and left the room, and he looked over to Katherine, sitting in a chair by the bed. "Where's yours, Kate?"

"I've already had mine, downstairs. How are you feeling?"

"Rather tired. But better."

"I'm so happy to hear it, my darling."

My darling. These, Hugo decided, were now two of his favorite words. He picked up a bowl of oatmeal laden with raisins, pecans, sugar, and cream. "While I eat, will you tell me again the things you said to me before?"

And Katherine did.

Hugo listened.

At the same time he remembered, last year, believing that he wasn't cut out for love. That he hadn't—wouldn't—find the right woman.

By God, how splendid to be proved wrong. And without having to spout poetry, either, or pretending to be something he wasn't. Life was good. Very good indeed.

When Katherine had done, and he had finished his breakfast, he said, "What made you decide to talk to me, all that time? Daresay most people would have thought it a hopeless endeavor."

Katherine had been sitting in her chair with her knees drawn up and her arms clasped around them, but now she unfurled herself and sat up straight. "Never hopeless. Do you remember Gabriel telling us, back at Surmont Hall, how he followed his instinct in searching for Livia? And then Livia said that perhaps there's more to life than we sometimes think. That maybe there's more inside us than we can know. I believe I was searching for *you,* and that the only way I could do that was with my words. By talking to you. And by hoping—trusting—*believing* that you heard me."

"Well, I'm awfully glad you did. Come sit next to me, Kate?"

"With pleasure." She stood up, moved the tray away, then eased herself onto the bed next to him where he sat propped up on pillows, his injured leg, well wrapped by Dr. Wilson, cushioned also by pillows. He took her hand in his and looked with a kind of wonderment into her lovely dark eyes.

"You," he said, "are so beautiful. Wish I could show you how I feel."

She smiled. "I know what you mean. But the words are nice to hear."

"It's good to say them, too. Powerful things, words, aren't they?"

"Oh, yes. Hugo, how long have you known that you love me?"

He thought. "I don't know, Kate. Months, perhaps, or longer. Maybe forever. Should've told you sooner. But you already know what an oaf I am."

"Dearest oaf," she said, with such warm, teasing affection in her voice that Hugo decided that these two words were now among his favorites also.

"Kate," he said, "it's come to me."

"What is it?"

"I hadn't realized it before, but now I do. What a tremendous stroke of luck it was, breaking my leg again. Otherwise you'd never have told me you love me."

She laughed, and, raising his hand to her lips, kissed it. "My own true love."

"Am I, Kate?" he said, enraptured.

"Of course you are." She kissed his hand again.

"Well," Hugo said, "that makes us even."

---

18 November 1812

Dear Percy and Francis,

Every day Hugo is better and better. Dr. Wilson says that he'll soon be able to come downstairs, using crutches. He wants me to tell you that he's very sorry that he won't be coming himself to fetch you from school, but his partner, Mr. Will Studdart, is, and we both think you will enjoy his company very much. We're all counting the days till you come home. Cook says she is going to make the biggest, most delicious Christmas pudding ever.

Love,
Katherine

"*M*adame," said Céleste, standing in the doorway to the little parlor Katherine had taken to using as her study. "May I speak with you, *s'il vous plaît?*"

"Certainly! Please come in." Katherine put down her quill. "Oh, Céleste, it's so nice to see you without that sling."

"I feel the same, *madame.*"

After several weeks of Cook's good food, Céleste had lost her haggard look and her dark straight hair had regained a glossy sheen; she looked neat and trim in her dark blue gown and spotless white fichu. She said, "I believe, *madame,* that *votre manuscrit* is completed?"

Katherine glanced down at her desk, on which the hundred or so pages lay in a tidy stack, next to it Claudia's illustrations, finished also, and so handsome that both she and Will had had to admiringly look them over a dozen times or more. Katherine didn't bother to inquire precisely how Céleste knew; that had always been Céleste's way. "Yes. I was just drafting a cover letter, but I don't know to whom yet."

"You are looking for *un éditeur,* I understand, to publish your book?"

Katherine nodded, and Céleste went on:

"It may be, *madame,* that I know someone in London, who may know someone . . ."

Katherine began to laugh. "Oh, Céleste, you truly *are* the most resourceful person I know."

Céleste smiled. "We all have our talents, do we not, *madame?* And it would be a very small way in which to repay your kindness to me. If you will but frank a letter for me, I shall write to *ma connaissance* at once."

"Of course. Thank you, Céleste."

"It is my pleasure. *Madame,* there is one other thing. The colleague of Monsieur Hugo, Monsieur Will

Studdart—you know that he is to move into his new house next week?"

"Yes."

"He has been making inquiries about finding *une femme de ménage*—a housekeeper. I went to him and offered my services, and he has given me the position. *C'est-à-dire,* if you do not object?"

"Of course not! What wonderful news! And you'll be close by, on Duke Street. I'm so glad for you, Céleste."

"Thank you, *madame.* It is odd to think it now, but when I first returned to Whitehaven, I thought my life was over. Now, I see, it is just beginning." Céleste smiled, and went away, and Katherine, filled with fresh hope, went back to work on her letter. And when she finished it, she took a new, blank sheet of paper. She looked at it for a while, and then she wrote:

> *Be who you are.*
> *To thine own self be true.*
> *Who am I?*
> *I am a human being, a person; a woman. A wife. A daughter and a daughter-in-law; a grandchild. A sister. A cousin. A friend.*
> *Mrs. Hugo Penhallow. Katherine Penhallow. Katherine. Kate.*
> *I am a writer.*
> *I am all of these things, and more.*

———

27 November 1812

Dear Katherine,

Percy and I are most awfully glad that Hugo is doing better. It was splendid of you to write to us. Also, thank you for the five-pound notes. We both hope that Mr. Studdart is a bruising rider as we intend to ride home as quickly as possible.

Faithfully yours,
Francis

P.S. Also, please could you tell Hugo to not throw away his crutches when he's done with them? We've always longed to try hopping around on them.

Chapter 21

November gave way to December, the winds blew, the rain fell, and waves crashed on the shore. Céleste took over the management of Will's new house with such unobtrusive competence that Will wondered how he had ever gotten along without her. Word came from Surmont Hall that Livia had had her baby, who was named Titania, and that everyone was healthy and well. The brusque, restless Christopher Beck spent so much time hanging around the harbor that Hugo, taking pity on him, hired him on as a temporary apprentice which, despite his father's uneasiness, seemed to be doing him some good. Céleste's contacts had produced the name of a likely publisher, and Katherine—using a pseudonym, as she didn't want either her surname or her gender to influence the decision process—sent the manuscript off to London. The *Arcadia* was sold for a very satisfying sum, and so, waiting only for the arrival of Francis and Percy, who traveled without incident under the cheerful aegis of Will Studdart, a party to celebrate was held in the big old house on the beach.

By afternoon the weather had obligingly cleared, the drawing-room was festively decorated by Gwendolyn and Diana Beck, Cook had outdone herself with the refreshments, Señor Rodrigo had never looked so sleek and handsome, all was in readiness and everyone was there—except for Hugo and Bertram.

One of the twins came into the drawing-room ferrying a platter of little ham sandwiches and Katherine, who had been helping Diana fix a sagging garland, said:

"Percy, do you know where Hugo and Bertram have gone?"

Gwendolyn looked over from the flowers she was arranging—both Will Studdart and Mr. Beck had arrived with great colorful bouquets—and exclaimed, "Katherine, how did you know that's Percy?"

"I don't know," said Katherine. "I just did."

Mrs. Penhallow nodded wisely, Percy said something about champagne, and then the dogs started barking; a few moments later Bertram came in bearing an enormous box from the confectioner's. Behind him, on his crutches, came Hugo, who unslung from his shoulder his rucksack in which were several bottles of champagne.

As Bertram opened the box with a flourish, Hugo explained, "I had a craving for marzipan," and looked so mischievous that more than one person wondered why, but, saying nothing more on the subject, he called immediately for glasses as, he said, there were so many good things to toast.

Everyone's health had been drunk, and various other tributes made, both solemn and comical, and glasses refilled more than once, when Katherine stood up from the sofa she had been sharing with Hugo, and said:

"I would like to propose a toast."

The room quieted, and Bertram said, "To what, Katherine? Or to whom?"

She smiled and looked around. Here, here, were the people she loved, and who loved her. Here was where she belonged; here, her heaven. And on the sofa, an arm's breadth away, was her light and her heart's joy, her ever-fixed mark and her guiding star. Hugo, always and forever.

Katherine lifted her glass high. "To me," she said. "For having had the infinite good sense to propose to Hugo."

"I'll drink to that," said Hugo, laughing, and raised his own glass. "To my Kate!"

"To Kate!" warmly echoed many voices, and everybody drank, and then someone cackled loudly and demanded:

"Kiss me, you saucy wench!"

"Oh, Señor Rodrigo, we love you too," said Aunt Claudia fondly, and went over to him on his perch which had been set near the fire, and Hugo said:

"An excellent idea." He reached for Katherine's hand, and she sat down next to him again. "Will you, Kate?" he asked. "My saucy wench?"

"Darling Hugo," she said softly, caressingly, "of course I will," and then, in front of everyone, she kissed him. And Señor Rodrigo cackled again.

Later, when the party was over and their guests had gone home, Hugo and his family gathered in the library. The dogs, the recipients of a great many scraps, lay dozing peacefully on the hearthrug. His mama was sewing, Bertram and Francis were reading, Percy and Gwendolyn were playing chess, and Katherine, leaning back on one of the sofas with her feet on an ottoman, was gazing into the leaping flames of the fire. He could almost hear the gears and wheels in her brain turning.

"Katherine," said Francis, looking up from his book, "this biography of Cornelius Tacitus suggests that much of his writing is flawed, though it may be difficult to perceive due to his persuasive style. Do you agree with that?"

Katherine didn't respond at first, and Francis had to say her name again, a little louder, before she blinked and looked over to him.

"I'm sorry, Francis, I had an idea for something. What did you say?"

He repeated his question, and after a few moments she replied, "It may be that I do. For example, he once said that gratitude is a burden, and I'm not at all certain he's right about that."

Francis nodded and went back to his book, and Hugo said curiously:

"What's your idea, Kate?"

"Oh, I was thinking about Livia and Gabriel's baby, and about a gift to celebrate her birth. I want to write a little story for her—about a fairy named Titania, who likes to ride horses and go fishing and fight battles."

"What a marvelous idea, Katherine dear," said Mama, glancing up from her sewing. "Such a unique gift."

"Thank you, Mama, I'm glad you think so. And I was wondering if perhaps Gwendolyn might be interested in illustrating it."

Gwendolyn looked up from the chessboard, delight on her face. "Oh, Katherine, really?"

"Yes. Aunt Claudia showed me some of your watercolors the other day. You're very talented, Gwennie."

"I don't know about that, but I'd love to illustrate your story! When can we begin?"

Katherine smiled at her. "Let's start tomorrow."

Hugo was already in bed, and Katherine, at her dressing-table, had just finished brushing out her curls and was about to weave them into a bulky plait, but Hugo said:

"Leave your hair like that, will you, Kate?"

"All right." She stood and went over toward the bed, next to which, on the little yellow table, three candles flickered.

Hugo said, "My God, but you're beautiful."

She smiled, looking down into his face. Never, ever would she tire of hearing him say that. Suddenly something came to her, and she glanced over at the rucksack which Hugo had brought upstairs and left by the door, rather than putting it back into its usual place in his armoire. "Hugo," she said, "what's in your rucksack?"

He had, now, an expression of sweet mischief. "A gift for you."

"How very kind." She went over to his rucksack. "May I?"

"By all means."

Lifting the flap, she saw within another, smaller box from the confectioner's. She pulled it out and looked at Hugo. "Is this what I think it is?"

He grinned. "Open it and see."

Katherine lifted the lid and there, as she expected, were a dozen chocolate conserves. She laughed and went over to the bed and climbed upon it, then held out the box to Hugo. He took a conserve, extended it to her so she could take a bite, and ate the rest of it.

"Delicious," Katherine said, with a little purr in her voice. "What a . . . *thoughtful* gift, my darling."

"Well," he replied, still with that look of sweet mischief, "I did think about it a lot. That is to say, I thought about how awfully *useful* a conserve can be."

"If one is creative."

"Which we are. Damn this leg."

"Never say that. I adore your leg. Both of your legs. All of you, in fact." Katherine offered him the box again, while with her other hand she drew down the bedclothes. She smiled. "Another conserve?"

Christmas came and went, Katherine and Gwendolyn worked on their project, and Percy and Francis one evening instigated such a loud and jolly pillow fight that the whole family simply *had* to join in—and Katherine learned that it was indeed a great deal of fun landing a pillow with a hearty *thwack*. On January 2nd she and

Hugo celebrated their one-year anniversary; she gave him a handsome brass spyglass, and he in turn handed her a small box about the size of a deck of playing cards.

Inside the box, nestled on a bed of amber velvet, was a necklace.

Its delicate links were formed out of silver burnished to a soft shine, and suspended from it, artfully wrapped in fine silver filament, were five pieces of sea-glass, white, green, amber, a deep ruby red, and blue.

"It took me a while to find the red piece," said Hugo, "but I was determined."

Katherine's eyes filled with tears. "Oh, Hugo, I've never seen anything so lovely. Thank you. I'll treasure it forever." And of course she put it on right away. It complemented, she said, her cherished seed-pearl ear-bobs so beautifully.

A week after that, Francis and Percy went back to school, Will Studdart graciously agreeing to accompany them; in the beginning of February, Hugo was able to walk without his crutches, which, faithful to his promise, he put into the twins' room until they came home again.

A fortnight later, on a crisp, cold afternoon, Hugo and Will were in their office, looking over some new hull designs, when Katherine came bursting in, her face alight with excitement. From her warm woolen muff she pulled out a letter. "Read this!"

15 February 1813

Dear Mr. Wolfe,

My staff and I have reviewed your manuscript with considerable enjoyment, and we are unanimous in agreeing that English Ships Out of Liverpool Harbor: A National Heritage would be a worthy addition to our list. I am gratified, there-

fore, to offer you the following terms: 200 pounds for the copyright, and a 5 percent royalty on each copy sold.

> *Believe me, sir, most sincerely, etc.,*
> *Samuel Brereton, Esquire*

Hugo and Will whooped with joy, and Will exclaimed, "Mrs. P., you're a wonder!"

"Oh, but I'm not done," said Katherine.

———

24 February 1813

Dear Mr. Brereton,

Thank you very much for your letter. It would be an honor to see my work published by your esteemed firm. These, however, are my preferred terms: 650 pounds outright, a copyright which reverts to me in 10 years, and a 15 percent royalty on each copy sold.

> *Yours very sincerely,*
> *K. Wolfe*

———

2 March 1813

Dear Mr. Wolfe,

While we all rejoiced to receive your acceptance of our offer, your terms, my dear sir, are a trifle steep. May I suggest instead the following: 300 pounds outright, a copyright which reverts to you in 15 years, and a 9 percent royalty on each copy sold.

> *Believe me, etc.,*
> *Samuel Brereton, Esq.*

———

11 March 1813

Dear Mr. Brereton,
    Thank you for yours of the 2nd. I am obliged to inform you, sir, that I am resolute concerning the terms I delineated in my previous letter. Should they not meet with your satisfaction, I must request the prompt return of the materials so that I may seek a publisher elsewhere.

                              Yours very sincerely,
                                      K. Wolfe

————————

18 March 1813

By express

Dear Mr. Wolfe,
    We accept your terms. A contract is enclosed.
    We look forward to hearing from you again at your earliest convenience.

                              Believe me, etc.,
                                      Samuel

————————

"**H**ugo."

"Yes, Katherine?"

"I want to publish the book using my real name. You don't mind, do you?"

"Of course not."

They stood at their windows. Outside, above, in the full dark of evening, the northern lights glowed and danced in dazzling arcs of green, yellow, pink, and violet. Hugo added:

"There's just one problem."

"Oh?"

"If I were any more proud of you, I think I might burst."

Katherine laughed, and brought herself more snugly into the circle of his arm around her. "Please don't. But thank you. I'm going to write to your Aunt Henrietta, to make sure she feels the same way. And do you remember that other idea I had, the one I mentioned to you and Will? I'm going to write that letter, too."

And not long after that, she got her replies.

———

22 April 1813

Dear Katherine,

   Thank you for your note. It says a great deal about the kind of person you are that you would consult with me as to the use of the family surname in such a public fashion. I think it is a splendid idea, and may I tender my congratulations? It sounds an excellent book and I look forward to ordering my copy in due course as well as quite a few additional copies which I shall give to the deserving among my acquaintance.

   You will be glad to hear, I am sure, that Titania now has a total of four teeth. We have several times shown her your charming story, with its equally charming illustrations, and though she is not yet quite capable of holding it herself, she has indicated her approval by blowing some very delightful bubbles.

   I cannot help but muse, my dear Katherine, that it seems somehow fated that you were to join our family. After all, "Penhallow," when one separates the word into its two components, is a name entirely suited for a writer and soon-to-be author, is it not?

                          Affectionately yours,
                          Aunt Henrietta

P.S. In future, if you like, you may address me as per the above, and leave off the more formal "Mrs. Penhallow."

P.P.S. Your second note has just this moment arrived, with your news regarding the Duke of Clarence. What a clever idea to ask if he would like to write a foreword to your book, and how very gratifying that he agreed. I daresay your publishers are at this moment tossing their hats in the air with jubilation.

———————

An image was forming in her mind's eye.

A blank page.

But not an empty, frightening sort of blankness.

Rather, it was an image of pure possibility—challenging and exciting.

The image continued to form.

She envisioned her own hand, a little pot of ink, a quill moving across the white expanse.

Then, words:

Some people seem to be born underneath a lucky star. Others seem unlucky from the moment of their birth. But Lucy Dale, in the course of her adventures, would come to learn that luck—seemingly good or bad—is a complex, even mysterious entity. She would learn that perhaps there's more to life than we sometimes think. That maybe there's more inside us than we can know.

She pondered these words.

She liked them, but it was difficult to know whether they would stay as she went along. She might shift them around, or change them entirely.

Nonetheless, it was a beginning.

You had to start somewhere, after all.

The rest would follow.

She smiled.

And then came a voice, deep, calm, patient, and beloved: "Kate."

Katherine blinked, looked over to Hugo, who stood behind Aunt Claudia as she worked at her easel. He had walked with her to the parsonage in the warmth of a lovely spring afternoon, wanting, he said, to see how the portrait was coming along.

"Yes, Hugo?"

"This painting of you and Rodrigo is simply ripping."

She nodded. "Aunt Claudia is a brilliant artist."

"Nonsense, my dears, you flatter me," murmured Claudia, her gaze, both dreamy and intent, moving back and forth between her canvas and Katherine, who said, her own voice rather dreamy:

"I've just had an idea."

"Tell it to us," said Hugo.

"I'm going to write a novel. It's about a girl who comes from an unhappy family and is sent to a ghastly boarding school, then goes out into the world a rather hard, troubled person. It's not going to be about me, though. It's just that I'm going to use my own experiences and reshape them. Play with them. Make them into fiction."

"That's what art is," remarked Aunt Claudia, dipping her brush into a little puddle of vibrant green. "Taking what we know and molding it anew."

"Yes, exactly," agreed Katherine, and Hugo asked, interested:

"What happens to your heroine, Kate?"

"It will all turn out well. I'm not sure how yet. But it will."

"I can't wait to read it," he said, and she answered, laughing:

"I can't wait to write it."

A few years later . . .

If, say, you happened to wander into a certain shop on Lowther Street when custom was slow, and decided to linger there for a little while, contemplating the purchase of a beef haunch or a nice flitch of bacon, it might be that the butcher's wife—Whitehaven's most fruitful source of information—would lean a dimpled elbow on the counter and regale you with some choice tidbits of news.

She might, for example, tell you, in a voice resonant with awe and pride, about the town's most well-known resident, Mrs. Katherine Penhallow, whose fame as an author was rapidly spreading. Why, she'd been to faraway London, not once but twice, where she had everywhere been fêted as a literary lioness, and her husband, the dashing Captain Penhallow, had frequently been heard speaking with the highest admiration of his wife's talent. (The talent which, the butcher's wife might add in a confidential tone, brought in a regular flow of cheques from the distinguished publisher Samuel Brereton, Esquire.) The captain and his missus had committed the dreadful gaffe of publicly being seen to be madly in love with each other but, as they were Penhallows—to whose illustrious ancestor the mighty Conqueror himself had bowed—Polite Society only smiled and pretended not to notice.

Word of Mrs. Katherine's success had even spread to the wilds of Scotland, made plain when one day she received a friendly letter from a chieftain's wife named Fiona who, thanks to their respective marriages to Penhallow men, was thus a newfound cousin to Mrs. Katherine. This letter, full of praise for Mrs. Katherine's celebrated novel *Lucy Dale,* had sparked between the two ladies a cordial, ongoing correspondence.

Meanwhile, the firm of Studdart & Penhallow, over at the harbor, was selling ships as quickly as their crews could make them and fast gaining a reputation as one of the country's best and most forward-thinking shipbuilders. Captain Penhallow and his partner Will were said to now be quite wealthy, though neither of them, being modest men, was ever heard mentioning it, much less boasting about it.

Altogether the Penhallow family was doing so well they had several times been to Seascale where bathing machines had at last been made available to the public, and—this interesting side note might well be conveyed to you in a lowered voice, given the radical nature of the disclosure—some of the ladies in their party went swimming in the ocean *without* the benefit of a bathing machine. And though Miss Verena Mantel said she only did it so she could keep an eye on her adventurous sister Miss Claudia, everyone could see that she was, in fact, having a wonderful time.

Speaking of Miss Claudia, wasn't it marvelous that her portrait of Mrs. Katherine and that handsome green parrot had been exhibited at the Royal Academy of Art during its annual exhibition, and was so widely acclaimed that no less a personage than the Prince Regent himself begged to purchase it for his own collection, offering Miss Claudia a sum so monumental that fashionable London was positively abuzz.

You couldn't help but admire Miss Claudia for refusing, saying that some treasures were ultimately meant to be kept close to home. And wasn't it lovely that after decades of genteel poverty, she now had plenty of money thanks to the clever illustrations she did for those books—money which generously she shared with her sister and papa, and also contributing to all kinds of charitable endeavors here in Whitehaven.

Yes indeed, thanks to her, and the captain and Mrs. Katherine, too, and their mama, and that pleasant Mr. Studdart, the charity home was running properly at last, and the indigents' relief fund was finally all nice and flush, and their dear vicar Mr. Mantel could even leave off writing those endless letters of appeal to potential benefactors elsewhere.

Well, well, what else? Oh, of course, the three Penhallow boys! They were all at Eton these days, doing splendidly in their respective pursuits, and absolutely thick as thieves with their cousin Owen FitzClarence, the Marquis of Ellington, who, after a lifetime of being extremely short, had in recent years shot up in height, a promising development which gave him enormous satisfaction.

Miss Gwendolyn, now, was all of eighteen and so beautiful that people were comparing her left and right to a Greek goddess—an accolade to which she responded with a mixture of embarrassment and (being only human) gratification. She was soon to embark on her very first Season and nobody had any doubt that she would enjoy a triumphant debut. Mrs. Katherine was hoping to join her sister in London, but having not so long ago given birth to twins—identical twins—and also being so busy writing more books, wasn't quite sure yet if she would.

It was remarkable, the butcher's wife might add, leaning a little closer to you over the counter, how even though the babies were only a few months old, everyone in the family could already tell them apart. You wouldn't think such a thing would be possible, and yet so it was.

But there, she might comfortably say, perhaps there's more to life than we realize. Maybe there's more inside us than we can know. Maybe—just maybe—we've all got inside of us a little bit of magic, all our own.

Author's Note

Dear Reader,

The Bride Takes a Groom is a story about love, of course, and it's also about hope, belonging, and the power of words—all things that to me matter a great deal.

I owe a debt of gratitude to the poet Emily Dickinson; this famous, exquisite poem of hers has long been a favorite of mine:

"Hope" is the thing with feathers—
That perches in the soul—
And sings the tune without the words—
And never stops—at all—

And sweetest—in the Gale—is heard
And sore must be the storm—
That could abash the little Bird
That kept so many warm—

I've heard it in the chillest land—
And on the strangest Sea—
Yet—never—in Extremity,
It asked a crumb—of Me.

In *The Bride Takes a Groom,* that talkative, rather mysterious bird, Señor Rodrigo, el Duque de Almodóvar del Valle de Oro, comes to represent the power of hope. I'm so glad that in the end he got his feathers back, aren't you?

All my best,

Lisa

**Continue reading for a sneak peek
at Lisa Berne's next Penhallow Dynasty novel**

Coming in 2019

London, England
Spring 1818

The first time Gwendolyn Penhallow saw the Earl of Westenbury, her heart seemed to lift and soar like a bird in flight.

He was the most handsome man she'd ever seen—had ever dreamed of—with his serene, even-featured countenance and his tawny light-brown hair neatly cropped *à la Brutus*, and he walked into Almack's with such easy, unaffected grace that she was, a little, surprised that the musicians didn't freeze, that all the dancers hadn't stopped dead in their tracks, that an awed hush didn't fall upon the room with the piercing sweetness of a long and exquisite grace note.

She had no idea, then, that he was one of the *ton*'s most eligible gentlemen. That he was an earl, fabulously wealthy, owner of several magnificent estates in Gloucestershire. That for ten years, a great many young ladies just like herself—come to London for the Season—had gazed upon him with eager, hungry eyes, hoping for his favor, waiting anxiously for him to choose a bride. And if Gwendolyn *had* known, she wouldn't have cared. What mattered is that he made her breath catch in her throat, in just the way it would when you suddenly stumbled across something rare, something very close to precious.

She was dancing with somebody else, but had just enough time, before she had to turn back to her partner, to see that the tall, handsome stranger was looking at *her*. That he'd paused, and onto his face came first an expression of astonishment, followed, quickly, by wonder and delight.

For a giddy moment Gwendolyn thought he might walk right into the dance, disrupting the intricate formations, and boldly sweep her away from her partner—what *was* his name? She'd forgotten it, could barely even feel her gloved hands in his—but he didn't move, didn't come her way.

Her heart sank low, foolishly low, and she could have kicked it across the floor like a sad little ball, but afterwards, when the quadrille was over and she was standing next to Mama, and she was doing her best to focus on their conversation and not let her eyes move searchingly around the room in a rude and immature way, the Honorable Mrs. Drummond-Burrell, the haughtiest, most minutely correct of the Patronesses, glided into view, at her side—as if by magic, a wish made manifest with all the dreamlike logic of a fairy tale—the handsome stranger.

He smiled. And joy shimmered throughout Gwendolyn, like a thousand lanterns lighting all at once.

"Mrs. Penhallow," said Mrs. Drummond-Burrell to Mama in her cool remote way, "may I introduce to you the Earl of Westenbury? He has just yesterday arrived in Town, and wishes me to present himself to you as a desirable partner for your daughter."

Gwendolyn watched with lips gone suddenly dry as the Earl bowed to Mama, registering more fully, now, how elegantly he was dressed in the dark knee-breeches considered *de rigueur* for Almack's, the dark long-tailed coat set superbly across broad shoulders, his snow-white cravat tied with marvelous precision. And then he was saying to her, with a smile in his gold-flecked deep-green eyes, "How do you do, Miss Penhallow," and that was that.

The fabled *coup de foudre*.

Love at first sight.

She was obliged to inform him that all her dances to-night were taken, but added, as if a casual afterthought, that tomorrow evening she would be attending Lord and Lady Mainwaring's ball. He promptly secured her hand for two dances—any more than that would have of course been considered *risqué*—and Gwendolyn had to wait a long, very long twenty-four hours until she could see the Earl again, and learn, during their cotillion and then a waltz, that he danced beautifully. He didn't step on the hem of her gown, or try to squeeze her hands in a vulgar way, or bring her too close to him during the waltz as some other gentlemen tried to do and which always made her feel all annoyed and prickly and icy inside.

The Mainwarings' ball took place two weeks and four days after Gwendolyn had attended her very first event of the Season (an intimate dinner-party hosted by her relation the Duchess of Egremont). In the days and nights that followed the ball, she and the Earl met at other gatherings, at assemblies and art galleries, at Vauxhall and at Venetian breakfasts, as frequently as propriety allowed.

Exactly three weeks after their propitious encounter at Almack's, the Earl sent a note to Gwendolyn's mother informing her that he was leaving Town on an urgent matter.

Eleven days after that, Gwendolyn's older brother Hugo arrived unexpectedly in London. The Earl had traveled to Whitehaven, and formally requested from Hugo—his sister's guardian—her hand in marriage. Was this what she wanted? Hugo now asked Gwendolyn.

Gwendolyn did. Oh, she *did*. The Earl was so nice—so

charming—so kind. And (she thought but did not say out loud) so handsome, so gallant. So unaffected and graceful in his manners. And the way he gazed at her, as if with his entire soul in those fascinating eyes of his. It made her feel so . . . cherished.

She was sure about this? Hugo asked.

Yes, she was absolutely certain.

It had all happened rather quickly, he observed.

It had, Gwendolyn agreed. But sometimes you just *knew*.

Hugo acknowledged the truth of this, having been most fortunate in his own marriage. Lucky to know in his bones he'd found his own true love.

And so on April 23, 1818, Gwendolyn and the Earl of Westenbury were officially betrothed. The Earl presented her with a singularly beautiful pearl ring which had been in his family for generations, a gift from Queen Elizabeth to a previous Lady Westenbury who had served as her Mistress of the Robes. In its warm gold setting, surrounded by tiny perfect rubies, the pearl glowed with a lovely milky luster which bewitched the eye.

When she was by herself, Gwendolyn would hold up her left hand and stare wonderingly at it. A symbol of her future happiness. Her life's great adventure. She was engaged. And to the most wonderful man in the world.

Seven years earlier . . .
Whitehaven, England
Autumn 1811

"Christopher, may I talk with you, please?" Gwendolyn Penhallow said, and Christopher Beck, annoyed at the interruption, brought his axe down with a *thunk* into a fat yew log and split it in two. They stood in the long yard to the back of his house, where he'd come to chop wood—over Father's objections, who said that it was a servant's job, not that of a gentleman—and all he wanted was to be left alone after yet another one of Father's longwinded lectures. So what if he'd been sent down from university? What did it matter? He rolled another log into place with his boot and lifted his axe high.

"Christopher, *please*," said Gwendolyn, and with a scowl he lowered the axe and looked down at her.

"Well?" he said curtly.

But she was silent, only gripping her fingers together till the knuckles showed white, and then, just when he was about to lift his axe again, she said, in a quick urgent rush of words:

"Oh, Christopher, we're in trouble. We've so little money, and Mama's so worried, though she never says anything. But I can *tell*. And Hugo's finally back in England, but he was injured and we don't know how is he is. Or even where he is. It's all so awful, and so frightening!" She took a tentative step closer to him, as one might, he thought bitterly, approach a fire-breathing dragon. "Diana says your mother left you a great fortune. And I thought—if you didn't mind it too much—that we could get married—and you could give Mama some of your money—"

"Get *married?*" he said, stupefied.

Gwendolyn nodded eagerly. "I know I'm only fourteen, and you're only seventeen, and a girl isn't supposed to ask a boy, but . . . but I'd do *anything* for my family. So will you?" She was looking up at him and suddenly it struck Christopher that her eyes were like great deep sapphire pools, sparkling with summer light. At this uncharacteristically sentimental thought he felt a rush of confused—confusing—emotions. Sensations. Gwendolyn lived next door and was his younger sister Diana's dearest friend; he saw her frequently. She'd been just a girl, as uninteresting and irritating as Diana.

But here she was, asking him to *marry* her. All at once Christopher realized, as if he'd been grabbed by the shoulders and violently rattled about, that Gwendolyn was beautiful. Tall, willowy, with delicate features and bright golden hair and a mouth the color of a ripe peach. Girls *did* get married at fourteen. His gaze dropped to her breasts, to their slight but unmistakably feminine curves, both revealed and tantalizingly concealed by the simple white bodice of her gown.

Lust, hot and piercing, rolled through his veins like fire and he was sharply aware that she might see it manifested. He could feel his face flaming red and, willing himself not to look down at his trouser front, awkwardly he shifted behind the rough pile of wood he had made and said to her:

"You mean it?"

Gwendolyn nodded again. "Oh yes, I do."

I do. The words of a marriage vow. Did she realize the implications of what she'd said? His mind was racing. How would they manage it? They were both underage. Of course: a bolt to Scotland—to Gretna Green—only fifty miles away. Ha! How furious Father would be. He was always prosing on about university, getting good marks, the need to be prudent and cautious, business deals, contracts, and how he was looking forward to Christopher joining him in his offices (a damned horrid stuffy place filled with people who sat around all day long shuffling papers back and forth), and on and on till Christopher all too frequently felt as if he would explode with anger and impatience.

Now, picturing Father's reaction upon discovering that his son had embarked on a runaway marriage—a decidedly imprudent, uncautious act—Christopher felt defiant glee overtake him. No more useless arguments with Father, ever again. He tossed his axe aside.

"Let's do it," he said.

Gwendolyn laughed and gave a little bounce on her toes. "Oh, Christopher, that's wonderful! It'll solve *everything*."

He barely heard her; he was already planning. They'd have to leave at night. And he'd need to pay for their coach fares, and lodgings and food also. After they were married, they could travel further north, up into the wilds of Scotland. How much money did he have on hand? He thought about it. Probably fifty pounds or so. They'd need to live rough for a while, but he'd find work. They'd be fine. And then he remembered something. A small, minute, critically important detail. Oh, bloody hell, but he was fortune's fool. He told her:

"I won't come into my money till I'm twenty-one."

Even as he said it, he saw the happiness fade from Gwendolyn's exquisitely pretty face.

"But that's four years from now. That won't do at all." Her voice wobbled with distress. "Oh, Christopher, I need the money *now*."

Well, that was that, then. His world closed in upon him again—his many failures, Father's disappointment, Diana fluttering round him like a small maddening moth in a house far too big for just the three of them—and Christopher could feel his scowl returning, his brows drawing together, the quick downturn of his mouth. He shrugged, turned away, picked up his axe. "Sorry," he said, and didn't wait for her to leave before he brought the axe down into the yew log and sundered it in two.

As it turned out, Gwendolyn's brother Hugo arrived in Whitehaven a week after that, healthy and well, and within a matter of days was betrothed to a rich heiress who lived just outside town, thereby neatly solving at a stroke all the family's money problems. Which was just as well, Christopher thought, because Diana had come trailing after him with the news of Hugo's engagement, and added in a low voice trembling with excitement:

"And Gwennie told me that her mama said that Papa asked her to marry her!"

He paused just outside the stable, stupefied all over again. "What the devil are you talking about, you nitwit? Father wants to marry *Gwendolyn?*"

"No, no, Papa asked Gwennie's mama to marry him! But she said no. Oh, Christopher, I do wish she'd said yes, she's the nicest, kindest, loveliest mama in all the world! And then Gwennie and I would be sisters! We'd all live together in the same house, and maybe, someday, I could marry Francis—or Percy—they're so very handsome— though I can never tell which is which. Aren't identical twins simply *fascinating?*"

"O God," said Christopher, nauseated to his very soul, then took one long step inside the stable and slammed the door in Diana's freckled face. He brushed aside the groom's offer to saddle his horse and did it himself, doing his best to keep his hands gentle despite the anger firing up inside him again, and within five minutes was on the wide, sandy beach, bent low over his horse's neck, riding hard and away, half-wishing he could plunge straight into the turbulent blue-green waves and disappear forever.

Four years after that . . .
Whitehaven, England
Winter 1815

"**O**h, Gwennie," exclaimed Diana, "you'd look like a fairy princess in that gown!"

The two girls were sitting close together on a sofa in the large, comfortable drawing-room of Gwendolyn's house, poring over the current issue of *La Belle Assemblée,* all around them the cheerful sounds of a convivial holiday gathering.

Gwendolyn studied the illustration of an improbably elongated lady wearing an elaborate dress of striped silver gauze, its glossy silver-edged hem drawn up to the knee (boldly displaying the white satin slip beneath) and ornamented with a large cluster of artificial pink flowers. It was difficult to envision herself in such a dramatic gown, and also wearing the pearl headdress, low-set wreath of brilliants, and the silver ribbons dangling negligently from the bodice—all of which were praised in the caption as the height of modish elegance. Doubtfully she said:

"Do you really think so, Diana?"

"Oh yes, do ask your mama to have it made for you! And you *must* wear it to Almack's! Every gentleman in the room will fall in love with you!"

Gwendolyn laughed. "One will be enough."

"Well, he'll be the *best* one, then," said Diana stoutly. "And he'll love you so much he'll want to be married right away. Maybe he'll spirit you away to Gretna Green, and you'll be a bride at eighteen! Wouldn't that be *romantic?*" She slipped her arm through Gwendolyn's and squeezed it. "Oh, Gwennie, I'm so excited about your Season! I *know* you're going to be declared a Diamond of the First Water! Everyone says so. Why, the other day I heard the butcher's wife tell everyone in the shop that you're as pretty as a Greek goddess!"

This was not the first time Gwendolyn had heard herself described in these terms, and although of course it was very flattering it was also rather embarrassing. One admired paintings and sculptures of the gods and goddesses of ancient Greece and Rome, but it wasn't real, really. *They* weren't real—they were works of art. Just abstract things. And it mattered to be real, because—

A burst of laughter over by the mantelpiece interrupted Gwendolyn's train of thought and she glanced over to see Hugo laughing at something his business partner, Mr. Studdart, had said. She let her gaze sweep around the room. How lovely it was to have her three other brothers home from Eton—and how tall they'd become, too, though they hadn't quite reached Hugo's great height yet. Percy stood next to Hugo, Francis was talking to Grandpapa, and Bertram sat next to Hugo's wife Katherine on a sofa, his hand on her rounded belly and on his face a look of deep interest.

"Did you feel that, Bertram?" said Katherine, and he nodded.

"It feels like an elbow, or a knee, kicking at me. How curious to think there's a person inside you, Katherine. Do you want a boy or a girl?"

She smiled at him. "I'll be happy with either."

"That's how I felt, Katherine dear," said Mama, who sat nearby with Mr. Studdart's new wife, Céleste, who had once been his housekeeper. Mrs. Studdart looked at Katherine, smiling a little, and Gwendolyn saw how her gaze went thoughtfully to Percy and Francis, and then to Aunt Verena and Aunt Claudia. Two sets of twins. Gwendolyn stared at Katherine wonderingly, then jumped when a mocking voice said from behind her:

"A fairy princess, eh?"

"Christopher, you frightened us!" said Diana reproachfully, twisting about to look up at him.

He ignored her and went on, drawling, "A bride at eighteen, Gwennie, how *romantic*."

Gwendolyn felt a hot blush coming over her as she too looked up at Christopher, into his dark saturnine face. She wished Diana hadn't mentioned marriage and Gretna Green within his earshot. That time she'd actually gone to him and *proposed*—what had she been thinking? After all these years it still felt a little awkward being around Christopher; there seemed always to be a sardonic, measuring gleam in his dark eyes when they rested upon her.

"Don't be a beast," said Diana. "Why are you here, anyway? You told us earlier you weren't coming."

His lip twisted in a sneer. "Father insisted." Casually he bent down, resting his elbows on the sofa-back, and so brought himself close to Gwendolyn, too close for comfort, but stubbornly she refused to budge, though with an abrupt prickle of awareness she realized that Christopher wasn't a boy any longer. At twenty-one, his shoulders were still wiry, but filled out with muscle now, and she could see a trace of stubble on his lean cheeks. Not a boy, but a man. He said, his dark gaze upon her:

"Looking forward to your Season, are you, Gwennie dear? Ready to sell yourself to the highest bidder?"

"I'm not *selling* myself," she retorted, nettled.

"No? Isn't that why women go to London, as commodities on the so-called Marriage Mart?"

"I'm going to enjoy myself, that's all."

"Really." In that one word was a wealth of skepticism. Scorn.

Oh, he *was* a beast. Why had he bothered coming home from university, anyway? For the pleasure of taunting her? In a low angry voice Gwendolyn said, "You don't know anything about it! I'm not just going for the balls and parties, I'll be going to museums, and lectures, and concerts, and all sorts of interesting things. You're just jealous! You wouldn't even know how to comport yourself in Society, or how to talk to people like a human being. You're—you're a *lout,* Christopher Beck, and a brute, and I *despise* you!" And she jumped up from the sofa and went over to where Aunt Claudia stood next to the perch of the family parrot, Señor Rodrigo, talking to him in her vague, amiable way.

"Do try, Rodrigo. Say 'I love you.'" Aunt Claudia held out half of a sweet rolled wafer and Señor Rodrigo only cocked his sleek green head and looked at it with visible contempt in his bright beady eyes.

"I love you," cooed Aunt Claudia.

Señor Rodrigo gave a loud, shrill, extended laugh, then said, "Blimey."

"I love you."

"Blimey."

"I love you."

"Blimey."

Finally Aunt Claudia gave him the wafer, which he accepted in an outstretched claw. Leisurely he ate it, scattering crumbs below him with total nonchalance, then looked up at her. "I love you."

Aunt Claudia laughed, and Gwendolyn, trying to shake off her bad mood, reached out her hand to allow Señor Rodrigo to climb onto her forefinger. "*Naughty* Rodrigo," she murmured affectionately.

"Blimey," he said, then made his way up her arm to her shoulder where he tried to nibble on her garnet ear-bob and then demanded, "Kiss me, you saucy wench," and she did, lightly touching her lips to his sharp black beak. And he laughed again.

From across the room Christopher straightened up, watching Gwendolyn, inside him a familiar roiling stir of anger. At her; her jibe. Anger at himself. Maybe he *was* a lout. A beast. Of no use to anyone. He cursed himself for having come to the party tonight against his own wishes, and again, later, when, home again, Father took the opportunity to mention just how well the Penhallow boys were doing at Eton, how bright were their futures, and if only Christopher could bestir himself to emulate them he'd likely be doing considerably better at university than he was.

Christopher listened, said nothing, ground his teeth, waited till Father had done, and then flung himself up to his room, paced around—back and forth, back and forth—until it was very late and his mind settled into something hard and sure, and from his armoire he pulled out a small valise and began to pack.

"**G**one?" repeated Gwendolyn. "Gone where?"

"We don't know," answered Diana, breathless with excitement. "He left a note saying goodbye, but he didn't say where he was going. He must have left in the dead of night! Papa's *so* upset, and says he'll hire the Bow Street Runners to go after Christopher and bring him back! Which of course I don't think he will. It's not as if Christopher committed a crime, you know."

After Diana had returned home, Gwendolyn went with slow steps up to her bedchamber, where she stood at the window overlooking the Becks' house. Almost level with her own room was Christopher's, though it was far enough away that she could only see the white curtains, left half-open, admitting the cool gray light of a winter's day into its new emptiness. Surely, surely, Christopher's leaving had nothing to do with their argument last night.

A fairy princess, eh?

A bride at eighteen, Gwennie, how romantic.

Looking forward to your Season, are you, Gwennie dear? Ready to sell yourself to the highest bidder?

Isn't that why women go to London, as commodities on the so-called Marriage Mart?

You're a lout, Christopher Beck, and a brute, and I despise you!

Suddenly all her joy, her anticipation in the coming spring, dimmed. As the days passed without word from Christopher, Gwendolyn found herself increasingly reluctant to make plans, consider her wardrobe, practice her dance steps.

And so when Katherine got a letter from their relation Henrietta Penhallow, the elderly, indomitable family matriarch in Somerset, who let fall the interesting tidbit of news that her former companion, Evangeline Markham, and her husband Arthur were planning an extended tour of Europe now that the war was finally over, intent on taking in the art and culture of France, Spain, Portugal, Italy, the German states, and—because Arthur was a Shakespeare aficionado and wanted to take his Evangeline to Kronborg, to show her the famous castle thought to be the model for the one in *Hamlet*—Denmark also, impulsively Gwendolyn said:

"Oh, Mama, do you think I might go too? May I write to Mrs. Markham, and ask?"

Katherine lowered the letter which she had been reading out loud to the family, and looked curiously at Gwendolyn. "But Gwennie, what about London?"

"I've always wanted to see the Louvre—the Rhine—Saint Peter's Basilica. And I'd love to see Hamlet's castle, too. This may be my only chance!" Gwendolyn knew she sounded a little too bright, a little too cheerful. A kind of desperation had overtaken her, and it felt as if she was lying somehow, even though she *did* long to see these famous places.

"You could go another time," Bertram pointed out. "After your Season."

"But—but war could come again, couldn't it? Please, Mama, may I write?"

There was more discussion, and in the end, her mother agreed, and Mrs. Markham graciously said yes, how delightful it would be to have a lively young person accompanying them, and in the spring, instead of going to London, Gwendolyn was on her way to Europe. If there was, deep within her, an ache of guilt, an anxiety, for Christopher, she did her very, very best to not to show it.

He could have gone to London, to their family bankers, to take some—or all—of the money his mother had left him. But he didn't. A few years ago, Hugo Penhallow had let him work in his shipbuilding firm in the Whitehaven harbor, and so he went to the house of an acquaintance he'd made, an older, somewhat disreputable man who ran a collier-boat back and forth to Liverpool (and, possibly, also smuggled French spirits). A good-hearted fellow, Barnabas asked no questions despite being woken from his sleep, and cheerfully agreed to take Christopher along on his next run, which, as luck would have it, was to happen the very next day.

Once on board, Christopher waited until the shoreline disappeared from view, then he went topside and took his place among the other sailors, who, as uncurious as Barnabas, accepted his presence without comment. In Liverpool he found a ship bound for Greece and hired himself on, wending his way toward the exquisite blue waters of the Mediterranean and the hot yellow sun. In Athens he boarded yet another ship, this one sailing to Crete, where he quickly found work in the olive groves despite his limited command of Greek. If he was homesick, if there was, in his thoughts, any longing for the people and places he'd left behind, he did his very, very best not to show it.

*G*ive in to your Impulses!

These unforgettable stories only take a second
to buy and give you hours of reading pleasure!

Go to *www.AvonImpulse.com* and see what we
have to offer.

Available wherever e-books are sold.

AVONIMPULSE

IMP 0811